Berkley Books by Kit Craig

GONE
TWICE BURNED

TWICE BURNED

KIT CRAIG

BERKLEY BOOKS, NEW YORK

TWICE BURNED

A Berkley Book / published by arrangement with
Little, Brown and Company, Inc.

PRINTING HISTORY
Little, Brown and Company edition / July 1993
Berkley edition / August 1995

ISBN: 0-425-14877-7

BERKLEY®
Berkley Books are published by The Berkley Publishing Group,
200 Madison Avenue, New York, New York 10016.
BERKLEY and the "B" design
are trademarks belonging to Berkley Publishing Corporation.

PRINTED IN THE UNITED STATES OF AMERICA

10 9 8 7 6 5 4 3 2 1

For Lois Gould
Girls just gotta have fun.

1

WE HAVE our instruments laid out.

Look at my twin shrinking from the task at hand. *No. Horrible!* Doesn't she know we have imperatives? *Yes, horrible!* My eyes bore into hers. *Exactly.*

We are alone in the latticed gazebo, where it is private. Far from the house. We sit on the floor, regarding the sacrificial item. Because of the badness yesterday there is trouble in the big house, and we are in danger. A sacrifice is in order.

We are the queen of Amadamaland. We do certain things to protect the kingdom.

And what are we doing exactly? This is one of our dark little secrets. Hers, mine. My twin grimaces and tries to squirm away as though she has a choice in this.

Can't she see we are the same person?

Whatever I *will*—happens. My hands dart out. She shrinks but does not fight me. I knot my fingers in her hair and twist until the knuckles gouge her scalp. *You like this. Admit it.*

No I don't like it, she cries, or is that me crying? *I don't! Oh yes we do.*

We do. We both know it. Gouging, I gouge with my knuckles until she starts to cry and I twist her hair until she stops crying and we resume. She relaxes into it. The sacrifice. There, that's better. She smiles at me. *Mmm, yes, we are one in this.*

A new voice jars us. "My God, what are you doing?"

Alarmed, we cry: "Janem!"

We cry: "Shut up, Emjane, we have to do this."

"Whatever it is, *stop it!*" Then we see her oh *yes,* the mother streaming downhill like a flight of banners. Look as she clears the patio steps behind Grandmother Archer's house. See her sprinting through the grass in her bare feet, Vivian the crazed and glorious. Beautiful in anger. Poor Vivian. Here comes our mother with her black hair wild and the silk kimono flowing. Her sleeves flash like pennants and her voice is huge: "Jane! Emily! *Whatever you're doing, stop!*"

Jane, Emily. Those are peasant names. Mother, don't you even know us? We are Jade and Emerald, the queen of Amadamaland, separate in some ways, yes, but always, listen! Always one person. Us.

In her rage, our mother is a thundercloud—we know that look. When she's angry she forgets we are the queen and treats us like ordinary citizens, like—*children.* "Stop it or I'll have to . . ."

What are you trying to do to us, Mother?

But the hill is long and our mother far away, so we pretend not to hear. Poor Vivian. Nothing she does matters. There is only us. When she is dead, there will still be us. Jade and Emerald.

"Jane," our mother cries in that big voice that means we have displeased her; "Emily!"

Fool. You don't even know us.

Queen Jade, we are, the queen of Amadamaland. We are her beautiful twin, Queen Emerald. Working quickly, we deal with the sacrificial object. And prepare to meet our mother. We will blink, all innocence. *Who, us?*

In Amadamaland, we can be who we want.

With Vivian, we have to keep our secrets.

"Girls!" Vivian Archer's voice is big enough to fill the distance between them, but her daughters act as though they don't hear her. She is shaking with anger. How could they? How could they do such an ugly thing? How could they call attention to themselves like this, after all her warnings?

Mother has sent her outside to tell them it's over. Next week they leave the genteel, musty safety of St. Margaret's for separate girls' boarding schools on the East Coast.

"Farmington for Emily, I think," Meredith said today. She means Miss Porter's. "And for our Jane, Ashley Hall."

Torn between rage and regret, she sobs. If only. If only this had come down differently! But Vivian can't escape the evidence: the bloody piece of silver, slapped into her hand like an ultimatum. If only the girls' riding teacher hadn't found the wretched thing. If only her girls would answer her.

If they'd only *look* at her: "Oh, Mom, don't be silly. Of course there's an explanation."

They are so beautiful, really, all sunlight and charm. They are so lovely and complex.

Then she homes in on the scene below. What they are doing down there in the gazebo. Everything in her quakes. *My God. What are you? What is this thread that runs through the generations?*

She runs and runs without coming any closer. It's like being in the old nightmare, where she screams her lungs to ribbons and nobody hears. The hill behind her mother's house is long, the velvety grass is spongy, her twin daughters see her coming. They will finish with the object on the floor of the gazebo before she can get close enough to see what they are doing.

What have they got down there? Their movements are swift and furtive. Panting, Vivian rummages through memory. Did they have somebody to the house to play today, did they? A girl from school? The gardener's daughter? And if they did, where is she, anyway?

If she asks, they will look up at Vivian with that bait-and-switch twin cleverness and say, "Who, us? Why, what do you want, Mother?"

Then her sly, beautiful daughters will turn away from her, basking in each other. At fourteen they still use that secret baby language that excludes the world outside the charmed circle of lifelong pairing. They use it against Vivian like a weapon. "Eemo. Eimo. Ey nay. Mo no Amadamaland letternay. Einel!" Their language conceals the meaning but makes clear their intentions: *Well, JanEm, EmJane, what are we going to do with her?*

What does it matter? She's only the mother.

The worst part is she understands. She too was born a twin.

Below, her girls keep on doing what they are doing. Everything distances them. Unlike most fourteen-year-olds, who run wild in jeans and T-shirts, Vivian's girls sit in the gazebo in flowered Laura Ashley dresses with their long hair pulled back in contrasting ribbons. They insist on quaint ruffled slips and tucked dresses straight out of *Little House on the Prairie.* What are they pretending here? Who are they trying to be?

If only you would yell *at me. If only you would get dirty.*

Diamond hoops nip their earlobes and their legs are covered with pale stockings. The shoes are pale leather, unscuffed, unmarred. Her girls have golden skins, and they have Steve Harriman's angular body. Their hair is light and full, like Steve's. They have Vivian's eyes, but with a difference—a glint that suggests that there are some things even a mother can't know. The brows curve like elegant, dark wings, and the hair is so thick and smoothly combed that even a high wind can't disturb it. The girls are always exquisitely groomed, perfect. Their profiles are perfect— left and right, Jane and Emily, unless it's Emily on the left, with Jane facing her. One is slightly taller, but Vivian cannot to this day say which; it's as if from one day to the next, the ratio changes. She thinks she knows who has the triangular smile, but they don't hold still long enough for her to make certain.

She needs to know, she needs to *know* which one is Jane and which Emily, and which girl put the silver charm underneath the hurt child's saddle and brought all this down on them. Isn't she their mother? She makes them wear colored watchbands to keep them straight—red for Jane, blue for Emily, but she knows they switch. Twins love to confuse, Vivian thinks, just the way Zane and I . . .

Vivian shakes herself; why is this so sinister? Sometimes when she tries to go into their suite, when she opens the door a crack, they freeze, as if she's caught them in the middle of something. Frowning, they rise with their arms folded, like—like *queens*. She is threatened by the heaped cartons, painted like castles with towers and drawbridges. Massed dolls in gowns, in helmets and bucklers reproach her. She knows better than to go any further.

If she tries the girls slip into the hall and flank her, laughing. "Mom, if you come in you'll only try to make us clean up." Their tone is light, loving.

"Plus, Mom, the queen is indisposed."

"Oh Mom, come on downstairs with us. We're going to sneak in the kitchen and make brownies."

This is how they head her off: with charm. "And if you show us your old school pictures we'll let you lick the spoon."

Laughing, she lets them turn her away from the door and hurry her along. Yet at the same time there is something running underneath, a dignity as firm as bedrock. *Do not think for one minute that you can oppose us.*

She knows better than to try.

Now she has to. She lingers on the hillside because she can't bear to begin.

They all know she has come running out of the house for good reason. Still the twins move slowly, as if enchanted. Their hands linger over the paisley scarf, ready to whip it over the thing between them. But they look so *sweet*, playing in the gazebo, like porcelain figures on a gilded music box—perfect, remote. If they see Vivian on the hill, they give no sign. If they hear her calling, they pretend not to. They are sitting flat with their thighs touching and their feet splayed, recklessly double-jointed, just like Vivian when she was little. Like Zane. In the gazebo, when Zane and I and poor Kurt Graver were little.

In the gazebo when we were grown and Kurt and I made love. It stops her heart. *God!*

Again Vivian feels the sick, sweet tug that brought her home to the big house on the cliff in the first place. She remembers the tangle of opposing forces—dark and light, yang and yin, good and evil, that drove her and her twin brother. Which was good and which was not? Nobody knew. She can't for the life of her say which side she represents. She and Zane could not know and now, oh God, history re-creates itself down there in the gazebo at the bottom of the hill. Once burned, she thinks, and is afraid to think: once burned, twice burned.

Oh God. Vivian is transfixed. The implications overwhelm her and root her on the grassy hillside, rapt and fearful. *In the next generation.*

She gropes toward complete memory but her perception is blurred, faulty. She won't or can't make herself remember. All she knows is that it began down there in the gazebo, the funny latticed bandstand her grandfather built in the last century when a string trio played while the family had tea. She had a twin brother then, a boy with her face and the same black hair and skin so white it seemed translucent. They used to lose themselves in their matched blue eyes, Zane fixed on Vivian's image, Vivian on Zane. What he thought, she knew. It was wonderful, terrible. Her mother Meredith shook when she held them.

They used to play down there exactly where her daughters sit now, on the weathered, silvery floor of the gazebo, spinning stories with Kurt Graver, the chauffeur's son; they were so *happy.*

Until it ended in fire and blood. Kurt went to the hospital and things were never the same again but they played, they did. When Kurt came back from the hospital they went on playing as if none of it had ever happened. But twinhood has its imperatives: the wicked thing that surfaced in Zane grew.

Then they were twenty and she and Kurt—she thinks it was love—like nothing she'd deserved to feel. But all at once instead of two lovers there were three in the gazebo— Kurt like a thunderbolt. It did not end that night. There were tears and reproaches, outrage and blood. The end came on the cliff. Memory beggars her.

Vivian chokes on it. The horror. The grief that followed. Pain and fear obliterate the rest, but somewhere deep she knows it's what makes her so afraid.

Now Zane is dead and Kurt has shut himself into the apartment above the garage and won't talk to her. She still cries for Zane. They were the same person. He was Vivian, she was Zane. Alike in everything. Even though her twin brother has been gone *for all these years* she misses him. It's like having a second self ripped out of her side. All these years later it's still raw.

After Zane died she spent a long time in the hospital. When they put her back together and released her she moved east. For a few years she managed to pretend that the evil thing between them, whatever it was, had died with Zane. She built a new identity, working in graphic design, everything ordinary; some nights she didn't even dream about Zane. She pretended her life was changing.

Then she met Steve and all her clocks struck midnight. *It's time.* She fell in love with bright, restless Steve Harriman but she used him hard because in spite of everything, she was compelled by the flicker of pattern. What was he—planning to marry some sweetfaced girl from the office? No matter; Vivian swept down on him like the wolf on the fold. He was astounded, flattered, dizzy, crazy drunk on her; it happened fast. And they did love each other. Steve thought marriage would bank the fires and leave coals burning steadily. He was so pleased when he found out she was pregnant. How could she explain that the children he wanted were not the ones she was carrying?

Whatever drove Zane had come to live in her. Caught underneath her heart, it still contains him. And she sees it in her daughters. Emily and Jane. Jane and Emily. When they were born she went into a depression. Having twins of her own, she has recreated the pattern. It grows, demanding completion.

Poor Steve! Did he notice how strange it was when Jane and Emily were born? Caesarian birth. They were simultaneous. *Good,* she thought. *Nobody's first. Nobody has to dominate.* Exactly the same weight and length. Only the hospital bracelets told her which was Jane and which Emily. *Perfectly formed.* Steve was so proud! And she? They were sunny, beautiful, but when she looked into them she saw Zane flickering.

They grew. Darkside, lightside, hopelessly entangled.

Looking into their eyes, Vivian saw herself. In their crib the twins' faces shimmered in uncanny comprehension: *Don't look too closely. Your eyes will burn right through to the retina.* She already knew they weren't ordinary. She prayed: Please let Steve see only the ordinary.

He did, she thought, until they were almost two. Then Vivian found Steve staring into the crib with such concentration that it frightened her. Babbling, she tried to distract him. "Aren't they beautiful?"

"I don't know," he said. Vivian saw they were not asleep. They lay entwined, communicating without speech. Steve shook his head. "Their rages. The silence. It's weird. I think we ought to have them tested." She saw her loving partner— their *father* withdrawing—*something's wrong.*

No, she thought. This is the way it is. "Steve, they're only babies!"

That night she woke trembling—could not figure out why, exactly, but got up and went into the babies' room. Steve was standing over the crib again. When he heard her low cry, the face he turned was tragic, haunted. "They're not . . ."

"They're wonderful!"

The girls were both awake, lying head to tail, watching her with those sly, sweet, terrifying smiles.

She loved her husband. She loved the twins. Like a tigress protecting her young, Vivian savaged Steve and stole the children. *I loved him, I did. But I had to do it for their protection.* The next morning she cleaned out their bank account. She left that night. She took everything he cared about and disappeared.

No. I did it for his protection.

It was late when Vivian reached the house where she grew up, pulling two little girls in their new dresses. She was surprised by how big the place was, how imposing the carved front door seemed when you were not sure of your welcome. As a child she'd taken it for granted—that everybody lived like this, that she belonged here. She prayed: *Please make her want us.*

Her mother answered the door herself. "Who's there?" With her white hair down and her pale blue eyes glazed with confusion, Meredith looked old for the first time. "Oh my God."

"I'm back," Vivian said.

"I see." Shivering in the chill of the California night, Meredith Archer filled the doorway, guarding against the incursion. Her look said, *Please don't make me do this again.* At first she didn't see the children. Shaken, she was too busy trying to close the door on Vivian. *She's never forgiven me,* Vivian thought. *She's never forgiven us.* Never mind that it was dark and the taxi was already plunging down the drive in the cold drizzle, slithering over wet gravel. There was a little battle over the front door. "I love you but I can't have you, I just can't *have* you."

The women pushed against each other. Vivian was stronger. After fifteen years, she was home for good. "I've changed," Vivian said—not quite the truth. This was the truth: "I need you."

"Go away." Zane's death changed the old lady forever. It was clear from her face how it had been. The velvet bathrobe hung on her; the fingers gripping the door were all bone and knuckles, as if her loss had somehow leached her flesh away. The tissue-paper skin of her face crumpled. "I'm begging you."

And Vivian? She was used up. Everything inside her shook. She was like a building about to cave in on itself in a slow, agonizing implosion. "And I'm begging you." She whispered into her mother's ear: "I'm sorry about Zane." She was. She wasn't.

Meredith drew herself up, trembling. "I'm not."

Then Vivian pushed them forward: the twins, her treasures. Jane and Emily. They were only two years old. They were drowsy, flushed. Raising their arms to her, they looked like little flowers. "Aren't they pretty?"

"Oh my God." The children smiled at her. Rocked, Meredith could not breathe. She barely squeezed it out. "They're beautiful." She finished with a sob. "But I begged you not to have children . . ."

Vivian wept. "But you wanted me to be married."

"I thought Steve would be good for you! I thought he could help you change your life." Meredith mourned for both of them.

Vivian's voice came from somewhere deep, "So did I."

". . . and now . . ." Looking at the children, the old lady began to shake. "Twins. You never told me."

On one side Jane curled her hand around Vivian's index finger; on the other, Emily clung with exactly the same pressure. They were like little generators with Vivian the connector; she could feel the current running through her. "Mother! I'm not the same." This was only partly true. How could she explain? Hope pushed her into a lie. "I promise. It won't be the same."

Tilting Vivian's head, her mother leaned forward, staring into her face as if studying it under a close lens. It was strange. The pause stretched to snapping before she said quietly, "I'd like to believe that."

Vivian took the gaunt, elegant old woman's hand, gripping until all her diamonds bit her fingers and she cringed. Glaring, she bore down. "You have to."

Something between them cracked and split open. Her mother's voice came as if out of the tomb. "Oh, my Vivian!" And with her face softened by love, she stood by and let them in, Vivian first, followed by the two beautiful daughters, Jane and Emily, or was it Emily and Jane? "We'll manage together." As she looked at the two children, her breath shuddered. "We'll do the best we can."

Then one of the children spoke—some little thing—and she got down on her knees and pulled them close to her.

Later Vivian heard Steve had hired a private detective, but a year passed and nobody came to the Archer house. In the end she did send word back: *I'm at Mother's. It's over. Please don't try to see us.* And her beautiful girls looked up at her with the smug smiles of the well-cared-for.

Until now, it's worked well enough.

Money helped. So did privilege. Everything the girls could possibly want was provided: a beautiful suite on the third floor—schoolroom, playroom, bedroom with four-poster beds under flowered canopies; paired cocker spaniel puppies, Chestnut and Cinnamon, matched ponies to ride on the grounds and in the hilly woods just beyond the stone walls, a perennially changing cast of servants, hastily paid off to avoid recriminations. Only Billy Graver, who had been with the family from the beginning, stayed on. And Kurt is here, although she never sees him. No. Can't.

What Vivian and her mother could not manage, quiet, constant Billy Graver did. Kurt's father. It's ironic. They've spun out the years in a fevered attempt to keep the girls happy, *quiet*.

("Do what you have to," they said to each new tutor, and to the sisters at St. Margaret's when the girls got too old and restless to be taught at home. "Just be careful not to make them angry.") They imported friends for the girls, on a rotating basis. Children came to the house for birthdays and special occasions, select guests at carefully planned parties. (Vivian remembers the high hum of anxiety as she tried to control the little outsiders, her own voice rising: "Oh please. Please don't do that." She looked into her twin daughters' faces and saw Zane. It made her beg. "Oh please don't do anything to upset them.")

It worked well enough, or she thought it had.

Until today.

2

NOW THEY ARE at the moment. Her breath catches in her chest.

Her girls! It's not their fault. It's that idiot girl in their riding class, the child got hurt when the runaway horse threw her. What did she say to Em or Jane, to bring this down on herself?

Vivian is still trembling from the confrontation. The girls' riding teacher stalked into the library with her hair pulled back so tight it stretched her face and her tweed coat flapping. She looked angry enough to crack open the house like an egg carton and spill the twins out and smash them. "The child will be in the hospital for weeks. When we finally caught the horse we found *this* jammed under the saddle." It was still bloody from the animal's flesh: a silver charm. Jane's, or is it Em's silver stegosaurus.

Vivian didn't have to see the bloody piece of silver to know what had happened. The fools. What could they have been thinking?

"It belongs to one of your daughters."

Foolhardy, careless. Giving in to anger like that. Hasn't she *warned* them? She thought she could protect her twins from the world. Or the world from them. Now this single stupid, vicious act has brought down outsiders, threatening the charmed circle.

The teacher was waiting. Vivian said, "That poor child. Tell her we're terribly sorry." *What did she do to make them angry?*

"If you can't control your twins, I'll have to notify the authorities. There's something strange about your girls. Something's not right. You need an evaluation."

"We'll take care of it." Meredith's voice struck Vivian cold.

The woman failed to catch her tone. "There's something strange about your girls. They're . . ." The riding instructor's words were blunt, ugly. "Capable of anything. You have to do something."

"I think we'll find a new riding instructor." The perfect lady, Meredith rose smoothly, glaring until the teacher looked away. "That will be all."

"You have to do something."

"I said, that will be all," she said, and without lifting a hand she forced the woman backward, into the hall. "And thank you very much for coming." Dignified and brilliant, she stood until the door closed. Then she turned to Vivian and her face opened like a chasm; she was beyond exhaustion. "Neither of us wants to do this, but it's time. Maybe in separate schools . . ."

"Mother, we can't!"

"They can't stay in school here." Meredith was all used up. "I will not go through what I went through with you and Zane. I love them just as much as you do, Vivian, but we can't handle them."

Vivian was already weeping. "Please, Mother. One more chance."

"I can't go through that again. And I won't let you go through it. Not for our girls, not for anyone. They're . . ." she doesn't know how to describe this, "not good for each other." Meredith produced letters from Miss Porter's and Ashley Hall. Acceptances. "They're at that age. There's the added problem of boys." There is also the unspoken. The Archers have stayed above the law so far; they've managed to protect the twins and cover up what they had to, but the girls are too old to be content here. They are beyond tepid parties in the garden with little friends from school.

Vivian said shakily, "I suppose we can't keep firing people."

"And we can't go on like this. It's all arranged." (It is—the tests Mother had them take last winter, "In case we decide to spend a year abroad." They did brilliantly. She made calls to her friends in the East. Everything taken care of. Except breaking the news.)

"God, Mother. Behind my back. How could you?" At this charge, Meredith's tears sprang. Still Vivian sobbed. "You can't send them away. I love them too much!"

"If we love them, we have to separate them." Meredith sighed. "Our resources here are limited. I'm not strong. You're only one person. Oh lord, Vivian, we can't let the same old story keep retelling itself. If we can just split them up . . ."

This was bitter. "You don't understand twins at all, do you?"

Her mother's voice dropped. "I understand better than anyone."

There was a long pause in which Vivian considered: herself/Zane, Jane/Emily, the past and the potential. "I tried so *hard*."

And before Vivian could turn the conversation Meredith issued her ultimatum. "It's time to break the news."

A crafty, secret part of Vivian can't stop running after other solutions, but they have no choice here. Together, the twins become a unit bigger than the two parts. She dipped her head in acknowledgment. *We have to separate them.* Then all her breath came out in a sigh. It was almost a relief. "You did this. You tell them."

"You know I can't." Meredith's eyes filled. "They'll put their arms around me and talk me out of it, or else . . ." Her face darkened as she reflected on the *or else*. "Let me send Billy with you."

"Mother, they're not going to . . ."

"You never know."

"They're my *children*."

Unexpectedly solicitous, Meredith followed her to the French doors, saying in a sweet voice, "If there's any trouble . . ."

"Mother!"

"Just be careful." Meredith grabbed the battery phone, clutching it like the ultimate weapon. "Please."

This is today, Mother. They are not me. Or Zane. This is nothing like the other time.

Vivian is right about this, but not the way she thinks.

There will be variations in the pattern.

Weaving a charm, she tells herself, *And they are not like us.*

Something small collides with her ankles and pulls her back to the moment—one of the twins' miniature cockers, furry and compact as a little meatloaf, solid and warm against her. The warmth of living flesh arrests her. "Oh, Cinnamon! Where's Chestnut?" Recovering her balance, she looks down at the animal, then up.

The sun is out; it's Thursday. Reality staggers her. Caught in midflight, Vivian hesitates, lost somewhere between rage and terror. The brute ugliness of necessity makes Vivian groan aloud. *My own girls, and I have to be careful how I approach them.* In spite of everything, she loves them. "Girls!"

Twin heads swivel. Blue-eyed, they regard their mother. Something makes her think of the little princes in the tower, waiting for bad king Richard to have them murdered.

Mother, what are you trying to do to us?

Vivian shakes herself. This is going to be worse than she expected. "Nothing," she says aloud, even though they haven't spoken. *They know without being told.* Another proof, she thinks. Another proof that they are different. She does not know what to do. Brightly, she lies. "Nothing." If only they would jump up, laughing. If only they'd come up to the house with her for ice cream, and be pleased by what she has to tell them.

They sit quietly. If the cards fall the right way this will be nothing; grinning, they'll rise and start kidding with her. They'll be bubbling, delightful, just ordinary teenagers.

They are waiting. And they are more than ordinary. They are twins.

If only she could turn this moment. If only she knew how to make it change! Don't they know what's at stake here? Can't they see what she and Mother have been trying to do, with their private school and extra tutors and symphony subscriptions and riding lessons, plans around the clock? Can't her beautiful, foolish girls see that everything they do is studied and weighed against their future? "Girls." She notes the quick movements, the furtive air as Jane—or is it Em—whisks the scarf over the object on the floor between them. She lifts her voice. "I have something to tell you."

"Yes Mother?"

Vivian recognizes the looks in the faces they turn to her. She groans. "Oh God."

Somewhere just out of her sight the old mystery is unfolding. Twin pairs of eyes study her and Vivian would like to keep her voice even, to match the quiet calm with which her beautiful daughters regard her, but she can't. She hears it quaver. They are quiet, regal; she could be just anybody standing out here in the grass, excluded, helpless. "Tell me you're not doing what I think you are."

Neither of them answers.

"Never mind," she says with her heart breaking. She's close enough to leap the steps and dart in and lift the cloth before they can stop her, but she won't. She's afraid to know what they are hiding. Instead she mounts slowly and sits down on the wooden bench that lines the octagon. The girls get up and sit on opposing benches. It's as if they are all three riding through the garden on a beautiful little ferry-boat. "You probably already know. Ah. You *probably already know* . . ." This is so hard! She clears her throat. "You know we can't go on like this."

Neither responds.

Without having to explain, Vivian takes the silver stego-saurus out of her pocket and tosses it on top of the paisley scarf; if it clinks against whatever they've covered up, she thinks, that will be a sign things aren't quite as bad as we think they are.

Instead it lands without a sound. What's under there? An inanimate object, *or one that has stopped moving*. She does not ask; she just begins. "Even you can see, it's time for some changes."

They look at the bloody charm with mild curiosity. "Why, what's that?"

Her voice shakes. "You know what it is. It came from your bracelet."

Their faces are bright and their voices sweet. "Not my bracelet, Mother."

"I promise, not mine." If only she could believe them!

She wants to, but she knows better. "My darlings. It's too late for excuses. It doesn't even matter which of you did it."

Their eyes brim; their mouths tremble. "Neither of us did it, really."

"We would never do a thing like that."

"The least you can do is to be honest. Emily? Jane dear?" They seem to sense that they are passing a landmark here, and their altered silence is worse than their denials. "Please." Vivian has her imperatives and she forges on. "If you'll just *tell* me, maybe I . . ." But they do not speak. When nothing happens she starts over. "I love you, but your grandmother and I . . . We've tried so hard, but now . . ." She gasps. "We have to do this."

The girls' faces are like porcelain, but as she speaks she sees fleeting darkness rush across the smooth surfaces like stormclouds across a quiet landscape.

There's nothing for it now, no way to turn them back into her little girls again so she can keep them close; she just keeps talking. "I'm sorry, but we do."

She sees their paired heads swivel until they are facing, Jane fixed on Emily, Emily on Jane in the troublesome old push-pull that hums underneath all her daughters' silent communications. As her belly quivers, they strike a balance and when they turn back to Vivian, it is as one person. They bestow strange, sleek smiles on her like matching Buddhas. *My God.* "Your grandmother and I . . ." She is weeping now. "It's all decided. We can't go on this way." Their eyes widen. Meeting the incredulous blue stares of her twin daughters, Vivian is staggered by foreboding. Gasping, she finishes. "We have something different planned for you."

Neither speaks, but their paired looks make her shudder.

3

THE MOST IMPORTANT THING about Carroll Lawton's life is that she was orphaned at ten, and sent to Jenkins, Florida. She's spent her life since then trying to ignore or overcome it—being the best, marrying Steve. She wants to go to live in Steve's life. She wants to surround them with family and never have to be that lonely child again. Still she is conditioned by the early loss. It lies at the bottom of her need to be strong and good at what she does and it lives at the heart of her best writing. It makes a part of her hold its breath each time Steve goes out the door and not relax until he comes back again.

Carroll lived at 553 Arbor Street with her aunts from the year her mother died until she married Steve Harriman. She was ten years old and she had just run out of parents. Talking about life on Arbor Street, her dead mother used to make the place sound like Tara. Poor Violet. She was probably homesick and trying to bring it all back. "When we went out people used to tell my father, 'You have a beautiful family.' Granddaddy wanted a house big enough to entertain the world. The place used to be full of people all the time," she'd say, as if Carroll could see what she saw and feel just as good about it: the parties, the Dickensian Christmases. "All the boys loved to come over and dance in the music room." Listening, Carroll used to feel guilty for being an only child and fatherless, and living in two rooms.

Then Violet died and Carroll was sent to Arbor Street to be brought up by Violet's sisters. It was definitely not Tara. Coming into the front hall with her books and the Teddy she'd outgrown but could not abandon, she was surprised by how shabby the place was and how awful she felt. Cut loose, feeling abandoned by her dead mother, she promised never to forget what it felt like to be little, and never to let anything like this happen to her children.

They tried to be nice. The aunts, grinny Aunt 'Laine, fat Patsy and lazy Suzy Larrabie circled her in the dusty old front hall in their Fabulous Fifties clothes and high heels. Behind them, just in from the nearby office where he sold insurance, Uncle Peyton lingered with a grin that made her squirm. They didn't know what to say to her. Finally Aunt Suzy found exactly the wrong thing to say to a little girl who's trying to pretend everything's OK and she's doing fine in spite of what's happened to her.

"You poor little thing, first you lost your father and now your mother!"

She does not recommend growing up without a parent.

Grown now, and married about ten minutes—no, ten months—Carroll is bent on creating what she never had: a real family. It's taken her some time to come to this decision. Marriage is wonderful, terrible, surprising, right for her. She loves living with this lover, partner, *friend* who closes his arms around her so tightly that their bones fuse. If her life is ticking like a time bomb or an alarm clock just about to go off, Carroll has no way of knowing it. Still, she ought to be aware of certain warning signs: the mystery that lies in the bed between them, as palpable as an extra person; the sweet, guilty feeling Carroll has that for the first time since she was orphaned, she's too happy.

And she's also a skilled reporter. Slight as she is, she carries herself with that jaunty self-confidence. Born pretty, Carroll has learned how to look tough and capable; she keeps her red hair short and her jaw squared. She's the master of the don't-mess-with-me look, and when she goes on a story she gets results. She worked for eight years on the Jenkins *Dispatch* before Steve came to town to sell off property left to him by a relative. They met one night at the old Yacht Club down by the sleepy river. She walked into the dining room with bright, aggressive Charley Penn, publisher of the *Dispatch*. They were there to make policy on a local scandal she'd uncovered: who to question, what to reveal.

Something drew her eyes to the sliding doors. She looked out and saw this new man at the porch rail, looking down at the sluggish water. He was not like anybody in Jenkins. The whole time she and Charley were deciding whom she should interview and whether to name her sources in the series, Carroll was watching the outsider. He paced in jeans and a safari vest, instead of the traditional lightweight business suit; unlike the southern men she knew, he was tall and restless, *wired*. He turned and caught her looking.

They knew each other at once. How to manage the introductions was never at issue. They managed the introductions. He was an architect, here to see whether he could do anything with his late uncle's property.

When he said he was in town for the week it seemed like a long time; by the time he left it was not nearly long enough. Sitting at her terminal in the newsroom or standing in a dirt patch interviewing some farmer, Carroll could still see him. Steve had a wonderfully untended look—collar too large, as if he'd just lost weight, hair too shaggy, expression too guarded. There was something going on behind his eyes that cast long shadows. It was as if a part of this man had been torn out a long time ago and he was still mending.

He held her so tight their bones collided. "Is it OK to say you're what I need right now?"

She didn't say it was exactly what she needed to hear. "You make me sound like a megavitamin."

"For the heart," he said, but he was laughing.

She had the idea that he was telling her more than he meant to. They couldn't stop talking. He knew all the last lines to her half-remembered poems. Everything they said to each other meshed; they were like two widely scattered jigsaw pieces destined to be pulled out of the jumble and put together. When he said goodbye at the end of the week Carroll wanted to leave with him, but she didn't. She was not about to risk her career for a maybe thing. He tried to convince her it wasn't "maybe." He told her there were better newspapers in Connecticut. He made it clear that sooner or later he was going to marry her.

It took him a year.

Carroll left Jenkins to come north with Steve Harriman; she wasn't sorry to say goodbye to the aunts or Uncle Peyton, but the rest was hard. She hated leaving the *Dispatch*. They were interviewing Russell, some squirt from Harvard, to take her place in the newsroom. She realized with a flicker of resentment that this Russell would finish her series. But she loved Steve so much that she'd come to the point of no return—that spot in the air over major oceans when it's too late for the pilot to turn back and there's nothing left but to go forward. Steve? She'd traveled so far in love with him that she couldn't live without him.

Charley Penn said, "One phone call and you have your job back."

Violet's death had taught her never to say never but she said it anyway. "Oh I won't be back, Charley."

But he looked at her from under that bush of hair that went prematurely white when he was thirty. "One phone call," he said.

It was only when they came back from the wedding trip and Steve went back to work that she realized she really was out of a job. Everywhere she goes, the story is the same: Your resume looks good; we like your clips. You know as well as we do that newspapers are collapsing, not expanding. We'd love to hire you as soon as our jobs get unfrozen. She keeps hearing Charley: *One phone call.*

To her surprise, she hears other voices. Alone in the house, she keeps seeing lonely little Carroll opening doors on empty rooms on Arbor Street: *Where is everybody?* She keeps hearing the silent reproach in Violet's sweet voice, "Everybody loved to come to our house because there were so many of us, and we all had friends." The day stretches before her like taffy and when it finally gets to be six o'clock and Steve comes in the door it snaps like a rubber band, leaving a surprised hush in which she hears the words as distinctly as if she's spoken them: *Always wanted children.*

She waits until they've eaten. She waits until they've finished cleaning up and then, pulling him into the living room, she says tentatively, "Maybe we should do the kids now, while I'm unemployed." Once she says the words, it's as if she's decided. It sounds right to her: *where we've been heading.* Let him build houses. I can build lives.

She does not expect the response she gets. Steve turns in distress. "Kids." A number of expressions cross his face—none of them expected. "Oh, Carroll."

Why can't she hear the bomb ticking? She thinks this is a momentary problem; she touches his arm. "What's the matter?"

"Nothing about you, OK? It's something about me." When Steve turns to look at her she sees a strange shadow flickering: a dark hint superimposed on his face like the negative of a bad photograph. *Something I'm not telling you.* "I just." It takes him a minute to bring out the rest. Looking into Carroll's face to see how she's going to take it, he says, "Can't right now."

She thinks Steve really does want her children, but there is a strange, jagged edge of distress running along just beneath the surface of all these conversations. If there is something ticking in Carroll's life, with the big hand on the clock closing on the designated mark; if it's just about to detonate, happiness has made her deaf. No. Dumb. She finds herself listening for something she is aware of, but can't yet identify. His untold story? The faint sound of ticking? She doesn't know. "Is there a problem?"

He turns his back so she can't see his eyes. She can't know what makes Steve so guarded and wary, or what makes him reluctant to talk about his life before they met. "I love you but I can't tell you." He's like a dog that's been badly burned—shivering with the cold but afraid to get any closer to the fire.

She is swift. "There's a lot of stuff you haven't told me."

When he turns she sees he's almost blinded by pain. "No there isn't." With an effort, he corrects himself. "Yes there is, but. It's not about us."

"Everything's about us."

He shakes his head violently. "Not this! You're the best thing that's ever happened to me. It's like being outside after

years of . . ." He can't finish. Instead he pulls close and
holds her as if this contact can draw out the pain. "Please
trust me."

Which is where they leave it. *I can wait,* Carroll tells
herself. *It can wait.* But she knows it can't wait much
longer. One of these nights when they make love she's going
to pull Steve even closer and talk to him softly, passionately,
drawing him along the path to revelation. Part of her wants
to know the truth and the other part is afraid to find out. *You
love him. If he can't tell you, you can wait. It can wait,* she
tells herself uneasily.

She can't know that in the life he's tried to leave behind,
nothing stays where you put it. And nothing waits forever.

Then in the night the phone rings. As Steve struggles up out
of sleep to answer it, Carroll draws her knees to her chest
and shakes with dread. They are at the brink of something.
Hearing Steve murmur into the phone, she understands that
even if she knew what was going on, it wouldn't stop what's
happening. Even knowing what happened to disturb his
sleep and make him so wary, she wouldn't be able to help.

Nothing she can do will protect him from his past or
prevent this. Nothing could possibly prepare her.

"I see. When?" He's talking to somebody he knows so
well they don't have to use names. Steve that she loves so
much but *doesn't really know* is muttering, "Wait. I'm
taking the phone into the next room."

"Steve." Trying to empty her head of dreams so she can
focus, Carroll reaches for him. "What."

"Go back to sleep." Gently, he disengages her fingers. "I
can't talk about this here."

Hurt, she says, "I see."

"No." He pulls her up in the bed so they can kiss; those
forearms cut into her back, like blades. "You can't possibly
see," he says, and with a final tightening of the arms, he
sighs and releases her. He takes the phone in the other room.

She turns on the light and for reasons she can't even guess
at, gets up and dresses: jeans, sweater, sneakers.

When Steve comes back from the phone in the kitchen,

his expression is beyond interpretation. He is ashen, trembling.

Carroll thinks she's ready for anything, her in her jeans and her purple Reeboks, combing her short red hair with her fingers. She expects him to tell her there's been a fire at the studio, or they have to go to some relative's bedside, but his silence arrests her. "My God, Steve! What is it?"

He just stands there with his hands hanging at his sides like dead weights and his face empty. "I thought it was over. I thought I'd never have to tell you."

Everything is different. There's something about the order in this pretty room, the lovingly placed ornaments in the house, her sense of comfort, of expanding love and, what, safety, that seems threatening now. *Your fault, for being too happy. If you're too happy, something will come along and take it away from you.* She has the idea that all their lovingly settled arrangements are trembling: this house, their lives, everything she and Steve Harriman are together, all these elements she takes for granted are just about to shift and crumble. Is this the warning tremor before a major earthquake or the stillness that presages a tornado?

"Tell me what?"

He can't seem to answer.

She finds it hard to breathe. Has her father been killed in a wreck again? Has her mother just been rushed to the hospital and is someone coming to tell her the worst? Is the sky falling? Her heart rushes ahead: Oh, Steve! What's happened, to make you look that way? What's the matter? What in God's name is the matter?

Therefore when Steve goes on, what he has to say astounds her. He says quietly, "You said you always wanted children."

She whirls. "Steve?"

"Oh look, if I'd had any idea . . ." He takes her hands, gripping so hard her knuckles grind. "Sometimes you get what you want and it turns out not to be what you wanted."

Alarmed, Carroll backs away but he's hanging on so tight she can't get free.

"Something's come up. I have to go to northern California."

Crazily she says, "No you don't."

"Their mother's been killed." He's looking into her face but it's clear it's not her face he sees. "Oh Carroll, my kids have lost their mother."

She finds he's let go of her. In shock, she says in a hushed voice, "Your *kids*."

"I thought I'd never see them again. I made a promise." That kind, blunt face she loves so much is stiff with pain. "I wanted to tell you but I couldn't."

Rage flashes. *You never even told me you were married.* "Kids!"

"Girls. My twins. She was in a bad way, so I had to promise."

This is killing her. "Who was?"

"My wife." In that second his face blazes. "Vivian! Something about having twins just staggered her and she was crazy. Crazy enough to take them away with her. Crazy with worry. Then when I tracked them down, her mother . . ." He does not explain, he just finishes. "It was part of the settlement. Complete secrecy. I couldn't tell you." He looks destroyed. "Now Vivian is dead and I have to."

"You can tell me anything," she cries. "Anything."

"This is not like anything. It's—something I can't explain. Something else. I was so sure it was over for good." Steve is upset and angry, loving and conflicted; somewhere behind all the confusion of expressions crossing his face, there flickers an unfamiliar little light she recognizes as joy. "My twins! I thought I'd never see them again."

"And you never . . ." She's trying to go with this, but too close to the surface, the betrayal, ten-year-old Carroll is clamoring.

"Oh God." His face is bright. "But now! I have to go."

". . . even told me." What he had just said registers. "When?"

"As soon as I can get a reservation." Dressing, he's swift and jerky as a cartoon character.

She can't just let him go; there's too much unresolved. "I'll go with you."

"You can't." He's trying to be gentle. "I'm going somewhere you can't go."

She doesn't mean to beg; it just happens. "Oh Steve, please."

"I can't." Stuffing his wallet into his back pocket, he looks up. "This is hard enough for these poor kids."

"I know something about poor kids," Carroll says, and she is ten years old again.

He's too busy explaining to hear what she's trying to tell him. "If Vivian was right—if Meredith is right, this may be harder than you think. I have to go without you. Oh look, Carroll, you'll meet them soon enough." Then he hits her in the face with it. He doesn't ask; he tells. "They're coming to live with us."

What she finds hard to take is the fact that in this spurt of decision, Steve looks happier than she's ever seen him. Her hands drop. "I see."

"My girls. Jane and Emily. They're little blondes, but they have Vivian's eyes."

"Vivian!"

Steve's face shines so brightly she has to look away. Even his voice is bright. "My wife," he says to Carroll absently, as if he's forgotten her. "Everything is different now." Then her *Steve*, whom she thought she knew, says in that disproportionately joyful voice that doesn't match the hour or the circumstances, "After everything I have them back. My beautiful daughters."

"Twins." She thinks with grim humor: One thing too many.

"After making me promise not to see them, their grandmother's begging me. She's getting old and she knows she can't . . ." A rushing shadow dims the light in his face. He's filled with things he isn't telling her. "I know this is a lot to ask." For the first time he sounds uncertain. "I hope you'll like them."

Orphans, she thinks. *You poor little* . . . "Of course I'll like them." But it's too much; she hears herself accusing:

"You knew I wanted kids and you never told me you had kids."

He is too distracted to answer.

With the jittery air of a man getting ready for a party, he's already packing, rummaging for extra socks, leaving her alone with this. She'll never know why it hits her the way it does or why when the words come out they are so bitter. "You never told me about Vivian." And without knowing how it happens, she finds herself both here in this beautiful room she and Steve have made and at the same time back in the front hall on Arbor Street in Jenkins, orphaned all over again. Stricken, she says something she'll regret for the rest of her life, Carroll Lawton, wife of Steve Harriman, who she loves and who she *thought she knew,* so hurt that she strikes blindly. This is how she reproaches him: "It makes everything that was ever between us into a lie!"

Then she says more; she says such terrible things to him that it will be hours before she can even take them out and examine them, much less find a way to make it right.

Trying to make it up, Carroll dismisses the cab and drives him to the airport in the still part of the night that falls between insomnia and waking up anxious. Even though Steve is ready to jump out of the car and send her back to bed, she insists on coming in with him. Early losses make you afraid of more losses, she thinks uneasily, or is it more vulnerable? It's as though she senses time running out and can't get enough of him.

She's glad the plane is late. It gives them some time together—not to mend, exactly, because she can't drag herself back to the bad moment in the bedroom long enough to figure out how to apologize—just a chance to be with him. Sitting on one of the generic impossibly conformed plastic seats that turn airport waiting rooms into torture chambers, Carroll seizes a last few minutes with Steve.

Beached in the harsh fluorescent light with coffee in paper cups and his legs stretched out in front of them, Steve just begins. "You'd have to see her to understand why I loved her—something behind the eyes that compelled you.

She made me forget who I was, and how crazy she was. If it *was* crazy. Maybe it was just—fated." He hesitates, bemused. He can't find a way to sum it up. "You'd have to know her to understand. We were married for a while, and when she left, it was . . . Never mind. It was already over."

She knows it isn't.

"Her name is Vivian."

Her voice is harsh. "You told me."

Shaking like a dog, he corrects himself. "Was Vivian. Her mother called from the hospital near the house. Meredith Archer. She was calling about Vivian."

"What happened?" She's not sure she wants to know.

"She couldn't tell me. Meredith could hardly talk. Poor old lady, this was one thing too many, on top of the rest."

He is raising more questions than he answers. The rest! She puts a hand on his arm as if to slow this narrative down so she can look at the parts, but it's as if he's talking for himself.

"She didn't tell me what happened. I'm not sure she really knows. They got Vivian to the hospital but it was too late, but that wasn't why she was calling." Steve is trying to line up the details so he can make sense of them. "She called to get me to promise to take the children."

Carroll understands this perfectly—what happens when a parent dies. "The children. Of course."

He says, "It's more complicated than you think."

"Aren't you glad to have them?"

"I think so."

His uncertainty staggers her. Carroll says firmly, "Jane and Emily."

"That isn't all." In falsetto, he mimicks something heard a long time ago but still remembered; it sounds like a secret code. "Janem. Emjane. Did you ever look into kids' faces and know they were different?"

She was afraid he'd go on, afraid he wouldn't go on.

"But I loved them. I really did. When she took them away I spent two years looking for them. Hidden in plain sight—Meredith's money made it work. Then Vivian decided to let me see them after all—at her mother's, playing in the grass. They were happy there—I don't know. Different. They were so happy that when Vivian begged, I promised never to see them again. It broke my heart but I loved them enough to agree." He seems to know there is no way to explain this. "For their sake. I had a hard time getting used to the idea, but when I did, you know what?"

"No."

He is battered by forces she can't see. "It was a relief."

"But they're your *kids*."

He takes her hands. "This is going to be hard for you."

So Carroll manages to say the right thing after all. "Well they're my kids too. I love kids. Will love them, no matter what. What I love, Steve . . ." It is as close as she comes to apologizing. "I love anything that has to do with you."

He can have both! Pleasure rushes into his face, quickly effaced by that old shadow, like a familiar enemy. "They're not just my kids." He finishes. "They're Vivian's."

And Vivian was crazy. "Just little girls."

"There are things you don't understand about Vivian." He puts down the paper cup and reaches for her hand, gripping it as if they're hotwired and he can put information into her directly. "Did you ever want something that was bad for you?"

She thinks, *Maybe this.*

"And you want it partly because it's beautiful and partly because it really is bad for you," he goes on. "That was my wife Vivian. Hard to explain. I loved her, but she was crazy as a bat in a wire wheel. From the beginning she had something driving her—unless she was chasing it. Vivian and this—*other thing*—going around and around somewhere inside her head, where I couldn't see what was happening . . ."

His plane is called; he's supposed to begin boarding but is intent on the recital. "And then we had the baby. Babies. Two, but both part of the same thing—it's hard to explain, but twins . . . They aren't two people, they're an *entity*. Same size, weight, same blue eyes, hands like starfish, even Vivian couldn't differentiate, and whatever was going on inside her . . ." He doesn't exactly finish. He just says, "I could see it in them. Something. I don't know what, just." He shakes his head. "Something."

He turns inward, as if looking for the imaginary wire wheel and trying to separate and identify the creatures circling ceaselessly inside it, tail to head to tail to head to tail until there is no separating end from beginning, captor and captive, master and creature, quarry and pursuer. The next words pop into the air. "I was afraid for the kids. The pairing, the private flow. Things happening. It was getting *weird*."

He drops the name into the space between them, where it lodges. "Vivian. I tried to get help. Remember, I loved her, they were my kids. And then she just *took* them. She took them away."

Carroll is aware of the passengers rushing by but she too is intent; she says, "And you just let it happen."

"I had to. It was part of the arrangement, and now . . ." He breaks off and starts over. "Carroll, there's something I have to tell you. About the twins."

But this is the last call; he has to go. She's aware that there are things she needs to say to him, an apology for the last bad moment in the bedroom, but there isn't time. "Steve, I just . . ."

"Oh Carroll, I love you so *much*." Everything she has to say to him is lost in the rush for the gate. Hugging her so hard that her ribs crack, Steve slips into the stream of passengers.

As he disappears Carroll calls, "I love you," but she can't be certain he hears. Sobbing, she is confounded by the past—Violet and Daddy, hugging like this just before he got into the car that last time and died in the crash.

Then at the very last second her husband, lover, the man she loves best, turns and over the passengers' heads he says, "Something you have to know . . ." She thinks she knows: *about Vivian*. But what she hears is, "About the twins."

Trapped behind the ropes, Carroll leans forward with her mouth wide, straining to hear, but a last-minute traveler rushes between them so she can't see Steve's face much less divine what he's trying to say. In minutes distance will fall between them and erase everything.

He's going and she hasn't made it up. Maybe it's the shock or the hour that decimates her on the echo of that bad moment in the bedroom, that she hasn't resolved, or maybe there is such a thing as prescience. Whatever it is, it flattens her. Later, back at the car, Carroll will sit in the parking lot for so long she loses track of time, sobbing for him. But right now even though he's ducked through the gate and headed down the ramp Carroll hears herself promising because she will do anything to make it up.

"Steve!" she shouts. Several people turn to stare. Steve is nowhere that she can see. "Don't worry," she said broken-heartedly. "Whatever it is, I'll take care of them."

4

"COOL," my sister says.

"Better than cool." We hold up the picture of our king, Saint Stephen. "Look at him!"

"And he's ours."

"All ours."

Look at us, the queen of Amadamaland. Aren't we beautiful? And triumphant. Yes. We have fought for the kingdom and emerged supreme. We declare a holiday for all the citizens in memory of the rival queen of the country next door, poor Vivian.

Poor Vivian.

Not poor. Just gone, she is.

But so sad. Our mother, lost . . .

Not our mother, OK? Just poor Vivian. Our real mother would never try to break us up like that, we are the queen, remember.

But she loved us . . .

Shut up! She was a witch! Why else would she try to take us out of here?

But she was our . . .

Wrong. She was just somebody the king got, to take care of us. We had to save ourselves, OK? Don't you think so?

I don't know, I don't know! Ow! That hurts! Please don't. Ow!

Well, don't you?

What?

Think so?

Ow! Whatever you say, now please stop hurting me.

That's better. Now rejoice and be glad with me and I'll let you be in charge today.

Hail to the queen.

*The queen is this and every dimension. Now smile, he's
coming!*

So I rejoice and my sister rejoices.

We are protectors and defenders. We have prevailed. Why
shouldn't we prepare a celebration? Our courtiers are safe;
so are the people in the villas safe; we have defended the
integrity of the castle. Rejoice for us, for all the cottagers—
everybody in the kingdom spared a fate, not worse than
death, exactly, but just as ugly and final. Not a single
Amadaman life was taken in the skirmish. And we have our
victory. Nobody can come in here, nobody can even begin
to dismantle the buildings or disperse our citizens. We are
the queen. No one dares question us.

But there is an astonishment. A fresh victory. Something
we did not anticipate. Even in Amadamaland, things you
don't know enough to hope for are often best.

Look down there!

From our parapet at the top of the house, we can see him
coming. Grandmother's solemn driver Billy Graver, circling
the driveway in the black car like a funeral cortege of one.
It takes him forever to reach the front door, sad old Billy
with his stern, judgmental looks. Willing or not, he is
bringing us a present. Leaning over the railing, we are glad
we put on our mother-of-pearl headbands this morning, and
our dresses of blue stone-washed silk. Billy gets out to open
the car door but his passenger is already springing out; he
looks so young!

It's just as Grandmother promised. He's here.

The special one.

It is amazing. Even from here we can see it. *He looks like
us.*

"There he is! Oh, Jade!"

"He's gorgeous. Oh, Emerald!"

One of us says, so slyly that neither of us can be sure she
said it: "We should have done it sooner."

To cover this, one shouts, ta-ra: "Throw open the gates."

Here he comes.

Our mother is dead, poor Vivian, but we are not an

orphan, oh no. We have gained, not lost. For the first time we're opening the gates to Amadamaland to an outsider. *King Stephen, the Expected.*

We just found out this morning. Grandmother called us down to the library when she got home from the hospital. After the ambulance came and took Vivian, we just—didn't hear. Nobody called. Nobody came. In spite of which, we understood.

When Grandmother finally got back at dawn, she called us down to break the news. Billy rattled the gates of Amadamaland to rouse us. He stood in the doorway and his face was like carved driftwood, colorless and stern. Sometimes he likes us so much he'll give us anything and at others he does not like us. Well enough. We do not necessarily like him. "Your grandmother has sad news for you." Not real news; we already knew. Only Billy was surprised.

His look told us he thought we wouldn't care. We did feel bad, we did. Some of us sobbed. She did not exactly tell us. Instead Grandmother hugged us hard without explaining and then she stood back and studied us. Then she took a big breath like a drowning fool: "Girls. I need to talk to you." *We know.* "Oh, Gran," we said, first one, then the other. "You look so sad!"

"I am sad," she said. "I just wish I knew what to *do* with you." At her wits' end. *I'm at my wits' end,* she used to say every time we walked into trouble.

We slid onto the sofa on either side of her and stroked her cheeks. "Don't be sad." "Please don't." We did things to make her smile; it always works; it worked today in spite of everything; with her eyes filled up like that, she smiled a little. Not hard to know what people want and give it to them. "Poor Gran, we hate to see you crying."

Poor Gran, so mournful. "If we hadn't been talking about separate schools . . ."

We stroked her face and breathed into her soft neck until she forgot what she was trying to tell us and promised there would be no separate schools.

"And then your poor mother, I . . ." She took a big breath. "When I tell you, you'll understand," she said. We already understood but we let her. She told us and we all three cried together and put our arms around her and said things to make her feel better.

But then! The surprise. "But, girls. Somebody special is coming."

"Not a new tutor."

"Not a new governess."

"Jane, Emily." Grandmother's hands got away from her and flew up and up. So did her voice. It came whistling out. "Your mother is. Something has. Your mother can't . . ." Poor old thing. "Somebody has to . . ." She finally got it out. "I've sent for your father, girls."

It was like a tidal wave crashing on the shores of Amadamaland, foam seething over us, washing away small objects, treasures, household pets, leaving us clinging for dear life. Janemjan, Jademerald, swept away by something new. We could hardly get our breath.

"You told us he was dead!"

She sighed. "It was a necessary lie. I had to bring you up the best I could," she said. "And now, without Vivian . . ." We stroked her hands until she calmed down. and said, "Now come upstairs with me."

Poor thing, she was so far gone in grief that she never even tried to read our faces. She just went through Mother's things with those shaky, *shaky* hands, while Emerald and Jade flickered in the shadows like fireflies, waiting to light up. She was looking for his picture. "Your father's name is Stephen," she said. "And he's coming. To."

Then didn't we lean toward her, listening. *Take us away?* But she didn't finish. There was something she wasn't telling us. *Yes there may be trouble. Nobody takes us out of the kingdom, no.* She had found the picture she was looking for, but she didn't let us see. She had it clamped to her front, bang among the ruffles of the dress she was wearing when it happened to Vivian. And she had that look.

One said, "Janem. Glena." *We have to watch out for her.*

One said, "Emjan. Femo naja." Sister told sister in the language only we two know: *She's nothing. Nothing at all.*

Our grandmother's eyes were all watery. She would not let us see the picture. "Oh stop it. Please don't."

We are steel and velvet. "What is he coming to do?"

"What's he coming for, Grandmother?"

Beaten, yes? But clever too. In her own way this lady, our grandmother, is as strong as us. She sighed. "I'll let him tell you the rest." And showed us the picture after all.

We smiled our smooth cat smiles. *Victoire.* No more Farmington talk, or Ashley Hall, no talk of separation. No, "Emily can study music in New York," no giving us: "Nice little school for Jane, in Farmington." Next to Amadamaland, New York is the hole in the middle of a zero. Farmington is in the sticks. No more of, "You need to make other friends, school will be good for you." No more resistance. She just showed us the picture.

Nothing comes between us. We are the queen. Our kingdom is here.

When she saw it, my sister shuddered and blinked. "Our father?"

Look at our grandmother's eyes, swimmy and so *grave.* "Yes."

"Fama. Emona." *Father, Emjan. Remember?*

Grandmother cried, "Stop that!" She hates our secret language.

"Fama? Emenola." Janem: *Not really.*

Sometimes in the deep of night the queen remembers someplace else, other bedrooms, another pair of arms, but it is in the book of the castle that the queen never had a father. In the royal book of Amadamaland it is written that the queen came into the throne room fully formed. Appeared. Us. No father/mother. Immediate and whole. A goddess, springing from the brow of a god. Even so, we knew. That is our face in his picture. Weaker, maybe, not so wise, but our face. We knew him at once.

We, the queen, pronounced on it. "Emo-*na*-mus!"

"Girls?" Grandmother kept waiting—for what?

We are the queen. There was no need to answer *her*. We took the picture of King Stephen and ran away. We put it in the Amadamaland cathedral, in front of old Dr. Archer's Visible Head with its glass eyes and articulated jaw. We flanked it with crystal bud vases we liberated from the kingdom downstairs. We put the little silk prayer rug Grandmother thought had been stolen in front of it and set candles in the silver candlesticks.

"King Stephen?"

We lit candles and watched the light flicker on the face. It was our face, but not. We look like him but we really come from Vivian.

"Maybe his name isn't King. He looks like a saint. Saint Stephen."

"Gorgeous."

My sister says, "Like us."

There is heat in my voice. "Gorgeous *man*."

"Exactly."

"I think I'm in love with him."

"Vivian said he was dead."

"Well Vivian was wrong."

Sometimes the rival queen was nice. When Vivian was happy with us she gave us things, she was sweet. Sometimes big as we were she used to hug us and try to get both of us on her lap. She cried over us. We feel a little bad. "Poor Vivian."

But now, the father.

Here he is. Look at him down there, standing alone in the driveway while Billy Graver puts the car away. Look at him waiting for Grandmother to open the front door. Seen from above like this, he looks so little. Like nothing. Watch him hug our grandmother and see how she backs away. Then the weak old thing forgets herself and almost falls, so he has to put out his arms and help hold her up. And all the time our grandmother is talking, talking.

We can only imagine what she's telling him about the Queen. Some lies. Well never mind, we have had enough of her. It's him we watch. He never thinks to look up at the parapet, where we are hanging over with our earrings dangling and our faces all pink from being upside down. He doesn't see us. We wonder what he thinks he is doing here.

We think: *Here he is.*

He is ours by blood.

The One who belongs to us, by our stars. Who all these years has been denied us.

"Vivian. Serves her right." She said it right out loud.

Wait. Who said that?

Janem, Emjan, Emerald, Jade. Who spoke?

It is us, the Queen of Amadamaland.

My sister does not have to say, *Daddy?*

In spite of which I hear, and do not have to say, *Idiot.* I know she hears. *This is no mere father.*

Our prince, my darlings, that's him going into the front door way below, and after he speaks with the grandmother, he is coming upstairs to the tower wing, where we will greet him by name. "Stephen." "Father." "Saint Stephen." "We knew you'd come."

Look, he has traveled all this way just to come and live with us! After we hug we will pull him into Amadamaland and we will live here together forever. It will be so fine! We'll be complete. We can be happy for the rest of our lives right here in our beautiful, perfect kingdom, Jade and Emerald and their king, Saint Stephen, together forever in Amadamaland.

And when the time comes?

When the time comes, we will marry him.

But we can't both.

Yes we can both. After all, we are the queen. Who would not want us, we are beautiful. Idiot, say it. Aren't we beautiful?

Everyone knows we're beautiful, but he's . . .

He loves us!

. . . Our father.

We will make him our king.

He may already be married.

Marriage is nothing. We are the queen.

"Look, here he is!"

Waiting, we are agog, aflame, suspended over our lives, like Rapunzel in the tower.

"Our prince!"

"Shh, he'll hear you."

Not prince. He's our father.

Father, prince, they are the same to us.

Together, we will be one. In Amadamaland.

5

GOING UPSTAIRS in the aging Victorian pile that belongs to his ex-mother-in-law, Steve Harriman finds himself walking softly, although there's no real reason to sneak. He stays close to the wall, as if putting his weight on the point where the tread is anchored to the wall may keep the stairs from creaking. He seems to need to go quietly. For some reason, he isn't ready to let the girls know he's coming. Jane. Emily. His daughters. His and Vivian's, that he thought he would never see again. It took him a long time to get over the loss and now . . . Now Vivian is gone and here he is.

All the bad memories slip away and he gulps in anticipation. The last time he saw his daughters they were tiny, with plump legs still bent in that baby way. His pretty, sleepy twins were like cuddly rabbits in fuzzy pajamas with feet. They were moist and fragrant from the bath, and Vivian had put on flowered hair ribbons to hold back their curls—roses for Jane and bachelor's buttons for Emily. They looked at him: not mirror images, but something more. The likeness was exact. Em. Jane. Or is it Janie and Em? No matter. They were so pretty he almost forgot.

But even in their sweet moments, some sinister current crackled between the two of them. It didn't have a name; it was nothing he could isolate and plumb. It was strange enough to make him ask for help. His friend the doctor was coming to evaluate. All he wanted the man to do was one simple thing. He wanted his friend the doctor to say, Don't be silly, they're fine. The night before, Vivian took them and fled. After all this time the memory is sharp as a hook dragged across an open wound. It took him two years to track her down, and when he did, she got a court order to keep him away.

"For your own good," she said the one time they spoke. Her mouth was filled with tears and she would not explain.

The daughters he said goodbye to are not the daughters he's coming upstairs to meet. These girls are adolescents, nearly women. Why should they be glad to see him when he hasn't come before, and never even tried to call or write?

He can't exactly explain to them about the court order, or certain threats made by Vivian. He can't be sure the girls will remember him. Here he is, Steve Harriman fresh in from nowhere and out of excuses, getting ready to pick these unsuspecting children up like puppies and take them out of their lives.

What is he supposed to do, open the door and say, "Surprise?"

He doesn't know.

He just knows he isn't ready.

Changing planes in Chicago, he shuddered in anticipation. He couldn't go in unarmed. Pressed, he dodged into the airport gift shop and picked up earrings for the girls—little crystal studs. Then he bought two more pairs: lapis and malachite. Then he worried because it might look like too much. Would they think he was trying to buy them off? He just wanted to have something to give them. He needed some way to let the twins know that even though Vivian told them he was dead, they *had*—no. Have. They have a father, who loves them. He just wants to show his daughters that in spite of everything, he never stopped thinking about them.

Now he bites his lip because he doesn't even know whether their ears are pierced.

And he understands he's a little afraid of them. On the long drive here, he tried to pump the driver. All he wanted was some little detail, anything he could build on to start a conversation with his estranged children, but at his first question Billy Graver went inside himself and pulled up the drawbridge, leaving Steve to ride along with his doubts. Meeting Steve, the driver could have been a doctor reporting a terminal disease, or a returning soldier bowed down by bad news from the front. Then there was Meredith. She wants him to take the girls; she doesn't want him to take the girls. It is confusing. She wants to tell him something but she can't.

Most of what fell between them didn't have to be discussed. When she pulled him inside, Meredith was breathing so erratically that her pearls jumped. Her elegant face was leached of color. She looked like a castaway who's spent too long staring into an eclipse and it was clear that it was not age that had done this to her, but the pressure of events.

"I tried to warn you," she said without preface or explanation. "She never should have had children. I never should have let her marry you."

"She would have married somebody else."

The old lady's hands flutter to his upper arms. "You had such a nice face. Viv was trying so hard. I thought it might even be all right. And now . . ."

"Shh, Meredith. They're my children too."

She pulled him into the ell under the stairs and gave him the rings he had given Vivian when they were married. "Here."

"She was still wearing them!" When they dropped into his hand it all became real. His breath came out in an involuntary groan.

She nodded and couldn't stop; her whole head shook. "I'm sorry. I'm just not strong enough. When they're bigger, you'll want them to have their mother's wedding rings."

"You haven't told me what happened to Vivian."

"It was very sad."

Vivian had died suddenly. This woman called him from the hospital in the middle of the night, dropping into Steve's new life to drag him back, and now he was here. He'd left home without really explaining, leaving poor Carroll standing in the airport with a hurt, puzzled look because Meredith said he had to come alone, and now? Steve prodded her. "How did it happen?"

She opened empty hands to him. "I don't know! Nobody's sure."

Was this all she had to give? Impatient, he said, "I need to know. I just need to know the details."

"A fall," she said. "It was terrible." Was the old lady trying to protect him from painful details? Or was she really baffled? He did not know. She wouldn't answer: Meredith Archer, who could only say, "I'm sorry. I'm just not strong enough to bring up another set of twins alone. I just can't. When you get to be my age, children put things over on you. They need . . . They need somebody else. Somebody young." Then when he thought she was about to start weeping helplessly, she drew herself up.

Staring at something he could not see. Meredith Archer turned a chiseled profile; she could have been a defeated general, looking out over the fields of a fallen country. "You can only carry a burden for so long."

He plunged. "Like Zane." The old business. Vivian was never clear about what happened to her twin brother, but she carried the full weight of their joint history. Their marriage broke under it.

Zane. The old lady's head seemed to spin on her neck at such great speeds that her expression blurred. "It's just too much. I just want them to have a chance! Now they're your responsibility."

Joy surfaced, surprising him. "I know!" God, he had missed them. Every night of his life he imagined going into their room and kissing his children good night. Feeling a little flash of disloyalty to Carroll, he realized how much he was in love with Vivian. How he missed her now.

"So," Meredith said, as if she'd explained everything, "there you are."

"Do they know about me?"

"I gave them your picture." Now that they had completed the transaction, Meredith had his elbow; he could feel the bite of her nails through his jacket. She was moving him toward the staircase.

"You still haven't told me exactly what happened."

"Nobody knows." Gracious, steely, his ex–mother-in-law had always been the perfect lady. Meredith, the master of denial. "They know you're coming, but I wanted the rest to be a surprise, so I haven't had them packed." By the carved newel post the old lady stopped, looking up as if she expected the girls to be hanging over the rail on the third-floor landing. She dropped her voice, in case. "They'll need all new things."

"I'll be happy to . . ."

She rushed on. "Once you get them away. The problem will be getting them away. Billy will have Vivian's car ready with the motor running. All you have to do is get them downstairs. And if anything comes up . . ."

"What could come up?"

". . . I'll pay."

He said, uneasily, "Why are you making this such a big *thing?* They're only kids."

"I hope so." Meredith's expression brought it back: the secretiveness, the strangeness that encircled his little girls and contained them—they were only *babies* but there were times when he looked at them in the crib at night and thought he saw something fierce and powerful there, a force bigger than the two of them that kept them locked, head to tail, spinning in a tight, furious, unbreakable circle, moving so quickly that faces, identities, everything blurred. Meredith's voice drifted between them and hung there, words quivering like discrete objects. "It's your turn now."

So.

Troubled, he rehearsed opening lines for this encounter, but he can't get much beyond, "Hi."

It's not the girls he's afraid of, its their reproaches. *If you really loved us, you would have come for us.* I couldn't. I promised. What if they don't want to go with him?

He tells himself this has happened too fast, that he needs to call home and touch base with Carroll before he faces them. He wants to be able to tell his girls, "You have a father who loves you and a nice stepmother. She loves you too. She wants you to come and live with us." He tells himself everything is fine, he just isn't ready to start doing what he has to do here.

This isn't the real reason. And it isn't anything Meredith has told him, either.

He can't say why he needs to be careful, or why he wants to surprise them. These are his daughters after all, his girls, and he's not the enemy, he's their father. They're only children.

He corrects himself. Not children. Adolescents. From all the pictures Meredith has, beautiful. They'll be young women soon.

When he comes into the third floor corridor heading for the girls' suite, he hears music. The Triumphal March from *Aida*. It lifts his heart and makes him smile. Swift and suddenly happy, he knocks gently on the door and waits for them to answer. He can hardly wait to see them. His girls, his children.

"Girls."

The Triumphal March peaks and then tapers off. Paired voices come from inside the door, silky and touchingly sweet. "Who is it?"

"It's me," he says. "Your father."

The blended voices say, "King Stephen?"

Surprised, he laughs. "Not exactly."

"Then you cannot enter," one says. Emily?

Maybe it's Jane who says, "We admit only the king."

"King Stephen. Oh, God, if you say so."

"Saint Stephen."

"Not exactly." He feels so guilty!

The voice is steely. It is an imperative. *"Saint Stephen."*

Sighing, he capitulates. "Whatever you want." He puts his mouth close to the crack and says, "I never got a chance to tell you girls this, but I want you to know that even when I couldn't see you, I loved you. I've always loved you."

"Wait," one says.

The other says, "Then come."

The knob doesn't yield.

"First give the password."

He feels in his pockets for the earrings. He was going to start with the crystals and save the lapis and malachite for other days, but now he pulls out all the little boxes at once, holding them out in cupped hands. "I've brought you some presents."

There is a scuffle on the other side of the door. "The password is: *Prenamo*," one says. He shudders. It is the old language.

The other says, "Present yourself."

"King Stephen. *Prenamo*." A grown man like this, locked out in the hall of a strange house with his hands full of trinkets and that *funny word* choking him. *"Prenamo,"* he says, louder. "King Stephen, OK? Or Saint, if that's what you want." Then on an inspiration he adds, "I have come to make homage to the princesses."

One says, in a voice so low and thrilling that it could have come from deep within a much older woman: "We are the queen."

"The queen," he says. "Oh *prenamo*. Please let me in."

The key is in the lock; chain latches are already sliding; in another second the door will open and he'll see his children: Steve Harriman, King Stephen to you, he thinks with a little edge of anxiety, waiting to enter the kingdom.

"You may enter," the other daughter says.

What does he expect when he walks in, hostility? Weirdness? It's neither. It's just two teenaged girls, flushed and beautiful and as uncertain and excited as he is. He still doesn't know what Meredith was trying to tell him but seeing them, he's relieved to know she's wrong. The twins fill the little opening. They hide their hands in their skirts like shy girls at dancing class. "Dad?"

They look so tentative that he says, "Hey, it's me. Your father."

Their smiles make his heart leap. "You're really our father?"

He nods. "You look *great*."

"So do you." Their eyes fill. "You heard about our . . ."

"Mother."

One corrects him. "Vivian."

"Yes," he says, feeling something twist inside him. "Vivian. That's why I've come. Your, ah . . ." He can't explain, not yet. "Your grandmother thought you probably needed me."

"And we need you," they say. They seem so *young,* so ordinary and easy with him, nice children with their smooth hair and pastel dresses, that he wonders what all the fuss was about. They hold out their arms to him.

Which is how Steve finds himself hugging them. His twins are beautiful, fragrant, standing so close that he doesn't see their faces. When he can swallow he says into their hair, "So, your mother. Vivian. Vivian is gone, but. Ah. At least you'll have me, OK?"

When they release him and back off one says, "We're so glad!"

The other says, "Really."

"We're so glad you came!"

"We thought you were dead."

"We just wish we could have had you and her together."

He hears the silent reproach. *Why didn't you stay married?* "She didn't want that," Steve says. "I guess I have a lot to explain to you."

"We have a lot to tell you too," one says. In spite of their grief they are both smiling, excited to have him here. Who wouldn't love them on sight?

"And things to show you!" the other says, and as her sister's face changes she rushes on. "The kingdom!"

He supposes they mean these rooms. "That's great," he says.

The other says hastily, "But not right now."

Her sister sees, and adds, "Not just yet, OK?"

"Whatever you say," he says. Something warns him not to tell them where he's taking them.

Like any children, his beautiful twin daughters want to forget their grief in the commonplace business of the day, two nice kids and their father, getting to know each other. They move him out the door.

"Let's go downstairs, OK?"

"Outside, where it's pretty. Out in the car."

"When we come back, we'll take you around the kingdom."

"Whatever you say," Steve says. He can't quite figure out how to tell them he's taking them away from here.

"To McDonald's, maybe."

"Or Dairy Queen." He's glad to hear them laugh. "Let's go spoil our lunches."

Now they're on the stairs, lingering until he catches up. "Wherever you say." Steve is laughing too, in spite of everything.

His daughters say, "You're in charge, Dad."

"Dad," the other daughter says.

Steve takes a deep breath. *Dad*. He feels better. He has plenty of time to break the news to them.

6

ALONE in Steve's house, Carroll wishes she could rewrite the last few hours. She wants Steve here so she can mend whatever is broken between them. She wants to take back her harsh words. But now he's on his way to northern California to change their lives.

When he comes back he won't be alone. He's coming home with his twins. She's a good reporter; she has to prepare. If she can get hold of some facts, she'll know how to proceed. Maybe she should be at the library, reading everything there is about twins: care and feeding, she guesses, or is it psychopathology? Do twins have special qualities that ordinary people don't know about? Are there specific things twins need, or things she needs to know?

She thinks there are.

There are characteristics unique to twins, she thinks, and doesn't know why this makes her so uncomfortable. Twins are unique. *Not like us.* She can't shake the bizarre double images in Jenkins, souls shadowing each other as if joined at the waist. There are pairs she met and talked to and others whose stories drifted up out of history, or is it legend: the Duvals, who shared a uniform in the War Between the States, confounding commanding officers, who thought there was only one Duval serving the Confederacy and had the wrong twin executed as a Union spy. Jane and Dansey Herbert slipped in and out of town history around the turn of the century; they fell in love with the same man and pursued him, flowing one into the other like water, beautiful girls who changed places at such lightning speed that they exhausted their quarry, loving him to death. The Archambaults had twin sons nobody saw and nobody wanted to talk about. There were the Soders. So ancient and dried-up that they were almost sexless, they still lived near the center of town when Carroll first came to Jenkins, two identical old people in matching overalls, stewing like wasps trapped in a kettle. If you slipped on the way home from school and accidentally put one foot on their grass, they came boiling out. Even the twins Carroll knew in high school were a little creepy: Betti and Bobbi Carter, who kept secrets, and answered for each other in class; the Benson boys—the dumb one always took the blame for what the smart one did, but when dull Blake got killed in a wreck, brilliant Bob had to be pried off his casket. That night the police found Bob sleeping on top of his brother's grave; when they woke him, he refused to leave; instead he started pounding on the dirt like the pillows of an unmade bed. "Get up," he screamed, sobbing to break the heart of the dead. "Get up. You've slept long enough."

Twins. Carroll has read that identical twins come from the same egg: not complete individuals, but discrete halves of a mystical whole. Joined in ways ordinary people can't know, they share, what is it: *the ability to know without being told.* One cries, "What is it?" before the other speaks. They don't debate; they act as one. Separated at birth, an identical twin will double over, gasping in pain at the exact moment that the missing twin is shot dead halfway around the world. It speaks of something alien to her, disturbing. *Not like us,* she thinks. *Not like any of us.*

And all this time the man she thought she knew has been the father of twins. Steve Harriman married and fathered twins and for unspecified reasons he walked away from that life and into Carroll's, hiding this central fact.

She is hung up on the lie.

The shock made Carroll say things she regrets. Blinded by pain and resentment, she attacked, hurting Steve when he needed her most. If she needs to go to the library and do homework now; if she wavers between research and compulsive shopping, buying too many things in pairs for Steve's girls, it's because she needs to make this up to all three of them. She's whirling now, torn between pain and guilt: pain at the lie and the betrayal, and guilt because she hurt Steve when he could least handle it.

"You've turned our lives into a lie!" He was ashen, shaken by the news from California, but she couldn't stop; it hurt so much! "You should have told me."

A long shiver took him by the shoulders. "I couldn't."

"Oh yes." She's ashamed to remember her tone. "Oh yes you could. You could but you let it go by and now it's, Oh by the way, in case you thought you wanted a family, you already *have* a family." She was crying. "I would have loved them, Steve. All you had to do was let me know."

"I was afraid if I told you, you'd stop loving me." The look he gave her then was clouded; she recognized the shadows rushing at his back—they had crowded Steve at their first meeting by the river in Jenkins, and in spite of all the vows Carroll had made to herself: to make him happy, to make him forget; in spite of the little song of safety she'd been humming ever since they married, the shadows had never gone away.

"Stop loving you? Me, *stop?*" Outrage shook her. "Who do you think I am that you had to lie to me?"

He put out his hands. "Carroll, don't. There's no way you can understand this. The weight. The responsibility." His voice was raw, as if he'd pulled it out of a place that was still bleeding. "Whatever it is they are."

"Nothing bad," she said quickly, like a maiden raising a crucifix against the unknown, or whistling into a whirlwind. "Nothing bad. They're only twins."

Everything in him shuddered to a stop. It was as if a bat had flown into the room and started circling. "My twins."

So this is how Carroll summed up her astonishment and pain at his betrayal, the anxiety that left her hurt and jittering. With her voice dark with resentment, she lashed out: "Exactly."

She might as well have smacked him with a board.

So she and the man she loves more than anything have this unresolved bad moment standing between them. There wasn't time to make it up. If Carroll is wandering the empty house now, bouncing from room to room like a Ping-Pong ball, it's because she wants a chance to rewrite all their sentences and give the scene an ending that leaves her feeling less mean and miserable. She can't wait to have Steve back so she can rewrite history.

It was this combination of love and regret that drove Carroll to shout after him as he boarded: "Whatever it is, I'll take care of them."

How badly has she hurt him? She doesn't know. She only knows she needs to see him soon, and in the ready superstition of those who have lost a parent in childhood, she thinks: *What if something happens to him and I don't get a chance?*

Stop it, Carroll. Just stop. He'll come back and find everything a mess—the house, your face. You don't want him to see you like this, so you need to wash your hair and put on earrings and a silk shirt. You have to focus on the ceremonial dinner. New furniture. You've promised to take care of the twins.

Twins. The word calls up a cartoon double stroller, with identical grinning doll faces framed in ruffled bonnets and identical pudgy hands brandishing matched rattles. It's like a practical joke.

But this isn't a joke, and they aren't babies. They're adolescent girls. Because it's less threatening, she's been thinking of them as little, but they're fourteen. Are they still kids or emerging women? She doesn't know. She doesn't even know what to buy for them. Steve left in haste. There are too many things he didn't think to tell her that she didn't have time to ask. Does their mother try to give them separate identities, or should she be out at Ikea and the Gap buying things in pairs? Carroll doesn't know. She thinks she ought to clear her things out of the front bedroom: books, her laptop, her files, to make a place for them.

She lingers at the door to the spare room, looking at the neat desk Steve bought for her, the open laptop with its blank screen reproaching her, the daybed that in a pinch they could use for guests. That first day, sunburned to pink and laughing, still shaking sand out of their shoes from the wedding trip, they stood right here. Hugging her, Steve opened the door. "I fixed this up for you," he said with a proud grin. Carroll was excited, touched. "It's your office. Plus. You can sit there and write a novel."

"In your dreams." She laughed.

When she writes her book, it will not be a novel. Carroll knows more than she ought to about how being orphaned changes ordinary lives. She remembers a quotation from a book on suicides: "The missing parent, like an open wound." She has spent her life since Violet died trying to fill the empty places; she thinks there's more to find out about what these early losses do to perfectly ordinary people, and considerably more to write.

Reinforced by Steve, she laughed. "Who knows what else I can do." Her tone was bright.

He crunched her to his side so they joined, flank to flank. "You can do whatever you want."

"Count on it." But even that first day she cast around in spite of her ambitions, secretly placing other furniture: the crib.

Now this will be the girls' room. His girls. In pain, she thinks: *He already has what he needs. He'll never want a baby now.* Then she thinks, bitterly, *He said he didn't know if he wanted kids. He never said he already* had *them.* Then she thinks: *Don't.*

Because to her astonishment she's come smack up against what's really bothering her. That rises in her throat and tastes sour in her mouth. It is the lie.

No, she thinks, leaving the room and kicking the door shut. It's discovering the lie.

No. She stops in the hall with her heart thudding. That isn't it at all. Standing there in the upstairs hall of Steve Harriman's house, Carroll is newly bereft. She wants to believe it's the shock, no, the *dislocation* that has leveled her and left her open to the winds, like a half-demolished house.

The fact that she left a job that was her life to follow a man who didn't love her well enough to tell the truth. She let Steve Harriman swoop down on Jenkins, Florida, and

pull her out of the sand like a shrub with shallow roots. He
shook the sand off her roots and transplanted her here,
binding her to him with love and promises while that idiot
Russell moved into her desk at the *Dispatch* and took her
place. Steve did all this—changed her life forever without
trusting her love enough to tell her the rest.

But that isn't the whole thing.

The real issue is deeper and more troublesome.

What bothers her now, what caught Carroll under the
heart with hooks was the way Steve's face changed in the
predawn light when he turned and for the first time said his
dead wife's name.

"Vivian."

It was like having her there in the room. *Vivian.*

Some unsuspected part of the man she thought she knew
moved out of the shadows for a narrow second, and shone.
And Carroll saw that happy as Steve had been with her, he
was not the same man he had been in life before Carroll,
before the explosion that ended his first marriage and
overturned him, changing his life. His look told her that
before whatever happened to change him so dramatically
happened, her lover, husband, her *only one* had been
delirious, exalted, drunk in love with Vivian.

It was jealousy that sent Carroll running at him, using
words like snares to bring him down in midflight and pull
him back.

She wants him here.

There are things she has to know. Like: Who was she,
anyway, this Vivian, who still lights up your face. And if
you loved her so much how could you end it in the first
place? If it's really over, why do you look like that when you
say her name, and if things between you two were so bad,
why does she still make you shine?

She wants to bang on his chest, hammering until it opens
like a cabinet and the truth spills out. She hears herself
crying: "Why didn't you tell me?" But she knows. No. She
thinks she knows. She's felt him shifting restlessly in the
night, murmuring in his sleep, chased by furies she can't

envision. His face when they first met was shadowed, as if at his back large shapes loomed, stalking him.

Short of sleep and parched—did she forget to eat?—Carroll roves the house, looking for something without knowing what. She may hope to find some object—photograph, diary, talisman—that Steve kept because he couldn't bear to throw it away, but kept hidden because he couldn't bear to think of Vivian. She just wants to find something that will prove the old marriage was really over.

No. That will prove Steve didn't love this Vivian after all. Or had stopped loving her.

Anything, she thinks miserably. After all, I'm into facts. It's an occupational hazard for any reporter. Get your facts to march in order and you can control your life.

Wait, she tells herself even as she rummages. It's over. You have him. The poor woman is dead. Listen, she tells herself with only a touch of guilt, you have to inform yourself; you're taking care of this woman's children now. Finally she admits that she's looking through Steve's things simply because she can't help it. She misses him so much!

This is what she finds. In the back of the drawer to Steve's drafting table, two snapshots. Steve and Vivian on some forgotten, happy day. They are only smears but they make her grimace; it's disturbing to see how lovely the woman is. Was. And in the pigeonhole in the desk in the front room, right where she could have found it if she'd looked, a fact that makes her ashamed of the search, she finds the divorce paper. It is official, bland and unyielding as a concrete wall. It's dated ten years ago, almost to the day, and it is a no-fault decree. Carroll knows the blanket terms for cases like these: Irretrievable breakdown. Irreconcilable differences. God.

Isn't this enough?

He loved her. It's over. She's dead. Carroll shouldn't mind that he used to love Vivian, but she does. Brace up, she tells herself. Feel better. After all, you're still here. You're both still here and you have him now. He's yours for good. But the selfish, jealous part of her stalks the house, slamming drawers and bumping into things, because if she and Steve live a thousand years together she'll always know that Vivian came first.

Looking at the twins, Steve will see Vivian's face.

Emily. She tries the names. *Jane.* She practices. Hello Emily. Hello Jane. Twins. For the first time Carroll forgets her own bitter preoccupation and thinks about the girls. Disturbed by the suddenness, the threatened incursion, she's shied off the central fact. She and Steve's twins have more in common than they know.

Their mother is dead.

Like Violet. Her insides shift.

Without knowing how she got there, Carroll is back in childhood, waiting for Violet to come home from the hospital. No. Inside she already knows Violet is too sick. She's waiting to be told. She is ten-year-old Carroll Lawton with her knuckles gnawed raw and the ear of her frayed Teddy gripped tightly in her teeth, ignorant kid in her striped T-shirt and matching polyester flares with her underpants drooping and her socks bunched up because when Violet got sick everything in the world seemed to let go all at once. She hears the elevator door and the almost intolerable pause while the person getting out collects herself. The sitter. She's coming back to break the news to Carroll that her mother is never coming home.

The twins. Everything in her rushes to meet them. *Poor kids!*

Carroll will do better than her aunts did when she came down to Jenkins, trying to be brave and not cry. She was doing all right until Suzy's gooshy sympathy brought her down. *Oh you poor thing, you've lost your mother! What's going to happen to you now?*

Please stop it.

She is crying. Stop.

She'll find some easy thing to say to Steve's daughters when they come, something ordinary, so they can pretend life is going on after all. She has to help them over the first hard places. She'll help the girls pretend that in spite of everything that's happened to them, they're going to be OK. Carroll will not, will *not* look at them and let her eyes fill up like Aunt Suzy's or say that awful thing. She'll love them because she loves Steve beyond loss and beyond all memory. After all, she's promised to take care of them.

The phone rocks her back into the moment.

"This is Meredith Archer calling." The voice is soft and elegant as old velvet.

"Vivian's mother!"

The old woman does not answer. "You're Stephen's wife?"

With the fear of the once-burned, Carroll cries, "Yes!" *What's the matter, what's the matter.*

"I'm the twins' grandmother. I thought I ought to call to let you know . . ."

Carroll is thinking *OhGodohGodohGod.* Her voice is too loud. "IS HE THERE?"

"Not any more," the woman says.

"What!"

The remote speaker seems not to hear her cry of fear. Instead she goes on in a careful tone that is not quite matter-of-fact. "He had to hurry down to San Francisco to catch his plane. I had him take Vivian's car." Cultivated as she sounds, organized and in control, the old woman betrays herself. "He might as well, she doesn't need it any more and I don't care what happens to it now. I just . . ."

Carroll prompts her. "Then he's on his way?"

"Yes," she says gratefully, "That's it. He's on his way." She pulls herself together and goes on as smoothly as a *grande dame* making arrangements for an afternoon tea dance. "He's on his way, and naturally you'll want to meet their plane. I thought the least I could do was call you with flight numbers and times."

Carroll is emptied out by relief. "Oh thank you," she cries, and is too fixed on this to think to ask the caller for any further details.

7

GOING HOME to the chauffeur's quarters, Billy Graver drags his feet in an old man's shuffle. He's reluctant to face his son. He knows what Kurt will say. *You will do anything for the Archers. Even lie.* Well he hasn't lied, exactly. When he helped Steve Harriman put the twins' things into Vivian's car, he just neglected to mention certain things.

They're his daughters after all, he tells himself. *They deserve a fresh start.* Another chance. They do! He and Meredith love the twins, but if they're going to help them, they have to let them go. Billy and Meredith didn't even have to discuss this. Like so many things that pass between them, it was understood.

He would do anything for her.

In his time he has done everything. Billy has worked for the Archers ever since he got his license. He was driving for the family when he and the orphaned Meredith were young. Last night he drove Meredith to the hospital to release the body of poor Vivian and he will drive her to the Church of All Saints for the funeral tomorrow. They've known each other all their lives, and if Billy thought he was in love with her when they were nineteen, if Meredith confided in him so completely that he could pretend she loved him, he knows better now. He is the driver and she is mistress of the house. Just friends.

In his time, Billy has taken her everywhere. He drove the limousine to the church the day she married Hal Oliphant, the unfaithful, drunken unfavorite son of some big family in the East. How could she love a handsome husk of a man whose family paid him to stay away? Whose mother sent a priest west to plead with her to change her mind? Poor raving Franklin Davage. Bushy-haired Father Davage with his warnings that sounded more like mad ramblings. They should have listened! It didn't matter what he said, Meredith was so dazzled by Hal Oliphant that she would have ignored a whirlwind.

They went to the church with the window between passenger and driver rolled up, sealing him away from Meredith. She sat in the back, lovely in her wedding dress, while he drove with his jaws locked tight so he wouldn't scream; his nails dug into the wheel until he could feel blood starting inside his gloves. At the church Hal Oliphant reeled in the road in his wedding clothes, already drunk. To this moment Billy wishes he'd done what he wanted, even if it meant prison. He should have run the bastard down.

To stop the pain he married Esther Beecham, and was surprised when nothing changed. Then Kurt was born and Billy told himself that if he hadn't stopped the pain he had at least begun to replace Meredith in his heart. *My son. My pride.*

But he is never through doing things for Meredith. When her twins were born it was Billy who drove her to the hospital and Billy who gnawed his knuckles in the waiting room. It was Billy who rejoiced when the long labor ended and he alone who saw the doctor's peculiar expression when he came out to break the news. If at the moment of birth something uncanny had happened, the doctor was not ready to give it a name. So it was left to Billy to tell Hal, who came in late, and drunk: "You have twins. A girl and a boy."

Hal said the strangest thing. "Not again."

"Don't you want to see them?"

"You've got to be kidding," Hal said. That was all. Blathering drunk, he muttered, "Better make Davage baptize them. Or say some charm." Crazy. Like a fool, Billy didn't pass it on. And like a fool, he let his wife Esther work in the big house. He let her go up there where handsome, ruined Hal Oliphant roved the halls, but that was not his greatest oversight. He let his baby grow up on this place with Hal Oliphant's beautiful, flawed twins.

It was Billy who drove Meredith to the hospital the night Hal lost control of the Mercedes and roared into a tree—the last in a painful string of accidents. Their visits to the hospital were like so many infernal worry beads. Police prying Hal out of the wreck found the drunken fool locked in Esther Graver's arms; Billy's wife was already dead. He did not mourn. This is what Billy hugged to himself and held tight: *At least I have my perfect son.*

Together in the hospital, Meredith and Billy clung, and when it became clear that Hal Oliphant was going to live, he drove her home. He drove her to her lawyers' offices the next day. Meredith divorced Hal and in an attempt to erase him, took back her own name. She finished with Hal too late. She had his twins.

And there was something strange about the twins.

He should have been warned! Billy has always been troubled by this deficit of attention. He and Meredith should have been wary; they should have combed the Oliphant family history, looking for signs. He should have tracked down the priest and laid open his soul and pried the secrets out. There were strange things hanging from that particular family tree that nobody talked about. There was more strangeness implied. The rest, nobody knew. It seemed better to put the past away and go ahead. Or so they told themselves.

But there is no anticipating the mystery and power of twins—one spirit in two bodies, good, bad, clothed in the same flesh, inextricably tied. There's no isolating and identifying the power that binds twins and no anticipating how it will be unleashed.

Because Meredith was left to bring up the twins alone, Billy ended up doing things he won't even admit to. After the first terrible business with Zane, he had to lie about the accident. He had to take poor Kurt to the emergency room and lie about how the child got hurt. "It happened too fast for me to see," Billy said, handing him over—his own son. "Hurry. He's in shock."

So there was the first lie. Then there was Kurt's injury. After that little Vivian needed certain injections just to keep her from waking up screaming, whether in anticipation or fear even her mother couldn't say. It was Billy who made the purchases. Later it would be up to Billy to cover up the last terrible business of Zane's death.

Then there are Vivian's girls. He loves them but delightful as they are they have their bad days, and in his time he has done certain things for the twins. If Jane and Emily are not like other children, it's his business to help Meredith pretend they are. If they sometimes fall into rages, if when they were small they got mad and broke things or beat their ponies or even, dear God, *hurt* someone, it was his business to help make the best of things, even if it meant covering up. He and poor Meredith have spent their adult lives covering up for things. It is too hard.

Still, Billy has been driving for Meredith for too many years to stop. He stays on. God help him he stays on in spite of everything.

He knows Kurt thinks it's because he and Meredith are in love; maybe he even thinks they sneak out in the deepest part of the night, but that isn't true. The truth is more complicated. They are old friends. No. Fellow sufferers. Partners yoked and moving down the long, unbroken road to the inevitable checkout counter. They are comfortable in silence because they've shared so much.

How to explain this to a man so young he still thinks love must necessarily include sex. Who shuts himself in above the garage, where there's no chance for either? He does business by fax and modem. His clients come to meetings in the tiny living room.

The tragedy is not Kurt's being hurt when he was little. It's his falling in love with Vivian. He's loved her ever since they were five years old. While the child was mending Billy sat by the bed and said, "Maybe we ought to go someplace else to live. I can get another job." Kurt flew into a tantrum and would not get up until Billy, who had his own loyalties, promised they would stay so he could play with "Bivian." They were children; it was sweet.

Lord, Billy thinks. *So it's my fault after all.* His fault for eating his pain in the first place, cleaving to Meredith after Esther died, for letting his vulnerable child ignore what had happened to him and play on with Meredith's dark, passionate twins. It seemed OK, his son got over the accident and grew up fine. They stayed on because Kurt was fixed on Vivian, dizzy and lost in love.

He should have known! He should have known from experience that only bad things come from this kind of love. But they were only kids! Children, and God help him, Billy didn't see it coming until they were in their twenties and so much in love that Vivian's twin circled them like a flame-crazed moth, trying to find some way to reach the center of the light.

Meredith saw it though, and sent her twins on the Grand Tour of Europe while Kurt went to Stanford. But they came back to the place; they all did. And picked up where they left off.

Billy let himself imagine it was OK; Kurt and Vivian would be happy in love—might even get married. He reckoned without Zane.

Crossing the driveway, he strikes his temple with his fist, grinding his face until tears come under his sharp knuckles. *So stupid!* He doesn't know exactly what happened after Kurt came back from Stanford, but by the end of that month Zane was dead and Vivian was in isolation in a private mental hospital. When it came time for her to come back here from the hospital she ran away.

And Kurt? He was never the same.

Something picked him up that night and broke him in two. He just went inside and never came out again. At the end of that terrible night Billy came back from the police station shaking with grief. For a minute he thought the apartment was empty. Like a kid in a horror movie he moved slowly through the rooms, calling. Then he found his son, crouched on the floor at the end of the hall with his head bent. Something had sent him so far inside himself that nothing could touch him. He stayed that way for a long time while his father wept and begged. When he came out everything changed.

Billy was about to call an ambulance when Kurt shook himself all over and stood. He had come to a decision. He made lists. Gave orders. He had turned into somebody else.

And if he never spoke to Vivian again it seemed all right. Immured as he is, he has made a success.

And seems satisfied.

It breaks Billy's heart to see him and know that at bottom it is all his fault. Groaning, he mounts the stairs.

8

SLOWLY, Billy enters the little apartment above the half-timbered garage. Kurt doesn't even wait until his head clears the opening. He snaps, "You didn't tell him."

"How could I, when I don't even know what there is to tell?" He doesn't, Billy tells himself. The hell of it is he probably does. Sadly, Billy surveys the living room: tired furniture, a brilliant carpet bought in hopes. He and Esther made a life here; they moved in when Kurt was born and they could have been happy here if Esther hadn't been killed in the wreck, if Kurt hadn't . . . He always feels heavy coming in. The Tudor beams make the ceiling seem even lower than it is. Computer screens flicker and smoke from his son's cigarette layers in the dim light.

"You'd do anything for Meredith Archer, wouldn't you?"

It is implicit: *even lie.* "I've done a lot of things."

"You just sent him off without telling him?" Kurt's accusation fills the tiny apartment like a dense coastal fog.

"It wasn't mine to tell."

Kurt lashes out. "Whose was it then, mine?"

Billy's voice breaks. "Oh, son." He hates this. It makes him feel a hundred years old.

"You should have done something." Darkhaired, lanky Kurt Graver pushes his chair away from the computer table, looking unnervingly like a young Abe Lincoln. He's hardly aware of thickly printed paper rolling out of the fax and urgent messages flickering on the various screens. He is handsome in his own irregular way, and in his own way he is strangely powerful. He is at ease with his body, physical—he keeps a battery of fitness equipment in his room—but except for the nightly runs he makes along the rugged coastal highway, Kurt hardly ever leaves this room.

"How could I do anything, when I'm just . . ." Billy breaks off.

Kurt's voice trembles. "How could you not?"

He is a living reproach. Of the trio of children who grew up on the Archer place, Kurt's the only one left. Wild, angry Zane Archer is long dead. Now Vivian is dead and he's afraid to ask Kurt how he feels.

Billy's chest clenches—dear God, how did it happen, really? He doesn't know. Were Vivian's eyes open when it happened and could she have saved herself? He thinks she may have welcomed it. The bond of twinship loosed at last. Darkness. Silence. The end. She may have rejoiced at the stilling of Zane's voice inside her head. Surviving, she contained both of them. Now the black fire has gone out. Or he prays it has.

Maybe her twins can grow up ordinary after all.

Poor Vivian's ex-husband is on his way back to the San Francisco airport with Vivian's girls. He's taking them away. Trembling, Billy helped him load their things into the trunk of Vivian's car, looking anxiously over the lid at Emily and Jane who leaned into each other, touching foreheads, and would not return his look.

Steve Harriman and the twins are gone now, heading for the airport. Soon the girls will be completely out of reach. When the car pulled away from the house this morning, Billy felt some of the same things he did after Zane died and Vivian ran away. Something lifted from the house. Relief. The engine that drove them all was stilled. He thinks they should count themselves lucky.

Kurt says nothing about Vivian. As far as he's concerned it ended years ago. Instead he charges his father. "You should have told him."

"Told him what? How could I tell him anything when I don't even know?" Billy doesn't have the heart. Not without proof. Of what? He doesn't even want to admit the suspicion. He loves them. They're only little girls.

"You don't have any idea what they're going to do."

"But they haven't . . ." Done anything. I think.

"You don't want to know, but you do."

"Oh, son." Billy wants to protest, and can't. He realizes how empty he feels now that Jane and Emily are gone. Twins fill more psychological space than they occupy physically. Like Zane and Vivian in the lost, innocent days before the accident, these girls are a *force*. Taken individually, they're not much taller than Meredith, but together, they are huge. For twelve years their joined, restless spirit has expanded to fill the Archer place, overflowing the house, the gardens and the cliff where the house sits, the ocean beyond. Now they are gone.

Kurt says doggedly, "You should have told him."

Even if Billy had wanted to stop Steve, or try to cobble some kind of warning instructions, notes for an unwary father, it's too late. He sighs. "He already knows."

"Sure he does," Kurt says bitterly.

"He's their father," Billy says, as if the rest naturally follows: caution. Full knowledge of the risks. "Of course he knows." But the secret guilty part of him is chiming: *Nobody ever really knows. Until you see it happening, you never know. And even then.*

Even then. Here is Kurt chained to this place. A reminder. Not for the first or the last time Billy thinks: *If only I could make it up to you!*

"You could have told him about Zane."

Stricken, Billy says, "No I couldn't." He is goaded, pricked by memory. He can still see black-haired, savage Zane Archer with his white-rimmed eyes and that dangerous grin. He falters. "How could I, when I don't even know the truth?"

"You know."

Billy cries, "Son, you never told me!"

Kurt looks up with that little jerk of the neck he has, showing teeth bared in pain. "You've always known the truth."

"Oh, son. I am so sorry."

"You know better than anybody," Kurt says, and Billy thinks: *Except you.* But Kurt won't admit self-pity and he won't permit it in Billy. Instead he glares, waiting.

"He lived with Vivian," Billy says finally. "He already knows."

Kurt says angrily, "He only thinks he knows. He's just like you were. Deaf and dumb and blind."

"For God's *sake*."

"You didn't want to know. They had to rub your face in it. Vivian." Kurt makes it sound like a whip crack. "Zane."

"With Hal gone we thought there was nothing left to be afraid of." Billy's voice drops. "When he left he told us to watch out. He never said what for. Oh, Kurt, at the beginning they were only *children*." His voice breaks. "Children . . ."

Kurt nails him with a look: Q.E.D. "Twins. So you just send this poor bastard off, like, 'Take care of the twins.'"

The twins are Steve's problem now. Looking out of the back of the car, Jane and Emily waved goodbye with such sweet looks that it brought tears to his eyes. He's trying hard to keep from crying. His heart rate is too high; it will take him a while to recover from all those trips from the third floor with the twins' things: cartons, clothes, certain dolls. He's shaky from all those stairs; he can't even catch his breath, and now here is the one person he loves most, half-turned from the computers with his yellow eyes flickering angrily. "Whatever you think I ought to be doing, I can't. I'm sorry. I have my loyalties."

"Loyalties." Kurt can't bear to look at his father right now. He turns back to the screen, moving his hand over the keyboard so swiftly that Billy can't follow.

"Son?" Billy holds his breath and waits. The air in the living room where Kurt works is tainted with smoke. He gestures with fingers stained yellow; he smokes so much he has the cough of a man three times his age, but he can't stop. Billy knows better than to say, Please don't smoke; do you want to kill yourself? Maybe he does. "I didn't mean to hurt you," Billy cries.

"We're not talking about that," Kurt says, chopping the air with his left arm. "We're talking about this."

"Oh Kurt, I am so sorry."

"You didn't hurt me," Kurt says.

"You know what I mean." Billy can hardly stand this. "I never wanted anything to hurt you."

"It's no big deal."

"It's terrible."

"No it isn't," Kurt says matter-of-factly. "It's the way

things are." With his right hand he gestures at the arrangement of tables and file cabinets behind him, the complex of computers and files and fax, the multiple phones. "You should be pleased. You sent me to Stanford and you should be proud. Look. I'm doing fine."

"But you're here." Billy does not know how to describe what's happened here. All he can do is sum it up. "You're always here."

"Yes." Kurt grins. "I'm here. And I'm doing fine." He has no life outside this room. He has no friends, no places he can go in town or in San Francisco where he can sit down and eat and laugh with other people, or listen to music or get up and dance. The only people he sees are clients, who come here for his meetings, do their business and go. Even tied to the Archer place as he is, Billy goes to town when he can, catches a movie, calls up people he used to know in school. Yet Kurt is terrifyingly contained. "I have everything I want right here."

Oh, Kurt. Billy thinks. *Oh, son.*

Now he snaps forward in the chair so quickly that his black hair falls over one eye. "Firms all over the country are installing my software. A million kids are playing games I designed. You know as well as I do how much money I make. Dad, I can afford to send you around the world. Anything you want." Irritated, he shakes his head to replace the black hair, but it keeps falling back in his eyes. "Name it and I'll get it for you."

If only I could make this right. Billy cries, "I only want you to be happy, son."

Kurt smiles. "Don't worry about me, I'm fine."

"It's you that ought to be leaving. With your money you could go anywhere."

"No I couldn't," Kurt says.

Billy chooses not to hear. "You could get a penthouse, take a cruise. Go to India or China, anywhere. You could give parties, you could start going out . . ."

"Like this?"

"It doesn't matter. It doesn't matter to anybody but you, and look at you. You're good-looking enough to meet anybody, and smart enough to do anything you want."

"Maybe this is what I want."

"You could have the whole world. Instead your whole life is on that screen."

Kurt's smile is strange. "And I know a million people. They all know me without having to see me. Is that so bad?"

"There's no reason for you to hide yourself away, like a . . ."

"Like a cripple?"

"If only you didn't let it bother you!"

Those yellow eyes are clear as unflecked amber. Kurt says in a sweet tone devoid of recrimination, "It doesn't bother me. It isn't even here." He means: You know that's not what's the matter with me. His smile is so bright it breaks Billy's heart.

"You're too young to bury yourself."

"I'm not burying myself. I'm reaching out." Even as he speaks the fax dings and two of his phones begin to ring. Without letting his eyes waver from Billy's face he keyboards a quick command.

Billy can't stop. "This is all my fault."

"No it isn't." Kurt shakes his head; he's troubled by the fall of hair that won't go back in place. Devoid of bitterness, he seems unwilling to place blame. "It isn't anybody's fault."

"I saw it coming." *I'm so tired,* Billy thinks. And for the first time in his life he thinks, *I'm so old.*

Gently, Kurt says, "You saw, but you didn't know what it meant. Now stop flogging yourself for something you couldn't help and start figuring out what we ought to do to keep it from happening again." The hair that won't stay in place falls over Kurt's eye one time too many and irritated, he raises his left arm and brushes it away. Without even noticing what this next gesture does to his father, whose breath finally returns in an audible sob, Kurt pats it firmly in place with the reddened, angry-looking stump that protrudes from the folded-back cuff of his shirt. Kurt's clear, untroubled expression tells Billy his son's mind is elsewhere; he's come to terms with the old injury and quite simply stopped thinking about what happened to the missing left hand.

9

WHEN THE CALL COMES that evening, Carroll is
emptying out the desk in the front room for Steve's
daughters. If she can just get through this hour it will be
time to go to Logan to pick them up. As soon as Steve gets
off the plane she can unsay everything she said to him and
everything will be OK. But the protective charm she's
weaving is broken by the bleat of the bedroom phone. She
goes to answer with a sense of inevitability. Conditioned by
childhood losses, she's never assumed anything is simple.
When Steve left she went into a defensive crouch: What's
next.

She's afraid to pick up the phone. Something's wrong.
He's missed his plane. He can't come back now. What if
he's never coming back? Stop it, Carroll, stop. Be cool, she
reassures herself; it's Steve, he's not on the plane but it's
OK; he wants you in California. He needs you; you're the
native speaker who can help soothe the old lady and
translate those awkward father-daughter talks. Or.

She's all jagged edges. Or.

The part of Carroll that is used to setbacks and losses
scurries ahead, looking for exits, but it can't outrun the fear.
She should never have let him go. She should have bought
or forced her way on board his plane, hidden in a toilet until
it took off, or taken the next plane out. She never should
have let him out of her sight.

She knows better than anyone that bad things happen to
people when you aren't looking. This is her fault, for being
so angry that she let him slip away alone. Listen, she was
still in shock: *not his first wife*. She can't wait to talk to him.

Before she left the airport this morning she checked on

available flights. In case. She's all but packed. She shouts
into the phone. "Steve!"

"No."

"Steve, where are you?"

"This is Meredith Archer."

There is something terrible in the air between them. Even
the old lady's voice is not the same. It sounds strangely
artificial, like speech produced by a computer thousands of
miles away.

"What is it?"

The caller doesn't answer right away.

"I said, what is it?"

"Something's come up."

Carroll's heart zigzags. "Steve!"

"No," the woman says at last. But when Vivian's mother
goes on the words are small and thin, as if she's forcing
them out. "At least I don't think so."

"What do you mean, you don't think so?"

"They just called." It takes the distant speaker a minute to
collect herself so she can go on. "The twins are in the
hospital."

"What's happened?"

She says helplessly, "They're still trying to sort it out."

"You'd better tell me what happened." Frightened, Carroll scans the room: her bag is here, wallet and charge cards
in the billfold on the dresser, over there. She can go without
taking any clothes. She roves the room with the phone
cradled on her shoulder, trying to listen and prepare for
departure all at once. Still she manages to keep the
reporter's cool tone, designed to create a sense of the
ordinary that helps interviewees keep talking, no matter
what. "Just tell me what you know, OK?"

"I think you'd better come."

The old lady is too addled or upset to tell her any more.
Somebody comes in and she rushes Carroll off the phone.
She's afraid she knows; she doesn't want to know. As long
as nothing's definite she can rush into the airport and make
the next plane. She can get where she's going and do what
she has to as long as she can tell herself Steve is safe.

She is all right, really, until the plane takes off. Until now she's managed to focus on details, moving through all the traveler's checkpoints like a soldier on a forced march, but once she is flying nonstop to San Francisco with nothing left to do, all her fears come crashing in.

What if something has happened to Steve? What if he's sick, or hurt? What if, what if? She tries and fails to focus on the girls, imagining accident, illness, throwing up a barricade of possibilities like so much broken furniture, useless against the juggernaut, because in the darkest part of her heart, Carroll knows her life is about to take another plunge into loss.

She won't spell it out, but in the practiced resignation of the orphan, she understands she is rehearsing for death.

Once caught unprepared by an unexpected loss, a child will do anything to keep it from happening again. She will build a circle around herself and the people she loves so strong that nothing can hurt them.

Yet in spite of a lifetime of struggle to win at work, to arm herself; in spite of Steve's love and everything she has shored up against future losses, she is in terrible danger. In spite of everything she's put between her and that terrible time, Carroll is never far from the front hall of the house on Arbor Street in Jenkins: "Oh you poor thing." She is that same person.

No! Stop it, she tells herself. Pull yourself together. You have responsibilities.

The twins.

I have responsibilities. She's like the survivor of a mine disaster pulling herself out hand over hand. Duty. This is the rope she will use to pull herself out of what follows. She will survive by taking care of Steve Harriman's girls. She swallows hard; she can feel her chest caving in under the weight of the next thing. *Whether or not Steve is OK.*

By the time she gets off the plane it is morning. As arranged, Meredith Archer's driver meets her at the airport—a greying man with green shadows in the hollows under the bill of his uniform cap. He is tall, too thin in the faded French blue livery that speaks of a long-lost era of great houses and chauffeurs; it hangs on him as though it has grown or he has shrunk. He looks beaten to death. Even though his head bobs like a windblown flower, the driver maintains a doggedly military bearing, greeting her with dignity. "Mrs. Archer sent me. I'm Graver. And you're Mrs." He seems to be having a hard time going on.

"Carroll." She says it without inflection. It is her business to be numb.

Shattered, he takes off the cap with a vestigial bow. He doesn't hear himself repeating her name. "Carroll." His faded eyes film over. He seems fixed on some remote point.

To pull him back to the moment, she says, louder, "Steve's wife?"

Without speaking, he takes her hand.

She tries to make sense out of what little she can read in the driver's face. Shaking off the hand as if that will help her avoid what's coming, she says urgently, "Is Steve here?"

"No."

"Is he in the car?"

He shakes his head.

All Carroll's fears escape her in a cry. "Steve!"

"They're at the hospital."

"They!"

His face is grey. "The twins. He was on the way to the airport with the twins. They're . . ." He could be choking on stones; he has to swallow them before he can catch enough breath to continue. "They're going to be fine. They . . . Oh." He falters. "Oh."

Carroll falls back on her steely reporter's tone. "Just tell me where he is."

"I can't."

She presses on. "I mean Steve. You know. Steve Harriman?"

When he shakes his head this time, there's no mistaking him.

Carroll's voice sounds like it's coming out of somebody else. "What happened?"

"Accident. There was an accident."

"Steve!" Everything in her shudders to a stop. "I have to see him."

"I'm sorry, you can't." Shattered, the aging man in the neat French blue livery that's mysteriously gotten too big holds his elbows and rocks as if he's about to sway out of control and he has to hold himself in place. "There was an explosion."

When Daddy died, she was too young and they didn't tell her anything. When Violet died, her sisters had her cremated and all they brought home to Carroll was an urn. She can't believe what's happened here until she sees Steve. Living or dead, she can't come to terms with it until she has looked into his face. She makes herself sound calm. "I can handle it. You can let me see him now."

There is only a negative: the shaking of the head that closes all doors. "There was a fire."

"It doesn't matter how bad he looks. Listen, I'm a reporter. I've seen the dead before." Her words are jumping up and down like butterflies, anxious to please. "Accident victims. Bodies after a fire. I've seen a lot worse things."

"Shh. No." He reaches for her but she pulls away.

"Listen, he's my husband."

"I know."

"Then you have to . . ."

"No." Billy Graver waits until he can manage it and says, "Everything burned. What didn't burn washed out with the tide. There's . . ." The rest comes out in a gust. "There's nothing left."

Now everything else in the world stops: the activity in the airport, all the clocks, the breeze, the movement of the earth. It is as if everything and everybody around them is momentarily arrested, like figures in a freeze frame. Carroll says into the great stillness, "Nothing left!"

"Nothing except a piece of the car." This surprises even Billy. He marvels. "Nothing at all." Then with dignity he steps forward and holds out his hands as if to support her in her grief.

What does he expect of her, public wailing? Complete collapse? Carroll has survived everything that's happened to her so far, up to and including the loss of her father and the death of Violet, by keeping herself to herself, and she is not about to collapse into anybody's arms. She knows how to do this; after all, she's done it before. Therefore in the practiced resignation of the bereft, she lets the numbness spread. She has no choice.

Later, when she's alone, she'll let grief come close enough for her to take a good look at it, and when she's had a chance to comprehend what's happened, she will cry so hard she'll understand why she was afraid to cry. She'll wonder why she hasn't spent her whole life up to now crying in anticipation; she'll cry and go on crying until she thinks she's never going to stop, but right now, she is silent, intent on being still. Right now she doesn't cry. She can't. There are more pressing concerns. She has to figure out how to get through the next few minutes, the next few hours. No. The rest of her life.

When she can collect enough air in her collapsed lungs to speak she says, "What happened?"

And the clocks in the airport click forward a second. If the crowd around them seemed to be in suspended animation, the world has started moving again. She will go on.

Billy is saying, "I want you to understand, there was nothing the matter with the car. It was Miss Vivian's, and I kept it in perfect shape." He finds it necessary to reiterate, "There was absolutely nothing the matter with the brakes. He was driving down to the airport by the coast road and the girls wanted something out of the trunk . . ."

"The twins!"

"Somebody wanted something out of the trunk. He had to stop. It isn't safe. He should have known it wasn't safe to stop. The road is too narrow, there are too many cliffs. I don't know why they didn't take the . . ."

She cuts him off. "Then what?"

In the tone of someone who knows, Billy Graver says, "I don't know." Then he corrects himself. "No. Even the police don't know. He was just taking them to the airport. All he was doing was taking them to the airport. By this time they should be in Connecticut."

Carroll understands that whatever's happened, the gaunt driver has not come to terms with it himself.

"It was at one of those laybys, where the road runs along the cliffs. The girls . . ."

"Are they all right?"

Billy nods. His expression is too complex for her to analyze right now but later on Carroll will take it out and study it like the map of an unknown place. "They say the car started to roll while they were getting something out of the trunk."

"My God."

That look again. "They don't know how it started to roll, but it did, and it was so close to the edge . . ." Then he adds more for his own purposes than hers, "Those roads are terrible. The cliffs are steep. He's from the East, he wouldn't know. He wouldn't know it was so close to the edge."

Carroll's tone is so large and stern that it surprises even her. "If I can't see Steve, I need to see the place."

"Yes," the driver says. "It's on the way."

Grief stalks like a huge animal, waiting to devour her. Pain blurs understanding. She says dully, "On the way to the hospital."

"No." He gives her a significant look. "Mrs. Archer wants you to come to the house."

"On the way to the hospital."

"No. She needs to talk to you."

"But the twins!" First their mother and now this. Those poor kids!

"They're still under observation. They're perfectly safe. When you see them, you'll see they're really perfectly . . ." For whatever reasons, Billy Graver can't say what he means. "You'll see them soon enough. Mrs. Archer wants to see you before you meet the girls. There are things you need to know." He puts one shaking hand under her elbow and Carroll lets him. Gently, he guides her out to the car which is waiting in front of the Arrivals building with the motor still running and the headlights on, like a limousine accidentally detoured from a funeral cortege.

Respecting the privacy of grief, Billy rolls up the window

between them so she won't have to talk. For the moment, Carroll is just as glad. Later, on the way to the hospital, she'll badger him with questions, wringing him dry of details about Steve; she'll want to know what her lover was wearing when he left the house and how he seemed, whether driving away with the girls, he was happy or upset. She'll beg Billy to replay every word Steve said in his presence, everything he did, because now Steve Harriman, the only love she has allowed herself, is lost to her and the details are all she has left of him. Except for his girls.

In a layby at a hairpin bend in the road, Billy stops the car. He leaves it parked on the shoulder next to a sheer rock wall, a possibility for a driver going up the coast from San Francisco, where the right lane hugs the cliff, and not, for instance, down the coast from the Archer place, where the road skirts the precipice so closely that in some places the road seems to hang in air. He gets out and opens the backdoor.

"They told me it happened here."

Trembling, Carroll gets out. She looks at the narrow layby on the far side of the road—no more than a sandy, crumbling shoulder too small to support anything but pebbles and a few clinging weeds. "I see."

"And now we have to go."

"Not yet." She crosses the road.

Billy cries, "Be careful!"

Mesmerized, she keeps going. "I have to see."

The edge is marked by tire tracks that tell it all. It's hard to know whether the rocks and sand were dislodged by the passage of the car or whether the cliff edge gave way under its weight, leaving the front wheels suspended over nothing until it plunged. She's having a hard time crossing the road. When she finally makes it, she sees how high up this is, and how far he had to fall. The drop is so steep that she has to lie on her belly to look down. She inches forward until she can look over the edge of the cliff at the rocks below.

Steve, she thinks, looking into nothing.

In the case of a death like this there is no body, so there will be no funeral in the ordinary sense. A part of her will always be running after him, perpetually crying out, *Oh, Steve!*

When this is all over, Carroll tells herself, not knowing precisely what "this" encompasses, I'm going to come back and find some way to mark this place.

At the moment, there is nothing to mark. It is high tide, and waves are boiling over the rocks where the car must have crashed and exploded and burned. Except for a slight blackening of the surrounding area, there isn't much to see.

She sees a single piece of metal protruding—all that is left of the car. Dwarfed by scale, it looks like a jagged claw, but she thinks it must be a substantial piece of the frame. The tide has come and gone at least once since the accident. The water is high right now and when it goes out, there will be nothing left.

It is as clean as a burial at sea.

Steve is truly gone. She supposes she should throw herself in after him or bury the ring he gave her in the ocean along with him, but she can't. Everything else they had together is gone: his life, their life together in Steve's house; grief is curled up by the front door of the house in Connecticut and she knows she can never go back. Without understanding why she does what she does next, Carroll takes her mother's ring off her right hand, the fire opal that came home from the hospital with the urn, and throws it into the sea. Her tone is even; the wind takes the words as soon as they come out of her mouth but she could be crying to heaven; she knows that somehow, somewhere, Steve is going to hear, and note the way she marks this departure. "Goodbye Steve."

10

CARROLL PULLS HERSELF BACK to her feet hand over hand; her promise is the rope she uses to save herself: *Whatever happens, I'll take care of them.*

The old lady meets her at the door of the Archer house. She is brilliantly dignified in pale grey silk that speaks of kinder times. This old spine has not crumpled with the years; she's tall and straight as a woman half her age. Although she will bury her daughter later today the old lady seems remarkably steady; her eyes are bright and her face has a healthy sheen. She wears no makeup, but there's color in her lips. She looks like a woman who has turned the corner in a major illness and is finally on the mend. She seems somehow relieved by the end of certain things. "I'm Meredith Archer. Thank you for coming," she says.

"I'm Carroll Lawton. Steve's wife."

Meredith Archer studies Carroll for a minute as if deciding how to proceed. Then she holds out her hands. It's clear that whether or not she knew Steve was dead when she made the phone call that brought Carroll here, the old lady knows now. "My dear."

The last time Carroll walked into somebody's front hall like this she was ten years old and they made her cry until she thought she was going to die of it. She will do anything to keep it from happening again. One kind word from this woman will demolish her. Scowling, she flashes the warning of the bereft.

Do not sympathize. Whatever you do, please don't cry for me. I can endure anything if we don't talk about what's happened to me.

The old lady seems to understand. Without condolences or further explanation, she begins in a light voice that makes her sound young. "When my mother was still living black was the official color for people in mourning, and you went through it in stages. Putting it on was like dying a little death. At a certain point you emerged into grey and finally you were allowed to wear white. I think the formal mourning period back then was a year, but there were so many members of Mother's family that something was happening to somebody most of the time. When I look back it seems to me she was almost always wearing black."

Grateful, Carroll greets her with her head lifted. Equals in loss, they stand eye to eye.

"As you can see, I can't live that way." Then Meredith Archer says the only thing to Carroll that she's going to say about this—about any of it. "And neither should you."

And so they are able to move forward.

Carroll follows her into the library, a high-ceilinged room brightened by daylight falling through French doors. The old lady indicates a carved fruitwood chair. Distracted by the opulence—the paintings and bronzes, the books, the graceful furniture, Carroll finds she can't speak. This place is lovely—yet in spite of all the treasures in this well-ordered room, in spite of the elegance, in spite of everything the owners have done to protect themselves, the Archers have been unhappy here. Carroll does her best to sound businesslike, in control. "You wanted to talk to me before I met the twins."

The old lady seems confused. "The twins?"

"Emily," Carroll says firmly. "Jane."

Meredith Archer flinches, as if it hurts to hear their names. "Yes." She collects herself and goes on. "We have to decide what to do. The teachers at St. Margaret's can't handle them. Without Vivian I can't handle them." In another minute she will be in tears. "I don't know what to do."

"Those poor *kids*." Carroll hears the first tumbler click into place. "After you called, Steve wanted to . . . No, we wanted to . . . I'd like to do this for Steve."

"I can't ask you to take them. Not alone." The cultivated

voice is like spring water, clear and cool. "Especially not now."

Uncomprehending, Carroll days, "They're only little girls."

"It's more complicated than you think." This is *their grandmother*, yet when she goes on it is with a strange uncertainty that informs even as it chills. "To be perfectly honest, I called their father because it had gotten beyond me." Her eyes fill. "I'm getting old, and without Vivian . . . Twins present certain problems. Vivian and I thought perhaps separate boarding schools."

"You were going to split them up?"

"So they could develop normally." She's trying to explain but all she manages is: "Alone. Vivian and I were making plans when . . ." She manages not to sob. "After she died I thought maybe their father could . . . They need special attention. Certain kinds of care."

"But now they've lost . . ."

"Everybody," their grandmother says.

Carroll says, too loud, "Except me."

"But you, you aren't even related. It's too much to ask."

"No it isn't. I promised Steve." Right now it seems like the most important thing in the world.

Sure as Carroll is, the old lady won't let them get where they are going. She seems intent on laying out cautions. "Twins can be too much for one woman alone. They're too much for me. They were too much for both of us, if you want to know the truth."

Why can't she just let them get on with it? Pain makes Carroll impatient. "I'm sure I can handle it."

"It's hard, I'm not strong enough. I love them but I just can't do it alone."

If this is a warning, Carroll is too deep in shock to want to hear. Speaking out of her own grief, she says, "I'm so sorry."

Meredith sighs. "It's not that I don't want to love them and take care of them just the way I did my own children, but my own children . . ." The old lady discovers herself on a byway she doesn't want to travel. She confesses, "I'm all used up. I just can't do it. Do you see?"

She doesn't, really, but Carroll nods.

"My daughter . . ." Her eyes fill. "You know I lost my daughter."

"I'm so sorry."

"It was inevitable." Meredith sighs. "At least she's at rest."

Carroll jumps. What does she mean, *inevitable?*

But there are no explanations, just steps in the progress they are making. "Now, the girls."

"I want to take them, Mrs. Archer."

"Thank God."

Unnerved, Carroll pushed ahead. "Can I see them now?"

"Not yet," their grandmother says. "I need to explain." She looks past Carroll at something in the middle distance—past events, perhaps, or past mistakes. "God knows we did everything we could for them. This thing . . . it's so hard to *contain*."

Like a runaway heading for the barn, Carroll keeps her head down and does not question. All she wants is to get through this, so she can be with the girls.

But the old lady goes on as if it is her duty to try to explain. "It's all so sad. You understand we were at an end here, or she and I would never have started this in the first place."

"I don't understand."

"Telling them we wanted to split them up. We thought maybe in separate boarding schools they could grow up normally. Distance, we thought. Maybe distance would diffuse the . . ." Whatever it is that troubles her, Meredith Archer can't find words for it. It's as if somebody has taken her by the ankles and rattled her. "The twins. There are things about twins that I hope you never have to know."

"Mrs. Archer, they're only children . . ."

She says, too quickly, "Don't be so sure."

Touched by their loss, with her heart taken by storm and rushing toward them, Carroll finishes anyway, ". . . why would you want to split them up?"

"You don't understand now . . . but you will." The old lady's voice drops. "You will." With this said she brightens.

"Maybe they'll do better with you." She does not explain; she just goes on. "You're sure you want to take them?"

"Poor kids!" Everything in Carroll warms to the girls. "Of course."

"I'm so glad."

"Let me go to the hospital and bring them home."

The old lady says too quickly, "They aren't coming home."

"But the funeral." She flashes on the twisted metal that will be Steve's only marker, the crashing surf; she has no idea where his body will rest. She can't even figure out how to mourn him properly. It makes her tremble. "Their mother's funeral?"

"I don't want them here for the funeral," Meredith says. "They can't come back here." Her face is just about to dissemble. "It's too hard. It's just too hard." Collecting herself she tries again on a more reasonable note. "You'll take them direct from the hospital. I'd like to do this quickly, for their sakes."

"I don't understand."

"With the twins, you never know. If you go straight to the airport it will be easier. For them. For me."

"Don't you want to tell them goodbye?"

She shakes her head. "I can't. It's too hard. Billy will take you straight to the airport from the hospital; there are tickets being held for you. It's Boston, isn't it? I booked you first class." At Carroll's baffled expression she lifts her voice an octave, hitting an accomplished, artificial social tone that implies genteel laughter. "It's just—easier. Easier. Don't you see?"

She is so distressed that Carroll says, "Mrs. Archer, if it will make you feel better I'll do whatever you say."

She grasps Carroll's hands. "Oh my dear." Now Meredith Archer finds it necessary to pile on reassurances. "But I want you to know that wherever you take the girls from here and whatever you have to do, it won't cost you a penny. Whatever they need will be taken care of. I know my duty, and as you might have gathered, I have means. I'm prepared to provide everything the girls need. And everything you need."

Offended, Carroll pulls away. "I don't want money."

"You can't do this alone."

She sets her jaw. "I won't be alone." She's going to take them directly to Jenkins, to her family home. Uncomfortable as she is with her mother's family, she needs them now. She needs dinner ready on the table and a place to go at night. She needs to go back to work. In Jenkins she has a place to live and a job. *(One phone call.)* She'll call Charley Penn from the airport and have him tell Russell, that twerp from Harvard, to get his things out of her desk. Then she'll call the aunts on Arbor Street and have 'Laine open the back bedrooms for her and the girls. And some day, a long time from now, when Carroll can bear to see the place where she was so happy for such a short time, she'll go up to Connecticut and clear out Steve's empty house.

"I insist. I expect to make a significant contribution."

"You can't pay me for this, Mrs. Archer." Carroll draws herself up. "I'm not doing this for the money. I'm doing it for Steve."

Meredith's voice is like a scarf brushing against her cheek and twining about her throat in a silken snare. "It may be harder than you think."

"But they're only . . ."

"Twins. When you get to know them, you'll understand." This is heavy with implications that Carroll is too stunned and preoccupied to mark. "I want you to be provided for. You'll need to give these girls everything they want before they ask for it. I can't explain, just take my word for it. It's important not to let them get mad. I just want to—I don't want you to . . ." She is unable to finish.

If she doesn't have anything else left Carroll has her pride. She's promised Steve and she says with great dignity, "Thank you. I'd like to do this alone."

"Very well. But before you go, I'd like you to see their rooms." Meredith stands. "So you'll have some idea what to expect." Her expression is a puzzle, fond, shadowed. "Then Billy will take you. The hospital bills are paid. I gave the doctors your name on the release. And I've booked your tickets to Boston: the seven-fifteen from San Francisco

Airport. So you can pick them up and go direct." The old lady adds, "Our surprise."

"I'm not going back to Boston. I'm . . ." Carroll interrupts herself. "Surprise?" Later she will think back on this conversation as ominous but at the moment she's just confused.

"The children respond best when they don't have time to plan ahead."

"You're going to send them off without *telling* them?"

"It's going to work better this way, that's all." She is intent on closure. "It's the only way. They're lovely children, but . . ." She has Carroll by the elbow now. "But first, their rooms. It's easier to show you than to explain." As if cued by the silence she creates, the driver slips back into the library. "Billy will take you up."

He looks at Meredith Archer out of eyes ringed with green shadows and does not move.

"Billy?"

Whatever they are to each other—employer and employee, equals, former lovers, accustomed friends—it is clear that the intent, handsome old man supports the elegant old lady as surely as she does him. Instead of doing as she says, he shakes his head.

Pressed, Meredith raises the old barriers. Her manner signifies generations of command. "I said, take her up."

Reminded of his place, Billy gives her a look of combined regret and pain that brings tears to her eyes. "Yes madam."

Carroll tries, "Maybe I can pick up a few of their things for them? Clothes, or favorite things?"

"They can have new ones," the old lady says hurriedly. "I think it's better for them not to look back."

This is how Carroll finds herself alone on the third floor of the Archer house, in the orphaned girls' rooms. It is like walking into another world. The place is like a warren, or a series of caverns, with niches and corridors leading from the main area into others. In this room velvet swags over the windows, sealing them against fresh air and compounding the shadows, so Carroll has to flip the wall switch to turn on the little chandelier before she can see. When she does, the shadows do not retreat, they just turn color. One of the girls has draped pink fabric over the flame-shaped bulbs so everything in the dimly lit central chamber is tinged with red. The close air is thick with the scent of death or lavender or of some rich, crushed bloom that speaks of both. It is as if life has fled, but some central part of the girls is still here. No wonder they hated leaving this place; no wonder they had to go. It is bizarre.

Where she can see them amid the mass of hanging banners and draperies and hastily assembled costumes, the walls are thickly covered with complex lines and crosses and lettering in ballpoint and colored Pentel and Magic Marker, whose significance is not immediately clear. The lines are as dense and tightly interwoven as diagrams of the central nervous system, and as hard to read. There are historical charts and genealogies and other things written on the walls in crabbed handwriting in characters as elaborate and mysteriously gorgeous as a military code, and where the walls are not otherwise covered they are thick with snapshots and formal photographs of vanished families and clippings from dozens of newspapers and magazines all arranged to no specific pattern, really, but unnerving nonetheless. She wants to get a strong light and a magnifying glass and decipher everything the twins have written; she wants to back out quickly and close the door.

There is too much here, it's too diffuse, all these toys and souvenirs and over here . . . Her voice emerges in a sob. There is a little table or altar complete with melted candles and dead flowers in crystal bud vases, and at the center, propped on something she can't quite make out, is an early picture of Steve with the same bright hair and dark eyes, but this is a young Steve with his eyes glad and his face unlined, untouched by the shadows that have hounded him since before they met. She is so busy stuffing the photograph into her bag that she does not immediately register the object supporting it: a detailed doctor's model of a human head with the skull flensed to expose the nerves and muscles, with lidless eyeballs goggling and pink tongue exposed

between teeth that open and close. Backing, she doesn't
know whether to laugh or go on sobbing when she sees that
the girls have given it a velvet tam.

She collides with something that falls over without a
sound; it is a life-sized rag doll in a ruffled silk dress and
organdie petticoats and pantaloons. She thinks there must be
at least a thousand dolls here, rank on rank—baby dolls and
elaborately dressed character dolls like Scarlet O'Hara and
Shirley Temple and Snow White as well as king and queen
dolls and legions of Barbies and Kens and Dawns all doing
their owners' bidding here in these silent rooms. They are
attended by trolls and Smurfs without number, along with
hundreds of stuffed animals of every kind—dogs and
pandas and koalas and horses and cows and Tasmanian
Devils and replicas of Maurice Sendak's Wild Things all
marshalled in daunting formations in front of dollhouses and
decorated cartons and wooden boxes painted up as castles
and cottages and shops and post offices and theaters that
represent a civilization whose nature she can only guess at,
structure after structure lining the madly figured Oriental
runners that connect the rooms. She cannot know that she is
looking at what remains of the country of Amadamaland, or
that it is as dead and deserted as the city of Pompeii. Or that
unlike the Pompeiians, who were caught in midflight by the
horrendous fall of ash, silent and fixed in place for eternity,
the citizens of this extinct kingdom have already taken their
valuables and fled.

Later Carroll will not be able to explain what she has seen
in these rooms, that makes her mouth dry out and her fingers
grow cold, but she can hear her breath rushing around inside
her mouth like wind in a cavern and she knows that if she
is going to survive this day in one piece, if she's going to
make it to the hospital and put on a cheerful face for Steve's
daughters, she has to back out right now and close the door.
She has to turn her back on the lost civilization and all her
questions and walk away, which is what she does.

No wonder, she thinks. *No wonder they're strange.* She
can give them a normal life in Jenkins, away from this
creepy place. They can go to high school and meet boys.

Instead of dolls, she'll give them a dozen new friends. She doesn't know why, exactly, but she staggers as she reaches the landing. It takes all her remaining strength to stay upright and keep from toppling down the stairs.

The old lady sees her face and does not ask.

Unable to speak, Carroll bows her head to accept Meredith Archer's swift, tight hug. Released, she touches the old lady's cheek with her lips, surprising both of them, and then with a tremendous effort clears the house and gets into the car. She will not speak again until she and Billy have passed through the gates and the car has turned off the winding access road onto the coast highway. Right now she needs to be someplace where the sun is shining and ordinary people are out doing ordinary things. She wants to sit down in some bright room and meet the twins. She needs to hug Steve's girls and love them and take them home to Jenkins, so she can begin to think about starting over. She leans forward like a mad coachman flogging his horses. *Faster.* She can hardly wait.

They are all she has left in the world.

11

"I DON'T KNOW what to make of them." The doctor looks up from the window where he's been fixed as if in front of a TV set, studying the pair in the hospital room.

Looking more like a kid than an official in the jeans and Adidas, the young detective squints through the one-way mirror. "They've been like this?"

"Ever since they came in. You'd expect them to be crying—unless they're in shock. I just can't tell."

The girls on the other side of the thick glass are as still as matched figurines. Even in repose they have a certain delicacy, an airy grace that makes them seem less like adolescents than models waiting to be draped in chiffon and feathers and sent down the runway to stardom, or displaced angels, lovely and diffident. Dressed in johnny coats and hospital robes, the twins stand with their backs to each other—one studying the TV screen as if there is something urgent written on its glassy surface and the other looking out the window. Without having to look, they move as one. The tilt of the heads is identical; each props the same fist on the same hip at the exact angle. They are composed, beautiful.

They are waiting for their new guardian to come for them.

The doctor says, "Look at them, Preston. What do you think is going through their heads?"

Bemused, the detective says, "You'd never know they'd just been orphaned."

"Shock does funny things to some people. God knows they've been through a lot. First their mother . . ." The doctor grimaces. "How did it . . ."

"A fall. We think. She was cremated immediately. The whole thing happened too far north of here for us to be involved. Out of our jurisdiction. Poor kids." Detective

Preston leans close as if the glass can magnify the figures on the other side so he can see what drives them. "And now their father."

The doctor says, "I can't even guess how they feel."

The detective says, "It's hard to know. What do you think?"

"Look at them!" The doctor and the young detective are progressing toward something they don't want to have to deal with. "They told our staff psychiatrist they barely knew their father, which explains it, I guess."

"Unless it doesn't explain." The detective lieutenant squints at the pair. "They don't look exactly griefstricken."

"It could be shock. It could be something else. Look at them. Composed," the doctor says, and then he says, as if it's a dirty word, "Serene. They're unwholesomely self-contained."

"Always the same story, right?"

"Always. A dozen people have talked to them and the responses don't vary. Nothing changes. Usually in these narratives something slides between tellings. With two girls involved, you'd think there would be a little slippage, but these two . . ."

The detective completes it. "Are picture perfect."

The doctor nods. "Sometimes you can get this with twins. Genetically, these things usually skip generations, but their mother was a twin. I think that makes the whole thing intensify. It's not two whole people. They're either less—or more. Look at them. Twins are in touch in ways we don't know about. Almost psychic. But never to this degree. It's eerie."

"I'd like to try once more before you release them."

"You'll get the same story. We've talked to them together and separately and it's always the same. Weird," the doctor says. "With twins sometimes, the only morality is what flows between them. The only imperative. They follow their own tune. And there's another thing." Disturbed, he taps his teeth with his index fingernail. "We can't tell which twin is dominant."

"Is that usual?"

The doctor shakes his head. "It's more intense than anything I've ever come across. There's no way to get at them. If there's anything wrong, we can't tell who's hiding it. Or making the other one hide it."

They consider this in silence. The detective is still for a long time. Then he moves closer to the mirror. "You're not satisfied it was an accident."

The doctor shakes his head.

"Neither am I." The detective says, "If you could just find a way to keep them for a while, study them. Separate them and see what happens. Take turns talking to them alone . . ."

"I'm sorry, we can't hold them. There's nothing medically wrong. No apparent trauma."

"On an outpatient basis, then."

"We can't. Remember, they weren't in the car when it went over; they weren't touched. No physical marks. We have no choice but to release them."

"Psychiatry." The detective is pushing hard. "You can call it grief counseling."

"Their grandmother is having them moved out of state."

His eyes snap open. It's as if he's just heard the tumblers click. His voice is harsh. "Out of our jurisdiction."

"Out of our reach, Detective Preston," the doctor says. "Their new stepmother is on her way here."

"Somebody who knows them?"

"Somebody who doesn't know them at all. She and the father were just married. He hadn't seen the girls in twelve years."

"And you're going to let her . . ."

"You know as well as I do what happens in these cases. The state has to place children with the nearest responsible relative."

"A perfect stranger. What are you going to tell her?"

"What can I tell her?" The doctor does not have to take the detective over the jumps: confidentiality, the uses of privileged information. He gnaws at the frayed fingernail as if he wished he still smoked. "I can't say anything that will prejudice the relationship. What about you? What are you going to tell her?"

"I don't know. I just think I ought to . . ." The detective breaks off and begins again. "I need to see them separately. I don't know what I'm going to tell the stepmother until I can find out what there is to tell."

"And if they won't talk to you?"

He shrugs. "Whatever happens next is going to happen in some other jurisdiction."

In the white room with white, white beds and more whiteness on the ceiling, the TV glows like a flower garden in a snowstorm. And we, in our white gowns, before the mirror that gives back the white room, we look like flowers. Our faces are like giant peonies bobbing under the weight of the *nice* the nurses have given us to make us calm and keep us quiet here. We are not sick, and yet they have given us druggy numnums. We are perfectly fine but we are in the hospital.

"Because of what happened," the psychiatrist told us. "You need some time to get over what happened."

But we are fine. It is Vivian and Saint Stephen who got broken. My twin wants to tell the doctors so they'll let us go but I squeeze her hand with my nails until she bleeds and we don't tell them anything. Then when we are alone in the room I look at her and suddenly she isn't fine.

"Don't let them see you cry," I say, and she makes her face completely still even though the tears are streaming. We make her stop. We do.

She and I are stuck here until Grandmother comes to get us. It is all right for now, I think, feeling the druggy buzz. But only for now. Now that the obstacles are removed it's time to go home, because there are pressures. The blue people and the green people are at war in Amadamaland. We must make peace so we can begin the celebration.

We have been standing long enough. I take a seat. My sister takes a seat. We have been silent long enough. I say, "What do you think, Emjan?"

My twin says, "I do not like this place, OK?" We who know without having to be told leave many things unspoken. I know it is not the place my sister dislikes. We have an interest in hospitals. It is that we have been too long away from the kingdom. We are needed at home. Her blue people and my green people have slaughtered each other in great numbers and there are probably fornications in the palace, gross secret mismatches. In fact, when King Stephen surprised us, we were in the middle of peace talks. We have numnums from Vivian's medicine chest that she won't be needing and Grandmother's liqueur candies for the truce party; we have liberated absinthe and port wine in cut-glass ship's decanters to celebrate the Armistice. Her voice teeters. "I don't like it at all."

"Manjennemma," I say, one of our many names for us. I use it to remind her who we are, and my sister lifts her head. I go on in the old language. "Prebo. Don't worry, we won't be here much longer." I am supreme in the only chair while she sits on the end of the bed and if you cannot tell which of us is which, doctor, well, neither can we some of the time. And if you, the doctor, are looking at us through that blatant two-way mirror, all you will see is two poor beautiful queens who have lost their father, the twins. You will see that they are upset perhaps, and under stress they fall back on their old cradle language, and if you don't understand a word of what we are saying to each other . . . Fine.

"But the doctor says we have to wait," she says. My sister, who is as one with me, at least most of the time. Her pink, pink nose and the red-rimmed eyes make her look like a poison bunny rabbit. What's the matter with her? In spite of what we found out about King Stephen's intention *to take us out of the kingdom;* in spite of what we agreed, my sister's eyes are running. She has been on the edge ever since disaster overtook him and now she has tumbled into open weeping.

I do not want them to see.

"Etrap," I say. *Stop it!* "Be calm. In short order we will be safe back in Amadamaland. It'll be as if all this has never been."

"But he's . . ." she sobs, and I think: *Don't do that, they are watching us.* Too late. She is sobbing aloud.

"It couldn't be helped," I say and in an undertone I try to put steel into her. "Never let them see the queen is crying."

"But he's . . ." She can't finish.

I can. "It is a very great tragedy. Naturally the queen will declare a period of mourning, but listen. This—this is, OK, the time of waiting. When we are home, then is the time to mourn him."

"He's gone . . ." She plucks her gown. "And we're . . ."

"Here." I touch the Band-Aid on her arm. The *nice* they gave us is buzzing between our ears; one shot and we are flying. "Not so bad. Shots now, later Seconal." Remember, we are talking in the old language that only she and I know because between us, we the queens created it. I can almost see them taking notes about our strange behavior; I can almost hear the scratching of their pencils.

Her eyes glitter. "Seconal?"

"Like Vivian's nice nighttime red ones? And maybe later, something to go home on. *Predibus,* and they will have to give it."

She nods. "Predibus." We will pitch a fit.

We will pitch a fit and they will have to send us home with Valium and other numnums, Seconal to sail the night in. I turn to the glass and go back to everyday language. The language of the boring outside world. "Of course they had to bring us to the hospital. We need a place to stay until they come for us."

"But who?" She is all anxious. "Who's going to come for us?"

"*They* are, stupid. From home." Grandmother, or silly Billy, her driver, who is groomed to do our bidding and keep us happy in Amadamaland, anybody but Kurt Graver with the yellow eyes. He doesn't like us; I have seen him looking, and if I have to, late one night I will crawl into Grandmother's lap and say to Meredith, my tool, *I love Billy but I don't like Kurt.* If that isn't enough to get him kicked off the place, I will tell the police that Kurt tried to touch me where I shouldn't. And then I will curl my hand around her face and make her agree that now that Vivian is gone she needs her twins together, and we will stay right there with her, safe at home.

But right now my sister needs attending to. "Grandmother would never leave us here," I say. "Remember we are the queen, so you can just stop crying."

But she won't. Or can't. "Janem, why aren't they here yet?"

"No matter, Emjan. See what's here that we don't have back in Amadamaland. Enjoy it. The boys, the men."

She sees what I am saying. "Something we don't have at home?"

"Something we don't have at home." They are everywhere in the hospital, young ones with big hands and hard, flat wrists and good-smelling bodies, and I think there is more to the kingdom than being queen and here are new areas that need conquering.

"Oh," she says, "they would be nice to have."

Indeed they would. The orderly who brought us here was one and the doctor who took our particulars was another, and when I brushed this doctor's hand with the best parts of me I think he looked at me a certain way. They are older than the stupid ones we meet in dancing class, who get creeped out that Emily and Jane are two, with only one face between them, as if we had not enough faces to go around. No matter; they wouldn't know what to do with us if we invited them.

My sister needs cheering and I say, "Tons of boys and men. The one who came with the mop after we spilled the orange juice, for one, the cute technician. Be nice and we can take him back to our house." *To Amadamaland.*

What's the matter with her? "But how can we look at new men while we are still mourning our king?"

"We need a new king, sister, and knights."

"But our poor Saint Stephen?"

"He loves us so much he died to make us free." I take her by the wrists and pull her up. I must put steel in her. "We are rulers, Janemana, we take what we want." Then I drop my voice so only she will know. "You wouldn't want anything to happen to Carlo, king of your blue people, would you?

You wouldn't want the greens to overrun your dresser and tear up all your pretty things . . ."

This makes her lift her head and chime in the old singsong, "We take what we want Amenanja. Boys too?"

"Boys too, some day." Soon, I hope. New knights we need. "Boys, yes." *Boys.*

But still she wavers, just a little. "But where from here, my Princess?"

I grip her tighter. "Home, Principetta. Amadamaland tonight. Tomorrow the world."

"I miss the father already . . ."

My fingernails gouge and my sister flinches. "Don't look back, Emenanja."

Soft, she is, too soft. "Still I am so sad."

"No," I say, correcting her. I say it to the mirror, which has become like another person to me. I go on, louder, in the other language. "We are so sad, after all, look at what has just happened to us. It's awful, isn't it?"

And my sister sees me looking into the mirror and she turns to it and says because it is expected, "Yes it is terrible."

Satisfied, I go on in the old language. "Terrible about our king, Saint Stephen. Lost to us. But listen, my selfest, listen here. Mourning we will have in the streets of Amadamaland, we will marshal the troops and all the courtiers for the funeral procession and in the square we will build a statue in honor of Steve the Great, who opened the gates of Amadamaland and found us, the princesses in the tower, and we mourn him properly from this day to the hereafter."

Then I stand so close our heads touch. "But look, see what I took from him." And reaching into the pocket of the hospital bathrobe I pull out the token I slipped off the king's wrist and onto mine right before we got out of the car on the Pacific Coast Highway: it is a silver bracelet. "We have a first class relic."

"My God."

"No. Your sister. And this will make us strong enough to do everything we have to."

"Yes," my sister says; she's feeling better. "Do you think we can get the cute one to come back in here?"

"Are we not the queen? Watch me." And then it occurs to me that to bring them running, to make them do us the way they ought to, the queen must cry after all. And let them see her crying for true. Big tears, loud howls. I move close enough to jog my sister; nobody but she will know that I am using Grandfather Archer's opal stickpin. *Ow!*

Here they come now. The kingdom is ours, I think.

Ours for the taking.

They are at the door. I say in the old language, "Koprictus." *Let us be ordinary.* Nice us.

My sister assents. "Koprictus." The queen recedes.

Nice us. When they come in they will find only ordinary girls.

"You remember Lieutenant Preston," the doctor says. He's waiting for the girls to look up so he can present the detective. When they don't he has to go on anyway. "You met him last night after the accident? You were probably too upset to remember."

"Yes," they say with their heads bent.

In the jeans and expensive running shoes the detective could be another kid, reminding them. "Like, we spoke?"

"Yes," they say to Preston. Speech flows back and forth between the girls so fluidly that there's no telling which says what.

"Afterward," they say.

"After the accident."

"But you were upset," he says.

"Upset," they say. One sobs. "So upset that we forgot."

He prods. "Too upset to remember what happened?"

They've buried their faces now. Without speaking, they nod.

"But now you've had a little time. If it's OK, I'd like to talk to you again."

"Whatever you say."

It is a relief to see them weeping. The doctor wonders whether, standing with their hands covering their faces, the girls know they have assumed identical attitudes of grief. He waits for them to look up, hoping to learn something from their faces. When they do, he's surprised to see how clear their blue eyes are after all that crying—with unmarred whites, like perfect marbles. The tears have evaporated. Their expressions are so open that he knows there's no credit accumulated here, no building on former conversations.

He's going to have to start all over again. *Interesting,* he thinks. *It's as if we've been writing on the face of a waterfall. Every time you start with these two it is right from the beginning.*

"You remember me, I'm Dr. Allison?"

They smile engagingly. "Of course." One speaks first, but there's no telling which. "Dr. Allison. Can we go home now?"

He doesn't answer. "And you remember Lieutenant Preston."

They say, "Right. Lieutenant Preston." Like any other girl their age, they look him up and down: *cute boy.* "Cool."

If you just wouldn't *echo.* "And you are Jane Archer, and this is Emily?" The doctor looks from one to the other. If one of you would just be a little taller, or more aggressive, or different.

"We're kind of hard to tell apart."

"He needs to talk to you before you go."

Even the detective is unable to figure them out. "I'd like to see you alone," he says.

Grinning, they turn to follow in an elegantly calibrated movement. "Sure, Lieutenant. Great!"

"One at a time."

They hesitate.

"If that's not a problem for you."

Without speaking, they confer. They shrug agreeably. "No problem."

"No, no problem."

One of them speaks first. Which one? Is it the same as last time or do they alternate? The detective doesn't know. He remembers his frantic third grade teacher tagging the Anson twins the first day: all that school year Jan was the one with the plaid hair ribbon and Jen wore the striped hair ribbon. He'd like to try that here but the girls' cool dignity unnerves him. If only one girl would push it a little, step forward, show him who's in charge here. "Who wants to go first?" He realizes he's waiting for one to give the other some kind of high sign.

Without consulting, they take a step backward.

"OK, who wants to go second?"

"Whichever you want."

"OK, if you won't decide, I will." The detective holds out his hand to the one standing nearer. "We'll take a stroll down to the day room and when we're done talking I'll come back for your sister. Doctor?"

The doctor nods assent.

Walking along with the girl at his side Preston says, "Which one are you, Jane or Emily?"

She smiles. "It doesn't matter."

"Well it does to me," he says sharply; he can't say whether it's the sleepless night that puts him on edge or the unyielding density of the child's serenity or the fact that walking along with her like this he can't be sure she really is a child and not an emerging woman. Tension makes him impatient.

"Are we almost finished here?"

"Sit down over there," he says, not answering. He lets her precede him into the empty solarium. When she is in place, sitting on the cracked leatherette with her knees and feet neatly matched and her head lifted, he pulls a chair around. They are facing but not touching so nothing he does here will be misconstrued. Then, moving openly so there will be no misinterpretation, he picks up her hand as indifferently as he would an empty bottle and turns it over so he can read the name on the hospital bracelet. Her fingers curl in her moist pink palm so suggestively that he quickly drops it. "Emily." He hesitates. "Emily?"

She smiles—*too pretty*. "Sure."

"I know this is hard, but we need to talk about what happened to your father."

"Terrible," she says, shaking her head.

"Yes, terrible."

"An accident."

He doesn't rise to this. Instead he watches carefully, as if he can read the details in the way she responds. "I think." Nothing. He lowers his voice significantly. "We're not sure."

She regards him in serene innocence. "Terrible accident."

"I see. Tell me about it again."

"If that's what you want." The eyes are like deserted ponds at the bottom of a deep cavern.

Later, when he returns Emily to the room, if this is Emily, there is a wait before the other twin comes out. "Jane," he says, and discovers he is in no respect certain whether this is a new twin or the same one who just sat in the sunny lounge, meeting his questions with the polite diffidence of displaced royalty. Even after he's checked the name on the hospital ID band, the detective can't know whether it's two girls he's questioned today or the same one twice.

Troubled, the young detective closes the door on the girls' room. Inside, they are dressing to leave the hospital, leaving him with an empty notebook and too many unanswered questions. Preston shakes his head. "They're so consistent—it's like talking to the same person."

The doctor nods. "All the reports match up, no matter which one you're with or how you frame the question. They all match up. Every one of them."

"They didn't tell me shit." They are at the end here. "So nice, and they didn't tell me shit."

"I thought maybe it was just me," the doctor says. "I was hoping you'd have better luck."

Preston says, "If only . . ."

The doctor cuts him off. "If only we had more time. If only we could get one of them to open up. If only they weren't leaving in an hour. I know." Inside the room, the twins are already dressing.

"This is definitely an if-only situation. If only you could give me a *few more hours*."

"Look, Lieutenant, the stepmother is in the lobby. What are we going to tell her?"

"Stall for time. Lie."

The doctor shakes his head. "Can't. She has a car waiting to take them to the airport. They're out of here tonight."

"To some other jurisdiction," the detective says sourly. "It would help if we had something definite on this. About them. We've got this enigma walking around with a mystery and we can't even tell the difference between them."

"All we know is that we don't know anything. Look," the doctor says because it's been a long day and because he is at the end of his energy, beyond improvisation and too honest to deal in invention. He knows better than anybody that he's casting around for a rhetoric to get them both out of this. "Let's let the stepmother handle it. She's family, she may know what to do with them."

"She doesn't know the kids," the detective says uncomfortably. "She doesn't know anything about them."

"What are you going to tell her then, that you don't know either? That you don't know anything but you're worried about something? Come on, here. How do you send these kids off with a bad rap when all you have are suspicions?" His index fingernail has split to the quick. He gnaws at it one more time and blows away a small fragment. "What am I supposed to tell her?"

"Tell her to keep in touch," the detective says.

12

JANE AND EM. Em and Jane. Carroll thinks Jane is the one on her left and Emily sits on her right in the big back seat of Meredith Archer's car, but she has no way of knowing even though the twins told her for the third time as they came out of the hospital. Laughing, they said, "Be cool. You'll know pretty soon."

Sandwiched between them, she is both touched by their warmth and at the same time unsettled and confused.

Following the uncommunicative doctor down the hall to their hospital room this afternoon she could hardly wait. She hardly marked the fact that he didn't tell her much, except that the twins were, what, internalizing their grief. Good, she thought. If we can keep from breaking down, we'll do better. She needed to hear Steve's tones again in his children's voices, to catch a last glimpse of his face reflected in their eyes. Together the three of them would try to handle what's happened—orphans together, Carroll thought. Afraid to plumb her own losses, she fixed on theirs.

"Oh, kids." Uncertain, she hung in the doorway. It was as if they hadn't heard her speak. Instead they sat on one of the beds with their smooth heads bent over their notebooks and did not look up. Oh God, she thought. Two kids, and I'm all the family they have now. What am I getting into here?

It was interesting. Suddenly there was nobody around—no nurses, no orderlies; she remembered a doctor friend telling her the secret of hospitals: *As long as they think they can help you, you're fine, but in a hospital you know you have a disaster when everybody starts to disappear.* The eerie sense of desertion made no sense in this context. Nobody was dying here; she and these girls were going home together.

She cleared her throat like an anxious child. "Emily? Jane? I've come to get you, OK?" Then she waited. Their lives together hung in the balance.

One spoke. "Koprictus."

Carroll blinked. "Ko-what?"

"Koprictus."

Everything changed. Absorbed, the twins were putting away their notebooks and their silver pencils. They moved like synchronized swimmers or Siamese twins separated at birth. Looking up at her with Steve's eyes, they smiled.

It was like the spring thaw.

"We're so glad to *see* you." They got up with gorgeous, enthusiastic smiles.

"You're so pretty!"

Carroll flushed. "Hey, thanks. Look, kids, I . . ." She shook her head; this with Steve was too fresh for her to be able to bring it into the room with them. He was dead and for the life of her, she couldn't come right out and say it.

"We know," one said gravely, as if sparing her. Strange. It was as if the girl had heard her thinking. "So sad."

"Terrible," the other said. "We do know." They put out their hands to her. "We're just so glad you came, OK?"

She shook tears out of her eyes and managed an uneven smile. "Me too."

"But what's your name?"

"Did you come to take us home?"

"Who are you?"

"Are you our new teacher or what?"

"No, I'm . . . Not exactly." She couldn't quite bear to tell them the truth. That she was the only person they had left to turn to. *Oh you poor kids you've lost your* . . . No. Not Carroll. Not yet. "My name is Carroll Lawton, and I've come to check you out of the hospital." She would wait to tell them where she was taking them.

"Hey, great!"

"We've been stuck in here forever."

They were bubbling at her side like ordinary kids. *My kids.* She was touched by their excitement and a little overwhelmed by their beauty. "Then let's get your stuff and get out of here."

* * *

They seem to be delighted to be in the car with her. They ride along so happily that she doesn't have the heart to break the news. If she isn't careful she's going to get weepy; tough as she is, the relentless march of hours has worn Carroll thin. She's at the end of a long, hard day that found her stumbling off the redeye in San Francisco early this morning. Now it's afternoon and she's heading for the airport again. She can hardly bear the idea of strapping herself into her seat on another of those flying coffins but she can't stand sitting in this rich woman's car much longer either, flanked by graceful girls whose hair makes hers look like something a bird made and whose flawless pale shoes make her want to hide hers under the seat. Even the twins' hands are perfectly kept, set off by heavy gold rings with flat squares of sardonyx the color of their eyes. They are so lovely that she may have to spend the rest of her life proving she's good enough to take care of them.

Travel makes the days blur. By the time she and the girls get to Jenkins it will be tomorrow. And Steve will still be dead.

How am I going to tell you about your father, she thinks, pressed and forlorn. And tries to sort them out instead. "One last time," she says now that she has them sitting on either side of her. "Which of you is which?"

"I'm Emily," the one on her right tells her. Is it the same twin as last time? The other?

"And I'm Jane," the other, with Steve's smile.

Dazzled by the duplicate likenesses, she blinks. "When we know each other better, I won't have to ask all the time."

"Either that or you will." They giggle and fall silent, fixed on the rushing scenery.

Yes it troubles her: the bizarre blurring of identities. Is this something they intend? She doesn't know. She thinks so. She has no way to prove it. Carroll doesn't yet know why it's so important to know which one is which, but she knows it is. She studies the twins with a certain urgency. She's skimmed their faces for clues—a chipped tooth, a fresh zit, perhaps, anything one might have that would distinguish her from the other; if these are mirror images she should be able to pet them, but the slight droop of the lip, even the slant of the head to the left is the same; they could be gold coins stamped from the same die.

Their clothes are the same: unreal Laura Ashley floral prints that make them look like large children, identical soft leather flats. *Well I can take care of that,* she thinks. *Running shoes in bright colors. Get you some jeans,* she thinks. *Gap for one and Guess? for the other. I can look at the trademarks and know.* She wants to ask the girls how they'd like this but she can't. Not yet. She doesn't know them well enough. She doesn't know them at all. Here she is, frazzled and unkempt after all her hours of travel and they are riding along as beautifully tended as little queens. They might as well be inside a crystal globe, perfect and unapproachable. *They'll probably want to put a bag over my head to keep from being seen with me.*

She wants to ask them about Steve, but she's afraid to start because she can't bear to find out whether they know he is dead. She wants to tell them where they're going. She doesn't want to tell them where they're going. She doesn't want to begin because she doesn't have the strength to follow through.

And so they sit with their faces turned as if there is nothing more important than what's going on outside the windows. Billy goes along in silence, protected by the glass that separates him from his passengers.

Then the car makes an abrupt turn off the freeway. The girls stiffen and swivel to face her.

"What's this?"

"Where are we going?"

Suddenly they are brusque, accusing her, "I thought you were taking us home."

"I am. Ah, kind of."

The other says, "You promised."

"I. It's." Her breath pops out: *pah!* "Not home. I'm sorry, something's happened and I can't. We're going to the airport?" Carroll says.

In that second, they changed. One minute they're going along as nicely as anybody else and in the next, she risks losing them.

"The airport!" The twins go rigid. Bracketed by the girls, Carroll is electrified by something that crackles between them; it's as if she is hotwired, conducting messages she can't even hear, much less translate. They vibrate like little helicopters, ready to lift off the seat, and then settle back again. The twins have communicated without speaking. When they do speak it is in tongues; they could be Martians, or angels talking over her head.

"Predibus?"

"Maybe. Koprictus?"

"Enemo."

This is no language Carroll knows. It is unnerving. "Jane?"

"Glena femo naja." The current runs between them, carrying God knows what messages.

Carroll tries, "Emily?"

They don't even hear. "Mo no letternay?"

"What?"

"Predibus."

"What are you two . . ."

"Predibus." The twins are agreeing on something.

Then the one on her left turns to her and says with great dignity. "We're not going."

The other's voice is sharp, commanding. "Turn the car around."

Oh God, she thinks, how am I going to save this? "I can't. Billy's under orders . . ."

"I said, *turn the car around.*"

"Or else," the other says.

It is a dangerous moment in the car. How can she think this? But there is something going on here that she doesn't know about. Can't guess. That made Steve's face go dark a long time ago, so that it brightened only when he fell in love with her. There's something going on that jerked him out of her bed and back into his old life at the ring of a phone, the old pull of blood so strong that she is just now beginning to comprehend its power. The two young women or old children bracketing her with their maturing bodies and smooth young faces are mysterious and stern as deposed princesses who can still summon armies, and a part of her knows that they are sitting in judgment. Wait. She is troubled and unsettled. They're only kids!

And I promised Steve.

They look ready to open the car doors and fly out, or turn and sentence her to death, anything to keep from going with her.

"Please." It's the wrong way to start, in this thin voice quavering with weakness, but Carroll is too used up to do better. "Oh please. Your grandmother wants me to take you home with me."

"No." The twin on her right looks like a marble Psyche.

"We're not . . ." The twin on her left looks like a marble Psyche.

"We're not going." Their chiseled jaws are squared.

"No. We're not."

"Look, it's . . ." Her mind is scurrying fast, but all their entrances are closed to her. "It's because your father is . . ."

"Our king."

"Saint Stephen. Gone forever. We know. So sad."

They have just let slip something extraordinary, but Carroll is so intent on completing this transaction, on getting them into the airport and safely on the plane that she doesn't register. Instead she says with desperate gaiety, "I'm taking you to Florida!"

They fall so still that she wonders crazily if they've been struck dead.

"Girls?"

There is a stupendous silence. The twins are considering. When she turns to the speaker she meets a cold blue stare; Carroll knows what she'll see if she turns to the other. There is something new in the car. They are something more than two fourteen-year-olds who happen to have been born of the same crazy mother at the same moment.

But they're Steve's kids too. "Look," Carroll says, too tired to care that she's built her career on telling truths. She will do anything to make them happy again. "It's kind of a vacation. OK?" At her back all the terrible hours since Steve left are piling up, pushing her toward closure at any cost.

She lies! "Oh look, your grandmother wanted to split you up, but Steve . . ."

"He tried to take us out of the kingdom."

"To a better place!" If the lie worked, it's a good lie. "Your father wanted you to go to Florida."

"Florida!" There is a pause. "Real Florida, like on TV?"

"Jenkins. OK? It's a small town, OK, but close to the ocean."

"The ocean." They brighten. The girl on her right softens. It's as if she's shut off the current. "Beaches, then. Not that old Connecticut."

Steve's house—she can't bear it. Not yet. She says firmly, "Not Connecticut." In her grief Carroll admits, "I can't do Connecticut right now. I have family in Florida."

"Can we go to the beach?" The girl says to her twin, "Florida."

"Fla-di-da." The twins are talking across her. "Lots of beaches." Their voices interweave, embracing a new word. "Boys."

"Beach boys. Cool!" They are turning into little girls again. It's as if she's promised to take them to Oz. Carroll knows better than to say, *We're going to be living there.* "Yummy boys for us."

"Beaches." Their breath is sweet. "Florida, Emangel. Plenem. Eemo?"

Puzzled, Carroll jerks her head around. "What?"

"Angelem. Florida. Eimo lettermay?"

One says, "Disney World?"

The other says, "Busch Gardens?"

"Anything you want," she says. Anything. "We'll make a day trip. Sure. Look," she says, remembering the arcane clutter in their third floor rooms, and even though Carroll wants to give them a normal life instead of all that complex decadence she offers, "if you'd like, I'll even have your grandmother send some of your dolls."

"Dolls?" Their eyes empty out. "Emenola. We don't have dolls."

She tries hard to please. "You know, your—things at home?"

That little current surges between them. "No."

Something flashes. "Nobody touches our things at home."

"Nobody." The tone is imperious.

Uncertain, she backs off. "OK, OK, no problem, we'll get you all new things in Florida." Caught between them, Carroll wonders which is the dominant twin here, because she has a feeling one is leading in all the exchanges and if she can just figure out which one it is she can win them both by playing directly to her. "Jane?"

But Emily says, "In Florida."

"Florida, Orlando?"

"Well, not exactly." If only she could work it out: which one's in charge. "We're going to my home town."

Now it's Jane who seems to be bargaining. "Miami?"

"Not really." What is it about these two that puts her on the defensive? She wants approval! "My town is called Jenkins, OK?"

"Jenkins. It's not in the commercials."

"Below Jacksonville. It's kind of small." They don't need to hear that it's not home but her old job that's drawing her. "You'll love it. It's only minutes from the beach."

"Beach club!" They don't give her a chance to say this is not exactly a beach club situation.

"Sailing," the other says.

She gives the best she has to offer. "Body surfing."

"And Disney World," they remind her.

"Whatever you want," she says, exhausted. And waits.

The twins begin their deliberations in the mad, jittery dialect that confuses Carroll; she wants to think they were taught to talk by a Japanese nanny, but they aren't communicating in any known language.

These two have taught each other to talk, and if their English is strangely formal, it's because English is their second language. This alien dialect came first. It is filled with sound, little clicks and bizarre inflections, so complex that they may have words for things she can't guess at. The syntax is so logical that she thinks that with an effort she might understand, but whatever they have to say to each other is embedded in a past so deep that she can't begin to touch it and the language itself is impenetrable. It's eerie, she thinks, defeated by the vocabulary and trying to make some sense out of the pacing, the gestures. She can tell by the tune that they're winding up their deliberations.

She can't figure out who's in charge and it makes her afraid. "Florida, Emangel. Plenem. Eemo?"

"Angelem. Florida. Eimo lettermay?"

Yes something is going on over her head. The girls are completing their transaction. "Plebo. Lettermay."

"So. Ah. It's OK?"

"Oh yes," they say, converging on her in a hug. The sun comes back out. It is all as if they're conferring a gift. And as before, they giggle like ordinary fourteen-year-olds, leaving her to wonder whether the rest was a product of her exhaustion and grief.

Their voices are light. "But we need new bathing suits."

"You bet."

"And T-shirts?"

"Sure."

"And party dresses."

She's so relieved she laughs. "Anything you say."

"Boys."

"And earrings. Are there lots of boys?"

"Oh God, I don't know. I think so." Gratitude pushes her into making promises she can't keep. "You'll meet plenty of cute boys at the beach."

It is only when they get to Arrivals and Billy Graver gets out of the car to open the doors for them that she has a second to talk to him. The girls get out nicely enough and their grandmother's driver speaks to them sweetly enough, but as the twins hug him and tell him to say goodbye to Grandmother, she sees him grappling with such conflicting emotions that it makes her afraid.

The twins stand by the automatic doors, waiting for Carroll to lead the way, but Billy draws her back. Surprised, she asks, "Are we all right?"

It seems to cost him to tell her what he says next. "They're sweet girls, ma'am, and I'm going to miss them."

His voice trembles. "But the thing about them is, you never know what to expect."

"But they're lovely kids," she says, more or less in his stead.

"Oh yes." He seems sorry to see them go. "Yes they are."

"And we're going to be fine."

His response startles her. "Oh, ma'am, I hope so. For everybody's sake." There is no making out what's flickering in the eyes under the shiny bill of the chauffeur's cap.

"Billy, is there something I ought to know?"

"It's just patterns." He shakes his head because that isn't it. Whatever it is, it hangs between them now, but he can't seem to find words for it. He says at last, "You'll be fine."

"Look, if there's a problem, you'd better say so."

But he's fixed on the girls, and whatever he needs to say or thinks he wants to say is lost somewhere, hopelessly out of reach. As they give him sweet little waves, he manages, "I think this is the best possible thing for them."

She wants to grab him by the shoulders and shake the truth out but she sees that the aging driver is weak with fatigue. "It's OK Billy. I'm sorry. I guess you've been through a lot."

He dips his head in assent. Then he looks from her to the girls, who are craning, intent on overhearing. "I'm sorry too." Is he apologizing for not being able to explain or about Steve or is this about the twins? Lingering, he tugs the bill of his cap so the shadow obscures his face. Then as the girls push through the sliding doors and Carroll whirls to follow, he grasps her hand so unexpectedly that she gasps. He squeezes hard. "Oh ma'am, ma'am. Take care."

She hugs him impulsively. "You too."

He says in a voice that has gotten old, "If there's anything I can do to help . . ."

The girls have slipped through the door and are heading through the airport, moving ahead so surely that she could be the child and they the women in power, preparing to yank her across the continent and stuff her into a completely different life. In another minute they'll be out of sight and because she can't do this without help, Carroll says, for Billy, who is incapable of speech, "I know I can count on you."

13

IT GOES FAIRLY WELL, really, until they get to Jenkins proper. No. Take that back. It goes fairly well until the cab pulls up in front of the big old house on Arbor Street. On the plane the girls took turns sitting by the window while Carroll took the aisle. If they had flown before, they didn't show it; they were like any children on a first flight, giggling and distracted by the novelty of magazines and soft drinks whenever you asked and meals on trays and sanitized earphones and the takeoff video. There were many goings to the bathroom and many conversations with the stewards, who provided cheap pins with the airline logo, which each girl pinned in the exact same spot on the front of her dress. When the cabin was darkened for the movie they whispered together while Carroll slept. Once she woke while the cabin was still dark and through slitted eyes saw them writing in their little books with silver pencils; when she squinted, trying to read over the near one's shoulder, she was daunted by the look of the page: as cryptic as the pharaoh's hieroglyphs or encoded chicken tracks.

Going through Chicago was OK; they led her from one shop to another in the boarding lounge arcade and this perfectly normal enthusiasm so relieved her that she bought them souvenir mugs and popcorn and frosted doughnuts so sweet they threw them away. She admired them for being brave, as she was trying to be brave. The stopover in Atlanta was even better because in the strange, skewed time scheme of coast-to-coast travel it was morning, and she was almost there. While the girls ate Belgian waffles she called the *Dispatch* from an airport phone and asked for Charley Penn. He was so delighted to hear that he didn't ask questions. The aunts in Jenkins were a little puzzled but two were headed off to work and the third, grinny Aunt 'Laine, who made a career out of housekeeping on Arbor Street, promised the wing above the kitchen for her.

Riding into Jenkins, the girls were so overtaken by the tacky commercial architecture and the bizarre differences in landscape that distinguished this place from northern California that they hung out the windows like sightseers from another planet. Excited, they asked each other if they could smell the ocean, could they see it yet, if that was sand, were they almost at the beach, going on in such sunny voices that Carroll was lulled into thinking that not only were things going well, they would keep going well.

Which they did, until the cab pulled up in front of the sprawling, weathered Larrabie house on Arbor Street.

Carroll is tremulous as matchmaker. "Well here we are."

They don't speak, not even in their arcane private language, but the shock is palpable. Carroll can almost hear: *Is this it? This can't be it. This dump.*

She gets out and pays the driver. He guns the motor, waiting for the girls to get out, but nothing happens even after Carroll leans in and tries to wave them out. "Come on."

They look at her without speaking.

Poor things, she thinks. They've been through a lot. "OK guys," she says. As the twins stiffen and press against the upholstery in stunning diffidence she thinks. Oh shit, I forgot. She tries to sound brightly matter-of-fact. "OK Jane. Ok Emily. Girls?" Once again they fix her with matched stares. "Time to get out."

"Here?"

"This is it," she says with that stupid matchmaker's lilt.

"No it isn't."

"This can't be Florida."

"I'm afraid it is."

"It doesn't even look like Florida."

"Not like TV."

"This is a different part of Florida." Exasperated, Carroll says, "Now will you please get out so the driver can go?"

"Do we have to?"

"Yes. Now are you coming?"

Their faces crumple in disappointment. "But it's . . ."

"It isn't forever," she says. "Right now we all need a place to recover." Poor things, she tells herself, trying to get into the right head. They don't mean anything by this, they're just tired.

The cab driver is gunning the motor.

Fatigue makes them sound querulous. "It looks so *old*."

"Do we have to, Carroll? Do we?"

Poor things. They're just tired and upset. "Please," she says finally. "For me." She hates herself for not being able to go on. Oh shit. She, who never lets anybody see her cry, is on the verge of blowing it right here in front of Steve's girls. "OK?"

Seeing she is on the edge, the girls exchange a look she will learn to recognize. In that instant they soften. "OK, Carroll."

"OK." With tight grins that suggest she's making a huge fuss over nothing, they thank the driver and get out.

Carroll is so grateful that she hears herself gushing as they go up the walk. "I know it isn't as nice as your house, but in the old days it was supposed to be beautiful, the columns are kind of a wreck now, but I used to sit up on this porch and it's so high off the ground that I could pretend I was on the deck of a ship . . ." *Oh my God,* she thinks, looking at the glossy oleanders flanking the porch rail and the morning glories starting up the columns, *I'm having an attack of memory.* There are those nasty flat-needled bushes overhanging the walk; the remembered smell of crushed needles almost overwhelmed her. *I don't think I can do this.* It's like sword-fighting with a monster: *Back, damn you. Back. Back!* But memory has overwhelmed her and in another minute it will have her pinned and gasping for mercy with her limbs wriggling helplessly, Carroll Lawton, who's managed to survive everything that's happened to her so far, pinned by the past and squirming like a doodlebug.

"Look," she says desperately, "at least it's big. There are a lot of places you can play and hide."

When she looks back to see if they're following she sees

the girls looking up in a concentrated moment of assessment. Dilapidated as it is, riddled with leaks and tunnels made by Florida insects, the old house is big. When Carroll's great-grandfather built it, he had pretensions. If he couldn't be a plantation owner, by George he could live like one, and if her great-grandmother wouldn't let him build outside town, where his property would be protected, too bad. Not his fault the neighborhood had decayed since then. Not his fault the house is crowded by its neighbors or that the Larrabies are the last private owners on this street. The aunts and Uncle Peyton would be just as happy in neat condos down by the river but the sad truth is, they can't afford to move.

At least the house on one side holds doctors' offices. On the other side the property has gone downhill—dozens of tenants, Carroll can hear somebody yelling; rusty appliances abandoned in the thick grass out front; gutted cars and several motorcycles parked alongside. The Larrabie house floats like a ship in the middle, pretentious, decaying, proud.

"A lot of places to hide," she says. "Are you two coming?"

There is a perceptible click: information noted and stored. Twin faces turn to her. The one on the left, she thinks, Jane, she thinks, is almost smiling. Maybe Jane's the one she can get to know. But even though she's at the top of the front steps the girls are still planted on the walk. Carroll realizes that the longer they stand there, making it clear that it is they, and not Carroll, who are in charge, the more helpless she is.

"OK," she says firmly. "Come *on*."

Then Aunt 'Laine opens the door with that grin and it's OK.

Magically, the girls start to move.

'Laine is as short as the other aunts but not as neatly put together; her hair was colored so long ago that the grey's showing through even at the ends and probably because she's been busy cleaning the bedrooms above the kitchen, the tail of her plaid Ship 'n Shore blouse is pulling out of her wraparound skirt. Although she's the youngest of Violet's unmarried sisters, in a funny way 'Laine's the most maternal, 'Laine the purchaser of colored Band-Aids and loving purveyor of junk food for afternoon snacks. "Oh, Carroll," she says, spreading her arms. It's 'Laine who took all her savings to pay for Carroll's first year of college and 'Laine who bought her the electric typewriter, which does not stop 'Laine from holding out her arms with that gooshy look that means trouble—tears and debilitating sympathy: *Oh you poor thing.*

And Carroll nails her with a look. "Please don't."

'Laine's grin smears a little but she pulls it back to rights and even though Carroll explained this over the phone she looks past her at the twins. "And who are you?" *Oh you poor . . .*

Carroll stops 'Laine before she can say it. She makes the introduction. "These are Emily and Jane Harriman."

"No," they say, ever polite.

"What?"

"No," they say.

"You're not who I think you are?"

Who speaks first? "Not Harriman."

The other says, "Archer."

'Laine's eyebrows go up. "Oh, I thought . . ."

"I'm sorry." Carroll manages to keep from calling them "guys." She swallows hard. "I should have asked. Archer," she says to Aunt 'Laine. "Jane and Emily Archer. And this is my Aunt Elaine."

"Archer?"

"They took their mother's name, Elaine."

"Well they look just like their father," 'Laine says. "You two look just like your father, you do!" Expansive 'Laine tries to pull the girls inside the house with her. Carroll sees them shrink.

Then 'Laine corrects herself. "No, you're the image of each other. Or Carroll, they're the image of . . ."

She says drily, "Themselves."

As 'Laine burbles on the twins draw themselves up and look that look, and judge. And in her exaggerated state of loss Carroll finds her glance shuttling from one twin to the other to her aunt and back again, shifting incessantly until it fixes on her own tattered reflection, looking back at her from the dirty glass in the front door; the eyes in the imperfect image are black sockets and the wide mouth makes another black hole. It looks like a painting of a scream. Then everything piles up: past, present, the exclusive bond between the girls and Billy's inability to come out with what was on his mind because she's convinced now that he was filled with it, whatever it was, but when he came right up to the moment, he couldn't say. Her heart clenches. What. What?

Meanwhile Steve's daughters linger on the porch, regarding her with clear, cool eyes.

Oblivious, 'Laine tugs their hands. "Oh, girls! Come on in, I'm so excited. Come on into the kitchen, I've microwaved a cake." As Steve's twin daughters go past Carroll into the dim front hall she sees their heads lift and their backs stiffen as the unwitting 'Laine goes on in a spasm of hospitality, "Chocolate, with sprinkles, and I got double Dutch chocolate ice cream, but first, I want you girls to tell me which is which."

Then, just when Carroll is about to despair of them the girls make a comic turn, looking past Elaine at her. In the second before they duck their heads and politely follow 'Laine into the kitchen, they do something that completely disarms her. With matching grins that demand complicity, they wiggle their fingers at poor 'Laine in a gesture that makes her want to laugh.

14

GETTING READY FOR DINNER in the old house where she was so unhappy growing up, Carroll wonders why in God's name she came back. Yet here she is. Again. She's uncomfortable enough with the relatives when she's feeling strong, and this is not exactly her best time. Coming in on the redeye this morning, she lost all track of when or whether she'd slept.

When she and the twins staggered into bed after lunch today, she didn't expect to sleep so hard, or to wake feeling so gritty and confused. It's already getting dark. Sitting up in bed in her underwear, listening to the clatter of the kitchen below, Carroll's lost track. Had she really grown up and moved away? What if she looks in the mirror and she's still ten years old? She forces herself to get up. The adult clothes still fit; the face in the mirror looks adult and assured, but an essential part of Carroll is forever little and marooned in that grim front hall.

Coming out of the room, she knows she's changed, but the house around her is the same. The labyrinth of upstairs hallways and bedrooms and closets is layered with past miseries, leaving her ankle-deep in memories. She perceives the upstairs hall as a series of closed doors leading to rooms where the aunts and uncle have slept ever since they moved out of the nursery. There are seven bedrooms on the second floor not counting the servants' quarters above the kitchen, where she and the girls are staying. A long screen porch runs across the back of the house and she's half-tempted to duck out there and wait for dinner to be over, just the way she did when she was little. Impatient Suzy used to ring the maid's bell to flush her out. When it sounded in her bedroom

Carroll fled to the attic, but when you're little and alone ghosts begin to stir.

They seemed to live amid the abandoned furniture and ruined portraits of forgotten Larrabies, and the rolled-up bedding and bare mattresses in the maids' rooms suggested sleepless nights and unshed tears. There was furthermore the unfinished space beyond, where one wrong step sent you into unknown territory where the flooring gave way to punky plaster and old lath. Therefore there are parts of the huge attic that Carroll has never penetrated, dark places toward the front of the house and crawlspaces under the eaves. Spooked, she always ended up coming back downstairs to face the family after all.

The worn pink hall carpeting stretches all the way from the servants' quarters to the large front room that has been kept just as it was when MorMama died. Great-grandmother, whom the aunts called MorMama, got TB and slipped away while Violet's Grandfather Larrabie was fighting in World War One. When he came home from the war he used to sit in his mother's room and talk to her. Like a monument to the past the great Eastlake bed still dominates the room, draped in the same dust ruffle and crocheted spread, with MorMama's satin bed jacket folded on the pillow as if she's going to come back and put it on some day. Violet said when she was growing up Grandfather used to slip away from the family and stretch out on MorMama's bed with the matching Eastlake side tables. Carroll was spanked for sneaking behind MorMama's striped chaise to read and she still doesn't know why dead people's things should be more important than a living child.

It makes her dizzy—so much family past piled up in one place. It makes her sad. She needs the girls to reassure her that this time, things are going to be different.

The twins aren't in their room. The beds are neatly spread and the clothes she bought the girls at the mall this morning are hanging in the closet like patterns—blueprints for rectitude—so straight and even that anybody who put them on must be straight and even too. The girls have laid out pink string sweaters on the beds with the arms folded across

the fronts as though these too are part of some obsessive
scheme for the future, and the beds . . . Carroll is uneasy
about the beds. They've pushed and pulled, rearranging so
the feet of the beds meet in a precisely aligned V. There's
something meticulous at work here—the twins imposing
order on their space. It seems strange until she remembers
herself moving in after Violet's death, marshaling her things
in ranks on the dresser to protect her, taping up pictures of
her fourth grade class and her and the ancient Larrabie dog,
her only friend here. She put them in a cruciform arrangement as though the order of objects could protect her from
whatever came next.

Fleeing memory, she starts downstairs. The shadows at
the foot are as forbidding as ever; the dark oak paneling is
the same and from a pedestal on the bottom landing a bust
of some unidentified poet greets her with a leer that always
reminds her of Uncle Peyton's. The dust in the place smells
the same. The genteel chatter from the dining room is
exactly the same and the scars in the pier table where
Carroll kicked it in some early tantrum are the same. The
living room, music room and the dining room are still hung
with faded brocade put in by Great-Grandfather in anticipation of triumphs that never took place, and his ornate
gilded chair still sits in the music room.

"Carroll, is that you?"

Starting, she realizes she's stalled outside the dining
room, unable to go back and reluctant to go in. "Hello,
Uncle Peyton."

"You know better than that."

She sighs, "Hello, Pay."

Uncle Peyton looks tired and older, with his collar open
and his coat off so she can see how soft he's getting around
the waist. Even though his prematurely white hair is
yellowing now, he's rumpled it in that same old boyish way.
"You'd better hurry, we're all at the table. 'Laine's been
holding dinner for you."

Still she hesitates, but she knows it's impossible to wait
him out. He'll stretch his neck like a hungry duck to extort
his greeting, and unless she sighs and capitulates, he'll take

her hand and hold her in place for the ritual embrace. "Don't I get my kiss?"

Interesting, she thinks. Men don't have to put up with this. There is something of the repressed lecher at work here and Peyton won't let her pass until she's brushed his cheek with hers and then just when she thinks she's well away, he'll sidle closer and drag his hand along her waist. Even more interesting is the fact that this happens even though she doesn't want it to because he is a Southern gentleman and he's family and she is a woman, and beholden. *Women have to do a lot of things they hate.*

She gets it over with. Peyton seems put out when she doesn't want to linger even after he points out that it's been such a long, long time. Pushing him aside impatiently, she heads into the dining room. Everybody turns to face her: fat Patsy, toying impatiently with one of 'Laine's buttermilk biscuits: lazy Suzy with her eyes already filling up: *Oh you poor thing.* 'Laine, whose expansive gesture indicates a series of burnt offerings, from her best sweet potato casserole with marshmallow topping to glazed ham with pineapple rings; the twins.

The twins. Silent, they sit on either side of Carroll's empty place in their matched Gap T-shirts and denim skirts, looking at 'Laine with dutiful smiles. Their hair is brushed smooth and they're so scrubbed that the only color left in their faces is in their matched mouths and their eyes the color of sky. Right now they look about ten years old. Carroll notes wildly that one of them is wearing a gaudy blue slap wrap bracelet in a flip feint at high school chic, and the other is wearing a red one.

'Laine grins proudly. "Red one's for Janey, blue one's for Em. Tomorrow, I'm getting them tiny little ruby and sapphire rings."

The twins twinkle. What else had Elaine promised them? Carroll's lips moved. *Ruby and sapphire rings.*

But if she senses disapproval, fluttery 'Laine chooses to ignore it. She is proud of her expedient, beaming. "Then we'll know for good and all which of these nice girls is which."

Only the twins will recognize the sarcasm in Carroll's intentionally weak, three-note delivery: "Great."

And then—surprise! They grin. "Where've you been?"

They're glad to see me. She grins back; she can't hide her pleasure. *They are.* "Sorry I'm late."

Suddenly she can handle this. She hugs the other two aunts, whom she hasn't seen since the wedding, and then slips into her seat between her charges. In a way, she's grateful to 'Laine. This is Jane on her left, wearing the red bracelet, and on her right side, Emily. She and Steve's daughters form a solid front as 'Laine plies them with food and looks hurt when they don't take seconds and Patsy wipes her mouth and asks polite, awkward questions and Suzy yawns and stretches her arms above her head with her hands linked like an aging sex goddess waiting for the old magic to take effect. Carroll is touched: *She's trying to impress the twins.*

Her twins.

While she wasn't looking the Larrabies seated around the table went crunching into their sixties, and Carroll is astonished to see that time has turned them into parodies of their younger selves.

'Laine, who was engaged three times when Carroll was little, is still pretty with her sweet motherly expression and her shoulder length white curls. The body underneath the neat shirt and skirt set is going soft—a funny, matronly contrast to the rounded collar and navy wraparound skirt and the polished penny loafers, an old style she adopted some time in high school in the forties and never changed. She talks in an apologetic little whisper and when she hugs you, you sink in. When she and the others grew up their mother was still living but bedridden. Violet ran away and got married. The other two girls had jobs and 'Laine was elected to keep house for Mother. She's never done anything else. "Only until you get married," somebody said, and 'Laine said that was fine for her.

Grandmother died some time in the early sixties but 'Laine had promised to take care until she got married, and in the happy expectation that the right man was going to

come along sooner or later, she was still taking care,
trudging up and down with loads of laundry and greeting
people at dinner with honey-glazed roasts and Bing cherries
embedded in Jell-O and pretty, inedible pies.

She still cherishes an old snapshot of Larry, a Jenkins boy
who got shipped to Korea after college. He's standing under
the palm trees out by the high school in his ROTC uniform
and even though he moved to Arizona after he got out and
never wrote to her, 'Laine is still in love with him. "When
Larry comes back," she used to say when Carroll was little.
"When Larry comes back . . ." It keeps her young. In spite
of the fact that she's old enough to be a grandmother, there's
something sweet and young about 'Laine—all the tremu-
lousness of an unfinished girl.

Aunt Patsy seems older. And she doesn't. Tightly girdled,
she goes in for big hair and small shoes. Perhaps because
she's worked in an office filled with men ever since she
dropped out of college, she is worldly by comparison, a
little loud. The black hair and aggressive makeup keep her
from being any age. Her face is so round there's no slack for
wrinkles and glossy lipstick makes her mouth look enam-
eled. Unlike 'Laine, fat Pasty changes her style according to
her self-image and throws in accessories picked out of the
pages of the latest *Vogue*. She's gone from slenderizing
blacks to carefully constructed brushed cottons that look
like slipcovers to gaudy prints in synthetic fabrics that flow
over the lumps in her.

Where 'Laine stays home waiting for the phone to ring,
both Patsy and Suzy make a point of going out. Slender
Suzy is the younger, not much older than Violet would be.
In certain lights she looks forty-something instead of what
she is. The dyed hair is not as aggressive a color as Patsy's;
as the years unfold her hairdresser makes slight alterations
in the styling. The clothes are almost chic; she gets a
discount at the downtown department store where she
works. She used to bring men home, but now she prefers to
stay out overnight. If she and Patsy sometimes hit singles
bars together, it's because Patsy thinks Suzy knows what she

knows: That you have to go looking for love because it won't come looking for you.

Oh God, Carroll thinks. *Here we are.*

Suzy says, "You look tired, honey."

Patsy says, "That color is good on you."

'Laine says, "I'm trying something special for dessert. It's got your favorite things in it."

Peyton eats without speaking but his eyes follow her.

The continuity is staggering.

Nobody remarks on Steve's death and nobody notes how long it's been. Dinner just goes on as it always has.

What's fascinating here is the fact that she and the relatives have all sat down together and fallen into the same old patterns without once marking the fact that Steve Harriman is dead, that after all her cutting of the ties after the wedding, Carroll has come back to them. The aunts and Uncle Peyton are sitting here with their heads bent over 'Laine's ham and sweet potatoes as if it's any ordinary week night ("Oh, and 'Laine, while you're at it, set an extra place"). It is a scene that unfolds without reference to anything that goes on outside 553 Arbor Street, an ongoing event waiting for Carroll to walk back into it.

It's Peyton's night to clear the table and as he leans past Jane to take her plate he accidentally brushed her cheek with his hand; moving quickly, he does the same to Emily and Carroll sees both of them go rigid with dislike. So they have that in common too. Later she can take the twins out for ice cream and brief them on the personnel.

Maybe when they're alone she can get them to loosen up a little instead of sitting there like polite dolls. Maybe she can get them laughing. She can start making friends with them.

'Laine looks hurt as they refuse her pie and Carroll tips them a wink and takes two pieces to make up for it. She murmurs to Jane, "I used to slip things to the family dog, but the dog died."

"The dog died." On her right, Emily snickers. *Good,* she thinks. If she can just get close to one girl, she thinks, maybe the other will fall into her hands. She reduces the pie on her plate to bits so maybe 'Laine won't notice she isn't eating it. Later she'll slip into the kitchen and deep-six it; it's awful but she'll go to any lengths to keep from offending the chef, who happens to be the only aunt she really likes.

Suzy has taken out her makeup and is brushing blusher on her cheeks. In another few minutes the doorbell will ring and without asking whoever the caller is to come in, she'll grab her coat and go running out. Sucking in her stomach, which she's convinced will make her lighter. Patsy complains about her weight. Carroll swallows a giggle and says, "Oh no, you look fine," while at her sides Jane puffs out her cheeks and Em begins to raise her elbows as if without her being able to help it, her body's begun to inflate.

The girls see how funny Patsy is. She's not alone here. She and the twins are together in this.

Maybe I brought them here so we'd have something to fight. If you fight hard enough, you don't have time to think.

When they're excused and everybody leaves the table she's surprised by warmth—the twins pressing on either side of her in the oppressive hallway, Jane and Em, Em and Jane, not putting their arms around her, exactly, but moving in so close that she is surprised by the solidity, the fragrance of living beings who are, right now, closer to her than anybody else in the world. Touched and grateful, she's barely able to speak. When she does it's to one, to the other, to both girls and to the extraordinary string of accidents that has bought them together. She murmurs, "I'm so *glad.*"

In the morning Carroll will make the necessary detour on her way to work so she can drop the girls at the beach. As they head down the walk that protects the sea oats and what remains of the dunes, she's going to hesitate, but only for a minute. Is it all right to leave them here, newly orphaned and brand-new to this place? Then she'll tell herself the sun's going to be good for them. It's fine as long as they wait for her to come back to go swimming. Who wouldn't feel better, wading in the surf? Later she'll come back and explain about the riptide and they'll go in together. She'll forget their funny, inscrutable jabber and their disappointment when they saw the house.

She'll think she dreamed the sound of thumping overhead and the voices murmuring in the night. In the sunlight, she'll be sure she imagined it. They'll look like any other teenagers, going down the path. Bouncing along in their straw hats and pink-and-white gingham bikinis, the twins will look less formidable, like figures out of a beach-blanket movie. Smiling, Carroll will wave even though they aren't looking. Then she'll be free to go where she's been heading ever since the accident ripped Steve out of her life.

After months away she'll pull into the parking lot behind the two-story stucco building on Flagler Street just as she used to every morning of her working life. She'll race upstairs to the newsroom to see her boss at the *Dispatch.* Charley's hug says everything without her having to say anything. Together they can acknowledge Steve: her loss, the grief. Then in the rhetoric of survival Charley will say, "I thought Russell was going to do that"

Then Charley will tell her exactly what she needs to hear. "Only you could do it right."

"I'll get right on it."

And sitting in her old spot by the front window, booting up and finding her old filename still in the company computers, Carroll Lawton will begin to feel better. Sitting there behind the tinted glass in the slightly stale recycled air redolent of cigarette smoke, she will smell all the old smells and realize that even though she spent her childhood trying to get out of Jenkins, Florida, this newsroom is as close as she's ever come to home. Although she told Charley goodbye forever after the wedding, her files are still in her cue. *Yes,* she'll think. *There.*

The twins are all she has now, but this job is what she is. *This.* It seems right to her. No. She knows it is right. *I came back here because of this.*

15

THE ARCHER TWINS lie on the sand with their chins propped on their fists, watching the beach parade. They are identical in the pink-and-white checked gingham bikinis; the green-and-white striped towels are identical and the pearly polish on their fingernails and toenails is in the same shade; only the slap wrap bracelets differentiate them— blue for Emily, red for Jane. Later, remember, they will have ruby and sapphire rings—the aunt has promised, yes! Gems are appropriate. They are, after all, the queen. Stretching, they look at the world through black-framed sunglasses. Their fair hair falls forward so it covers their faces like a widowed queen's veil, giving them the illusion that they see without being seen. They love this new beach! Sunlight sparkles; the sand is white and fine.

Everybody in the world is going by—boys near their age and men three times their age; some are as old as Uncle Peyton, the only man they can find in that big, messy house on Arbor Street. There are so many here! The men all do that strange dancing double take when they see the twins laid out on their matching beach towels. Men and cute boys alike let their eyes slide here, there, over the girls' sleek bodies. It feels—strange. As they pass, the men turn that proud three-quarter face that tries to pretend it isn't looking, and then hesitate in mid-step, hoping the girls will speak. Every last one sucks in his belly as he goes by, while the twins wriggle in the sand and murmur as if they hadn't noticed. It is exciting.

This is nothing like Amadamaland. In Amadamaland the courtiers and knights stand in respectful ranks as Jade and Emerald pass among them. They worship from afar. Everybody in Amadamaland does as the queen says, but these men look at them with different eyes.

Jane and Emily, Jade and Emerald, the girls are so tightly linked that they communicate without speaking: *Men, Emajena.*

And that are all looking.

What do they see?

Us, Janemela. They are all looking at us.

Why does it make them smile?

They must see something they like.

The twins consider this with royal diffidence. The eyes raking them make them feel strange. New. Oh yes this is weird. Emerald asks aloud: "Do they know we are the queen?"

And Jade considers. The twins have no basis for comparison. When she and Emerald leave the kingdom and go downstairs in Grandmother's house in California, there is only Billy, who is too old to figure, and when they go outside there is only Kurt, with the missing hand and the puzzling black looks. Kurt doesn't like them. Even before the business with the gardener he didn't like them; he never has, and even though each of them in her turn has rubbed against him, purring and cozy, he's refused to talk to them, really, much less say why. At home Jade and Emerald can go for days without meeting a stranger. The cute boys they see they see only from a distance, at the monthly concerts given at St. Margaret's, when St. Anselm's comes to their school. In northern California they are children in a garden in shiny shoes and prim flowered dresses, lovely and untouchable. Here on the beach in new bikinis, they are something else.

The eyes of the men make Jade feel good and bad, special. "Don't be silly, everybody knows we are the queen."

"Then why are they looking at us like that?" The eyes of the men make Emerald feel good and dirty, powerful.

They're staring because they can't puzzle it out, you know?

But they think it is beautiful, right?

Right. They think it is beautiful, but that's not all they think. Turning in the sand as they roast slowly, Em, Jane still move as one; it is their power and their distinction, this pairing of beautiful flesh. *They see* us. *They see it is different.*

Yes. Jane, Em, Em and Jane alike, they sigh a satisfied sigh. *Yes, different.*

We are the queen. Stretched out like this, the twins feel special, extraordinary, and the passing parade of oglers? *Another proof of the existence of the queen.* If one of them is getting hungry or one of them needs to get up and go to the bathroom, it's not important. The only thing that matters is the unit they make. The engine that drives them is the will of the pair.

Pressed, the twins could not tell you who is the leader and who is the follower here.

Their identities blended in the crib: Jane and Emily tangled and howling—rather, in the economy of joined lives, one twin howling so both will be fed. They act as one. What one twin does, she does for both. It's always been this way. If the girls get up now and move their towels closer to the beach parade it is without consultation, and if they arrange themselves on the towels like Playboy models, it's because some part of them needs what's coming even as it fails to understand exactly what that is.

All they know is that they're greedy. They've never felt exactly like this before.

Like the men, the twins see things they like—strong sunlight beating down on polished bodies. They study a procession of biceps and pectorals and laterals mounted on frames of all shapes and sizes; they study boys' long bellies and the tightly muscled bellies of body-builders corrugated like washboards, lean men and fat ones, bodies there is no need to look at and bodies that seem to say, *follow me.* It's like seeing their lead soldiers magically realized: life sized and marching past on a conveyor belt—the Lucite Visible Man multiplied, but with each fresh body clothed in tanned and oiled flesh.

Mmmm.

The beaches are too cold in their part of California for this kind of exposure; in their part of California there are only the cliffs, and winds laden with mist. If the twins want to swim Billy Graver takes them to the club and Grandmother sits by the pool with them and pops towels around their shoulders.

Grandmother, what are you afraid of?

Why are you covering us up?

She said it was so they wouldn't be cold but they knew it was so nobody could see. Their bodies are perfect. Why is she ashamed?

In their part of California they never get to see boys undressed like this. They don't get to *be* undressed like this. Or get these looks. Maybe this is what Grandmother was afraid of. They giggle. *Interesting.*

Interesting. They are excited and pleased.

One of the girls stretches, digging her fingernails in the sand like a kitten. *Useful, perhaps.*

The other yawns. *We'll see.*

Yes, I think we'll see.

The queens of Amadamaland wear bodies that look older than they really are. Are they new women or large children? Even they don't know. Although the spoiled child rages inside, at a distance they look mature. In a strange way the girls' bodies are just that: something they put on to confuse the onlooker. Like their faces, the bodies are beautiful, smooth and flawless, paired.

Janem, our outsides do not look like our insides.

Exactly, Emangena, they would be frightened if they could see.

Her sister finds it necessary to remind her. "Emerald," she says aloud. "And you are Jade." *And we are beautiful.*

Jade says, "And we are queens."

Regal, Emerald says, "Together we are queen of Amadamaland." *Look at them looking, Jade!*

Jade warms under their eyes. *Yes! See the way they look at us!*

"Well I think we can be queen of this. Right, Jade?"

"And queen of Disney World and all the other places that

Carroll woman promised she'd take us." Jade looks at her pearly fingernails. "And we will make her take the boys."

"We don't know that she's going to take us anywhere," Emerald reminds her, running her tongue over her own fingernails. "A woman we don't even know."

"She married King Stephen."

Emerald does not say what they are both thinking: *He should have waited. He should have married us.* "We should have gone home. Why did we ever agree to come with her?"

"You know. To get out of the hospital."

Everything—the threat to the kingdom, the overnight flight, their seedy new surroundings—everything's left Emerald tired and disrupted. "But it isn't any fun."

Jade says, "The beach is fun."

Emerald can't help it; she frets. "She promised to take us lots of places, and all she's done so far is bring us here."

"Well this is not so bad. I'd rather have these . . ." Rolling over, Jade puts her arms down at her sides and then drags them up in a sweep so that she makes angel's wings in the sand. When she rolls back and sits up, her gesture takes in the three new boys who have just come down from the parking lot. The trio is standing far enough away to keep from alarming them but close enough to see everything they want. With the back of her hand Jade flips her long hair over her shoulder and gives them that look she's been practicing. Now that they're watching, she's ready to complete the thought. "I'd rather have these guys than a hat with Mickey ears."

Somebody laughs. They are close enough to hear but too far away to touch, three lean guys with chipped teeth and raunchy grins. The Florida towheads look closer to twenty than fifteen, tanned to peeling by too many weeks in the sun and just a little edgy, rocking back on their heels in lowslung, faded cutoffs, studying the twins from underneath lashes flecked with sand. The one in the lead rubs his hand across his bare belly, leaving a sandy track. *Three. One too many,* Jade thinks. *Or one too few.*

She pretends not to notice. "Emanjela. Premo?" *You want?*

Like Jade, Emerald flips her long hair over her shoulder and looks at them. "Janema. Preemo." *I want.*

Born at the exact moment they are identical, line for line and bone for bone, same flesh. Thoughts flow. *And they will do what we tell them, like our subjects?*

As they consider this the girls turn and stretch like kittens getting ready to grow into tigers. Without looking, exactly, they can see how the boys respond. *They have to want to. We have to make them want to.* They both know the imperial we.

That's a problem.

Unless it's not a problem. When they lift their shoulders and tilt their heads just so, their hair falls in a way that makes the watchers shift their weight on their feet, straining to get closer.

This might be better than Amadamaland. Yes they are just beginning to comprehend their powers.

Or something we can take home.

Oh let's go play with them; they're just big dolls.

And as if something palpable has shifted the balance here, the leader of the trio licks and licks his salt-rimmed lips and rubs his belly and grins.

The anticipatory buzz links them. *Mmmmmmm.*

With a gesture of magnificent indifference, Jade stands up. It could just as easily have been Emerald ducking her head to mutter a final question behind the shimmering screen of blonde hair. "What if they want us to do what *they* want?"

But Emerald chooses not to hear. Her body goes through the same sequence. She says, too low for anybody but her sister to hear, "Jade, if we catch some, can we take them home with us?"

Not yet fifteen—old, young, dangerous women and vulnerable children, they move out. But in the last second before they lift their faces to the strangers, Jade says in a strangely gutty, adult voice, "Queen Emerald, I think it works the other way."

16

WE COULD KILL Aunt 'Laine.

Just when everything was going so well.

Standing by the refreshment stand, we are, and we are just about to take our hot dogs and get into their car—these boys are so *cute*. What are their names? Tod and Randy and Jake. They all work down at the marina and they want to take us out on their boat, and if this is a little scary because they're over twenty, it is also exciting, OK? Look, we are the queen. Our eyes are glossy with it. *New realms.*

Real knights.

They have their hands on our waists and the next thing is just about to begin when this Larrabie woman that we hardly know comes down on us and ruins everything. No kin and she says call her aunt, no way. This walrus comes galloping down into the sand with her ankles rolling in her gummy shoes until one foot turns over and she stumbles into us. 'Laine comes gasping with her elbows flapping and her shoulder bag sliding, sad old woman with the dyed hair and the wrinkles, fluting, "Oh, Jaaaaanne."

Don't call me that. It is humiliating.

"Emileeee . . ."

I told you never to call me that. Like to murder her.

One of the guys says, "Who's that?"

"Nothing. It's nobody."

I can feel his fingers moving. "Don't look like nobody to me."

"Nobody we *know*." But I am thinking: the rings. Maybe she is bringing the rings.

"Oh, girls . . ."

The boys mock. "Oh, gi-rulls . . ."

"*There* you are." Her mouth is quivering.

We are looking at her: Woman. We can forgive you if you've brought the rings.

In hell. "Your stepmother was afraid you'd get too much sun."

Stepmother! The bitch. "We don't have any . . ."

"Now hush. Come on." Woman, don't you know you are dealing with the queen? This 'Laine will try to drag us away like children. She tsks at us. "You don't want to get burned on your first day."

I turn; my sister turns. "Let's get out of here," my sister says to Randy, or is it Tod. But the boys are intent on the tableau we make, the queens surrounded by courtiers, bare, sandy arms around bare waists, his around my sister's and get this: in the middle, another *his* around *ours*, and at this end, the third—*his* around mine. His arm and *his* arm. I love the heat.

So as 'Laine crunches down I duck into Tod's shoulder and pull Randy closer and my sister does the same. Shall we say to no avail? Nothing halts this galumphing woman who is hooting like a fool, "Oh, girls . . ."

Tod has his mouth on my ear and I am stretching to feel his sandy lips slide the length of my neck to my shoulder and all the time this creature is getting so big she obscures the sun.

"Oh girls, please come on."

"Go away!"

I hear my sister shouting, "Go away!"

"Who do you boys think you are?" Aunt 'Laine is so loud and out of place here in the sharp-edged sunlight, so angry and insistent that the boys' arms slide off us even though I try to hold Randy's hand on my waist. As we face her, our courtiers fade away. See them disappearing. *Some knights you are.* "You damn well better get out of here," she shouts and this speeds them along. She shouts, "You want to go to jail?" Yes she is angry. Instead of quaking before the queen, this 'Laine yells at Tod and Randy and the world at large, *"Do you have any idea how old these children are?"*

So she has said the one thing that will ruin us, at least in that company.

The boys split. Forget about the night on the boat.

This 'Laine is red in the face, bustling and indignant. "What do you children think you're doing?"

My sister shows a flash of royal anger. "We are not children."

But this does not even slow Elaine. "I know what you are," she says. "You're my responsibility. Now come on."

Still we are not sorry. Cute as he was, Tod smelled like a stale mattress; his fingernails under the strap of my bathing suit were sharp and when I looked at Randy, there was green stuff on his teeth. *We can do better, yes? Plenty more where they come from.*

Yes we can do better. And will.

At the wheel, Aunt 'Laine is indignant. "Trash trying to pick up my girls."

We are not your . . . The sun and the water and the ice cream she buys us on the way home have made us mellow and too drowsy to take her up on this.

"I saw those boys." She surprises us. "To tell the truth, you girls were meant for better." Her voice gets furry and confidential. "You just have to wait. The right man will come along . . ."

We do not ask if she's still waiting for the right man to come along. *Our king, Saint Stephen,* my sister thinks and does not say. I know what she is thinking and I murmur, "Better." Our saint is in heaven, where saints stay. All the living, sexy ones are here. "Better." *Yes.* Dumb Aunt 'Laine thinks we are talking to her.

"Better," she says, driving along and driving along. "One of the first things a girl has to learn is who's the right boy for her." We let her talk because she has promised us the rings.

She promised but she doesn't give. Instead she sits us down in the big kitchen and feeds us grilled franks and more ice cream, this time with fruit and jimmies, three kinds of syrup—until our bellies get as fat as the grabby Peyton's. She winks as she pours on Marshmallow Fluff.

It is strange, like sitting down with the maid. My sister the queen does not say anything and I don't say anything.

We need time to study the situation here.

The house is almost big enough for us. In the cavernous kitchen we're like chess pieces on the dingy black-and-white linoleum. Me. My twin. Elaine. There are glass-fronted cabinets and a rusting two-door refrigerator. The big gas stove has many burners and two ovens so big that you could perform cremations here. Something about it makes 'Laine sentimental. "In the old days the family had a cook. When our mother was little every day was like Thanksgiving, with three starches on the table at their dinners, and for dessert, three kinds of pie." She says this as if she's reciting an old prayer that used to mean something to somebody else. "Of course our grandmother had ten children, nine living, so things were a lot different here." It is awful, having her try to make friends with us. All she had to do was give us the rings. Instead she tries to make us love the house.

"I see."

She tries to make us love her.

"I see." *Love.* Imagine. Yeugh. What about the rings?

"I suppose things are a lot different at your house." She is all tremulous. "I mean, were."

My sister the queen does not say anything; I the queen will not say anything. The Felix the Cat clock on the grease-spotted wall above the giant stove is wagging its tail, tick-tick.

"Do you girls like movies?"

Tick tick.

We are sick of her trying to make friends with us. We shrug.

"TV?"

Tick tick.

She sighs. "I just wish I knew what you girls liked."

You have no way of knowing what we like. Better not say that. Better not say anything. Better just roll our ice cream over and over in our mouths until everything is gone except the jimmies. Better eat and then get shut of her. If we are in exile, so be it. This is temporary. We are still the queen.

The woman cannot tolerate a silence. "Poor Carroll must

be . . ." She breaks off. "They were just married last year, and now, poor thing . . . First her mother, and now this. Awful. Devastating. So sad! Poor Steve!" She sighs. "Terrible thing. And such suspicious circumstances, you know?"

This brings our heads around.

"Killed *so fast*. Freak accident. At least they *said* it was an accident, but from what Carroll says . . . I don't know."

Suspicion makes us squirm. We are sick of Elaine talking but we don't know how to make her stop. I run my finger around the bowl and my sister runs her finger around the bowl. She licks her finger and I lick mine and all the time the woman talks on.

"And your mother too. So fast!" She sighs again. Then her eyes slit. She looks at us sideways. "What happened to her anyway?"

Somebody shudders. *I know.*

Disturbing. *But I don't know.* Do we or don't we?

Disturbing, yes. *Don't want to know?*

Don't know! It is confusing. We do know, but we don't.

This 'Laine is waiting. Naturally we do not answer. "I just don't know what we're going to do with you . . ." Then she sighs again. After a while she can't handle any more silence, this woman we hardly know staring, us staring, nothing going on. Even she is getting sick of trying to make friends with us. Elaine gets up with this little quiver. "If you girls want to go play . . ."

Play?

Queens don't play.

We have more important things to do.

We are the queen.

She can hardly wait to have us gone. She gives us a hug that is more of a push and everything comes out of her, quivering. ". . . just go ahead."

We shake off Elaine's strong hands and go upstairs. We get into clothes, but they're not *our* clothes. Pink gingham halters and ruffled shorts. Tawdry, like the room. Carroll what's-her-name says this is our room, OK? This is nothing like *our* room. See the twin beds, cheap and tacky plaid spreads. Matching maple dressers with identical mirrors. Matching windows. One gives on the back screen porch. The other faces the house next door. I say to my sister:

"We can't stay here."

"Look," my sister says. She is at the side window. "Look over there."

And so we do. Unlike this place, the house next door has lots of apartments. It is like the movies. In every window, secret lives are going on. There is a woman hitting her screeching baby. Over there, some fat girl in her underwear tries on clothes; she is getting ready for a date. On the first floor, two people are having a fight. Up on the third, a man with black belly hair pulls up his T-shirt and scratches. He sees us staring and stares back. In the attic window we see a woman so old she's probably been there since it was built. In the driveway are motorcycles; we hang out the window, trying to see if the owners are around. We need cute boys. Nobody. Too too bad. My sister is sagging. "Where are the boys?"

"The boys aren't home now," I say, "but they will be."

"If not, we're going home." Florida is hard! We are so tired! "When this Carroll comes."

"We'll make this Carroll take us home."

"After Grandmother begs us to come back."

"After we get the rings." Sapphire for her, ruby for me. At least we will have one thing to show for this. To take back to Amadamaland. Outward and visible signs we are the queen.

We fall silent. We watch the window movies in the house next door until we hear a motor start. Somebody's backing out the shared driveway. "Look!"

It is the Larrabies' spare car. "Elaine. She's going out."

OK Elaine. Well might you go shopping. Meanwhile, we're alone.

Then we have a time. Oh yes. The house is ours, and so we have our way. First we go into the big front bathroom where the aunts pee and we take all the pills out of all the bottles and mix them up and put them back. Oh yes, we take a few for us. Numnums for later, who knows when?

Take that, Elaine. Uppers and downers so mixed up that you won't know whether you're coming in or going out.

After that we have the whole house to explore—the other bathroom, gangs of bedrooms and big closets, which we skim. We find the top styles from old years in Aunt Suzy's closet, outgrown clothes in Aunt Patsy's, candy wrappers in her dresser. A woman's hair on the pillow in the Peyton's bed, no color that we recognize, but you never know. Poor Elaine has a shelf filled with withered corsages, from dances a hundred years ago. It pleases us to stick the pearly corsage pins inside our halters with the smooth heads against our skins and the points sticking out of the folds; squash us and you'll feel them right enough. We study the room where this Carroll stays—a few sad clothes, underwear. No clues.

Bored we are, so it is up the back stairs to the attic. It's big and scary and hot, probably from sun beating on the roof for centuries with no rain. There are more maids' rooms up here, how many servants did they used to have?

Rooms there are, and in the attic proper, gangs of trunks and boxes filled with used-up clothes and over here, oh boy, piles of old-fashioned hats sitting on wig stands and look, pins we find, beautiful with jewels and devices on the end, long enough to stick the biggest hat to the biggest hair, so nice we have to take them, yes. Pins we find, and family portraits piled up like people in a doctor's waiting room and behind the rooms a crawlspace where the roof meets the eaves. If we wanted, we could duck inside and run the perimeter of the house like rats but it is hot and dark and when my sister kicks over a box at the opening, insects run. The attic's big; there are a dozen places to hide, but not now, not now.

Down the back stairs we go, but nobody's in the kitchen. Wherever this Aunt 'Laine is, she doesn't come back and bother us, not even when we mix up eight dozen things from the shelves, starting with ketchup and hot sauce and Hershey's syrup to make an ugly drink and then dare each other to take a taste. I do. My sister does. Nobody dies. Nobody wants it, either. It is disgusting. We talk about feeding it to this Carroll, but we decide not, at least not until she's bought us more clothes and bikinis and taken us all the places she promised, yes? We take the mess outside and pour it out in the dirt under the huge back porch.

We're bored so we go around front. The columns are strangled by creepers. It looks like Tara, if Scarlett O'Hara got poor and the jungle started eating up her house. We sit in the rockers and rock and curse, curse and rock.

If she wants to give us rings she can damn well hunt for us.

Nothing in this awful place goes the way it's supposed to. She doesn't come looking. We are alone on the porch. We sit in the high-back rockers working on the royal chronicles and talking about the boys. Tod and Randy no-last-name, and call-me-Jake.

In the absence of the Great Book of Life, that went over the cliff in the death chariot with our late King, Saint Stephen, we write their names in our books. This will have to do until we are at liberty to enter their names in the Ledger of the Realm which my sister keeps, along with her novel, in the back of the dresser in the Royal Bedchamber in Amadamaland. Sir Tod and Sir Randy. Milord Jake. How we wanted to enter their names on the roster of knights!

But she came and got us. Elaine. Doesn't she know we are Archers? Beware, bitch. We have the power. Paired Archers can send the arrow into the center of your brain.

Right now we are armed, but not dangerous. After all, she's promised us those rings. Today, she said last night, but probably she means tomorrow because it's getting late. The queen is stern but she is also gracious, and so we are inclined to wait.

Besides, here's a new guy. Yes! And pretty cute. He just got out of a cute car and now he's crunching along the driveway next to our porch. We go to the rail and look down. "Nice car."

"Say what?" He catches us looking. He *looks that look*. And we? We say, "Do you want to come over?"

"Can't, I came to see my girlfriend."

Oh yes we saw her in the upstairs window, deciding what to wear. But look at *us* in our halters and shorts. We sit on the rail so he can see us. "Come see us instead?"

He sees. Oh yes he sees. He's cute enough; he will do for now but he's soft as Mr. Poppin' Fresh in polyester pants and shortsleeved shirt where we are thin, lovely. Quick. He should be flattered, thrilled. "Sorry. She's expecting me."

But we have seen her. We know we are prettier. So does he. "Oh," we say. "Well she isn't there." There is a little roll where his neck meets his collar but the smile is cute. We hang over a little farther, feeling sleek inside our skins and skimpy Florida clothes, with the pearly heads of the corsage pins rubbing us *there*. "She's gone, OK? What's your name?"

"Ed." Our expressions make him blush.

"Well come on over, Ed."

Instead he shakes his head. "Too bad you're too young."

We are sultry. Sexy, yes. "Old enough to be queen."

But he just—blows us off! "Sorry, kids." *As if we are nothing at all*. And turns and goes.

Clouds roll in. "Hey wait, you. We are no *kids*."

He doesn't hear the thunder. He just goes on.

Doesn't he know what forces he is awakening? *Kids!*

Too bad there's nobody to tell him: Nobody crosses the queen.

"Eemo." *Shall we?*

"Eimo." *Will we?*

You betcha. Us. The Archers. We don't even have to discuss it. Yes. In spite of which, one of us calls after him. "Glena." *Watch out!* But he, this Ed, is already out of sight. Inside with that ugly girl. Never mind. We can wait. The queen's temper is short and her memory is long.

Therefore we sit back and wait, and plan. Our knights. Tod and Randy and call-me-Jake. Maybe they're still at the beach. When this Carroll woman gets back from wherever, we will make her take us back to the beach. And if they're gone? There are plenty more where they came from. The beach is a feast of lean boys and raunchy men. Forget cute Ed with his slick car and his superiority. *Kids.*

Tough rocks for you, Ed. We are the queen.

And we are hungry, yes, but not for ice cream with jimmies and three kinds of syrup. We'll be going home soon, so we need to work fast. When this Carroll comes back we'll make her say how long this little *vacation* is for. How much time we have. Two weeks in Florida, is it? Or is it three? We left in such a rush we didn't ask. Time, we need, but not too much of it. Time here, in this ruined house. Time we need to find and catch and use and have. We need time to get us the best and cutest knights, to take back with us, but not so much time that we get bored.

After we see Disney World and Busch Gardens and maybe even Universal City, after we have our just due and this Carroll has bought us all the Florida clothes we can wear in two lifetimes, we will go home. Then and only then. Let the Archer grandmother beg us to come. Then we can decide what to do. There are things going on back there that we need to see to. The Blues and the Greens are at odds in Amadamaland and only we can sort it out, but when we go back into the kingdom this time we are going back on our terms. And we're not going alone.

Knights we need, we know this now that we have seen so many nearly naked, tanned and strong with flat muscles in their bellies and long round muscles in their thighs. Nearly naked and that close! Knights we need and knights we'll have, and take them all back to live with us in Amadamaland, where I the queen have my way and my sister the queen has her way because we are the queen and we will have everything we want in Amadamaland. We will . . .

"Oh, there you are!"

That awful voice! Priss-priss: *eohh, theah you ahh.*

Too easy to see that there's nothing in her hands and nothing in her pockets. No rings today. One of us says, "Go away."

She grins that everlasting pink lipstick-on-the-tooth-y grin. Elaine it is, oh see her clomping along the porch. *Put away our notebooks, quick!* She knows we hate her but she won't quit. We throw looks like armed grenades but she doesn't stop and she won't shut up. "I'd thought you'd gotten lost." *Ah thowut you'd* . . .

I make a face.

"Oh, girls." *Aww, guhls.*

My sister makes a face.

As it turns out, she *is* bringing something. Something nasty. Cards. "I just brought you these forms, for registration?" She drops them in our laps. Cards with our names on them. Archer: Jane and Emily. *Ah just brawt* . . .

We glare. "You—what?"

"You know, for school?"

"School!"

"After all," she begins, and the next thing she says shakes our hearts inside our ribs and sets our brains and eyes and tongues all rattling in our skulls like china. It unseats huge and terrible shapes in Amadamaland. Just out of sight tall buildings shudder and start to fall. Watch out! We can bring everything crashing down around us like the city of Babylon around the raging Samson and his tormentors. In a flash we see the ruin of civilization, the world engulfed in molten lava, the dreadful termination of lives. While Elaine says, "Now that you're living here . . ."

Glena. Watch out.

Does she understand what she is unleashing? No. She pulls us up. "Let's go inside and fill these out."

Feel the volcano boiling up. Beware the Archers. Beware the wrath. Beware the fire in our hearts and in our veins the molten steel hardening. Yes we are *becoming*.

Elaine the ignorant, marching us along the porch. Fool. Beware the queen. As she blunders on we are aware of activity in the driveway; through the vines we can see that Ed person coming out the side door of the house next door. He is alone. Here he comes, down the drive. In another minute he's going to get in his car alone, when all this time he could have been getting in the car with us. *Ignore us, hey.* He sees us and waves. *Call us kids.* Slow-moving target. We wave back.

He hesitates just below us.

Call us kids. Something in us stirs. *Better call us destiny.*

Rage weaves between us as we fix on him. Fury crackles and I think: *Eemo*. I switch my behind and when I look over my shoulder, he smiles. My sister looks back over her shoulder like a model. *Eimo*. Unwitting Ed person, stopped in his tracks. The slob.

Ed lingers while Elaine is so intent on her cards that she doesn't see what's going on.

Krazgo. Not good enough to be a knight. Watch out, careless Ed. We need him for other things, OK. *Glena!* Watch out.

While I wiggle my fingers at Ed and my sister sees him run his tongue around his mouth, heedless 'Laine holds the screen door open. "Are you girls coming?"

No answer here. Just us hanging by the rail in the early spring heat. And 'Laine jiggling. And Ed. Yes, Ed.

My sister clicks and I click in a transaction that needs no explanation. There is no external sign that it completes itself. Elaine just babbles on while we drift back to the rail and look through the vines. At the far end of the driveway this Ed lingers, licking his round mouth and rubbing his fingertips along the hood of his cute car.

Krazgo.

They are both fools, yes, but we still have use for her, while he . . .

We know what we must do.

No one knows that we are about to do it.

Beware the lack of outward and visible signs.

Elaine's mouth trembles. Can't she feel the wrath? "Girls?"

Beware Jade and beware Emerald, Emerald and Jade.

Too bad for you that you don't know Vivian's warning. Instructions for anyone who's ever taken care of us, Grandmother's help and all the staff at school and all the ships at sea, it goes right over her head. *Whatever you do . . .* Never mind.

Too bad.

Too late. In her fiercest nightmares Elaine won't see it happening. For the moment, her circumstances protect her: this Ed out front, stroking his car; the rings she promised, our position in the house. Now Elaine, getting-old Southern lady goes on as if we are ordinary, not the queen but children, *children.* Seals their doom. "Of course school. Now that you're living here for good."

For good. She just lets it fall out of her mouth.

Rage rips through us. *Kaaaaaa.*

17

IT DOESN'T MATTER how far Kurt Graver rows on the machine adapted to his missing hand or how many miles he runs along the coast road every night, he doesn't sleep much now. He hasn't slept since the Archer twins were whisked away. More than their being here, their absence has left him jangling. For him it's like knowing there's a bomb ticking somewhere just out of sight. He can be physically exhausted and still not sleep. No matter how late he stays up or how long he sits in the dark in the cluttered living room, smoking and staring at the changing displays flickering on the VDTs, he doesn't even get sleepy. Instead he sits there waiting as if the answers to all his questions are just about to come up on one of his screens. He is ordained to do something. But what?

He's trying to figure out what to do about the twins.

He doesn't want to believe something terrible is going to happen, but he does. The others may want to ignore it but the bad old history is still writing itself, and the outcome of the next chapter is up to him.

If Kurt had his way all life would be on some gigantic data base and all he'd have to do to get to the bottom of the mystery here would be enter the right password and get into the system. Without leaving this room he'd shake the twins' family tree until it yielded the twins' grandfather Hal Oliphant and then he would squeeze Hal Oliphant until he gave up his secrets. He could modem into Trappist monasteries one after another and on one of his electronic forays he would raise this Franklin Davage, S.J., who is hiding out in one, the priest who knew the Oliphants so well that he tried to prevent Hal's marriage here some forty years ago. And when he could not prevent it, fell off the earth.

The priest knows something we don't know.

When Hal and Meredith Archer married, the clergyman performing the ceremony came to the ritual moment: "If anyone here present knows any reason why these two should not be bound together . . ."

Meredith gasped. Handsome Hal just gave a boozy smile. Until the Jesuit sprang out of the shadowed vestibule shouting, "Wait!"

Turning from the altar with a poisonous scowl, Hal Oliphant raised an army of ushers and had him thrown out of the church.

Kurt reflects: How many times has Billy told me this? Over and over ever since I was five and Zane Archer blew me apart. "He tried to stop the wedding," Billy says, "but she wouldn't listen. I drove him to the bus. He told me there was something wrong with Hal but they were married by that time, so he wouldn't tell me what it was." Considering his son, Billy says over and over, "If only she'd listened to the priest."

If there was a bad seed in the Oliphant family, Kurt thinks, it fell close to the tree. Zane. He flinches. Vivian's twin brother, Zane, with his uniquely black vision and a lust for destruction. And yet the three children played together; they played until . . . Sometimes Kurt still feels the ghost of the missing hand. Flexes the imagined fingers and lets them play across his keyboards. Zane. Sometimes Billy rages. "He should have been smothered at birth." From the beginning Zane's silky malice set him apart. Now it flowers in the next generation: Vivian's twins. They smile and wave at him; they flirt with him underneath his window. Pretty as they are, he still sees Zane in them—handsome, malicious.

He doesn't know what to do.

After the accident—after Kurt's left hand exploded in his face, his father went half-crazy trying to locate the priest. The child cried, "Why, Daddy?"

Billy whirled on him, weeping. "Because he'll know what to do!" And the sad old story came out.

The deep, superstitious part of Kurt believes in the power of the Jesuit. *He'll know what to do.* But the priest hasn't been heard from for years. Now Kurt is grown. Now Vivian is dead, leaving only Kurt, with his dark suspicions. She's dead and her twins are gone. And he's still here. Stuck. What will it take to blast him loose?

Nobody knows it but until this week Kurt's perimeters have been defined by Vivian. Until Zane died she was his sun. That night it was over, but still! He is surprised by how close she's held him all these years.

As kids they were desperately in love; he loved her when they were five years old: Vivian clutching his spurting wrist to stop the bleeding, looking at him out of those beautiful, tragic eyes. Kurt survived the early accident all right; he went back to kindergarten the next Monday because he was tough. Vivian loved him, and no matter how the stump hurt, he was fine.

Love kept him on the place. He was safe and happy with her here, going to town in the closed car with Billy at the wheel. They left reluctantly on school mornings, coming home as soon as the last bell rang. After the explosion Kurt needed the safety: beautiful Vivian and her brilliant, funny brother. The Archer place. Him.

Until he left for Stanford, he didn't know how bad it really was. Without Vivian, he panicked, gasping for air. Cut loose, he couldn't breathe! He taught himself how to feel safe within certain boundaries: the classroom buildings and the dining hall. The computer lab. His room. He could go other places as long as he had a friend to ride post. Nobody knew. Clever as he was, Kurt dissembled. He didn't *have* to go out much. People liked him. They came to him. When he graduated he and Vivian would be together again. Together, he thought, they could go all over the world.

Then he tangled with Zane and it ended. They weren't children any more. He looked into Vivian's face after Zane died and for the first time saw her naked. It was over. They never spoke again. After the hospital she ran away. Kurt would not see her again until she was married and divorced. Until she came back with twins of her own. When she came back it was the same. Yet he's still here.

But look. He has the world at his fingertips. He is

surrounded, reinforced by technology. Disturbed as he is now by Vivian's death, by the sense of large shapes shaking loose and beginning to move, Kurt spends these nights keyboarding.

Logical as he is, he sees ghastly patterns, the flashing dark-light-darkness that ruined his life. He can't let Vivian's twins have their way out there in the world. If he can just come up with the right information, he'll know what to do. At least he's trying to help. Or has the illusion he's trying. Before he's done he will have exchanged with every hacker and consulted every computer directory and accessed every database in the world. The right electronic hop, skip and a jump and he will be, as it were, face to face with Father Franklin Davage.

Where is the bastard anyway?

"In seclusion," Billy said in one of those agonized sessions they've had every night since Vivian died. Kurt pressed for details until Billy groaned, "Oh, let the dead bury their dead."

"This isn't about the dead. If you know he's in seclusion, you must know where."

"In some Trappist monastery, I think. Anything so he wouldn't have to see what happened here. Oh hell, maybe he went to Mount Athos."

"Greece?"

"It's possible."

What if Kurt could modem into the place where the priest is hiding out? What would this Father Davage say? Keyboarding, he would charge him.—*What is it with these people, Father? Is it something in the blood?*

—*I can't say anything. I'm in seclusion.*

—*So am I, Father,* Kurt will say.

—*Please go away.*

If you're worried about it, Kurt will say, *we're quite alone here. You. The computer. Me. The seal of the confessional.*

He can almost hear the priest:—*That's another thing.*

Speaking through computers is a lot like confession, Kurt thinks. The most intimate place in the world is not the 900 number, it's a computer bulletin board. You can say anything from behind the screen.—*Come on, Father, you can tell me. What is it with these twins?* His mind always supplies: twins, but in his heart Kurt knows he's trying to locate and attach some meaning to his own life. He won't admit it but his dialogs with the priest go back to the first weeks after his injury, the maimed child trying to make sense of the accident. Trying to reach the priest by phone, by mail, Billy supplied the rhetoric. It stuck with the child. "Father Davage will know what to do." *So. What about it, Father?* Kurt holds imaginary conversations with the priest more often than even he would care to admit. In the absence of meaning, the mind constructs it. It's one of the reasons he got into computers in the first place.

The last bad business with Zane split his world in two, separating hope and expectations, love and fulfillment, Kurt and Vivian. And in its wake Kurt Graver marshalled all his Apples, IBMs, faxes and modems, for God's sake a VAX against his enemies, and shut himself in here. He likes his controlled environment. From here if he had to, he could control the world.

Or he thought he could. But his assorted systems are not doing the job. Vivian's death demonstrates that he's not complete or even protected here in the snug garage apartment, barricaded behind technology. No matter how many computer systems and copiers and other electronic toys he shores up, Vivian is dead.

And Kurt? He's isn't safe. He isn't even self-contained.

There are just too many things out there in the world that he has to see about, information that computers won't yield. What the twins are doing. What's going to happen next. God, he's hacked, phoned, faxed and modemed and for all his megabytes of memory, for all his megahertzes of power, he can't even turn up one missing Jesuit.

He's spent the last three days researching this Franklin Davage, S.J., onetime friend to the Oliphants of Manhattan and the Eastern Shore, apparent Cassandra, luckless early warning system and custodian of certain secrets, he thinks. He actually thought he'd find the guy through computers.

Fat chance. The Trappists are not on line, no way. He's also phoned every Trappist monastery in the country without any luck. The externs who give and take messages have never heard of anybody by that name. The Manhattan directory yields no Oliphants and there are none listed in Palm Beach either, the last reported address for Vivian's wastrel father and his second wife. Using certain codes he's accessed credit ratings, the major credit companies, everything, and as far as he can make out, by modem at least, Franklin Davage, S.J., and the foolish Hal Oliphant and all his kin have simply disappeared from the map.

The more he can't find this Father Davage, the more he needs to find him. It's weird. If he can't find the answers on the electronic bulletin board; if he can't control the environment from here, he's going to have to venture out.

It's been a long time.

What if I can't?

It is this that leaves Kurt Graver edgy and restless, circling like a gerbil in an exercise wheel. If he can't sleep now it's for more than one reason. With Vivian's twins gone the Archer place is so quiet that once Kurt gives up and goes to bed he can hear his father tossing and sighing in the next room. The stillness makes him acutely aware of the sound of his own breath. It wasn't the noise the girls made, he thinks; it was the space they occupied. They were more than just two girls living here. They were more than that spooky kingdom with its armies of dolls that Billy deplored. Giggling, they pretended to flirt with him. God help him, Kurt felt flattered. Every time he saw them, his stump throbbed. Superimposed on their faces he saw Vivian and Zane. Again and again he relived the agonizing moment in which fire bloomed in his left hand and seared his veins: the moment that changed him for life. He can still hear Zane's wild laughter. Twins were his past and in mysterious ways, he thinks, they are his future.

With them gone, the place is preternaturally still. A single light shines in the big house, marking Meredith Archer's room. Yes the house and grounds seem unaccountably empty. Yes the stillness is keeping them both awake. Like

Meredith, Kurt's not ready to admit to himself that Vivian is gone. No. Dead. He will never get over her death. It marks the end of the passion he's nursed ever since that first bad day. While Zane laughed, sweet Vivian cried and cried, hugging Kurt's wrist to her white shirt with the little yellow ducks while the blood spurted and Kurt howled to break your heart.

Because he will do anything to keep from repeating his own history, Kurt fixes on the twins. Gone, all right. He wishes to God he could forget them. Beautiful as Vivian, but underneath, he thinks, as wild as Zane. Why don't people see? This fills him with irrational anger. Was it the girls' fault Vivian died? What about the accident with their father? He doesn't know. And what about this Carroll, who took them away? Is she OK? He would like to go back to his life in this room, but he can't; his missing hand aches.

Damn them anyway.

The girls are all he thinks about. Out of sight like this, Jane and Emily Archer don't disappear; they don't even begin to fade. They just get bigger. They loom in the mind. What are they doing, out there in America? What are they doing with Steve Harriman's widow? What are they doing to Carroll Lawton, who walked into this scene too late to understand it, and scooped up the twins thinking they were ordinary kids?

Although he's always been wary of them, Kurt knows he loves Jane and Emily Archer in some of the same ways a secret sinner loves the sin. He loves them because they're all that's left of Vivian; he also hates them for being like Zane. Withdrawn. Intent. Dangerous.

Strangely, he wishes them back. *At least we knew what they were doing.* Out of sight, they could be anywhere. The possibilities keep him awake until dawn, heavy with unrooted dread.

Sunlight shafts into the little breakfast nook, picking up the color of the orange juice, the yolk of Kurt's soft-boiled egg. He puts a perfect two-minute egg in front of his father and waits. His father claims to have put the whole thing out of his mind, but it's clear that he hasn't. This morning Kurt sees Billy's hands tremble as he tries to hold his egg so he can tap it open; last night Kurt saw him circling the telephone like an obscene caller without the faintest idea what to say.

"Who are you calling, Dad?"

"Nothing. Nobody." Poor Billy, he went white. What was he trying to do, call this Carroll Lawton and issue warnings? "I wish I knew."

So there's that, but that's only part of it. With Vivian dead and Steve Harriman dead, Kurt feels an added obligation to the widowed girl—Steve's wife, whom he saw standing in front of the main house three days ago, waiting to get into the car.

She had her fists on her hips in a brash attempt to look tough. It made Kurt want to go outside and take her by the shoulders: "Look, it's OK to cry." *Hurt, like me.* Like drawn to like. He was stopped by the blunt image of his stump on her arm. Still Kurt knows from experience that like him, this Carroll Lawton is the kind of person who says, "It's fine" when the exigencies make it clear that it isn't fine and she isn't fine.

Unexpectedly widowed: Strike one.

The least I could have done was warn her.

Strike two: Carroll Lawton sent away without warnings and with no operator's manual to draw on, unarmed and cut loose in America with those extraordinary twins. Kurt can't be sure why this leaves him so disconcerted. No. He looks down at the stump, which in ordinary circumstances he never looks at. No. He knows exactly why.

It is his duty to protect her from strike three.

"Dad. We can't let this go on. We can't just let it happen to her."

Tapping the egg, Billy turns empty eyes to him. "Let what happen?"

"You know."

He does know, but too spent to embroider, Billy denies it. "Nothing's going on."

"The twins. They ought to come with warning labels, and she doesn't even know."

Billy's spoon flies off the end of the egg without even denting the shell. Tears spring. "There's nothing to know."

"You know better and you know it." Kurt is on his feet now, standing over him. "If you're not going to tell her, I am."

"I know I've promised Meredith to give them another chance."

The sudden decision makes Kurt dizzy. "Then I am."

"Oh, son!" Billy studies him with those watery eyes; Kurt has never seen his father look so old. Even his voice quavers like an old man's. "You're really going?"

He can hardly breathe. "Somebody has to."

Billy is torn here. He has secrets to keep, but there's something else going on: what he wants — what he's nudged and nagged and hinted at ever since Kurt finished college and shut himself in here. Whatever Billy wants, it's near. He's on the verge of a smile. "They've gone a long way." He starts over. "They're down in Florida. Florida." He tries to make it sound ordinary. A little vacation. "I don't know. Maybe the trip would do you good."

Kurt thinks: *Is that all he wants?* He doesn't know what Billy wants. *To see me go out?* This is terrible and wonderful. It is so sad. "Somebody has to follow up on this. Somebody has to be sure it's all right." He's a little afraid. It's a little like being kicked out of the nest.

"You mean that the twins are all right."

But informed by the pattern, the ghastly possibility of repetition, Kurt says, "You know what I mean."

"They're only children," Billy says. "Maybe they deserve a second chance. A fresh start," he says wearily, as if concluding a long dialog he's been having with himself.

Kurt snaps, "So they can hurt somebody else?"

Billy backs off. "I'm just afraid you'll . . . No, it will be fine. The trip will be good for you, I just . . ." He's blathering. "Just be careful," he says, and he just can't help himself; he adds in a motherly tone, "and have fun."

This is frightening. He's really going. Kurt draws himself up. "I'll do what I have to," he says.

18

WHEN CARROLL COMES IN, nice old 'Laine meets her in the front hall with her floured hands raised high because she's in the middle of rolling out cookie dough. "I thought some cookies would be in order," she says without explanation. "What with everything." She is a one-woman charade today; the trouble is, Carroll's too preoccupied even to guess at what her aunt is acting out. Fluttering, anxious, 'Laine lowers her voice and mutters through tightly matched teeth, "They're upset."

One day in the newsroom and her view of the world is so nearly returned to normal that Carroll says automatically, "Who's upset?"

"The twins. Jane. You know, and Emily, except they want us to call them Jade and Emerald." Then 'Laine adds something that the distracted Carroll dismisses as so silly that she's sure she misheard it. "Queen Jade and Queen Emerald."

"The twins!" My God, she'd almost forgotten them. She doesn't hear herself making the automatic correction. "Jane. Emily." *What am I going to tell Steve?* She rushes on. "Tell me you didn't forget and leave them at the beach."

"Of course I didn't, I . . ."

"All that sun after so much fog. They'll be burned to cinders," Carroll says. If they're damaged, how is she going to explain to their father?

"I went and got them just the way you told me, and I brought them home and gave them lunch and everything was going fine until . . . until . . ."

Their father will be . . . Here's trouble. She can't quite admit their father is dead. Something makes Carroll say, "You didn't make them angry."

"God knows I didn't mean to," 'Laine says.

Dead. She whirls. "Where are they?"

"I don't know what I said to set them off." 'Laine's soft face is quivering with distress. "Whatever it was, I lost track of them for a while."

She hears herself trying for a patient tone. She hears herself losing it. "What do you mean, you lost track of them?"

"I just did."

"All I asked you to do was take care of them."

"I couldn't help it. I don't even know what I did." 'Laine's eyes fill. "We were having such a good time. Then they got mad and went off somewhere."

"You just let them go?"

"I didn't know. They were out on the porch? They got so mad that I didn't want them to look at me. I went inside to see what I could find to make it up to them—candy, cookies, you know." Standing there in the old-fashioned apron with her old-fashioned hands floured up to the elbows, Elaine starts to get old. The last time Carroll looked her aunt was a spunky middle-aged flirt who would make some man a good wife someday, but in the last year the sun has crossed the meridian and it's too late. She wonders if Elaine knows.

Sympathy makes Carroll gentle. "Cookies aren't always the answer." It's all she can think of to say.

"They always worked with you. I thought a little chocolate would . . ." She brightens momentarily and then sags. "Then when I came out to see if they wanted to lick the bowl, they were gone. They weren't anywhere. I didn't know who to call."

"You could have called me."

Even though she's twice Carroll's age, her aunt looks sheepish, like a bad child brought to the accounting. "I kept looking for them in the house."

"Why did you think they were in the house?"

Elaine's gesture is expressive: hands raised, as if holding the past—all those lives spun out in all these rooms. "You know the house. A person could get lost in here." She waits for Carroll to say, there there, which she does not. "Besides, where would they go? They haven't had time to meet any boys." Elaine won't look at her. "No place to go, but they were gone. I'm sorry, I was frantic. I looked for an hour, I was just about to call the cops when I heard the front door open. They didn't say hello, they didn't say anything, they were just standing there. The two of them with those cold, cold eyes."

"Where were they all that time?"

"I don't know. They wouldn't talk to me." She sighs. "It's a sad world when two teenagers can make you feel like a worm in your own house where you've lived all your life."

"I'm sure it isn't that bad."

Her aunt goes on. "Lord, I said, I'm so glad to see you! I tried to give them ice cream but they wouldn't talk to me. Now they've shut themselves into the second floor back porch and they won't come out and they won't let me in." Elaine stops. "Is something the matter?"

"I'm all right." Oh no I'm not all right, Carroll realizes. As long as she has calls to make and stories to write she can pretend, but Steve's death took all the blood out of her. She can hardly put one foot in front of the other to go upstairs.

"Where are you going?"

"Up to see about it." She corrects herself. "Up to see about them."

The twins are, as advertised, locked onto the screen porch that runs across the back of the house. The hall door's still locked; they must have gone out through their back bedroom window.

She taps on the glass. They've stationed themselves at the rail in the white wicker rockers where Carroll used to hide out when she needed to cry. Silent and serene in white dresses she doesn't remember buying for them, the girls are facing out like matrons on an ocean liner, waiting for the next sitting in the dining room. When she taps again they turn and recognize her with faint smiles and listless waves. She calls, "Hello?"

If they've been close these last two days, they are

different now. They give her their grandmother's smile: frosty, remote. The one Meredith reserves for the help.

She calls, "Open the door."

They smile and pretend not to hear.

She hears herself shouting, "I *said*, open the door."

After a while she gives up and goes into her bedroom and opens the window that gives onto the porch and climbs through. Without even turning to look at her the twins go on rocking, pointing at something beyond the rail, as if they've sighted whales or an iceberg or another ship passing in the pink late afternoon light.

She says drily, "I don't suppose you're going to tell me what's the matter."

After a long silence in which the twins murmur little things about the view off the back porch—the trees, the two-story garage, the shed, she says, "No, I didn't think so." Troubled, she asks, "Did you really tell 'Laine to call you queen something?"

They don't even dignify this with a look.

After a while one of them turns in her chair, and as she does, her sister turns. As the girl points to the apartment above the sagging garage, Carroll sees the red slap wrap on her wrist—this must be Jane. She says, "Are those the slave quarters?"

In the dim dead days, the male cook used to live up there. "No." Using the slap wrap Elaine put on the girl last night to verify her identity, Carroll says, "Jane."

She lifts her head at the sound of her name.

"Believe me, there aren't any slaves."

The twin wearing the blue slap wrap says, "But you could put slaves up there if you had some."

"Nobody wants slaves, Emily."

"Somebody's got to do the work around here."

Carroll makes a mistake. "Emily, that's an ugly thing to say!"

The eyes the girls turn on her are lovely—blue and cold. Without answering, they swivel so they're facing the rail again. She might as well be gone. As one, they prop their feet to make it hard for her to move around to a place where she can see their faces while she talks to them. This means that when she begins, she has to address their backs. If they're up here, it is for a reason, and if they're baiting her, that's for a reason too.

"Your aunt—I mean, Elaine, I mean, 'Laine says you ran away or something?" She wants to sound stronger, but it's been a hard three days and she can't help the nervous little lilt. "Please smile at me. What's the matter with you girls?"

Jane rocks and Emily rocks.

After a while the silence gets to her. "Listen, dammit, just tell me *what is your problem?*"

She can almost see the air between them vibrating; it's thick with unspoken communication. As if agreeing after several minutes of silent consultation, the twins shift in their chairs so they are not looking at her directly, exactly, but turning partial profiles so they can, what is it—see, without being looked into.

"School," Jane says.

Emily says, "School."

This leaves Carroll baffled. If she can just position herself right, she'll be able to look into the twins' faces so she can see what's going on. She approaches from Emily's side but the girl ducks her head, leaving Carroll to talk to her smooth, thick hair. She says anyway, "Your problem is school?"

Speaking, Jane seems disingenuous. "She said . . ."

Em is quick and cold. "The bitch."

"Don't call her that." Carroll sighs. If she's going to make a friend here, it's probably Jane. She moves around to Jane's side.

Emily says, "The aunt."

"Her name is 'Laine." She slides along the rail, trying to address Jane, but Jane turns away.

"She said since we were going to be living here we might as well start school. She said we would be *living here!*" Emily's elegant brows rush toward each other in an arresting frown.

Jane lashes out. "For good!"

Oh God.

Jane says, "But she doesn't know anything, right?"

"Just say she doesn't know anything."

Even seated, they are formidable. She stammers, "I can't."

They charge her: "All you have to do is say she's wrong."

This shuts Carroll down. When she starts up again it's on emergency power. Bare bulbs hanging from frayed wire light her brain. "I'm so sorry," she gasps.

"You said this was only a little vacation."

There are tears in her voice. "I would have said anything to get you to come with me. I'm sorry."

They lash out. "Sorry!"

"I love you guys but . . ." Embarrassment confounds her. *Oh Steve, I am so sorry.* She finally manages to finish. "I haven't been straight with you."

The effect is chilling. Without seeming to move at all, the twins come to their feet. Young as they are, they stand tall, so imperious that it makes Carroll fall back. They circle their chairs and finally after all this shifting and dancing, she and Steve Harriman's twin daughters are face to face. Angry with her as they are, stranded in Florida with their backs against the wall, newly orphaned and betrayed, the twins are beautifully composed, as still as a pair of marble nymphs. Ordinary kids she could have dealt with, but they are not ordinary. She would have preferred tantrums, hitting, anything. As it is, their perfect mouths are relaxed; their brows are unmarred and like the eyes, the faces are lovely, but empty. It's like addressing paired porcelains.

Oh please say something. After too long she says weakly, "Kids?" God, if only they were ordinary kids. Kids, she could understand. This is different.

They don't speak; they don't change.

What is most alarming is the fact that their uncanny stillness in no way means nothing is going on. In mysterious ways she senses but can only guess at, these two, Jane, Emily—whatever they want to be called—are completely in touch.

Downstairs 'Laine is calling, "Supper, *supper*," in that tremulous, hopeful voice of hers. From here they can hear

Suzy and Patsy jabbering in the driveway while Uncle Peyton's car rumbles into the garage, but here on the second floor porch there is nothing but silence, one desperate woman at odds with two remote girls, threatened by the current that runs between.

She has to explain. "Your grandmother begged me to take you. She said she couldn't keep you there."

"Couldn't keep us together?"

"Couldn't keep you," Carroll says and her heart falters. She's afraid of what they will say. No. She's afraid of what they will do.

As it turns out, they don't do anything. They just stand facing her with those eyes that don't waver and—perhaps it's an illusion—don't seem to blink. It's as if they've suspended everything: breath, heartbeats, the flow of blood, until they have this resolved.

The silence is almost more than she can bear. "Please?"

When they finally decide, what they have to say is astounding. Jane is the first to yield. She comes to herself with a little shiver and inadvertently, Carroll lifts her hands as if aching for a hug. Jane moves back a step. Emily moves back a step. Jane blinks like a waking sleeper and says, "The rings."

"Rings!"

"If we're going to stay here, you have to take us out to get the rings."

Emily says, "Sapphire. Ruby. The old aunt promised us."

Jane says, "But we think she can't afford it, so we think she was making it up."

"The rings." Carroll keeps shaking her head in hopes the particles will settle, but she still can't sort it out. She realizes they are holding out their wrists, indicating 'Laine's silly red and blue slap wraps.

They say, "We can't keep wearing these."

"They're ugly."

"They look bad."

She is looking at their left hands: those flat, layered stones in the brutish square settings. "But you already have rings."

"Oh, these." Their looks shame her. Fool, they say, don't you know what's important? "These are only sardonyx. We want ruby, sapphire. So you can tell us apart. She promised."

"God, if it's that important . . ."

"You mean you'll get them?" Jane begins to soften.

"If that's all you want . . ."

Emily pounces. "Tonight?"

To make them smile? Cheap at the price. "Sure," she says, relieved to see their faces are changing in a brilliant flash of teeth. "If that's all you want." Like a fool, Carroll hears herself giving in. "Absolutely. Fine. Right after dinner, OK? We'll go out to the mall."

"Not later, OK?" They are swift and fragrant, crowding her.

"Let's go right now."

"But Elaine is waiting dinner on us."

"The rings might be all gone!"

"We can eat later, OK?"

Somewhere in the back of her mind Steve's voice rings: *OK, babe?* The twins' breath is sweet; their voices are sweet. "Come on, Carroll." They are twining their hands in hers, soft, wheedling. "Let's go, OK? Let's go get us the rings."

"The beautiful, beautiful rings."

"Oh Carroll, we'll buy! We'll buy your supper at the mall."

"Wait a minute. I don't know."

They are like judges at the Olympics, waiting to see whether she'll make the last jump or fall.

Downstairs, she can hear the tempo in the kitchen picking up—her aunts and uncle chattering as they carry dishes back and forth. Everything is ready; 'Laine will have the table laid and Carroll is expected to sit down just the way she did every night when she was stuck here as a child. The familiar tugs at her but the twins' eerie insistence keeps her rooted here. The strange plays off against the commonplace. And underneath everything there is the manner: as if these beautiful children are somehow *entitled*.

Does one of the girls really say, *Don't make us wait, OK?*
She doesn't know. But she might as well be under orders.
The effect is the same. The strange plays off against the
commonplace and wins.

"All right." A sigh that starts somewhere deep rocks
Carroll, but she catches her breath and begins again on a
bright note. "OK kids. Let's go."

They hold up their scorecards: perfect marks. "So, yay!"

She doesn't know what makes her want to thank them for
being pleased with her, but she does. Touched, she lets them
take her hands and pull her along.

19

WATCHING THE TWINS chatter in the sunny dining room the next morning, Carroll is reluctant to go in. They look so happy! Pretty heads bent over the new rings—ruby and sapphire solitaires set in gold. When the jeweler at the mall told them how easy it would be for their mother to come in to the shop later and add diamond chips, their eyes shone. "When you graduate from high school," he said. "And two more when you finish college. Right, Mother?" Looking at Carroll they said, "Our mother is dead." After a moment's hesitation, Jane, who was wearing the ruby, said, "Now we have Carroll." When Emily assented Carroll felt herself go weak somewhere at dead center in an almost sexual rush of warmth.

They like me.

Never mind that she maxed out on her plastic to do this; cheap at the price. In the part of her where checks and balances are noted, Carroll put the twins on the plus side; they can't begin to replace Steve but look, here's one good thing to set against the bad.

On the way home she put Jane in front. Emily said, "My turn next time?" Warming to them both Carroll said, "Your turn next time." They left Suzy's car in the porte cochere and went in the side door to the dining room, where the aunts and Uncle Peyton were sitting around in the ruins of Elaine's shepherd's pie. The three Larrabie women and their rakish brother swiveled their heads to look at her, Carroll's only relatives looking like nothing so much as stuffed owls.

God how she remembered all those sad evenings, seeing them sitting there in the dining room and having to go in.

Suzy always grilled her about her schoolwork and criti- cized her clothes; Elaine plied her with food she didn't want while Patsy ate food she didn't need; thin, squashy, fat, the sisters bore the family stamp on their faces and if biology really were destiny, Carroll could end up the same way. Worse yet, every night of her life as a child Uncle Peyton raised his face for the obligatory kiss and would not let her sit down to eat until she'd sighed and given it.

Now things are different.

Since Carroll's childhood, her relatives have run true to type. When they came in last night—late, admittedly, but for good reason—Suzy tapped her American Beauty nails on her glass with an annoyed look and said, "The least you could do is get these children to the table on time." Plump Patsy said girlishly, "We waited and waited." The rubble on her plate suggested she, at least, hadn't waited for long.

Elaine was distressed. "I tried to save a little for you, but this is the best I could do." She was like an octopus, trying to gather the remains of the salad, some bread, the destroyed pie and press them on her niece. She was wheezing with good intentions. "Oh let me go out in the kitchen and heat up some hash."

"It's OK," Carroll said, feeling unaccountably rich. "We had something at the mall."

Uncle Peyton stroked his yellowing moustache. "You could have been more considerate."

With Steve's daughters flanking her, she could handle this. Confronting the relatives, she and Jane and Em stood arm in arm in arm—if not exactly family, then friends. The coldness that fell between them out there on the porch had dissipated; Carroll doesn't think it's the rings. She wants to think she's broken through. They like her! At least Jane does, and if Emily is more reserved, just give her time. Together, they form a solid front here in the old house where she soldiered through her own hard childhood alone.

She woke in the night and heard the girls talking— excited, she guessed. They were so sweet at bedtime that she heard herself promising to take them to Orlando. It's expensive—hotels for three nights, three theme parks, but she's back at work so she'll have her paycheck to add to her and Steve's joint checking account. She's still too shaky to confront the exigencies: selling the house where they were so happy for such a short time. Insurance companies, banks. Final things. Add them to her grief, subtract Steve and she's left with the sum total of their short marriage. And the twins. If keeping them happy costs more than she makes, that's fine. In a strange way, the twins are the last barricade between her and the totality of grief. As long as she can keep busy pleasing them, she doesn't have to face the rest.

She's so relieved to see them laughing in the sunshine that she doesn't even wonder why they're downstairs so early today when they were up jabbering all night. Once she thought she heard thumping overhead but she discounted this as another sad waking dream prompted by the last few days of tension and pain.

Seeing them this morning, she knows she imagined it. They look so pretty! They have on their new Gap T-shirts and khaki shorts; they look less imperious and more like well-meaning campers with their pink espadrilles and morning light playing in their shiny hair. See them sitting by the window with their right arms extended in the sunlight, starfishing their hands so they can study the sparks glinting in their new stones. It makes her feel—not maternal, exactly, but proud. This is her doing, hers. Carroll can't wait for them to look up and smile. She's about to go in and speak when in a beautifully synchronized passage they lean in until their heads touch. She can almost hear the buzz. Their communion is so intense that it excludes the world.

The twins are chattering so fast that the words don't separate into any language she can recognize. They don't see her; they don't hear, even when Charley Penn honks his horn out front. Even so, Carroll lingers. She wants to say goodbye before she goes to work but the girls are so engrossed that she sighs and backs out.

Rumpled, grinning Charley Penn leans across the front seat and opens the car door for her. "How are the kids?"

"OK, I think. Being twins makes it easier." The house is big, old, depressing. She feels guilty for leaving them alone there while she goes into the newsroom and looks for her old self. Carroll past present and future flickers in front of her. "I'm so glad they have each other."

*   *   *

It just breaks out of me. "Amanenjanamamenjanama . . ."

"Stop you should, just cut it out." Protesting, the weak sister feels what I do; is disturbed by what disturbs me. We can't afford to feel this way. "Shut up," I say. "Shut down. The aunts."

I know. I can't. Never like this before. "But oh shit oh glena-glena sister."

Stern she is, we are the queen. See how thought flows back and forth between us. "Strebidibus." Forget it. Things to do. We have *things* to do. Forget it! "Strebidibus, OK?"

But my voice keeps going, OK? "Frenemo oh my ooh oh amanenjanamenamenjama . . ."

"Shut up," she hisses.

"Ahmo frenemo." I'm so sorry. Grieving, I protest in the old language and in the old language my sister answers me, but before I can stop her she slides into the common people's talk in a brutish conjunction that strikes my heart.

"Naja dummy and don't you forget it."

I try to raise her up. "Glena hemo krazgod."

"Etrap!" *Stop it.*

"Krazgod," I say. It's true, we did. We got him. Looked into that face and did the thing. Saw the fear and did it anyway. "Krazgod, sister."

"Menemene sisterno." I know what she thinks: We did the thing and it felt good. OK, I feel it too. She says, "We are the queen, remember."

I sigh. "We are the queen."

"Queen Jade," she says firmly. "And Queen Emerald."

She's right. We are. "Queen Jade." I sigh. "And Queen Emerald."

"Queen of Amadamaland and queen of here."

"I guess so," I say; I don't feel so good.

"Look, my queen. Queen, remember. Queen everywhere we go, OK? They know we're queen and you know too. Why else would they give us the tokens?"

Right, the tokens. "They're nice, but still."

"Queen, OK? In this and every other kingdom."

"Queen wherever we are," I say, because she expects it,

I mean, what else? But look! We feel so bad from it or I do, and what I don't know is, is it only me that feels bad or is it *we?* Things blur until there is no knowing. What I know is that in spite of everything the excitement leaves me twitching—the old feeling only more. Because we *looked into that face* while it was happening. Maybe that's why I don't feel so good. Feel bad even though at the tippy end there was that grin on his face, so good it was for him in some way, I guess, or at least my sister says it was.

"The queen does what she must and never looks back so smile," my sister says, but it makes me crawly, OK? We've been sawing back and forth over this all night: what we actually did. What to do with the trophy we took. The trophy makes the whole thing special, because of, or in spite of the part that creeps into my belly and won't leave. It makes me want to throw up today, although it didn't seem like much while we were doing it. Not my fault I am staggered by second thoughts right now.

Not my sister's fault she has only first thoughts.

Mine pile up in my throat. I cry, "Krena?" What shall we do?

She tells me, *nothing.* "Naja."

Hear me groan, "But look what we did!"

"Shh!" She comes back in the old language. What does she say we did? She says, "Naja." Nothing.

"Oh, agh." I can't help myself. We did do something, in spite of what she thinks. No pretending we didn't. We have the trophy to mark it. "Oh sister, frenemo." I'm so sorry.

"Sisterno. The queen, remember. Etrap." Stop that.

I can't help it, see! I feel *things* about it, different. I mean, this is *huge.* What's the point of doing, if you aren't supposed to feel? "Fregel," I say even though I know what she'll say to this. "Fregel." *Guilty.*

My sister the queen brings me down. She does it in the common people's tongue. "Queens don't have guilt, ass-hole, so forget it."

And what's done is over, OK. I pray in my heart that we won't have to do it any more. "Frenemo," I say again, so sorry!

But she lifts her hand and mine so the red stone and the blue one are cold on my cheeks and she goes on in the old language. "Etrap, OK? Naja." Then she spreads her hand and I see the colored fire on her finger and she says, "Etrap, and I mean it."

"Yes," I say, "OK." It is, I guess. Besides, we have to figure out what to do with our trophy. Where to put it then, that they won't see, but we will enjoy it because we know it is there.

Watch out, the thin aunt is coming. This hard-looking Suzy woman trips through on high heels, followed by Patsy who is too big for the spikes that carry her. They give that look they save for the twins. Then the Peyton, who has another kind of look for the twins.

She says OK, but I'm afraid she doesn't mean it. It took long enough to bring my weak sister around. "OK," I say, sealing it. My twin swallows so hard I can see the lump on her throat glupping, glupping; how can we keep our position here when she is so craven?

"Bye," Uncle Peyton says.

We say, "Bye," as nice as can be expected.

Then up we go—to our room, we tell pink, sweaty Elaine, who asks have we filled out those cards yet. We say we haven't but we will, we promise we'll do it real soon. Then we go up but past our room and up the attic stairs into what will become the annex to our kingdom. Away from Amadamaland, we must colonize. In our time we'll go from kingdom to empire to world.

The attic is vast. It's almost big enough for us. It's hot and dusty, empty of life except for the insects, squirrels, ourselves. We have our uses for every part of it but right now we're concentrating on our special place. Never mind which room it is; never mind which part of the attic we have found; we make the map and then destroy it because here in the colonies as well as back home in the kingdom, we the queen have to keep our secrets. The place is nice; the *thing* we carry between us is nice—the best we could get yesterday, rushed as we were, pressed for time and hurrying to completion. Take that. Take that and that. And give us *that*, while you're at it. Never be missed except by the one who gave it up—in hopes, I suppose, although we don't know what he was hoping for. He gave it up to us at the very last minute. With that smile.

The space is nice, but not as nice as it's going to be. We've already done a few things, a start. We have our trophy, yes; we have our notebooks and our pictures from home—beloved Saint Stephen! and we have collected forgotten treasures from this used-up Larrabie family from every corner of the attic. See the portraits of glassy-faced ancestors propped here, the vases there, and three-legged chairs from an old gazebo teetering in the four corners of the room we have selected. Not as good as it should be, but better than we expected. Away from Amadamaland, we are the kingdom.

Alone.

Carroll is gone. Newspaper, she says. To get money to buy us things. She says she is a reporter, like Lois Lane. Well we think she should put us in the paper. Put our pictures on the front page. The working aunts and uncle are outside in the car now, quarreling in the drive. We can't wait for them to leave. Then Elaine must go, even if we have to send her—to the mall for more presents; now that Carroll has given us the rings Elaine promised, it's up to the poor bitch to give us something too. A cinch. No problem. She would do anything to make us like her. Then while the aunts and the dirty uncle are good and gone, we'll fan out through their rooms and take the best of what they have without their even knowing it and bring it up to reinforce the outpost which already looks less like an outpost.

Now that we have the first treasure.

We take some time arranging the right setting. By the time we have it put more or less where we want it my sister has stopped sniffing under her breath and is feeling better. So—good! She feels better; I feel better. It's a relief. Sometimes I think we must be joined at the head, unless we are joined at the belly.

Then we hear the voice. "Emily."

My sister turns. Somebody's at the bottom of the attic stairs. It is Elaine. We quit breathing.

We hear her starting up the stairs. "Oh, Jaaane."

"Oh shit," my sister says.

"No," I say. "This is good." I put my head close to hers and soon enough she sees what I see. "Really." So I answer, lilting. "We're up here."

"What are you girls doing?"

My sister says. "Nothing." I am proud of her.

I say, "Be down in just a minute."

"Well hurry, it's hot up there."

And my sister answers, "Just another little minute."

"Too hot for you children. Pretty soon it will be stifling." She is working hard on lilting. "It's getting hot down here too."

"Yes ma'am," I say.

This Elaine wants to bribe us. "It's getting so hot I thought I'd take you girls to the beach." We exchange looks. So easy! Still we linger. We aren't finished here. After a while she says, "Hurry up, I have a surprise for you." We hear her clopping away.

We look at each other again. It is like looking at myself. We still haven't decided about the trophy. I have it on a marble-topped table we've dragged out from under the eaves but that doesn't seem right. It wants something more, or better, or different. My sister had it on a little shelf but that wasn't right either. Now we have to quick decide so we can go to the beach. Finally I take it off the table and without having to consult my twin I spread my scarf in the middle of the floor and take the trophy.

"Yes," she says.

"Yes," I say.

We put it there.

When they stand like that with their elbows planted on the counter of the refreshment stand and their cute, pert butts facing the ocean, Lanny Raynor can hardly bear not to touch them. He would like to just reach out; his mouth waters and his hands cup in spite of his best intentions. He's been watching them for an hour.

They caught his eye when he came down to the beach this morning after he got finished at the gym. When he began his walk up the beach he just ran into them. They were planted on their bellies in the sand with their feet twined in the air, succulent little things, could be any age. By the time he came back they had turned over to toast the other side. Beautiful. Since then they've been down to the water and back three times, parading like little models. But they don't go in. Instead they jump in the wavering, changing foam line and then come back, giggling, to their matching towels. It's still north of noon but now they're ordering hot dogs, flirting with the counterman and twitching those asses. Watching, Lanny blesses the fact that it's a school day because it makes him the only game in town right now. What is the old saying? Good things come in pairs.

And he has a lot of fun out here, cruising the beach until he meets somebody he can make music with. He's always subtle, smooth, mind if I help you dig, or, walk a little way with you, or: can I lie down next to your blanket? And never violent, just furtive. For Lanny the best pleasures are the ones his partner is least expecting. No big whup, just a few gentle touches, a kiss or two, he is not after all a rapist. Funny old word from the old funny papers fits him exactly: lothario. Most of the time the girls he finds go along with him willingly, surprised, maybe, but grateful. And the twins, the twins!

He thinks there used to be a thing on TV where Hayley Mills was twins and he's been going nuts trying to remember whether there was one good twin and one bad one. He's been going nuts trying to decide which of these girls might be bad enough to want to go places and do things with him, but when girls come in pairs like this they don't always want you to separate them, and there's no reading what's going on inside those sleek bodies.

These twin bodies look perfect without any effort on their owners' part, and their fair hair catches the light without benefit of peroxide. They are so pretty it makes his palms sweat. How old are they anyway? He tries not to think about how old he is. He doesn't look so bad himself, but it takes him a little longer. All those hours in the gym. Lean and well-muscled in the thong bikini, Lanny knows he looks like an ad for some heavenly health club, and if his body matches up with theirs, if he already knows the three of them will look good together, well it's up to him to call this to their attention. Cute. Not from around here, he can tell by the red lines that don't match yesterday's tan. He sidles closer.

"Where you girls from?"

When they turn, their sunglasses give back Lanny's image in quadruplicate: muscular shoulders sloped, pelvis slanted forward, tight, ridged belly. He looks like the big bad wolf in one of those old cartoons; it's a little unnerving.

"You're not from around here, are you?"

When the girls don't answer he says, "I'll take off mine if you'll take off yours."

One of the girls giggles.

"Sunglasses," I mean," he says disarmingly. If he hits on one will the other get mad or peel off and leave him alone with her? He doesn't think so. Somewhere inside he's humming, "Double the . . ."

They are mumbling together, God they are pretty; what is it they're saying? "Anamana."

It doesn't sound like anything. He tilts his head. "What?"

"Premo?"

"Preemo."

They raise their hands and lift their glasses. The eyes are staggering: china blue, glassy, perfect. But with an attitude.

Lanny falls back a step.

Hard to explain the effect of their cold scrutiny. It's a little like dressing for a barbecue and discovering you've wandered into the wrong party. He touches his throat, feeling for the bow tie he ought to be wearing. Oh, excuse me, I didn't know it was a tuxedo thing.

He's just standing there and they're just standing there.

One says, "You forgot."

"I'm sorry." Now why did he say that? He doesn't know. It was just automatic.

The other says, "Your glasses. You were going to drop your glasses so we could see each other."

"Oh, right." He's so relieved he can't quite understand it. He drops his wraparound girlwatcher shades and blinks at them. They're watching him intently. Without moving their eyes they seem to be gauging his quads and pecs and triceps and counting the ridges in his tightly muscled belly.

One says, "Now the suit."

The other says, "Jade!"

"Might as well see what's what," she says.

"Jade," he says. She's waiting. What makes Lanny most uncomfortable is the fact that it seems like an order. In another minute they'll have him stripping right here on the beach in front of everyone and the beach cops will be on him in seconds. If they're underage he's cooked. Buying time, he says, "That's a pretty name."

The other giggles. "And my name is Emerald."

He looks at her. "Emerald." He flashes on one time when he was little. He was springing up and down in the surf, just jumping waves until he tangled with an undertow; he didn't even know how it happened, just suddenly he was way over his head with nothing underneath his feet but a million gallons of the Atlantic; panic moved him fast but the ocean pulled him the other way and it took him an hour to swim back to where he could touch again and by the time he did he was frightened and exhausted. "That's beautiful."

"The suit," Jade says.

"Oh," he says. "Not here."

She is looking at him intently. "In the water."

"In the water . . ." He'll do anything to make friends with them. "Would you girls like to go swimming?"

"Yes!"

The one called Emerald reminds her, "We can't go in."

Jade explains as if this kind of thing happens to everyone. "The aunts won't let us."

"How old are you girls anyway?"

"She says not without a lifeguard."

Maybe they're younger than he thinks. But maybe they're not. "Would you girls like to go somewhere?"

"We can't."

"She told us not to leave the beach either."

"I don't see how we're going to get to be friends," he says.

"She made us promise."

Jade starts. "But we can go in."

Emerald finishes. "If there's a lifeguard."

"Well then," he says. "Before I . . ." He doesn't know how to finish this. Before I lost my job? Not good. Dropped out of school? True, but a long time ago. Instead he gives them the bald lie. "Did you know I used to be a lifeguard?"

"Really?"

"Sure. Once you start saving people, you never forget how."

Warm flesh bumps warm flesh as they close in and jostle him. He can feel the sand particles rubbing between them. One says, "So it's OK for us to go into the water after all."

"Sure it is."

"And we'll swim out?"

"Sure. A little ways."

"Eeemo?"

"What?"

"Eimo?" They are talking over his head again. "Einel!" they say, tugging him toward the water.

"Wait," he says. The girls are moving so fast now that they have him confused: Jade, Emerald, or is it Emerald and Jade; double the . . . Lanny thinks, and more or less stops thinking. If they asked him to drop his suit a minute ago, now that they have what they really want they have forgotten. Well, he hasn't forgotten.

"Water, come on."

"Come on, water!"

"Sure," he says. His voice is thick with anticipation. He can already imagine the three of them bobbing together and the warm soapy feeling of his bare hands on those perfect bodies in the beautiful salt water. Who is he to know what they expect or what makes them angry or what may happen to anybody foolish enough to stir them up?

20

KURT GRAVER is on the redeye, flying east. He is blindsided by excitement, stunned. Being up so high. After all these years, being exposed. Somewhere inside a part of him is running around waving its arms and giggling like a little boy.

The rest is rock-bottom terrified. This is the first time he's been off the Archer place in the daytime since Zane died. When he gets into open places can he still breathe or will all his life systems just shut down? Can he handle being so exposed?

Although she's used to assessing the moods of all kinds of passengers, the stewardess would never guess. Kurt sits facing front with his dark hair falling straight from the part so it almost covers one eye and his face fixed in a forbidding expression of reserve that says: Don't touch me. Don't even try to talk to me. There is something rusty-looking about him, as if he is somehow unused.

Handsome, she thinks, looking at him. But there is that scowl. Except for the amenities, she leaves him alone.

Kurt's heart levels off with the plane and at cruising altitude, he discovers he is still breathing. He begins to consider.

Things about the Oliphants. What does he really know? All he knows, he knows by extrapolation: the weirdness of the girls, the strange, dark streak that ran through Zane, hidden until it exploded in blood. It was like a geyser splattering the world.

What else? Things his father knows. "Well," Billy told him, "the Oliphants were rich before they lost all their money in some bad deal. Rich enough to send Hal away. Except for him, I think they were perfectly ordinary people.

Plain. Fine. What I do know is that they wouldn't come to the wedding. Wouldn't have anything to do with it."

For his father, the pain is still fresh. "Hal Oliphant was a terrible drunk. Meredith, I mean Mrs. Archer, never should have . . ." Billy has left off trying to finish that sentence; there's too much grief implied, too many bad things have fallen between then and now. "There was something about Hal; from the beginning Meredith knew there was something wrong with him, but she was in love and she refused to see. I'm not sure she knew what it was." He sighed. "And she married him anyway. At the wedding, she didn't want to know."

Billy's voice hit bottom. "Then she didn't want to tell."

Right, Kurt thinks. The fatal fact, or flaw, that brought out the priest. Some flaw that runs through the generations, Hal to Zane. Kurt is convinced it's surfaced in Vivian's twins. He's convinced the truth is locked up in some monastery with this Franklin Davage, S.J.

If he's on the plane now, it's because he has to be.

If he knows where he's going, it's because Meredith Archer has supplied him with a place to start.

He doesn't know what Billy said to her exactly, only that for the first time since the accident when he was little, the old lady got in touch with him.

She sent word. She didn't talk to Kurt; she never could. Since the old accident Mrs. Archer has found it impossible to face him. She was kind enough, quick to pay the bills and send presents to the hospital; she even offered to pay for the best in artificial hands, but she—could—not—be with him. Even when he and Zane and Vivian were kids Meredith used to see him coming and disappear; one look at the rapidly healing stump and she'd fade. It took Kurt a long time to figure out that it was nothing he did. It was what he was. Maimed, and by her own son. Kurt embarrassed her. OK, lady, he thought. OK. And he stayed away. Easy enough to do back then when Kurt was little and in love with Vivian and he thought she was in love with him. Now Vivian is dead and he's left with the sad legacy of warped pathology that he has no way of knowing whether he can ever identify, much less straighten out.

At least he has a lead.

The information came to him secondhand, by note. Meredith sat up there in the big house and wrote instead of phoning. It came on one of her engraved correspondence cards, formally delivered by his dad, who was accustomed to doing such errands for her. When Kurt looked up his father was standing in the living room in full uniform, holding his cap. *God,* he thought. *Is that all you ever wanted to be? A chauffeur?* Billy didn't have to speak; Kurt already knew the answer. *All I ever wanted was to be near her.* She'd put Kurt's name on the envelope and, forever the lady, had written in the lower right-hand corner, "Kindness of William Graver."

"Something for you," Billy said. He just handed it over.

Kurt didn't have to ask: Do you know what it says? It made him furious to know that Billy would never dream of reading it. All his life with the Archers Billy has obeyed orders without question, carried notes without reading them. Dignified as he is, kind and intelligent, Billy is a servant.

Well Kurt is something else. Still he has to thank the old lady for supplying the one piece of information he could not pull out of his extensive network of data banks. Of course Hal Oliphant has living relatives. Of course his sister would be listed in the Manhattan directory under her married name.

But they are landing. Has he slept? He doesn't know. He's flown into night and come out in broad daylight. More time has passed than he was aware of. It's dizzying. Still he's been through this airport so many times in memory and imagination that he makes the transition to a taxi almost without noticing. Puts on his mirrored shades as if they'll hide him from the world. Riding along, he is turned in on himself, mulling it—where to go from here. What he has to ask. What he has to do when he finds out. Before he's aware that he's paid the cabbie and gotten out Kurt is hatched, blinking and shaky, on the corner of the building where Hal Oliphant's married sister lives.

The freedom staggers him.

He loses several beats before he comes to with a jerk and realizes where he is. Outside, in one of the biggest cities in the world. It's like waking up in any one of a dozen movies. And discovering that although he has a part, he doesn't know his lines.

He is almost blown away by the city of New York.

It is too much! He could hyperventilate right here, spinning in place until his eyes rolled back in his head and he collapsed; he could get into the next taxi and go back to the airport and go straight home to his computers, where it's safe. Or else he could stand here and wait for something to happen—mugging, drive-by shooting, arrest for being crazy—hanging in air until he got busted or the ambulance came and took him away.

Or he could get his act together and do what he came to do.

Dizzy, he puts his hand in his pocket and it closes on Meredith Archer's card. It is rigid, crisp. He can read the raised monogram with his fingers. He takes it out. Carte blanche, he thinks. Telling him where to go, Mrs. Archer has added a note that will make them let him in. The doorman reads the card, dips his head and lets Kurt inside. He buzzes the apartment and when there is no answer he tells Kurt, "It's OK. She's always home. She's a little—you know. You'll find her on the roof."

Hal's sister is older than Mrs. Archer. She looks ninety-something in her terrycloth bathrobe with the flapping basketball shoes and the big straw hat. She's up on the roof watering her plants. They sit in flats warmed by artificial light. She's been living alone for so long that until she sees herself mirrored in Kurt's sunglasses, she isn't even aware that she's not exactly dressed. She greets him with dignity nonetheless.

"Are you a friend of Hal's?"

"No ma'am."

"Of course not. You're too young." Approaching, she squints into his face. "You're not one of his children, are you?" She's so close he can see the ripening cataracts on her pupils. "Nope. Not one of *his* children, I can tell. Don't ask me to tell you where he is, because I don't know."

"I just need to know . . ." What's wrong with him. That must be genetic. Where did it begin? How can it end? There is no way to say this. Just as well, because the next thing the old lady says betrays grief.

"If you want to know the truth, I don't want to know."

"Oh, ma'am, ma'am . . ." *I am so sorry.*

"Please don't ask me about Hal."

"I won't. I just . . ." Need to know what to do.

"Don't beg, it won't do you any good. I haven't seen my brother for fifty years."

He knows better than to press. "No ma'am."

"Or heard from him either. So don't."

"I won't." Instead he asks about the priest.

Her face softens. "Franklin," she says. "Poor Franklin." It's as if she's been waiting for this question half her life. "In seclusion, don't you know?"

"I know," Kurt says. He's getting weird. This is the longest he's been out in years. The highest up he's been. Pull yourself together. Breathe. "But where?"

Moving even closer, she stands on tiptoe to take off Kurt's sunglasses so she can study his face. Whatever she sees seems to be OK because she nods and begins. Remote, she says. Small town, she says. Dominican monastery somewhere in Vermont. Kurt nods. Not the Trappists after all. Franklin's the chaplain there, or he was the last time she heard from him, but it's been years. She stresses this. Years. She stresses it so he'll know what to expect. Father Franklin Davage, S.J., is at least her age, perhaps a little older and after all these years there's no telling whether he's still alive. She doesn't even know if he's still a priest. He doesn't write. The nuns are the only Dominicans left. They operate under the vow of silence, she says. That's why there's no phone. "What a waste."

"Him shutting himself away like that?"

"Him going into the priesthood." To his surprise she sounds girlish as a jilted teenager. "He could have broken a dozen hearts, and almost did."

"I'm sorry."

"It's all right." The old lady's skin is so transparent he can see the veins and for a second he sees how lovely she must have been. "We got over it. Women always do."

He's about to thank her and go when she says, "Wait a minute. You can't leave until you've seen my violets."

Then before he can back into the door and plunge down the stairs to safety Hal Oliphant's big sister grabs his hand and pulls him toward her plants. Rank and file and officers, she has the plants in their pots standing on what look like plant bleachers like a little audience. She keeps them where they can get reflected sunlight during the best hours of the day. Dozens of potted African violets. Frankly, they're revolting with their whitish stems and hairy leaves. Kurt tries to back off but she's insistent now, holding him in place so he can hear her naming them: genus, species, variety and variation, bred and cross-bred to produce remarkable results. He could spend the rest of his life out on this rooftop, meeting every plant personally and learning to call it by name.

"And this," she says when he's just about to despair of ever escaping. "I want you to see this." The genteel gardener lifts the corner of a rag to reveal a plant hidden under the bleachers. Kurt kneels so he can see. The thing is enormous, grotesque. Even in the shadows the thing flowers, and the flowers are hideous. "This is one of my failures. I hid it under here hoping it would die." She sighs. "But it's doing better than ever. You see?"

A genetic freak. Kurt doesn't know what to say.

She goes on. "With the best possible intentions I crossed two strains and instead of something beautiful, I got this. Even the best possible intentions can go wrong. Even the best strains can go bad." She fixes him with her filmy eyes. "Do you understand? Sometimes you get a wild card that doesn't seem to come from anywhere."

"Oh ma'am, ma'am."

"It's nobody's fault," she says, standing. "Nobody's fault what blood can do when it's mixed wrong, you see? But you couldn't possibly know."

It's as close as she comes to talking about Hal Oliphant.

"Thank you." He tries to pat her reassuringly and back away at the same time. And in his haste to escape, exposes his stump. Hearing her gasp, he looks down. The cuff has fallen away. In the sunlight like this it looks blunt, bad, embarrassing. He blurts, "I'm sorry," and flees.

"Oh, you poor thing." As he opens the roof door and plunges into the stairwell he hears her pattering after him. As he begins his descent she opens the door. Her voice follows him down. "You poor thing. You do know after all."

By the time he gets to the cloister after a short flight and a long drive, the day has disappeared. The monastery where the Dominican nuns are located is on a hillside in rural Vermont. Kurt parks outside a rock wall that must have been put together by some fan of King Arthur and his court. The gates are locked but the garden door bears a sign.

NO TRESPASSING
To Make Deliveries
Ring the Bell.

When nobody responds Kurt gives the gate a little push and when it yields, he opens it and starts up the dirt road to the main building. The place is a strange combination of farm and fairyland. What must have been formal gardens in the old days have been turned to vegetable plots. The dirt road goes between rows of last summer's plants still staked to posts. Beans, he supposes. Tomatoes. Squash. The nuns live in a fake castle built out of nubbly rocks by some dreamer whose descendants probably liked it less than he did and donated it to the order. From here he can see gun slits instead of upper windows, and at the roofline, carefully replicated crenellations; if they wanted to the nuns could pull up the drawbridge and repel all boarders. They could mount cannon on the roof.

He crosses the drawbridge and finds the buzzer. Nobody comes. At first he thinks there's nobody around. But this is a living institution, not a dead one; he has the sense of several complete lives going on somewhere just out of sight. He doesn't know the religious order of the day but thinks maybe the sisters are at evening prayer. Therefore he's surprised when someone actually comes. She doesn't look like any of the pictures of nuns he's seen. This is a wiry, capable-looking woman in black with a thin band of white showing where the half-veil meets her dark hair.

"I'm not a Catholic," he blurts.

"No problem," she says. She squints at him through the slit in the door. "We weren't expecting anybody."

"I'm sorry I didn't call ahead."

Her look suggests he's insulting her intelligence. "We don't have phones here. Nobody calls ahead."

"I thought you couldn't talk."

That look again: "I'm the extern. There are three of us and between us we take care of all the outside business here."

"And the others?"

"Nobody enters the cloister," she says.

"I . . . came to see Father Davage?" He expects her to slam the little window: never heard of him, and so he adds quickly, "Somebody told me he was here."

"He's . . ."

"In seclusion. I know."

"He's one of our burnouts. So sad."

"I'm sorry. I've come all this way and I just." He just what? He doesn't know. He has the sudden, crazed idea that he expects the priest to restore his missing hand.

"I don't know whether he'll see you."

"Tell him I'm here about the Archers." He rethinks. "No. Ask him if he remembers Hal Oliphant." But that isn't it either. For whatever reasons, he keeps seeing Hal's sister among her African violets. He sees the plant she kept hidden. That she made him see. *Even the best strains can go bad.* "Tell him I'm here because Hal Oliphant has grand-daughters."

She says cautiously, "He hasn't seen anybody in years."

He can't shake the image of that horrible, sprawling, bulbous plant. "Tell him they're twins."

"He says he doesn't want to see anybody."

That plant. Cut it out Kurt. Stop it. That plant. The missing hand. Cut it out! He isn't going to fix your hand he may not even tell you what to do about the twins. I've come as far; this is so precarious! Everything piles up and comes out unexpectedly. "Oh please let me in."

She considers for a moment. Then she does, pulling him inside and shutting the door behind him quickly, as if she's afraid of letting in the world. "Wait here. I'll go and see."

He is in a generic convent parlor: good but shabby furniture donated by some genteel family, bad reproduction of Murillo's virgin in a dark frame over the sofa, surprisingly good figure on the contemporary crucifix by the door. The unexpected element in the room is a sliding window in the inside wall. There is a grill over the glass and in the open space between the grill and the bottom of the wicket, there is the little ledge where he supposes books and messages are passed. Beyond the grill a translucent curtain hangs. It makes him think of a confessional. Do Catholic people kneel in front of that little window and spill all their secrets here? He wonders if the families of these cloistered sisters come on Christmas or birthdays and whisper at them through the opening. He doesn't know. His breath catches. He doesn't *know*. This is what's killing him. He doesn't know anything.

After a long time the extern comes back. She seems surprised. "He says he'll see you. Pull your chair over to the wicket and wait."

After another long time Kurt hears the glass window slide open. The curtain stays where it is but it moves slightly, as if stirred by somebody's breath. Kurt has a wild impulse to get down on his knees and say what Catholics do—Bless me Father for I have sinned. He says, "Father Davage?"

"It took you a long time to get here."

"What?"

The priest's voice is dry, as if his throat is papery from disuse. "I expected somebody long before this."

"You did!"

"I thought . . . How long can it go on?"

"Oh, Father!"

In the silence that follows, the priest moves the curtain a little to one side so he can see out. Kurt hears him grunt with pain. He must be crippled by age or arthritis or something worse. Apparently satisfied by what he sees, the priest says, "I suppose you want me to tell you something useful."

Kurt leans closer; if only he'd pull back the curtain so they could be face to face . . . "Anything!"

But the curtain stays closed. "I can't. Not really."

"Why!"

"Most of what I learned, I learned from Hal and his brother in confession . . ."

"His brother!" Kurt discovers that he's on his feet with his fingers tightening around the grill. "Hal's brother?"

"A twin."

"Hal has a twin?"

The priest corrects him. "Had. His twin brother died when they were sixteen. The police declared it an accidental death."

"But Hal confessed to you."

"No." His breath is shaky, as if charged by things he can't say.

Kurt says urgently. "Look. You have to tell me what he did."

"I'm sorry, I can't do that."

"The least you can do is tell me what he said."

"Don't you think I want to? Don't you think I would have told everybody if I could? The police? That poor girl, his fiancée?" The priest's breath hisses out in a little burst of frustration. "I can't."

"You can't?"

"The seal of the confessional." When Kurt does not immediately say, Oh, right, he explains. "Everything that's said there . . . Everything I do there . . . Understand, I carry it to the grave. And if I'm killed for not telling, fine."

Then Kurt hits him with it. "You know Hal Oliphant had twins."

The priest's voice comes from somewhere high behind his forehead in a thin, perfect tenor that falls into the room like a celestial groan. "Oh God. I heard she was pregnant, I never knew . . ."

"That it was twins? They were twins. One." Kurt's breath catches. "One died."

"Was it. Is it . . ."

Kurt thinks the priest wants him to answer a question that this seal of the confessional, whatever it is, won't let him ask. Sobbing, Father Davage wants reassuring, he wants to be told Zane's death was an accident. Kurt says, "You mean, who died?"

"Please."

The priest is so closemouthed that it makes Kurt cruel. "You mean, was it the good one or the bad one that died? The bad one, for what that's worth." As he says this he thinks uncomfortably: At least I think it was the bad one. Then he hits him with it. "An accident." At least the police said it was an accident.

"God!"

"There's something else you need to know. Hal has grandchildren."

Without having to be told he says, "Twins." The priest's sigh shakes the curtains. "I was afraid of that. I didn't come down to the parlor to help you, son, I'd like to but I can't. I can't help anybody any more. I . . ." The curtain trembles as if the man behind it can't stop shaking. Finally he manages, "All I can do is pray for you. I'm the last person to ask for help in any case. I don't even hear confessions any more. I have done worse things than any of the penitents who come to me. Sins of omission, you understand?"

"Omission," Kurt repeats. All those years he hid behind his computers, up there in the garage apartment. "I think I do."

"I still say Mass for the sisters but when I elevate the Host all I can think about are my failures—Hal's brother . . ."

"What happened?"

". . . that poor girl. I can't tell you."

"Yes you can."

"If only I could!"

Kurt's patience snaps. "That's enough!" For the first time

in his life he uses his disfigurement instead of hiding it. While the priest behind the curtain sighs and stirs with arthritic slowness, he unbuttons his cuff and rolls it back to expose the stump. Then he says harshly, "Lift the curtain."

"I'm sorry. I won't."

Kurt growls, "I didn't say open it, I said lift it, OK?"

"I don't have to keep the curtain closed," the priest admits. "I'm hiding."

"Just lift it a little. I have something I want to show you. That's good." He lays the mutilated stump on the little edge and slides it underneath the grill. "One of Hal's twins did this."

"Oh son, son!" There is a stir as the priest gets up with an effort and with an even greater effort pulls back the curtain from the wicket so at last they are face to face. The failed Jesuit is still handsome, with clear eyes under disorderly white brows and the profile of an eagle. His face lies so close to the bone that the soul shines through, as if he's been purified by pain.

It is such a nice face that Kurt almost apologizes for upsetting him. He almost cries, *Bless me father, make me well!* But he has this to do. Now that he has his audience Kurt continues. "You see what drives me. This is why I have to know."

"All I can tell you is what I can tell you. It won't be much. Hal trapped me, you see?" The priest can't seem to stop sighing.

Kurt hangs in place, waiting.

After a while, the priest begins. "You know how it is. You go along and you go along, you think there's something *wrong* but you don't say anything because you're ashamed of yourself for suspecting; there's still something wrong but you don't know what it is exactly until it boils up and explodes in your face."

Kurt winces.

"So I didn't say anything. Then it was too late."

Kurt echoes. "Too late."

"It was like seeing a volcano erupt. Hal . . . His brother. It was terrible."

"He killed his brother?"

"There was a fire. We never knew. But the business about the girl . . ."

Kurt barks. *"What about the girl?"*

"I can't tell you any more. I'm sorry I can't tell you, but I can't."

Kurt puts his stump on the ledge again.

"All right!" The priest groans. "After his brother died, there was something about a girl. Terrible thing. Hal caught me in the confessional. After he made his confession and I gave him absolution I sat there trembling. I thought, At least he's sorry. I hear him get up; I thought he had left the church. He was waiting outside. Laughing. He laughed and laughed.

"You should have heard him: 'I couldn't let it go by. Somebody had to admire what I did. Now I have bound you. You know and there's not one single thing you can do about it.' " It's too much. The priest breaks off. When he resumes his voice is thin. "All the time I thought he was truly sorry he was putting me in a trap. Chapter. Verse. Terrible details and not a word I could say. That poor, poor girl.

"And then we heard he was engaged. I tried to prevent the marriage but I was under the seal. I tried to warn the Archers but when they asked what was the matter, I couldn't say. They just laughed at me and went on with it. I tried to do so many things and there was nothing I could do; I tried to tell them but I can't. Here at least I don't hurt anybody." He looks up at Kurt. "Are you the twins' father?"

"Their father is dead too."

"Oh dear."

Bearing down, Kurt repeats, "They said it was an accident."

"Oh dear!" It's as if he's struck the priest in the face.

Now Kurt lays out his trail of escalating incidents and growing suspicions, from early vandalism in Meredith's morning room to the death of her pet. He makes himself talk about Vivian's apparent accident. One day she was getting ready to send the girls away to school and the next . . . He describes the day Steve Harriman got into Vivian's car with the orphaned girls and set off down the coast road, heading for his death while he, Kurt Graver, sat upstairs above the garage and did nothing. Yes he's guilty as hell.

"And what did I do? Nothing, Father. That's what I did." What does he want, absolution? "Now this woman their father married, this Carroll Lawton is taking them to live with her."

"That's terrible." The priest covers his mouth. "I mean . . ."

"It is terrible," Kurt says. "She looked so young. So not prepared. I don't know what they're going to do to her but they're going to do something." Doubt makes Kurt falter. "At least I think they are." He sees the girls' faces and just beneath the surface Zane's face coming and going, flickering until their pretty smiles are one with his savage glare. He remembers the last day, Vivian's twins riding away in their flowered Laura Ashley dresses. What was he supposed to do, run down and shout accusations? "God, Father, they're only little girls!"

The Jesuit is on his own track. "Hal was only a boy."

"How can I warn her when I'm not sure?"

Their narratives overlap. "That's what hampered me," the priest says as Kurt says:

"What if I'm wrong?"

"I kept thinking, What if I'm wrong? This is what I'm paying for. This failure. I've been paying for it ever since."

Kurt is studying him. "Father, all I want you to do is give me something to go with."

"I can't do anything. I couldn't do anything, my God, that's why I'm here. Helpless in the face of . . ." The priest whispers, "My own failure." His mouth clamps shut. His face is glazed with tears.

"Then there's nothing I can do." Kurt looks into his open right hand as if he can see its missing mate there, complete down to the curling fingers, stares into it as if the answers sit in the palm of the spectral hand. He says hopelessly, "Maybe nothing will happen . . ."

"Please God."

"Maybe she'll be all right." He's studying the priest and

he plants the next information carefully, waiting for it to sprout. "If she doesn't make them mad."

This brings the priest around smartly enough. "The temper."

"The temper," Kurt says.

Everything he's been trying to suppress assails him. His groan rattles the little room. "Oh my God."

"The temper." Kurt has him now. "With the girls so far it's only been little things—I think. But with Vivian's brother . . ." My God, he thinks, what did I do back then to make Zane so angry? All I did was fall into his mud castle and break it, I was crying, *it was an accident.* What Zane said to him after the explosion, Kurt's blood splattered his face but he was laughing, laughing! *It was an accident.* For God's sake was it because he knew I loved Vivian? Another minute and Kurt will be hanging on the grate and sobbing out his story. He'll pull the bars out of the wall so the priest can thump him on the back: there there. He leaps for safer ground. "Hal's sister says even with plants things go wrong. You end up with a mutant strain."

"Into the last generation," the priest says.

"Three generations of twins. This poor woman has taken the girls to Florida and she doesn't have a clue. If I walk in cold, what am I going to say?"

"Maybe you shouldn't walk in at all."

"Then I would be just as responsible—sorry, Father."

"As responsible as I am. I know, I know. I just wish there was something I could tell you. I wish there was something I could do."

"Goddammit, father."

"Exactly," the priest says. Then he says so naturally that he surprises even himself, "Why don't you just go to Hal?"

Kurt leans forward with his eyes glinting. "Do what?"

"Maybe the years have improved him."

"He's still alive?" Kurt pounces. "Where is he?"

The priest says as if it's the most natural thing in the world, obvious, "Palm Beach."

"Palm Beach. No he isn't. He dropped out of sight. He

dropped off everybody's computer screen. He's not in any police network, he . . ."

"He put everything in his third wife's name."

"And you know what it is." Bitterly, Kurt pushes back in his chair and makes as if to leave. "But you can't tell me because that was in confession too."

Now the priest is angry. "Don't belittle me. Don't think you know what binds me and sets me free. He did it after the second marriage foundered. He got religion. Then he fell in love again." He stands up quickly, so angry that he doesn't even feel the stabbing in his joints. His eyes are bright with rage. "I have his new wife's name. I even have an address. The fool imagined I could help him get the first marriages annulled."

21

WHAT HAPPENS is probably Carroll's fault for being so late. She never should have left the twins alone with the relatives for so long, but things happened at work.

Not her fault the Jenkins police came up with a death so tasteless, odorless and colorless that until the coroner finishes, they can't even identify it as a murder. But it was her fault for hanging in after the police P.R. officer told her there wouldn't be anything conclusive until tomorrow. She just wanted one more thing to put in to make a solid story. As it was they went with the bare facts. "Found dead in a mall parking lot . . ." Even though she didn't have much, Charley gave her a box on One A. ("Glad to have you back.") *Glad to be back.* For the first time since her wedding she's going to wake up in the morning and see her byline in the paper, at the top of a story she worked on until the pieces fell in place and she got it right. *Nature's way of letting you know you're not dead.* Maybe it means more to her than it should right now, but, hey.

Because she can't bear to examine her own grief, she focuses on death. The least she can do is make Steve proud of her. She has to get this story out, and get it right. It keeps her well after quitting time.

Coming home late, Carroll walks into trouble. When she calls out nobody answers, although she can hear voices escalating in the kitchen. Her aunts are having words; she can recognize the tune from here and her whole life in this house boils up in her throat. The familiar sour taste makes her want to walk out of the scene and keep walking, but she doesn't. *That poor kid.* Struck in the same place by the same old sadness. She corrects herself quickly. *Those poor kids.* She can't afford to think, *Poor Carroll.*

She has this pressing need to make up to the twins for her whole life as a kid.

Still it takes her a minute. Every time she sees these women she has to remind them she stopped being the orphan child a long time ago. Every time she sees them she has to come on strong just to prove what the rest of the world knows. She's a grownup now.

She runs her fingers through her short red hair, pushing it back, and with a little shake lifts her head and straightens her shoulders. She holds herself like a tall person, lifting her shoulders as she goes through the shabby family living room. With misgivings, she opens the kitchen door. Although it's crunching toward the Larrabies' dinner hour, there are no signs of preparation here. Instead she sees 'Laine's grocery bags leaning against each other on the counter with their sodden bottoms leaking and small items spilling out. Her aunt Elaine and the twins seem to be at some kind of standoff. Jane and Emily have carved out their own territory in the middle of the kitchen. They're standing quietly with their eyes fixed on something Carroll can't see while 'Laine scolds them and chic, angry Suzy stands framed in the back door. The girls are pink from the sun and their fair hair is plastered to their necks in salty ropes. Their expressions make it clear they're far away; this fight is going on without them.

They don't stir when Carroll says, "What's the matter?" She turns to Elaine. "What's the matter?"

Flushed and angry, 'Laine growls, "I told them not to. They know perfectly well I told them not to but they did it anyway."

Suzy is impatient. "I don't see what difference it makes."

"And now Suzy wants to act as though it never happened."

"I want to get this settled," Suzy says.

"What?"

'Laine's shoulders are hunched and her jaw juts. "This is not the time for presents."

Carroll looks from 'Laine to the twins for some clue as to what's going on but the twins blink and don't respond.

"They disobeyed."

Rattling matched candy-striped shopping bags, Suzy begins tapping back and forth in her high-heeled patents. "All I want to do is have them try on these dresses."

"I told them what to do and they did as they pleased."

Suzy snaps, "Well don't make a federal case out of it."

'Laine says to Carroll, "Do you think behavior like that should be rewarded?"

"What did you guys do that you shouldn't?"

The twins turn faces smeared by daydreams or memories; she can't know which.

"No dresses now. They don't deserve it."

"What's the matter?" Carroll looks at Emily, at Jane. "What's the matter here?"

Jane doesn't answer; she just extends her hand and studies the ruby ring. Emily turns her hand, looking for lights in the sapphire chip.

"If I want to give them nice dresses I can give them nice dresses." Suzy looks with scorn at the wet patches on their Gap T-shirts. "You can't let them run around in wet bathing suits."

'Laine says doggedly, "I can't reward them for being disobedient either."

Suzy ignores her. "We're going to be friends, aren't we, girls?"

"Dresses to match the rings," one of the girls says dreamily, and the other says, "Pretty. Strapless."

"You're trying to make them look like hookers."

"'Laine!"

One of the twins says, "Just exactly what we wanted."

Carroll says quickly, "What?"

The girls swivel to face Carroll, saying in counterpoint, "The dresses."

"You know, pretty."

"To match the rings."

"We told Aunt Elaine we were sorry."

"The first thing we said was, Aunt Elaine, we're sorry."

"And we are."

It disturbs Carroll how nearly interchangeable they are. One says for both, "And now, the dresses."

"Silk ones."

"She promised."

Suzy says, "I did."

Elaine sniffles. "I told them not to go into the water."

They turn blue eyes on her. "You told us not to go in without a lifeguard."

"Well we had one."

"We did."

'Laine's face is pink with distress. The tail of her perky blouse has come out of her wraparound skirt and the collar is sadly crumpled. "There was no lifeguard when I dropped you and there was no lifeguard when I picked you up."

"He had to leave."

She turns to Carroll. "There wasn't any sign of one."

"He was there but he left," Jane says to Carroll.

"I looked and looked."

"He was there but he left," Emily says.

"It took me an hour to find them."

"We were right there."

"She just didn't know where to look for us."

"We said we were sorry."

They have Carroll by the hands now, Jane on the left, Emily on the right, sweetly urgent. "We said we were sorry. Carroll?"

"Caa-rull?"

"So can we have the dresses now?"

"They don't deserve . . ."

Carroll can feel the pressure building up in the room. What's been going on here while she was so busy at the paper? What have her girls been doing while she was tied up with her possible homicide? How many alliances have been made and tested?

One of her twins tugs on her hand. "Can we?"

Suzy is rattling her twin shopping bags with an impatient look. She and 'Laine have been wrangling for so long that she's reached the end of her patience. "The least you can do here is decide. All they want to do is look nice . . ."

"That's all we want."

Suzy finishes, ". . . just like all us girls."

"All we want to do is look nice."

"Oh Elaine, I'm sorry." Carroll frees her hands so she can hug the girls. Side by side by side they face the Larrabie sisters. "They'll do better next time."

"We will." They hug her back. She's so grateful it makes her mouth water.

"We will do better next time."

"All right," 'Laine says grudgingly. Released from combat, she looks sadly at her groceries. "It's getting so late we're going to have to order out for pizza." She tries to perk up her tone. "Do you girls like pizza?"

"Pizza. Right. I'll spring for watermelon for dessert."

They don't even hear. Carroll is aware that they've flowed away from her like quicksilver, attaching themselves to Suzy and her shopping bags.

"Dresses. Can I see?"

"Can I see?"

"Of course you can. After all, you want to look nice."

"All we want is to look nice. Did you get us shoes?"

Elaine asks mournfully, "Is pizza OK?"

As Suzy bridles and giggles, they look back at Elaine. "We're sorry, we can't."

"Everybody likes pizza," Elaine says.

"We're going out."

"But you haven't had dinner yet."

"Aunt Patsy is taking us to Dairy Queen."

"That isn't dinner."

"First Uncle Peyton is taking us to the Charthouse . . ."

"Uncle Peyton!" Carroll starts. "Did he . . ." *put his hands on you?* But they're happy, bubbling.

". . . at the top of the Bradley building . . ."

". . . the restaurant that goes around."

Suzy says firmly, "After you get into your party clothes."

"All right, all right," Elaine says while Carroll is still standing there with her mouth open. "Party tonight, but tomorrow morning, school."

They look from her to Carroll and back. Then after one of

those lightning exchanges that Carroll has learned to recognize they nod. *Click.* "Tomorrow morning, school." There is a little pause. "But we'll need clothes."

"I'll take you shopping before you register."

Upstaged, Suzy begins, "I'll . . ."

"You'll be at work. And after, we'll have lunch. At . . ." Elaine is groping. "At Binky's. It's the best. OK kids?"

"Yes Aunt Elaine."

The speed with which all of this has happened leaves Carroll unsettled and bemused. She can't work out the scenario in which all these dramatic changes took place. Frosty Suzy out shopping for Jane and Emily, Peyton promising dinner at the most expensive restaurant in town. Did Peyton slide in with his dinner invitation just now while Elaine and Suzy were fighting or did the girls go to work on him and Patsy at breakfast before Carroll ever came downstairs? What are these two up to? What happens while she sleeps? While she's away? She doesn't know. All she knows is that since she first walked in with these two orphaned strangers, everything has changed. Steve's girls have been at work here, playing on the relatives' needs, and the balance of power in the house has tipped. They've set the aunts and the uncle against each other, all the Larrabies so bent on winning them that everything—parties, presents—comes to them.

Yes they're older than Carroll was when she first came here, they're a pair, which leaves them stronger and better equipped to cope; they're pretty, no, lovely with their fair hair and blue eyes with flawless whites that shimmer like porcelain, but there's something else at work.

It's not so much the twins' good looks as it is their bearing that signals this: the assurance that brooks no refusals, the clever expectation that everything good will come their way.

She wants to stop and consider this. She wants to ask the girls a thing or two. She wants not to be home alone tonight. At the very least she wants to ask Suzy and Peyton if she can come along but her tall, stylish aunt has Jane and Emily in tow now and whether unconsciously or by design, the girls adopt her stride and the arrogant angle of her head, moving out of the kitchen like the Spanish Armada under full sail. Suzy and the twins will pass through one more time with Peyton in his white suit and a black shirt and tie that might look right on a man half his age but make him look like a cartoon gigolo. He's shepherding the two in their soft, full silk dresses and Suzy's dangling earrings; he has his hands cupped under their elbows and as they exit he pulls them close so the three of them will fit through the door. She can hear them laughing as they get into the car.

This is how Carroll finds herself having another of those sad tuna melt suppers at the kitchen table with her aunt Patsy, who is put out because at the last minute Suzy and Peyton fobbed her off with some excuse, and poor Elaine. Patsy's angry and hurt. As she usually does when she's brooding about her weight, she's picking at her food. Some time during the evening she'll say, "I don't know why I can't lose weight. I eat like a bird."

This is what she's doing now. Eating like a bird. "They're all at the Charthouse now." Patsy pushes her plate away. "Suzy says she didn't invite me because eating dinner this late is bad for my digestion, when what she means is, she doesn't want me along."

"Well they don't want me along either," Elaine says.

Carroll says, "Of course they do."

"They think I don't look right with them." Patsy's face is quivering. "Like I don't match."

"You have lovely clothes."

"It isn't my clothes. They think I'm fat."

'Laine says automatically, "You aren't fat, honey, you're just . . ."

And Carroll finishes as she has—how many times? ". . . statuesque."

Patsy keeps worrying it. "Peyton will keep them up too late. They need their sleep."

"Never mind their party. We're having our own party here." Elaine has melted squares of Hershey bar and marshmallows on top of graham crackers just the way she used to in her Girl Scout days.

The whole thing is so sad that when the phone rings Carroll lunges. *Thank God.*

"Kid?"

"Oh, Charley!"

"I'll pick you up early tomorrow. There's been a drowning."

"Who?"

"He washed up naked. They don't know."

"Accident?"

"Undertow, maybe. Or a cramp. But the guy was in shape. Strong."

Her mind is running ahead of the story. "Something else?"

"They aren't sure yet. Whatever it is, I want you on it."

"You want me on it." She's surprised and a little embarrassed by a surge of joyful excitement. Most people told about a sudden death think: How sad. A reporter thinks: Good story. *Great.*

"First thing in the morning. And I need a follow on the death at the mall."

"They haven't . . ."

"No. It's weird."

She'll be out before the twins get up. She ought to be taking them to register at school, not 'Laine, but her aunt would be disappointed and besides, she has work to do. *I have work to do.* "Right, Charley. I'm there." She wants to hang on the phone talking to Charley because it extends the, what, the *useful* feeling she has when she's working, but her aunts are fidgeting over their gooey "Some-mores."

She'll sit through the evening with 'Laine and Patsy as if watching TV with them is the most important thing on her mind, but as she does, Carroll finds herself sorting the details of the day: the discovery of the body in the last car at the far end of the parking lot in the local mall, her inconclusive interview with the investigating officers. Grinning politely at a rerun of "Cheers," she will itemize the calls she has to make and the questions she has to ask in the morning to come up with a second day story that's stronger than the first, so there's that. And now there is this drowning. If they haven't made an identification, that's where her story is. She can comb the beach looking for people who knew him, telephone all the local gyms. If they have an ID she can go to the victim's house, try to get a picture, find friends or neighbors who have some background on the guy. Jenkins is a large enough town, or small city, for any unexpected death to be potential news. Watching "Knots Landing" unfold on TV, she finds herself hoping it's murder.

Fleeing grief, she rushes headlong into reporting death.

Her second phone call comes as Elaine and Patsy are heading upstairs after the late news. Carroll turns off the set and tests the silence. She's not quite ready to be alone with herself. She's hunched on the sofa in the musty family living room picking at the frayed flowered slipcovers and waiting for Peyton and Suzy and the girls to come in when the phone rings. She answers quickly. "Yes, Charley. What've you got?"

The man at the other end is abrupt. "This isn't Charley."

"Then who?"

Instead of answering he says, "You're Carroll Lawton?"

He sounds so urgent that she says crazily, "Steve?"

"No. I'm sorry."

Why does he apologize? How did he know? She hears background noise: crowd murmurs, amplified announcements over a remote P.A. "How did you get my name?"

"I'm sorry to be calling so late, but I had to get to the airport. This is the first chance I've had."

"Who are you?"

The speaker sounds rushed. "You're guardian of the Archer twins?"

"Yes. No." *Guardian.* It sounds formidable. Final. Like more than she can handle, but there is another element here. "I think so. Who gave you my name?"

"You don't know me but I think we need to talk."

"Who are you?"

"I'll explain tomorrow."

"Tomorrow!"

"If I can make it. There's somebody I have to see first."

"Why can't we talk now?"

"They're calling my plane. Shut up and listen. There's something I have to tell you. This is going to sound crazy, but until I can get there, I . . . Look." He seems to be having a hard time getting it out. "It's." When he does, he gets it wrong. "Be careful with the twins."

Or she does. "Of course I'll take care of them." Tears spring. "I'm going nuts trying to take care of them."

"That's not what I mean."

"And now my aunt and uncle have dragged them off." She doesn't mean to sound so weak and stupid but it's late, she's pressed, she's been left the one last treasure Steve had to give to her; she thinks she knows what she's supposed to do and she can't even do it right.

"I don't mean that, I mean . . ." The anonymous speaker breaks off. "Why is this so hard? Listen, why I called was, I . . . What I'm trying to say is . . ." He blurts, "There's something strange about the twins."

Carroll jams her knuckles into her mouth. She doesn't want to hear this. She definitely doesn't need it. Not tonight. Not now. "You don't know what you're talking about."

Suddenly he sounds very young. "Yeah, right, I knew it was a mistake, trying to do this by phone but I got, I got worried, OK? I knew it would be tomorrow or Saturday before I could get there and I can't explain until I get some kind of proof but then I thought anything could happen and I just . . ."

She hears the front door opening; she hears laughter; she hears Suzy and Peyton laughing and the twins' high musical giggle, coming as if from a single throat. "I can't talk right now."

Suzy calls, "Carroll, are you still up?"

He growls, "I just didn't want you to be down there unprepared."

Now it's Carroll who is rushed. She feels guilty and furtive for listening to whatever he's trying to tell her. She feels guilty about being on the phone at all. "I'm sorry, somebody's here."

"Don't hang up!"

But now they are in the family living room, twins and Suzy with their hair flying, laughing and brilliant in their contrasting silks; has Peyton given them champagne? Yes, she thinks. Too much. The rooms fills with colliding perfumes—Suzy's Chanel and the spicy cologne she's splashed on the twins, Peyton's aftershave and second-hand smoke from the expensive restaurant dining room. Flanked by Suzy in her black sheath and Peyton in his crumpled whites they move into the shabby sitting room in a burst of glamour that leaves Carroll giddy and uncertain. Looking at the girls' pink faces, their blurry smiles, she smiles foolishly; why is it so important to her to make them like her? "Hi girls." She's only half aware that she's still on the phone.

"Ma'am, *ma'am*. One thing?"

"I'm sorry, I can't talk."

"Hey Carroll." Jane sidles close. "We had the best time."

Emily curls an arm around her. "We had the best time."

"*Listen*, whatever you do . . ." The next thing pops into her ear at the same time that the girls circle her, hugging and putting their faces close to hers; they smile, she smiles, and right before he hangs up the caller says, or she thinks he says something that snags in her memory and flutters there like a rag stuck to a freshly plastered wall. It goes by too fast for her to take it in but even now she hears the echoes— Meredith Archer in her drawing room and somebody—her driver Billy Graver?—saying this, exactly this. It's something that she will have to take out and examine later, but not now, not now. His voice rushes into the receiver. "Don't make them angry, OK?"

But by this time the girls have taken the receiver from her and lovely Jane puts her thumb on the button, disconnecting the speaker, and sweet Emily hangs it back up on the wall.

.

22

—ONEMUS EENAMUS YES! And the feeling, and more things we will be feeling, I think I like Florida.

I know I like the beach.

We hate the school but that's where you get boys, cute ones to follow us home and wait with the motor running while we lied to Aunt Elaine; here we are at the beach! We let them play until we got tired of them. The sand is like a dessert cart. Take as many as you want, there are always more. Knights for our very own, as many as we want, laid out on towels rank on rank on rank, so fine! The queen will take only the best onto the throne with her, so let the trials begin. Want to run fastest, jump highest? Want to come into the water with us?

Jade and Emerald, no, Amanenja queen of Amadamaland separates the bold from the worthless in the royal tournament. We will take the finest and the strongest into Amadamaland with us; only the winners will sit at the feet of the queen. Beautiful bodies like gold sculpture, holding up the throne—only the best, OK? And the others—too bad. Tough rocks cute boy, you failed that test. Offend the queen will you, so much for you, take that!

But that was yesterday. No time for that. We are the queen.

Now here comes a good one, stalking in the tight leopard suit, the kind the sun tans right through and he's all built up with those big chest muscles, like yesterday's, great bleached hair and four-alarm tan, but maybe cuter, maybe not so . . . Whatever. Maybe no problem, just right, OK? Let's see.

—*Not ready. I'm scared.*

—Scared are you, well you weren't scared when it counted, my queen, I saw your look.

I saw your tongue circling, licking your lips as if you couldn't get enough of it—the excitement, the power; I felt our tongue on our lips; it was fine. Fine, yes, how it came down yesterday and how it felt to us, yes, doing what we had to do after he did what he did. Beware of the ones that look The Look. Offend the queen, will you? No way! We had no choice, you know? I know you know. What I feel, you feel: if we are not the same person, we are close enough. What one thinks, the other knows. Sister, what a rush! In all our lives since we came into the kingdom and set up shop there, this is the best it's ever been—this feeling, Queen Jade and Queen Emerald together, supreme.

—*Fregel.*

—Fregel! Forget guilty. When we are done here in this Florida, we will go back into the kingdom, and when we do, we'll be a thousand strong.

—*Still scared.*

—Don't be scared, feel glad. All the *things* we have because they think they can make us happy here! Garish. Expensive. The fools. Florida clothes from the housewife aunt and silver barrettes she bought to make up for forcing us to school. New shorts and skirts we have, and funky shirts from this Carroll and silky dresses from Suzy, the money extravaganza, with her Diamonique and classy suits right out of fashion magazines. Grandmother would never let us go out in shiny dresses like the ones Suzy buys for us, low in the front and low in the back, and she would never approve of big jewelry with bright stones. We look like queens; that's what Suzy says, 'You look like little queens,' well yes, you know, and right you know, there may be a place for you in the kingdom; Suzy the One Who Shops, Lady Suzy, who gives, and takes us out at night. The mother would never, ever let us go to the Charthouse or dance after bedtime like that, no not the mother, the Vivian . . .

—*I feel bad about Vivian.*

—Well don't. She never understood we were the queen. What she did see, you don't want to know.

Look how it was, the way she treated us. You'd think we were disease that you had to keep in an isolation ward so it wouldn't spread. If we hadn't—You Know, we would still be there. We had to You Know before they sent us off to those terrible separate schools. If they split us, then what would happen to our powers? The Grandmother, the Vivian, they kept us like Rapunzel trapped in the towers of Amadamaland and now we're out, so, good! Good lying in the sand in our bikinis, good feeling the sun on our bellies and good letting the boys look into our belly-buttons like frog princes looking into pools. We will take the best into our army, and into our lives.

This Jenkins, this Florida. Not bad! From here we can go anywhere. We can get anything.

Look what we've got so far! Silks we have, from this Suzy, and from Elaine, silver barrettes; Patsy doesn't know it but she will give velvet capes next winter when it's cold enough for us to convince them it's really cold. The Peyton gets to buy ermine tails for the aunts to sew on the collars, raiment fit for the queen we are, plus, this Carroll already gave crown jewels.

—*Crown jewels! Pinhead jewels. Pretty, but so small!*

—Fine one you are to complain. Small maybe, but stones rolling in the right direction toward bigger ones. I think, and see them shine, OK? We have our rings and Suzy's things, Diamonique earrings the size of caramels, plus the gold chains Aunt 'Laine is going to buy us to make up for not being first with the rings. With more to come, and the food! This Patsy eats for regiments and she brings food for armies because she wants us to like her, yes, and what she brings, we store. Cakes Patsy gives, blueberry muffins from Dunkin' Donuts yesterday and frosted honeydips today, that we sneaked upstairs, to put with the five-pound box of candy Patsy left on our dresser last night that we took straight to our armory, provisioning for battles to come.

—*What battles? Not here.*

—Wherever we have to fight.

—*Not here. They want us to like them, and so they get us things.*

—Yes, you think, sister, and yes for now, and things we get, but who knows what else we get, and when? Let's take what's now and take it good, but remember. Tomorrow, you never know.

Tomorrow it can go sour.

Like Patsy. She promised Dairy Queen because she wanted to go to the Charthouse last night. She wanted to flounce in and sit down at Uncle Peyton's table and pretend to be pretty and thin, like us. When we left without her she got burned up. The note with the candy: *This will make you sweet to me.* Sorry, you are fat. When she goes out the queen of Amadamaland wants only beautiful people in her entourage, not big things stuffed into flowered satin and tiny, tiny shoes. But we'll make up. We need the food. We'll let her take us out to some drive-in where they bring burgers out to your car and nobody sees how you get grease on your mouth or how your chins tremble when you start licking up the crumbs, and between times we can swank around town with Suzy and the Peyton and get presents and put them on, yesterday the Charthouse and tonight the Rainbow Room.

—*About the Peyton one. He looks . . .*

—He looks The Look.

Beware all you who look The Look, you too, you Peyton one, with your white suit and your yellow teeth, but with your plastic, man, we live like queens. When we get dressed up the Peyton can afford to take us where we want to go. Out, where the people can look at us and be amazed. We saw those men with their homely wives and their mouths watering, courtiers ready to bow down.

—*The Peyton wants to give us presents, but what does he want to take?*

—Ah, that is the whole thing. Never mind what he wants. We take what we get, and more, and more, and forget the wants, OK? It doesn't matter what he wants. All that matters is what we need.

Expensive clothes we need, to make up for the ones we left behind in Amadamaland, and rich dinners in all those places to make up for leaving the kingdom and scooters to make up for the no ponies, and we need gold and silver things to make up for the rundown house and ugly new bedroom and trips to Disney World to make up for the having to go to this terrible new school.

—*I hate the school.*

—Ugly, you know, not like our St. Margaret's where every class was a party with us and some nice teach sitting around a table in those elegant rooms, like, What would you girls like to talk about today? This school is a factory, with tacky cracker teachers playing like they know more than us, and if we say yes ma'am, yes school to Aunt 'Laine it's for the boys we see hanging on lockers and slouching down the halls, not all cute, no, but all boys.

And who else for our knights, but all these beautiful tanned long-bodied boys with their muscle shirts and their bleached blond heads and their chests out to here, we'll try them out and the best will come to the top like cream, you'll see when we begin the trials. But the school building! Yeugh. We aren't going to like it, no. No secret corners and no soft places to hide in with the boys, everything by the bells.

Aunt 'Laine flirting with the principal while we smiled, *Ko-prictus.* Nice us. She flirted while he winked. Both of you, shame!

This Dr. Foster Goss, that laid it out for us. Go from this classroom to that one in this order, sit in this seat in this row. Be quiet or else. Fine for commoners too poor for St. Margaret's, but we are the queen. Separate home rooms, no way! The only order we accept is our order. The only orders we follow are our own.

And look at Dr. Foster Goss, the whole time this poor Aunt 'Laine is simpering, he's sneaking sly looks at us. We know. He thinks we don't see him looking The Look. The queen doesn't let people like that get by with things like that. He'd better back off or the Goss will learn what happens to fools who are thinking about One Thing Only while they try to make you think they're thinking about something else.

—*Wait. The Peyton thinks about One Thing Only.*

—That's different. He buys us things. This Dr. Goss, we

have to show. Like all the jerks who play like they're talking ordinary talk when all you see is them working their mouths and looking The Look. We can handle the school. We know how to look like we're going there without going there, OK, we only have to do it until summer, which is soon. Then we're free and by fall we'll have the best knights marching in our army rank on rank on rank, cute knights on our left and marching in front of us when we invade. Then Grandmother will be dead and we the queen will inherit the kingdom, we will move all our cute knights into the castle, we'll march in triumph back to Amadamaland.

—*I miss the Blues and the Greens. It was so sweet, and now . . .*

—This is bigger than the Blues and the Greens.

—*Scarier.*

—That's why it's fun. Now put some stuff on my back, OK? OK. So school is just a little while, OK? OK. And all we have to do . . .

—*OK. Now you put some stuff on my back, OK? OK. Emenanja, I'm scared. I don't know if we ought to do what we have to do.*

—Shut up. All we have to do is pretend to go to school. Mornings the school and then the beach, every day the beach, OK, and you know what happens at the beach.

—*I don't always like what happens at the beach.*

—In hell you don't. I saw your face.

—*It happened so fast!*

—It had to happen. OK? Don't think I didn't see your face when we did it, I can see behind your eyes to the place where you are thinking, I can see into it and I know. It felt good. It did. It felt like more. So here we are. Again.

—*I'm sorry, I just. I don't know.*

—Yes you do. I can feel it writhing inside you, don't think I can't, because I feel it traveling in me. *Yes*. OK? And, *more*. So it's again, OK? And soon. It's the beach for now and the beach whenever they will let us, and knights for us, cute ones, and we will make them do whatever we want them to, OK? And *things* to get for the kingdom in the attic, and trophies for our shrine.

Oh sister, look. Up by the refreshment stand. Randy. Alone.

—*S-scared.*

—But it's a *good* scared. We're quicker than they are and the things we do, they'll never know.

And good it feels, it does feel good, right twin one? Right sister, my peer, my queen? Everybody gets scared sometimes, if you aren't scared, where's the rush?

"You Randy. Over here."

"Hi Randy. It's us."

23

KURT IS DELIVERED, squinting, into the strong sunlight of Palm Beach. He feels bedraggled and shaky as a new chick. All the houses in this neighborhood have sharp edges. Even the shadows on the dazzling cement look different, black and stark. Heat shimmers in waves around his ankles. The cab rounds the corner leaving him marooned here with the hot air parching his throat and drying out his lungs. This is Florida.

It's taken him too long to get here; he blanked out in the terminal in Atlanta and missed his connection. When he came to himself he was sitting on one of those moulded plastic seats with his head bobbing and his wrists dangling, going: Uh. Oh. Uh, just like your classic sixties burnout or disrupted Nam vet, some beleaguered stray turned out of his institution too soon and left to scavenge in public places, spending nights scrunched up on unyielding seats. Even now he doesn't know what happened to him.

One minute he was waiting for his plane and the next, it was gone. The time just disappeared. Whether he was overtaken by exhaustion or by what he now recognizes as acute agoraphobia, he can't say. If Kurt had his way he'd go home this minute. He'd go back upstairs to the garage apartment and spend the rest of his natural life at his work station, zipping through time and space electronically, the only travel he considers safe.

Stupid, getting this close to Hal Oliphant and then blowing it just because he phased out. By the time he had a new ticket and another flight scheduled, he'd lost the morning. By the time he located the Oliphant house, half the afternoon was gone.

Now he is here.

The house is exactly where the city records said it would
be, but if Hal Oliphant has a phone Florida Information
doesn't know it. If Kurt wants to talk to Vivian Archer's
father, if he wants to find out anything about the family, he's
going to have to go up to that pink front door and ring the
bell.

He wants to, but he can't.

He doesn't know what freezes him here in the middle of
the deserted street, dangling in place in front of the Oliphant
house like an oversized coat from an invisible hook. Is he
afraid this old guy Hal Oliphant will refuse to see him, or is
he more afraid that Hal will ask him in?

*Be cool, he tells himself. What do you think, he's going to
try to hurt you? What can he do to you, force your one
remaining hand into the Dispos-all or blow it off with an
exploding drink?*

Still he lingers. He can't figure out what keeps him
planted in the cement in the middle of this empty heat-
blasted street.

It's a lot deeper than simple fear for his person. He has the
idea that even though he came all this way to do something
hard and complicated, it's going to be harder and even more
complicated than he thought.

And there's this.

Now that he's here, he knows which he's really afraid of,
Kurt Graver who has found beauty and logic in the world of
the computer where options chosen open new options in
gorgeously complex but ultimately predictable map of
possibilities, where actions and reactions, decisions and
consequences are inexorably linked. Sitting at his terminals
he can scan the world and control everything he touches, but
now he is unshelled in front of a closed house on a deserted
residential street in Palm Beach, Florida, and when he goes
to the front door anything can happen. Anything.

What Kurt Graver fears most is not the unpredictable, it's
the uncontrollable.

He's afraid he'll look into Hal Oliphant's face and
discover Zane smouldering inside, the same evil spirit
flickering behind the eyes. Stretching like a waking tiger it

will unfold, greeting him: *Oh, it's you. I thought you'd never come.* It may be the same force that propels Vivian's twin girls. When he confronts Jane and Emily, he's going to see the same shadow flickering in their faces—something nameless and hidden stirring just beneath the surface, flexing like a tiger preparing to spring.

So what keeps Kurt Graver hanging here is something he hasn't exactly fathomed—the nature of the evil he's come out to deal with—what he's afraid the twins will do.

He is increasingly certain that the dark force that propelled Zane Archer didn't die with the person. It lives. He has seen it behind the faces of Vivian's twins. He's seen the danger all his life but until now, he never saw it clear. He doesn't know whether it was the priest who put the last piece in place for him or whether the knowledge has struck him like lightning, but standing in the street in front of Hal Oliphant's house, he knows. It lives. Whatever it is that links the Oliphants—bizarre electrical current, or spirit, or evil genius or driving energy or worse—it is pervasive. It has tracked these twins through the generations, through Hal, whose twin brother died mysteriously, to Hal's son Zane. And then? God, he thinks, and then? Through Zane. No, he thinks. He knows now. Through Vivian. It lives in Emily, he thinks and he can feel his belly quiver and knot itself. It lives in Jane.

And as far as he knows, he's the only person in the world who cares enough to try to find the girls and confront this. He doesn't know how to begin; he doesn't have a clue. Awkward Kurt Graver, an agoraphobe even on his best days. What can he do?

Who do I think I am anyway, riding out like the masked avenger or a neogothic vampire hunter, ready to nail evil with a stake through something's heart? He manages to uproot himself, but only to kick a piece of tail-light reflector out of his path. *Who I am is, I'm a jerk.*

OK, the house is daunting. It is. It's an expanded Florida ranch, glittering white in the sunlight with reflective shades pulled down over the plate glass windows and a neatly raked white gravel front yard and dead palms in white cement urns on either side of the front steps. Except for blue roof tiles and some red things blooming in a bed next to the lavender front door, there is no color here. The house is bland, faceless, with that hermetically sealed look that signals prosperity in hot climates—everything closed up tight against intruders, central air conditioning, security system, live-in maid, complete lives going on inside, unthreatened by contact with the outside world.

No wonder he doesn't want to go to the door.

And what am I going to do when I find him, grab him by the throat and not let go until he tells me what to do? Or tell him, Look, you've got these strange *granddaughters. How about you hold still while I drive this stake into you?*

Some jerk I am, thinking I can do this. He thinks maybe he ought to go home and work on something he can handle, like changing the tax structure of the state of California, or writing global war games for the Joint Chiefs of Staff.

He supposes he should be grateful when the vintage silver Cadillac with tinted windows rounds the corner and almost hits him. Jumping out of the way as it swerves into the driveway, he discovers that once moving, he can keep going. As the garage door rolls up automatically and the car glides in, he bounds up the front walk and rings the bell.

"That won't do you any good."

He whirls. She's old, north of sixty and beautifully veneered, with aggressively tanned legs in the short-shorts and a blonde hairdo that would do credit to the top of a wedding cake. The face tells him she could be any age behind the dense black sunglasses, but the body tells him she is not. Her legs are too skinny and her midsection is too thick, as if the muscles that held her in place have begun to let go. "I'm sorry," he says automatically. Why is he always apologizing? "I'm looking for Hal Oliphant."

"Well, you're in the wrong place." She takes down her dark glasses to look at him.

Her expression makes him say, "I'm sorry" and mean it. "I'm so sorry, Mrs. Oliphant."

She says in a tight little voice, "I took back my name. I'm Veda Faller again." She has pretty blue eyes in the middle of that too-tan face but the lines around her mouth remind him of certain carvings of saints being impaled by arrows or killed by rocks. Turning away, she unlocks the door. "Nice talking to you."

Oh please!" Without even thinking about what he's doing Kurt grasps her hand and cries, "Can I come in?"

She studies him. Does she think they have something in common or does she think he knows something she doesn't know? He isn't sure. "Maybe you'd better." She disarms the alarm. "You don't look so good."

He moves into the cool, dim front room without hesitation because he knows Hal Oliphant isn't here. It's a well-ordered house with a day-to-day calendar on the little side table with little notations for almost every hour. The gilded frame around the mirror above it is thick with business cards—anybody you might need to call for goods or service, help in case of any contingency—if he looks closely enough Kurt is sure he'll even find a supplier for artificial limbs. The place is as stone quiet as a model room in a museum—no newspapers strewn on sofas, no piles of hastily opened junk mail waiting to be thrown away. This is the home of a single person who cleans up the entire kitchen after breakfast and fluffs up cushions every time she gets up from a chair. There may be one incredibly messy junk drawer in this woman's kitchen, but he doesn't think so. Like Kurt when he's at his multiple terminals, Hal's ex-wife has all the parts of her life under control. He's unaccountably dizzy—sudden change of temperature or disappointment, maybe, or maybe it's relief. After a while in which he waits for her to double-latch the door and turn on a china lamp with shepherdesses twined around the base, he says, "Is it OK if I sit down? I think there's something the matter with me."

She says quickly, "I'll get you something to drink."

"Water would be fine."

She's rattling at the bar. "Then I'll get me something to drink. You sure you don't want something stronger?"

"No thank you," Kurt says. He wants to be safe at home but he's here, with this woman who has shed Hal Oliphant's name and he has to ask her something. The hell of it is, he doesn't know what to ask.

"After all," she says, nailing herself firmly in the older generation, "it's half-past the cocktail hour."

"Water will be fine." Oh God, he thinks, now that I'm inside, what if I can't go out again? What if instead of being stuck at home with my computers forever, I end up stuck here?

As Hal's ex clicks across the terrazzo in her high-heeled sandals, he's touched and temporarily distracted by the fact that she has iridescent toenails. In a house where nobody else lives, this woman is brushed and polished and made up down to the extra ring of green eyeshadow around the dark eyeliner, carefully put together just in case somebody comes. She sets down a glass of water and a plate of stale Pepperidge Farm goldfish and watches until Kurt takes a drink and puts a handful in his mouth. "You asked for Hal Oliphant. What do you want?"

Kurt flushes. "It's hard to explain."

"No it isn't." She is looking at his arm: the wrist.

"It's nothing." Embarrassed, he hides it between his knees.

"Yes it is." Her face is changing. Rimmed by shadow the same color as the flowers in her shirt and heavy with mascara as they are, her eyes brim. Her mouth quivers; she's about to tell him more than he wants to hear. "It's Hal. He's hurt you too."

"No." Kurt had never met the guy. But without Hal Oliphant there would have been no Zane and no explosion and no Vivian, nothing about loving Vivian, so you might say it was Hal who changed his life. "Not exactly." Then Kurt flashes on Hal and his own mother, her dead and him walking away from the wreck, and he's burned by tears he can't help. His mouth is quivering too; he knows he'd better shut up but he blurts, "Yes."

"It's OK," she says. "I know the look. I saw it in Mildred's eyes, she was his first wife?"

"She wasn't his first wife."

This doesn't surprise her. "Whatever."

"She was at least the second."

"Third, eighth, she had the look. I thought it was because Hal loved me and not her. Do you believe that? Just goes to show how charming he was. How convincing he could be." She squeezes her eyes shut as if to keep him out. "Is. And then one morning, after . . ." Whatever he did, she can't or won't spell it out.

"After what?"

"I can't." Her voice is getting thin. "Not yet." Carefully put together as she looks with her perfect makeup and big hair, Veda Faller is no sounder than Kurt. They both sit there for a long time and then she finishes with a brave little lilt, "But I got over it. At least I thought I did. And then one day I looked in the mirror and I had it. The damaged look. Like you."

"There's nothing the matter with me."

This makes her angry. "I may look all right to you, kid, but I'll admit right now there's something terribly the matter with me, and you're welcome to get up and walk out of here right this minute if you aren't willing to admit there's something the matter with you."

He'd like to get up. He'd like to excuse himself and go, anything to escape her scrutiny, but he can't quite move. "I can't."

"I can't tell you where Hal is," she says as if he's asked, "but I can sure as hell tell you what you're looking for."

So he sits in her neat little brocaded chair in that perfect living room with his hand on the water glass and his wrist clamped between his knees and listens.

"I married Hal Oliphant five years ago," she says. "He and Mildred came into the dance class I was teaching at the time and he swept me off my feet. Too bad about Mildred, he said she didn't understand him; he said she was insanely jealous; he said she was losing her mind. He could tell you anything and you'd believe. At the beginning we were very happy," she says. "We went out at night and came home and hugged and lay down together and laughed and hummed, and everything was fine except for Mildred's phone calls, you know, his ex-wife? She called at night when he wasn't here and she'd always say, Aren't you wondering why he isn't there? I thought she was crazy, that's all, when all the time she was trying to warn me, but you want to know the truth?"

She's pulled her chair up so they're almost knee to knee. "Even if she'd spelled it out—what he'd done to her, what he was really like, I wasn't ready to see. I was too much in love, you know? He charmed."

Kurt flashes on the twins playing underneath his window— gracious, lovely; when they caught him watching, they looked up with those sweet smiles and raised their hands in identical waves.

She sighs. "He had all that charm." She lapses for a moment, reflecting, and then with a little *hah,* resumes. "Oh, God if I'd only listened to her! If she'd only listened to the one before! The calls I wouldn't listen to were only the first sign. Next came voices in the night. I used to wake up and hear him in the bathroom, talking, but to who? I never knew. Sometimes he seemed to be arguing with himself, man to man but other times I thought I heard a child's voice, I think it was a little boy's, it was strange, but I loved him and he never mentioned it, so I never asked.

"And then one day I picked up the phone and heard him on the extension with a woman—not Mildred, somebody young, and she was giggling, these strange things started turning up in the laundry, once a handkerchief with lace edges, another time a woman's blouse and when I asked him about it he said it must have come back from the cleaners with our stuff, he was sure it was a mistake but there was a price tag still on it—strange! And all the time there were these voices in the night . . . And me? I was so much in love that I just dreamed along, OK Hal, OK, OK fine."

He says, "Are you all right?"

"I'm fine." She shakes her head as if she can make the tears fly away for good. "You know, when you take a man into your life you're always taking in a puzzle and an enigma, but lord, I never expected to find my gold tank watch missing, or go into my jewel box and discover my grandmother's diamond earrings gone, any more than I wanted to believe there were strange things in the laundry, a perfume, not mine, coming from his dress shirts, lipstick on his undershirts and in the night these voices. You want to know what I thought? I told myself, 'There must be some explanation,' like a fool I thought: This must be a mistake. And you want to know the worst thing?"

Kurt discovers he can't speak.

Her voice drops an octave. "I thought, oh dear, it must be something I did." This leaves her angry and ashamed. She doesn't want him to see her face crumble so lowers her head, leaving him to study her burnished, indestructible hair.

"You know how it is when you're in love with a man, you think he's so perfect, you don't want to hear one bad word. Well I'm here to tell, love doesn't only make you blind. It makes you deaf and dumb. Especially dumb. There I was seeing these signs and dodging these crazy phone calls from Mildred and strange girls who wouldn't give their names; I didn't want to hear. Hal wasn't home much but when he was, the voices got louder and louder so we could never sleep through any night and then the police came— something stolen from a store—a leather case I had found in the top of our closet the day before. I thought Hal had bought it to surprise me and yes he was drinking and yes the money was leaking from our account and yes I still loved him, I loved him even after he stayed away for three days and never even called. When he came back that time there was blood on the right front fender of the Mercedes and I believed him when he said a cat had run in front of the car. His voices seemed to bleed over into the daytime, I could come into any room and hear them but if I knocked or called, they stopped, and then one night . . ." She can't stop gasping.

Kurt says gently, "It's OK. If it makes you feel bad to talk about it, stop."

She shakes her head. "I can't."

"And then one night . . ." It takes her a minute to control her breath but she manages finally. "I woke up and they were talking in our room. In our bed." She looks at him as if this explains everything. "So now you understand."

"You haven't exactly told me who."

"Who was talking? I didn't know at first. It was dark. I was scared. I thought he was having a nightmare so I turned on the light. There was nobody in bed with us. But there were voices, Hal and this—*other* were arguing as if they'd been at it ever since we went to bed and turned out the light."

"Who?" Kurt leans forward as if he expects to hear her say it was Zane.

"I don't know. I've thought about it and thought about it and I still don't know. Hal, of course, but more than Hal, this *other,* and I don't know whether it was some split personality thing or if he was possessed or what. 'Evan,' he kept saying, my Hal, my husband *that I thought I knew,* 'God damn you, go away,' and this other voice kept coming back, 'I can't,' and Hal sounded so savage that I thought hell had opened up and vomited monsters on our bed, he was screaming, 'Go away and leave me Evan, I've had enough!' and first it answered in a child's voice, 'It isn't me, it's what you did,' and when he started screaming 'I didn't do anything,' it answered in a man's voice, it was coming out of Hal but it wasn't coming out of Hal, 'I am the victim and the proof,' it sounded so *sad,* 'you have to stop.' Then Hal screamed, 'Leave me alone,' he was rocking the bed like somebody falling into a fit. The man's voice said, 'I won't let you kill any more,' and Hal was thrashing and my God, I should have seen it coming but I couldn't, I was too busy trying to shake him out of the nightmare; I tried so hard; he was grappling with the enemy by that time, trying to throttle it and he was shouting, 'Get out or I'll kill you again.' "

Stunned by the significance, she repeats. "Again! Did you hear that. He said, 'Again.' "

Not even being aware of what he's doing, Kurt touches her cheek with his stump. He is asking, not telling. "He killed his twin."

She gasps to keep from sobbing. "I don't know who he killed; he was screaming and fighting and then . . ." She is on the brink now but determined, the narrative so fluid that Kurt can't quite follow, "And then they talk so fast I can't tell what they're saying and Hal is vicious, pounding the woman to a pulp."

It's strange; forced to talk about the unspeakable, she flows into third person as if the terrible scene she is recounting is happening to somebody else. "The poor woman can feel his teeth closing on the blade of her hand and grinding in, he is all flying knees and nails and elbows and fists hammering until she is crying for mercy OH HAL PLEASE DON'T, the woman is writhing to get away and Hal is screaming, I'VE GOT YOU NOW. IF I HAVE TO KILL YOU AGAIN I'M GOING TO KILL YOU TWICE and he almost does before she struggles away and falls off the bed and rolls all the way underneath into the middle where he can't reach her and she stays there until morning when he leaves the house and it's safe for the woman to drag herself out . . .

"She calls the police and has all the locks changed and I don't know who Hal killed or who he thought he was killing but the woman lived even though he beat her half to death, and it took doctors months but she recovered, or the outside of her did. She lived in spite of everything he did to her and when she got away from Hal Oliphant that night she heard him howling, it was dreadful, terrible, MY GOD HOW MUCH I HATE YOU, and in the last second before she tore free he looked into the face of his victim *this poor woman* without even seeing and all the time, oh God . . ."

Her voice gets so small that Kurt has to stand and lean close to be certain that she's actually still breathing, and it is leaning close like this that he hears the last, the worst, part, Veda Faller, who behind her reconstructed and carefully polished face is forming the words she finally exhales—"The woman . . .

"It was me."

It is later, sitting together over canned cream of tomato soup and bran toaster cake and a Jello-O salad at the gold-flecked Formica kitchen table, they are mending. Her recital has bonded them, and in the same spirit of giving, Kurt has given back. He's told her more than he's ever told anybody, even Billy, whom he loves. Softened by the way she fussed over him, strangely touched by the sprig of mint floating on his soup, he just started talking and found it hard to stop.

He's told her almost everything he knows. Starting with Zane, he told her about what happened to his hand. Open to her as he was, he skipped the next part, going on to Vivian's death, Steve's accident. If he doesn't tell her about him and Vivian, if he can't talk about what happened when Zane found out, he's sorry, but he can't. He thinks about it all the time but he doesn't want to. He doesn't like to talk about it at all.

Instead he cuts to the chase. Leaning over the tiny table, he tells Veda Faller about the Archer twins. "I don't know what's going on with them," he says finally, "I can't name this—I don't know—*dark thing* I think I see, but, whatever it is . . . I think it's the same thing that was going on with Hal."

Her voice is shaking. "Some family curse."

"I don't think so. I don't know what it is. Something about . . ."

She speaks, so they finish the thought in unison, ". . . about being twins."

"Paired."

"Driven." She's looking at something he can't see. "Separated but never separate."

"Too close. Good and bad."

It is almost as though they are engaged in a meditation, or litany; she finishes for him, "No way to know which is which."

Mesmerized by the progression, he murmurs, "No way to sort them out."

She finishes, "No way to sort anything out."

For a moment, they don't speak. Then she says, out of a profound hush, "I think Hal killed his twin brother."

Kurt hears a click. "Yes." He's not surprised.

"And the voice in the bed . . ."

"Yes?"

"I didn't recognize all the voices in the bed. Some low, some high . . ."

"And the Archer twins are his granddaughters." When he lays out his fears, she's not surprised.

"These children. Where are they?"

"Not far from here. A town named Jenkins? Their grandmother has passed them on to somebody new. A woman named Carroll Lawton. She was married to their father. When she took them nobody warned her," he says.

"Oh dear," she says. "I hope she's up to it."

"Her husband just died. Right now I don't think she's up to much of anything."

"That poor girl." She touches her face and without having to be told, Kurt knows she is tracing the invisible scars of one of the old injuries. "You'd better see about it."

"I know."

As he gets up, she stands. "You'd better see about it now."

On his feet, he's surprised to discover that in spite of the food, in spite of all her kindness, he's still unsteady. "These kids," he tells her, "they're so pretty."

"Like Hal."

"They're amazing."

"Hal's charm. He could make you do anything for him."

"The charm. So until you see it at work, you don't believe it. There's no way for anybody to know. I just don't." He breaks off. "I don't know if I can make her believe me. That's why . . ."

"It's why you came looking for Hal."

"Oh look, I am so sorry."

"I'm sorry Hal isn't here." She studies him for a minute, considering. Then she shakes her head. "I. Oh dear. There isn't time. These children. Something could happen." Then she corrects herself, striking echoes that frighten Kurt more than anything else she could have found to say. "Anything could happen," she says.

"You know where he is, don't you?"

"He's a long way away," she says. "Tennessee. There isn't time to get there and back before . . ."

"Tennessee." His head swims at the idea of another plane trip. His stomach lunges like a bucking horse. Getting this far almost did him in. "Maybe you're right." Even though all his parts are moving, worry keeps him planted here; he doesn't know how to sum it up. "What am I going to do?"

Reluctantly, Veda Faller reaches the point they've been approaching. "Your last chance is probably Hal."

So at last Hal Oliphant's ex-wife gives him the information he came for. "After—after what happened to me, I pressed charges. I went to the hearing with my face still bandaged up. My throat was so raw I could hardly talk. I couldn't get Hal convicted for what he is, they said he would always be too crazy to stand trial. I couldn't send him to jail, but I got him put away. It's a private institution." She pulls one of the cards out of the mirror by the door. As she hands it to Kurt, she surprises him with a hug. His last impression of her is of one of those funny old-fashioned brassieres poking at him through her silky shirt like a pair of empty twenty-inch shells.

24

THE MEDICAL EXAMINER is so backed up that he can't get to the death at the Gateway Mall until Friday morning. Thursday's preliminary examination showed no signs of foul play so except for the victim's youth there are no apparent anomalies—nothing significant to push this case to the top of the priority list. He will dictate his report into a Perlcorder and the clerk who transcribes his tapes won't fax them to Jenkins until near noon. By the time the report on the late Edward Middleton reaches the local police chief's desk Carroll will be deep in another story, a drowning.

The hall phone wakes her shortly after dawn. She staggers out and throws herself on it before the ringing can bring Peyton out to study her in her pajamas or wake the twins. The sleep-drugged part of her can't stop thinking: *Steve.* It's Charley. "Oh, hi. Early!"

"Something's come up."

There it is again—that surge of electricity. "Great!" Greedy for the story, Carroll crouches over the receiver, stroking it as if she can coax details out of thin air. Charley's augmented Walkman picks up the police band and he heard what little he knows while he was out running. She's all over him with questions but he only knows what he knows. As soon as he hangs up she calls Lacy Cotwell at the police station. She's done Lacy favors over the years, which Lacy returns by keeping Carroll informed. At first glimpse this death at the beach looks like natural causes, Lacy says, but, she adds, there are a couple of things . . .

"Like?"

"That's all I can say, OK?"

Carroll dresses in seconds and heads for the scene.

Clipping a PRESS sign to her sun visor in case she gets pulled over, she manages the drive to the beach in half the time. No matter how fast she drives, she isn't going to catch up with her racing imagination. A part of her is always running after—what: The Big Story. The story she was born to write.

Somewhere deep the ambitious part of Carroll is already looking for a pattern. If her luck has turned, today's death will have something in common with yesterday's, some thread that suggests that there's more going on here than other news people see. She wants to be the first. If this is murder and she can break the story, she just may be able to live with herself.

Writing about sudden death, she can move on. If she can't replace Steve, she has to find a way to live without him—as the toughest reporter who ever walked. The next time she leaves Jenkins it's going to be for a reporting job in Miami or Washington. She'll be the best crime writer since Edna Buchanan of the Miami *Herald*. If she can just write about enough murders, if she can make herself isolate the ugliest details and get them down in stark, uncompromising terms, maybe it will help her get over Steve's death and make her tough. She'll get strong enough to handle anything, even the fact that she's ripped wide open every time she reaches out in the night and collides with that empty place in the bed.

Two deaths isn't exactly a pattern, but it's a start. This second body washed up on the beach in the night. Lacy told her it was a white male identified as Lanny Raynor, an out-of-work beach regular who always staked out his blanket in this area after he finished his daily walk. The difference this time was that Lanny was on the beach well before dawn and he was lying face down in the swash. The first beach patrol of the morning found the body. Like the one at the mall, it bore no traces of violence, no lacerations, no tissue insult, nothing to suggest the victim died an unnatural death. It was middle-aged, fit and remarkably well muscled, which presented a puzzle. If a cramp hadn't gotten Lanny, what had? He was in shape; he worked out. He was strong enough to make it back even if he got caught in deep water, and if there was no getting back he was certainly fit enough to hold out until the guard in the tower or other swimmers or one of the half-dozen of windsurfers spotted him. Unless a riptide snagged him and held him under until his lungs filled and it was too late.

Whatever happened, nobody saw. Even the lifeguards reported nothing unusual.

If the ocean didn't get him, what did?

She parks in the beach parking lot and without wasting time taking her shoes off, goes crunching through the sand. The whole scene is unfolding just beyond the dunes where she can't see. It's like one of those dreams where you run and run and find yourself mired in the same place. Cursing the long drive, she is aware that she spent too long on the phone with Lacy; it took her too long to get here; it's taking her too long to wade through the deep sand now and too long to catch up with her story. Since Charley first called the sun has climbed into position; the color of the morning sky has gone from pink to silvery white and the top of her head is getting hot.

By the time Carroll finally reaches the spot where the body washed up, the coroner's wagon has come and gone. She sees the tire tracks crumbling; in some places beach walkers have already trampled the marks, effacing them. The police are gone and the last onlookers are drifting away. She wants to question them but like criminals dodging TV cameras, they cover their heads with their windbreakers and hurry by. The old couple she does manage to stop has nothing to say. The old man blinks at her from under the bill of his baseball hat; his wife is so indignant that the flowers on her straw sunhat are bobbing. "Death and dying. Is that all you reporters can think about?"

Carroll thinks but does not say, *Yes ma'am.*

"Why can't you write a story about how pretty the beach is, or how nice it is for the young people to have a beautiful, healthy place to come and play?"

"Yes ma'am." Carroll pretends to scribble in her notebook. "Thank you ma'am."

As she approaches his tower, the lifeguard ambles down

to make certain she spells his name right. "LoBelle," he says. "That's Robert LoBelle. I'm a senior at Tufts."

"And the—guy who drowned?"

"Believe me, he didn't do it on my shift. As a matter of fact they don't know when he did do it. Nobody reported anybody in trouble, nobody saw any swimmers beyond the buoys."

"I mean, what can you tell me?"

"This Lanny Raynor? He lived at the Y." The guard is earnest and bulky in his orange T-shirt. His face is smeared with zinc oxide and under the orange pith helmet he has the classic long-distance squint. He looks like an extra in a beach blanket movie; the difference is that this time it's a murder mystery.

When he doesn't go on, she doesn't speak. A clever reporter, she pretends to be absorbed in her notebook; when she does this right, she disappears. It makes people start talking just to fill the empty space.

The guard muses. "He was kind of a scuzzball, if you want to know the truth."

"Uh-huh." She keeps her head down. Think of me as your psychiatrist.

"In a way, it kind of serves him right," the lifeguard says thoughtfully. "He was one of your local beach creeps. He's what we call a heavy cruiser. Looks for the youngest and tenderest and picks them up, and after that, who knows? Whatever he does to them, we've never been able to catch him at it—he's too smooth—and we can warn the girls about him but they don't believe us, so that's all we can do. And none of the girls ever files a complaint." He muses. "Maybe they were asking for it."

Carroll wheels on him in an angry flash. "What makes you think victims want to be victims?"

"Sorry."

She can't stop. "What makes you think you know anything at all?"

"I said I was sorry, now back off!"

Mistake, she realizes. She's strung tighter than she thought. "When was the last time you saw him?"

"Yesterday, I guess, but if he made a pickup yesterday, it wasn't on my shift."

Carroll's mind is already scurrying: interview the hall-mates at the Y to find out if Lanny had a history, check the police books for prior arrests. With guys like this around, she's glad the girls are safe in school today. "What do you think killed him?"

The lifeguard shrugs. "He could of O.D.'d. He could of had one of those heart attacks you get from too much blow."

This brings her up short. "He was a user?"

"Lady, I don't know."

"Are there a lot of drugs on the beach?"

"Ma'am, there are a lot of drugs everywhere."

Make a note, she thinks. Ask Lacy about drug arrests. Do a series about how they handle drug problems at the beach. She makes another note: warn the twins. They're good girls, but there are things they need to know about survival here. It makes her feel marginally better, having somebody to care about. That may even care about her. She's been through too much with Steve's daughters to let anything bad happen to them. "Thanks."

"That's Lo, not La, like Patty. L-O-B-E-L-L-E."

Stopping at an outdoor phone, she calls Charley with what she has. "Terrific," he says. "I think I want to banner the story. Second Mysterious Death."

"We don't know yet that they're both mysterious."

"I sent Russell up to the coroner's office, and he . . ."

"You sent *Russell!* This is my story."

"Well you can't be in two places at once."

"What do you have him doing, backing me up?"

"Relax, I've got him waiting for the Raynor report. He called in about the other one, the guy from the Gateway Mall?"

"What does he have?" As they talk, she looks back toward the dunes. The sun is climbing; the breeze stirs the sea oats and two children on the path start fighting over a plastic bucket. The day is going on as if nothing had happened and here she is, strung out because she's afraid Russell will get something on this before she does. Then she and Russell will share the byline, unless she ends up in a slug at the bottom, "Additional reporting done by . . ." She can't have this. She won't. "Come on, Charley. Speak."

"Be cool, the coroner won't talk to him. But he overheard something." Charley sounds wired too. "There's something."

"What?"

"Some anomaly."

"Anomaly!" As soon as she hangs up she'll call the coroner. So it surfaces and takes over—the old excitement. *Good story*. Somebody's dead, but, hey. "I'll get right on it," she says.

Between calls to the coroner's office, she looks for people who knew the victims. Because the gym is near the beach, she starts with Lanny Raynor. Stringy and weatherbeaten, his acquaintances don't look particularly pumped up. They look sad, polite, like people who have been sitting in one of life's waiting rooms too long without ever being called. They tell her how many pounds Lanny could press and how far he ran when he was training. Anxious to please, they keep dribbling banalities with one eye on her notebook, which means she has to write down quotes too dull to use. Even the owner responds with a shrug. Back in Jenkins she goes to the Y but the teenager on the desk says it's too bad and the two hallmates she can collar eye her suspiciously: girl, they think. Girl with a notebook. You have your nerve; they sniff and turn away.

Carroll can't figure out whether Raynor was the kind of man people don't want to talk about or whether, worse yet, there's not much to say about him.

There are even fewer people who know Edward Middleton—no relatives in town, no friends that she can find; he was one of those colorless guys who slide through life without leaving a mark. Only his employer seems to know him.

"He was a nice enough guy. I liked working with him because he didn't have any rough edges." He shrugs. "If you want to know the truth, he didn't have any edges at all." He tells her Middleton was dating a teller from the bank across the street. "He thought it was a *thing*, but it wasn't anything."

Standing just inside the bank door for so long the guard gets suspicious, Carroll studies the teller. Seen from a distance like this, she looks faintly familiar; context, Carroll thinks—supermarket, maybe, or cruising the local Marshall's, or T.J. Maxx. "Sally Schultz?"

The pretty, indifferent teller blinks as Carroll asks delicately if she minds talking about Edward Middleton. "Oh," she says, "no problem." Sally adds hastily, "I felt terrible when I read about it in the paper."

Carroll looks deep and understands that she doesn't feel terrible. She probably hardly knew him. Scraped raw by her own loss, she says anyway, "I'm so sorry."

"It's OK." Confronted with a death, Sally Schultz seems unsure of her obligation but she seems to think she has one. "You know what's sad about it? I was supposed to go out with him the other night, and I blew him off? Like, if I'd known anything bad was going to happen to him, at least I would have, you know, said goodbye nicely, you know?"

When Carroll comes into the station her friend Lacy hands her the coroner's report on Middleton. There is indeed an anomaly. The cause of death was trauma to the brain. The coroner found a tiny puncture wound under the hairline at the base of the skull.

Lacy says, "We haven't had one of these for a long time."

"Puncture wounds?"

"Oh, we've never had one of those. I mean murders." Lacy is scowling as though she doesn't know whether to be scared or not. "Drive-by shootings, maybe, a couple of drug deaths, but not something like this." She looks up. "It's like the person, you know, *thought it out.*"

"How would somebody know you could kill a man like that?"

"Movies," Lacy says. "Or TV. The air is filled with these things. You can learn eight million ways of killing a guy, just by watching TV." She adds, "Plus, our people didn't find any prints in the car except for this poor jerk's."

It's strange, Carroll thinks as she tries her source at the

county medical examiner's office one more time. He's nice enough but she knows he's stonewalling her. It's frustrating, like being told Waldo is buried in a plate of spaghetti that's so drenched in sauce that there's no way of knowing where to start looking.

At six she cruises the station one more time and comes up empty. Sure she can look at the Middleton report again but the chief of detectives refuses to speculate and nobody wants to talk about Lanny Raynor. As far as public record is concerned, it's still an accidental drowning. Nobody's willing to say otherwise and nobody will admit the two deaths are linked. The detective in charge is so bent on keeping what they know a secret that he doesn't even tell her that the Raynor report is in. She's on her way out of the office when Lacy Cotwell clears her throat wetly. Carroll turns to see Lacy blinking so rapidly that she's afraid her friend is about to faint. Instead Lacy puffs out her cheeks like a bird trying to warn away attackers and rattles her nails on the clutch of manila folders she's carrying.

Carroll drifts closer.

Squinting significantly, Lacy fans the folders so Carroll can read the tabs. RAYNOR, one says. Then she shrugs and heads into the chief's office. She's given Carroll everything she can.

OK, Carroll thinks. It's late; Charley's waiting but she lingers long enough to pounce on the chief as he leaves his office to go to the bathroom. He's one of those good old boys who prefers to believe that no matter how bright she is, a slight woman is just a little girl. "I understand the Raynor report is in."

"Oh, that," he says easily. "What makes you think . . ."

"I saw it."

"Right. Well it's closed right now, OK?" His broad, earnest face is bland and studiously empty. "All in good time, OK?"

"Come on, Hank. I'm on deadline."

"You don't want to see this stuff, which fish nibbled which parts off the body." He grins. "Not a nice girl like you."

She snaps back: "I'm not a girl, I'm a reporter. What was the cause of death?"

His face closes. "I'm not at liberty to say."

"Is there anything that links this to the Middleton case?"

They are at the bathroom door now; he maneuvers her out and himself in and as he slams and latches the door he says, "I'm not at liberty to say."

By the time she files her story the paper is closed except for the right-hand column on the front page, which Charley has saved for her. Except for Charley, she's the last one in the newsroom. Dinnertime has come and gone but she's too pressed to remember whether she ate. Russell called in an hour ago to report he'd come up empty, which she notes with a grim little smile because she doesn't have much. Beyond the bare details she has only the quotes from Middleton's boss and his erstwhile girlfriend Sally; she weaves in the more presentable quotes from Raynor's friends and after consulting with Charley doubles back and rewrites the lead.

The new lead does not link the deaths, exactly, but describes them as the first two sudden deaths in the Jenkins area since a drug shootout in March. Charley won't let her cite Lanny Raynor's arrests for possession because at the moment he's only a drowning victim, whose record isn't relevant. Instead she calls the chief of lifeguards at the beach so she can fill with descriptions of undertows and riptides in the area and the guard's warning to swimmers to stay in the guarded areas and never go out beyond the floats. The story carries her byline with nothing from Russell, which takes out a little of the sting.

It isn't a bad story. The details make her wish she had more details. Edward Middleton of Jenkins, found dead in his car at the far end of the Gateway Mall parking lot early Thursday, was an apparent victim of murder, according to the county medical examiner. According to police the weapon was a long, sharp instrument smaller than an ice pick but longer and heavier than an ordinary needle, causing immediate and fatal trauma to the brain. Middleton leaves no survivors.

* * *

How awful, Carroll thinks, to die like that, alone, so that when you go, you aren't much missed. Driving home late, sour-mouthed and empty after a day of digging that has yielded scant details and unprintable innuendo, she broods over the dead.

Two single guys with no survivors. How sad it must be to die with nobody left behind to care. How terrible to sink beneath the surface without a trace. Two people without families, without *lives* as far as she can tell, two men with no living parents, no true lovers and as nearly as she can make out, no children to care when they don't come home tonight and tomorrow and the next day—two lifetimes spent with nothing left behind to mark the place.

She can hardly wait to see the twins. She hopes they haven't already eaten. She'd like to take them out to dinner at some nice place and forget all this. She wants people in the restaurant to look at them and think: What a nice family.

Her heart skips a groove. *Family.*

She'll be cool about it, she'll let the girls have their lives and try not to be voracious; after all, she has her life. No. She has her career. She doesn't want to hover but she's touched by their trust and grateful for their attention. She'll hold the twins loosely in order to keep them, sitting in the front row at recitals and graduations knowing that there will in fact be somebody left behind to mourn if she falls off a cliff or gets knocked out of her socks by a truck.

Approaching the house on Arbor Street she sees them on the porch, sitting with their feet propped and their smooth blonde heads shining under the yellow light. She leaves the car out front and hurries up the steps. "So glad to *see* you." She hesitates on the top step, waiting for them to speak. "Emily? Jane?"

They regard her with eyes so bright they look almost feverish—too much sun, she tells herself. They're dressed in pale blue cotton sundresses tonight, simple lines that fall straight from their sunburned shoulders, probably something picked out by 'Laine to match their eyes. The arms of their big rockers are pushed close to support a box of chocolates and they turn pink sunburned faces to greet her with big brown melted-chocolate smiles.

"Hey, I'm so sorry I'm late!"

"Hi Carroll," Jane says through caramel.

"Hi Carroll," Emily says.

She's getting better at telling them apart; she's sure she is. It isn't just the rings. Jane has a little comic twist to her smile and Emily looks slightly more serious—something around the eyes. "I didn't want to be late but I got hung up on this story?" She thinks it's better to spare them the details. "Did you kids have a good day?"

They smile secretive smiles. "It was OK."

Her heart bounds ahead of her. Do you need anything, do you want anything, what do you want that I can give you? "Are you having a good time here?"

They nod. God, how she wants to please them!

It's late. She sees Patsy has been here ahead of her with candy. "I suppose you've already had dinner."

"Not really," Jane says.

"You haven't eaten? You must be starving!"

"Not really." Emily gives her a beautiful chocolate smile.

"You should have eaten." Fine surrogate mom she is, letting them go hungry. "You should have had dinner by now."

Jane shrugs. "We got home late from the beach."

"The beach!" Lanny Raynor's life flashes before her eyes. She has so much to tell them before they can go back to the beach! "I thought you were supposed to be at school."

"We were, but we got out early."

"We got early and the boys took us."

This turns her around. "What boys?"

"From school."

"Aunt 'Laine said it was all right."

"But she was mad when we came home late."

"Wait a minute." Carroll remembers herself at that age, hitchhiking. But things were different. The beach wasn't quite as harsh. "You didn't hitch, did you?"

"Oh no."

"Not really." They study their nails.

"How did you get home?"

Emily goes on as if she's answering, which she isn't. "Then Peyton and Suzy wanted to take us out to dinner . . ."

"You mean Uncle Peyton and Aunt Suzy?"

Jane has a funny, entitled air. "They want to be just Peyton and Suzy to us. You know, friends."

"Right, Carroll. Like, friends." Em's little scowl suggests Carroll had better lay back if she wants to stay friends. "So Peyton and Suzy wanted to take us out to dinner but Aunt 'Laine had already cooked her special chicken pie and she got mad plus Aunt Patsy was mad because they didn't want to take her out with us and things got worse and I don't know . . ."

Jane finishes with a smirk. "They're in there having a fight." Emily's smirk signals trouble elsewhere and the superiority that comes with not being involved. "They've been fighting for an hour."

Carroll sighs. "I know what that's like." Her aunts and her uncle fight like tired children, they've been fighting together ever since they were little and even their arguments are stale. They say all the same things and stamp off to the same old corners of the house. She of all people ought to know. She can hear the familiar buzz; it's as if the whole house has been whining for years. Sometimes the whining gets a little louder, that's all. Suzy and Patsy and Peyton have been fighting for so long that they fall into all the same old patterns—one on one in various combinations until finally in spite of everything 'Laine gets pulled into the tangle. Carroll has tried to deal with this and can't. She most especially can't deal with it tonight. It's like trying to separate the tigers after they've melted into butter, nobody alive can stop them streaming in an unending circle around the bottom of the tree and no power on earth can sort them out. "And the whole time you two are out here starving."

"It wasn't our fault," Emily says hastily and Jane confirms it. "It wasn't our fault."

"Of course it wasn't your fault," Carroll says. Inside somewhere the relatives are fighting; it's more than she can face right now. "Come on," she says, "let's go out and eat."

"Someplace nice?"

"Someplace really nice."

So it's sweet to be sitting there across the table from her girls in the nearly deserted Yacht Club, watching the waitresses fuss and the chef come out to ask how they liked the bluefish, and it was sweet seeing heads turn as they came out through the bar although Carroll can't for the life of her say whether they look like guardian and lovely young charges or three friends. She may be imagining it but it seems to her as though the twins have matured in the few days they've been with her, so that the eyes that follow them may register three women passing, one not bad looking and the other two extraordinary, gorgeous and perfectly matched and in spite of their youth so fully formed that they could be any age.

Coming back from the restaurant one says, "Oh, we forgot to tell you, Aunt 'Laine said be sure and say you had a phone call."

"Was it from the office? Was it the coroner?"

The other says quickly, "He didn't leave his name."

"You're sure it wasn't Sam."

"Not really."

The coroner is an old friend; Sam would have left his name. Uneasy, she asks, "Then whoever it was—did he leave a number?"

"I don't know. I think so. Probably it's too late to call."

"Jane's right, it's probably too late to call."

"You wouldn't want to wake him up."

"If it's the coroner . . ."

"It wasn't the coroner."

"Really. You wouldn't want to call the wrong person."

"If it's the paper I have to . . ."

"Besides, he said it wasn't important."

"He told Aunt 'Laine he'd try again in the morning."

"It's really too late to call."

"Right," Carroll says with relief. "It's too late to make any calls."

She's glad. When they get back everybody else has gone to bed. They have the family room to themselves. The girls

watch TV without any other light on and Carroll finds she
likes this too; it turns the room into a cave, safe as a nest
with the three of them gathered around the electronic fire.
Sitting on the sofa with one girl on either side she is bold
enough to put an arm around each and pull them to her in a
hug. They don't resist; instead they flow against her as if
they've made a pact to do everything she wants. The human
contact is like a little shock. She can taste her tears. Their
slender bodies are warm and fragrant; their hair flies around
her face like silk and she hears herself saying again, "I'm so
glad you're here."

One gives a little sigh that sounds somehow snug,
protected, and the other says, "We are too."

One of the twins touches the remote and they find
themselves watching the TV with the sound off so that it
seems easy for Carroll to say, "Look. Kids. I was in your
rooms, back there in California? Everything was so . . ."
For a minute words desert her. Finally she manages,
"Special. I . . . I mean you had a lot of really nice stuff. It
looked like—some kind of castle?"

"A kingdom," Jane says, pulling out of Carroll's embrace
even as Emily collects herself and withdraws.

"Our kingdom," Emily says.

"It's—it was . . ." They are at a delicate point. If she
stampedes them they won't tell her anything. Therefore
she's up against it—what she thinks, no, thought about that
cluttered and slightly spooky place when she first saw it and
what she thinks about it now. She treads carefully, trying to
creep into their secret life before they can shut her out for
good. "Beautiful. Like nothing I've ever seen." Bemused,
she smiles. "All those glass ornaments, the beautiful fabric
you used everywhere, and the pictures. The toys." When she
first looked into the place it was creepy; now with the girls
flanking her, it seems magical. "Where did you get all those
wonderful toys?"

"We picked them out," Em says.

"We did. And anything we didn't like . . ."

"We threw away."

"No. We gave it to Grandmother for the needy."

"I see. Well you have . . ." How to approach it? Through flattery. "You both have a perfect eye for what looks right."

A ripple passes through her: the girls agreeing. "Yes, we do."

"And all that—imagination." She is hushed. "You had whole stories written on the walls . . ."

"Our novels." Who speaks? In the dark like this they sound so much alike that there is no telling.

The other makes a slight alteration in the text. "Records of the kingdom."

"Records. Yes. Records."

"Special," Em says, sliding closer.

Jane snuggles. "Our place."

They both say, "Our lives."

"Next to that, this place doesn't look like much." Carroll's voice is furrier than she intended. God, am I making some kind of mistake, keeping them here when they have all that wonderful stuff at home in California? "You must miss it a lot."

The girls seem to sense that she's unsure of herself because they wriggle closer. "No problem," Jane murmurs.

Em says dreamily, "We'll get back to it."

For the first time in a week Carroll feels snug again—surrounded, maybe even loved. Because it's dark and they can't really see each other's faces she says, "Your grandmother—I don't know—I don't know if she's going to let you go back."

"Not go back," Em says. Now she sounds more deliberate.

Jane says, "We don't need to."

"But your kingdom!" She's thinking, you poor sad kids, your parents, your lives!

"It's OK."

"It is." They answer so fast that their voices twine and she can't tell whether one or both of the girls say the next thing. What she does note is the steel-under-velvet quality of their resolution; they could be vanquished generals, marching out of the territory. "Not go back."

"No. Not go back. We're going to get it back."

She is thrown back on herself, at ten, in exile. She loves them for being so brave.

They sit for a long time while the girls think their own thoughts, whether on the same path or widely diverging ones she doesn't know, and Carroll reflects on the brief glimpse she had into their kingdom, the ranks of stuffed toys, the regiments of dolls, every figure and every object disposed according to a pattern that even now she can't divine. What were they doing there, cloistered amid their ranked playthings? What do they think they're going to do now? Brave, she thinks. They're wrecked by the loss of their parents and they're doing everything they can to be brave. She tries, "I'm so glad you don't mind being stuck here with me."

One last time they hug and snuggle. "We don't, really."

"We like it here."

"We're having fun."

"We are."

"I'm so glad," Carroll says. She kept going today on the big story, or the illusion of the big story, and she kept going after that for the sake of the orphaned girls. Now in a strange way they are giving back more than she has to give to them—company, distraction from her pain. Solace, she supposes. She has the illusion that she and the girls are in this *together*, bereft and mending, safe for the moment on this old sofa that bobs like a life raft through the seas of loss. She wishes she could sit here with the twins all night and not have to say good night and drag herself upstairs to her miserable empty bed.

Next to her, Emily yawns and stretches and Jane kneads the arm of the overstuffed sofa like a cat and she too stretches silkily.

Then suddenly the twins get up, so abrupt that Carroll sits there, bemused and cooling, long after the girls brush their lips across her cheeks in a polite good night and excuse themselves, saying in chorus:

"It's late."

Startled, Carroll says, "I guess it is." It is. It's half-past

Arsenio. She's exhausted and reluctant to go upstairs because she's scared of being alone in bed.

At the door Jane says, "It's late and we have things to do."

Em echoes, "Things to do."

"If you want," she offers, "I'll make popcorn. We can watch a tape."

"We can't."

"It's late and we can't."

There is a subtext: We have *things* to do.

Loneliness makes Carroll craven. "It's OK, tomorrow is Saturday, you can sleep as late as you want."

"Too much to do tomorrow. So, night, Carroll."

"Tomorrow, yes. Night, Carroll, OK?"

Like dutiful children, they back out.

Loosely, Carroll reminds herself. She feels like a mother parting with her young for the first time. Hold them loosely and you can keep them all your life.

25

—NICE UP HERE in this nummy secret place we make for us, little gold chairs we pulled into this room from the attic jumble, lovely prayer rugs and fringed pillows and naked statues from dusty places under the gables; we have marble-topped tables. Next, we fix the throne room. Then we bring our gorgeous knights and it is perfect. If we don't have any knights yet—well, soon.

—*Dark up here.*

—That's the whole point!

Plus, look at all our lovely stuff! Presents from the aunts and the uncle, and see our trophies, that we pulled out and wiped clean to put on the altar in the trophy room, and look! We found this beautiful, beautiful mounted horsehead with the silver mane and the lovely blue glass eyes that follow us. Either our king Saint Stephen shot it in the jungle and had it stuffed especially for us or else it was his favorite mount, the Challenger. Yes. When he died King Stephen was so sad that he had Challenger preserved so he could *always keep it with him.*

Alas, poor Challenger is dead and our king has died. Now it's up to us, the queen, to keep the holy kingdom forever.

We do it in his honor.

See the trophy room with three splendid trophies lying in there on the altar, signifying. And all those other rooms waiting to be used. We can surround ourselves with beauty, and wait for worshipers to come. *Look on my works, you mighty, we are the queen.* We are the queen and no one crosses us.

Next, we make the throne room. We want the carved gold chair with velvet in the downstairs sitting room. Seats two.

Perfect. Our knights can sit at our feet on pillows while we hold court.

So private, so nice! We can do anything we want here. Right, my sister, O queen? Anything. So stop whining and be glad.

—*I want to go home.*

—This is better than home, OK? When they stole us from the grandmother's house—just—like—*that*—when they dragged us into exile and boarded up our beautiful lost kingdom, we the queen Emerald thought it was the end, yes, we the queen Jade thought it was the end. Gone, our beautiful palace. Gone, all our beautiful fierce knights. Left propped and gathering dust back there in Amadamaland, stacked like so much firewood.

But look, our new knights breathe, and when you hurt them, they stay hurt!

Who would have guessed that all these thousands of miles from Amadamaland we could make a new kingdom? Who would have imagined living knights?

Funny, my queen, how these things happen. Knights-in-training at the beach lined up and waiting, and smarmy courtiers downstairs, and up here, this beautiful secret place, all dark and private, where we surround ourselves with pretty things, and wait.

—*Oh shut up, it's just dark.*

It's dusty here and creepy. Oh Emananjena, Janamenjena, I don't like it here. There are things *scutting out in the dark attic, who knows what? Hear them crawling through the junk, land crabs or night lizards, big orange scorpions making tracks in the hundred-year-old dust. We're breathing dust and tiny bugs; there are mosquitos trapped in my ears and it's horrible, trying to sleep in this silly old bathtub . . .*

—The royal swan bed!

— *. . . this silly old bathtub with the high back and the big claw feet, I don't like it here and I don't like us.*

Look now. We are in big trouble. Oh sister, what have we done?

—Naja.

—Done again. And they will wash up! No matter how deep we go you know what will happen. Sooner or later they will wash up on the land, and then they'll come and get us.

—For what? It was an accident, OK? Well, sort of an accident.

Like, look at that Randy. What are you going to do when your knight won't do like you say?

The queen does not brook disobedience.

She has everything *our way*. Our knights go where we want and do what we tell them. When we say, "March," they march. When we say, "Kneel," they kneel. If *even one knight* won't do what we say . . . You know what we have to do.

When you are absolute, sometimes you need a nice execution to make an example. Those are wonderful days. Everybody assembles in the courtyard, knights and ladies in their best are all ordered to watch. It's always like a party, remember? Yes they take our message. That's how the queen stays absolute.

—But that was at home. Those were only . . .

—Knights, just not flesh-and-blood ones. Listen, sister. A bad knight is a bad knight wherever you find him. Nobody opposes the queen and lives. We had to act fast, OK? Look how bad that Randy was. The lying! He said he'd get us everything we wanted, when all he wanted was to do things to us. Body things.

He offended the queen. Nobody offends the queen. Try it and you feel her wrath. So it was Randy's fault, for trying us.

—It was awful.

—It was a mistake. Besides, it felt *good.* You know it did. That new, strange feeling. Don't worry, OK? Tomorrow we'll find a good knight, you'll see. He'll be good and cute and he'll do *everything we say*.

—What if he doesn't?

—Well.

—My queen, what about our mistakes? Oh sister, Carroll will be mad. What if somebody finds them?

—We'll fix it so they won't be found. Nobody washing

up. No more accidents. No messes. Just royal trials, and new
knights to come.

—*Promise?*

—The queen keeps her word.

And look! We have *all Saturday* ahead. Cute Saturday
boys walking and swimming and lying on their fronts in the
sand with their butts sticking up, new knights just waiting to
be found.

We'll get us a good one. We'll bring him to the throne
room and give him drinks and Patsy's candy and he'll fall
down and worship us. We can make him bring another one
so there will be one knight for each, a beginning, yes? Then
we'll have fun playing on all the chairs and sofas and never
notice if it's hot up here.

And when we get tired of him we'll go out and get more.

Oh sister, queen, we can raise an army of knights! And
when we do we'll get in the car and set out for the kingdom,
us and our great knights that talk to us with real mouths and
look at us out of real eyes, better than our knights in the old
Amadamaland, with their plaster and plush faces and staring
glass eyes.

—*Pretend knights do like you tell them.*

—But it's more fun with real ones. You'll see. So
Grandmother, here we come, California, watch out, when
we come back we're going to have cute boys with us! A
whole cute army! Now stop sniveling, your majesty, OK?
It's lovely and private here, we have our *very own nest*, OK,
with brocade curtains to sleep on and this deep feather
mattress, that turns our beautiful old bathtub into a swan
bed, or a glass slipper stolen from a giant queen . . .

—*It's hot up here. I don't like it.*

—*Strebidibus*, sister. *Etrap*. Shut up. Tomorrow, the
beach.

—*I can't shut up, it's dark and it's hot and I don't feel
good. Frenemo. Really. I'm sorry about everything.* Fregel.

—Guilty? *Strebidibus*. Like, forget it! It's not our fault
Randy brought it on himself.

We are the queen and we do what we have to.

Listen. We had to do it.

—*Not we. You. You did it. Oh frenemo, this is so awful. Krena? What shall we do?*

—Look, bitch, I am you and you are we and what I do, you do.

—*And we are the queen. I know. So hard, sometimes, too much.*

—We are us and no other, and don't you forget that either.

So you can damn well forget all this *I* and *you*.

We are *US*.

We are *us* and no other, *so you can stop it*.

Listen, sister. Listen hard because you *will hear me*.

We are *us*, we are this unto the death.

And we don't cry.

In Meredith Archer's granite heap at the top of a high hill in California, Billy Graver sighs and tosses. He is touched that she feels shaky, and needs him to sleep in the house. It doesn't matter where he lies down. He hasn't been able to sleep since his son Kurt left on his desperate mission. The selfish part of Billy was glad to see Kurt go. It gets harder and harder to bear the pressure of his son's suffering, to look at that maimed wrist and know that somewhere back there, Billy is to blame. He should have gone to the police and charged Zane Oliphant with battery; he should have killed Hal Oliphant before he could marry Meredith and visit her with twins. He should have taken Kurt and fled this place right after the accident but he loved Meredith and he just couldn't.

Whether at risk or safe or going into certain danger, at least Kurt is free. He loves the boy; Billy wants him to go out into the world and do better than he ever could. More than anything he wants Kurt to be all right, but he has no way of knowing how he is. Kurt hasn't phoned since he left two nights ago. He hasn't wired. Billy can only hope the boy hasn't gone to ground somewhere, overwhelmed, no, thunderstruck by the wide open places.

In his greedy father's heart he cares less about what the twins are doing than about seeing Kurt restored to health.

He wants him whole. He wants him to be able to go outside and have a life.

Two days and he hasn't heard from him.

Billy would like to turn on Kurt's computers to see whether there is a message on one of the screens for him, but the garage apartment is locked right now, because he is sleeping in the big house. Meredith has asked him to spend these next few nights in the downstairs maid's room because she admits that like Billy, she's staggered by guilt and by worry.

What are Vivian's twins doing now that they've moved out of Meredith's control and Billy's ken? What are they doing now that they're freed of the lessons and concerts and all the other rituals Meredith devised to keep them occupied? Are they being good girls as he and Meredith so fondly hoped or are the two of them just being fatuous, the Oliphant grandchildren's soft-hearted dupes? What's happened to Carroll Lawton, who volunteered to take care of the girls and rushed off with them before Billy could find words to send her away fully prepared?

Worse, what are Hal Oliphant's grandchildren doing out there in the dark right now? Billy faces what he's known in his heart and yet refused to recognize all these years. The fact he's refused to face, for Meredith's sake. Ignore these things and they don't go away. They only get worse.

Savagery like chain-lightning spans the generations of Oliphants. He saw it in Hal. He saw it in Zane and he sometimes thinks he saw it in Vivian.

Worse. He knows it has surfaced in these pretty twins, but as long as they were here to smile and say nice things to him they kept him too bemused to see. Now he's sickened by his willingness to be fooled. Why didn't he see? Why couldn't he tell that poor girl who took them away?

It is this that makes Billy stare dry-eyed at the ceiling with his arms outstretched and torn nails gripping the edge of the mattress as if he's taking his place on a torture rack.

Then he shudders and snaps upright. Twins.

What if they hurt Kurt again?

He wants to call the police, but there's nothing to say; he

wants to warn his son but he can't reach him; he wants to hurl himself into the car and go looking for them but he can't. He can't do anything, he realizes, weeping. He's promised Meredith.

The twins wake at first light and climb out of their bower in the heavily cushioned bathtub. Threading their way through the cluttered attic, they pad toward the staircase. Their pretty little sun-dresses are damp with sweat and rumpled from being slept in. Their breath comes slowly as they pick their way through the abandoned trunks and broken furniture in the cavernous attic, taking care not to make any noise that will wake the sleeping family below. They are rosy with the heat and sweaty from sleep and if one of them is still groggy and wants nothing more than to throw herself on the twin bed in the room Carroll has prepared for them and go on sleeping, the other won't let her.

They have things to do.

Today we are going to start early.

The queen slides open the dresser drawer and pulls something out—paired ruffled bikinis with the price tags still attached. She rips off the tags with a kitchen knife she brought up to the room on their first night and shakes the suits at her sister the queen who rubs her eyes, yawning. The new bikinis are sea-green and yes the queen will look like mermaids in them, just right for today she thinks, yes. She slips hers on. Why is her sister still standing there, rubbing her eyes? Without speaking she holds the other suit out and stares at her sister, hissing until she puts it on.

Then they pick up their rubber flip-flops with little daisies jiggling where the straps meet and they reach for T-shirts and without looking to see what her sister is picking out, each puts on the new blue one with spangled waves picked out in green sequins on the front. In pink sequins, each bears the legend, FLORIDA.

They are dressed now, but not quite prepared. They kneel in front of the maple veneer dresser. One pulls open the bottom drawer and they study the array of hatpins still left to them. It is a glittering collection. There are long ones and

short one, delicate, sharp pins with ornamental heads like
Spanish fans and butterflies and gaudy peacocks and there
are pins with pearl heads held in a gold filigree and
tarnished silver pins with long steel points and pins with
points that look like stilettos. This battery of pins has
anchored a hundred hats and dozens of corsages and now
they all lie side by side here in the dresser. Without
consultation, the girls reach for two of the longest and most
beautiful—a five-inch pin with a carved jet head for one
and for the other, a pin with an ornamental metal head
studded in brilliants. Careful not to stab themselves, they
slide the pins diagonally into the warm place between their
bodies and the skimpy tops of their ruffled bathing suits, and
if one girl's fingers tremble and she prays that nothing will
happen today, she has become so clever at dissembling that
the other never guesses.

They are almost ready.

Holding their breath the girls come out into the hall and
are momentarily nonplussed. At the far end they see raffish,
white-haired Peyton shuffling back to bed from the bathroom. At this distance he could almost be mistaken for one
of the boys from the beach because the shock of hair is
combed in the same way and they are too far away to see the
moustache. He looks rumpled and sleepy at the moment, but
they already know from being in the car with him that his
breath is warm and rummy and his fingers are sharp. If he
turns they will have to think of something—to say? To do?
They may have to slide into his bedroom for a little sweet
talk and many promises they don't intend to keep before he
will snuggle and then release them to begin their day.

Frozen in the dim hallway, the girls stand embracing like
nymphs at the lip of a Roman fountain. When he staggers
back into his room without noticing them, it is a relief. It
makes it possible for them to slip down the back stairs and
into the kitchen where 'Laine has left out boxes and bowls
and jars of jam and bottles of syrup in preparation for a
ceremonial pancake breakfast. Too bad! Scooping out the
middle of the cake she has made for their dinner, they eat
with greedy hands and when they're done, they dump the

remainder in the garbage. Then they lick their fingers and wipe their hands on the tablecloth and head outside, into the soft morning. They make one more stop in the garage, where they stand for a moment with their foreheads touching. An observer would have no way of knowing whether they are communicating or only reaffirming some decision arrived at in the night. With the kitchen knife, each cuts off a three-foot length of nylon clothesline which she loops around her waist underneath the T-shirt. The effect is so funky and stylish that admirers would have no way of knowing this is more than a fashion statement.

Then they slip out of the garage and around the house, heading off down the shady street for the Kash 'n' Karry that stands at the corner where Arbor Street stops being neighborhood and turns into commercial desert.

They have the idea that if they hang around long enough at the counter, they'll find somebody coming in for ice to stock his cooler. "Going to the beach?" they'll say, and he'll say, "Want a ride?" These things are so easy!

There is somebody parked in front of the house, a dark figure slouched behind the steering wheel with his head resting against the metal windowframe. There is something about him that looks familiar. Drawing in deep breaths that they won't release just yet, the twins tiptoe closer.

Jane grabs Emily. Now her breath hisses out but slowly, so that she whispers almost without sound. "Look!"

Emily grasps Jane. "Big Kurt!"

They are frightened and thrilled. "He loves us!"

"No, he's come after us."

One says, "What are we going to do?" even as the other says, "Told you he was in love with us."

Drawn, repelled, excited and wary, they communicate without speaking but, strangely, in the old language. *Glena.* Watch out. *Fridibo.* He has come to get us. *Krazgo.* Get him.

Something profound trembles in the air between them.

Sleeping Kurt Graver stirs and they scramble backward. Yes he is everything they remember, big, craggy and good-looking. Asleep like this and in this light, he looks vulnerable. Anything or anybody could hurt him. Yet even in sleep, he's dangerous. They know what they have always known. Big, brusque Kurt with the severed hand has eyes that look deep. He sees right past the disarming smiles and hears their true intentions no matter how they dissemble.

—Now we know how, we can do him, yes?

—Shh. It's OK. He's asleep.

—*Krazgo*, and I mean it!

—No, my queen. We still love him.

The other sighs. It's true.—No. We still love him.

There it is. Their savage hearts back off.—We do.

Therefore they tiptoe backward and keep on backing until they have faded into the soft shadows at the far end of Arbor Street and swiftly whisked around the corner, at which point they turn around and, hampered by the frivolous flip-flops, the twins start running.

Without having to speak they know that they need to act fast. Today's the day, whatever that means.

At the 7-Eleven, a nice old guy comes in to fill his cooler before he heads for the beach to go surf casting.

Jane smiles her best smile. "Going to the beach?"

"Yes ma'am," he says, smiling broadly. "Want a ride?"

"Yes sir," she says. "Right, Em?"

"Yes sir," Emily says. "We have a lot to do today. Right, Jane?"

"Right," Jane says, being careful to make sure that her sister doesn't detect even a second's hesitation.

Ted Madison is on the beach early today because he broke up with his girlfriend last night. The fight was ugly and it went on for so long that it left him too angry and disturbed to sleep. Emerging from a sweaty, knotted mess of bed-clothes at dawn, he decided the best thing he could do for himself at this point would be work out some of the pain and rage by running. He's walking back from a six-mile run when he blinks to be sure he isn't so crazed that heat mirages have left him seeing double.

*   *   *

Bad, she thinks, treading water while her hair fans out behind her like a mermaid's veil of curls. So bad. These things start so well, but in the end they always come out the same.

I thought *this* new boy would kiss us and be nice to us without getting ugly. Who knew he wouldn't want to kiss us at all?

Look, how can we make it come out right when these knights won't *do* the way our good knights used to do at home?

In the old kingdom we told the knights, *Stay there*. We could tell them *Wait* and they would wait, and, *Do this,* and they would do it. They did everything we wanted, even fight and kill each other, yes. Yes. They would even kill themselves. *Do it.* And if they were dead and gone, no problem. They were only toy knights. Pick them up in the morning and play with them again.

But these knights are alive, so warm and nice at first. Then it goes wrong and they get weird or gropey, or get nasty *down there* that we don't like. Or they disobey, like this one. Then we have to make an example. Thwart the queen will you, take that. And that.

And when they die, they don't come back like the toy ones do.

Oh, why do they have to do us wrong when they're so right?

When it's right, why do they have to make us angry?

Patience, my sister says. What good is patience? *Temporary inconvenience*, she says. But here, executions are for keeps. No picking these knights up in the morning to play again.

Not this one's fault we wanted things he didn't want to do for us, him going, "Take it easy, I just broke up with a girl," my sister growling, "Never mind." My sister the queen wants to spend the rest of her life kissing knights and so do I. So now we are out in the water again, swimming way, way out like three beautiful fish and then we the queen dive like mermaids, twining around his legs, so fun! But this one doesn't get all, like, hands and fingers in soft places like the

other ones. He doesn't do the way we like, kissing and stuff
until we can't make them stop and so we have to stop them.
He doesn't even want to kiss.

We're getting mad. My sister is like, "Blow off the queen,
will you." Oh please, watch out, don't make us mad. He's
like, "I'm not trying to . . . oh look, just *don't*, OK? I'm
just a little wrecked right now." Bad knight, beware, the
queen is warning you . . . "Sweet knight, we can make
you feel better *all over*." "Just don't, OK? You kids are only
kids." *Kids*. Warning. Warning. Wrong thing.

Warning. Wrong thing to say.

Then he does a surface *flop* just like a fish and we move
in, but he is like, "Wait a minute," and we are like, "Can't!"
and when we beg for nice kisses and he *will not promise*, my
sister takes it out, the pin, and I know what I'm supposed to
do and therefore even though it is awful, it will happen—so
fast! She pulls the pin out of her front and because she will
kill me if I don't, I pretend to hug him from behind and in
that moment the three of us are one as we hold him, me and
my sister, my *self*. We submerge together, and my breath
trembles as she drives it in. He jangles like an electric wire.
And we feel it: the rush.

Then we use the ropes.

Then we spring to the surface like blowing whales.
Everything bubbles up in me and I cry, "Oh noooo, we let
it go wrong again!"

She purrs: the ropes. "But they will never find this one."

Oh look, I think, this has got to stop.

Got to. I don't dare let her hear me thinking it. Part of me
howls, *I loved him* as my sister says, "Tough luck, bad
knight!"

And then once more we broach the surface of the water
and swim away underneath the surface, like two beautiful,
spangled fish.

26

HE IS AT THE DOOR when Carroll comes down the next morning, a tall, rangy man in jeans and a khaki jacket. 'Laine hisses, "I thought you'd never get up. I asked him to wait on the porch because he said he knew you but that you might not know him."

She finds him leaning against the doorframe with one hand in his pocket.

"You can't let just everybody in," 'Laine says.

He's good-looking in a rough-cut way but seriously rumpled, as if he's accidentally spent the night in a dumpster. Maybe he washed up in a water fountain and combed his hair with his fingers. He looks drawn, like a marathon runner pushed to the limit.

He seems to be deciding what to call her.

"Ms. Harriman?"

"Lawton. I kept my maiden name." She's surprised by the next thought: I loved him and I didn't even change my name for him.

The stranger is saying, "I called last night?"

Distracted, she pulls herself back. "Oh. Mr. Ah. I was supposed to call. I'm sorry. My aunt forgot to write it down."

Behind her, 'Laine hisses, "Ask him if he's come about the twins."

"Yes, 'Laine, that would be wonderful," she says heartily, as if Elaine has said something else altogether. "I'd love it if you'd go and make me something different for breakfast. Something that takes a long time."

"Make your own breakfast." Her aunt wheels and goes upstairs.

Have to mend that later, Carroll thinks, and turns back to

the stranger. She doesn't know this person but something
about him—the profile, perhaps, or the diffidence—seems
familiar. "Carroll Lawton."

"Kurt Graver. I think you know my father."

For a minute she doesn't and then she does. Billy Graver.
The lovely, somber man who told her Steve was dead. "Of
course. You look just like him. He's Mrs. Archer's . . ."
She's at a loss.

"He does a lot of things for her. I know there's no reason
for you to talk to me. I've come because . . ." He goes at
it from another direction. "I wanted to have more information before I . . ." but that doesn't work either. "Oh hell,"
he says, "this is going to sound crazy and you're probably
going to kick me out . . ."

"You aren't inside yet."

"Oh look, it's about the twins."

"Come in."

When they are sitting in her great-grandparents' overdone
Victorian parlor with the sliding doors closed, he begins. "I
don't have any proof and I know you're going to think I'm
crazy but I couldn't go any further with this until I'd had
a chance to touch base. I have to go to Tennessee today but
I couldn't leave without talking to you. It's the twins. I think
the twins are . . ." His expression is sliding all over the
place.

"What I mean is . . ."

As he starts to tell her and fails and tries again Carroll's
mind scurries in several different directions: her aunt's hurt
feelings, the coroner's report on Lanny Raynor and what
Charley's going to expect from her; her girls, who are
sleeping later than they ever have—she's glad, they've been
through a lot. Poor kids, she thinks and will not let herself
think: poor me.

Whoever this guy is, nice as he is and probably well-
meaning, he doesn't know anything about grief or he
wouldn't be here right now. Still she thinks he means well
and she knows he isn't going to leave until she's let him say
whatever he's having such a hard time bringing out. She
studies Kurt Graver. Centered on the elaborately carved

ancestral love seat, he leans forward with his right fist
clenched on one knee; he has the left one stuck in his pocket
as if he's got something he doesn't want her to see. This is
so obviously hard for him that she tries to help him along.
"You were trying to tell me something about the twins."

This surprises it out of him. "I think they're dangerous."

"Not Steve's girls." No. She can't stop shaking her head.

"There are things you don't know."

"They're my girls now. I don't need to know."

"Things they did in California," he says, overlapping.

"The past is past."

After all that effort, he is strangely still. When he speaks
again it is in even tones. "It may be only the beginning."

"Don't, OK?"

"I'm sorry, I have to," he says. "Look. Some bad things
are going on. They've been going on for years. Like this
week. I don't know how what happened happened, but I
have my suspicions."

She is too upset and defensive to mark what he has just
tried to tell her. "They're only girls."

"I can't pin it down for you because I don't know what
they've done, I don't even know what they're going to do.
I just wanted you to be careful. I know you probably love
them and all . . ."

"I do."

"But I want you to watch out for them. They hurt people."

She is surprised by anger. "You don't know that."

"I wouldn't be here if I wasn't pretty sure."

This makes her mad enough to confront it head-on.
"What is it then? What exactly are you trying to tell me?"

"That's the whole problem! I'm not sure. Look," he says,
"I'm going to see their grandfather. If I'm right, he can help
me figure this out, but until I do . . ."

"Until you do, maybe you'd better keep quiet," she says.

"I can't. I, ah." She can't know what makes him grimace
and bite his knuckles before he says, "You might as well
know, I . . . I have a hard time going out. I wouldn't go all
these places and say this stuff if it was nothing. What it is,
is. There's a thing—about the family?" He tilts his head as

if it will help him find a way around her barriers. "Either it's in the blood or else it's something with twins?

"Whatever it is, it's awful. I think."

Listening, Carroll sorts a series of impressions—the shadows that haunted Steve, the legacy of pain that seemed to come with these relationships—Vivian, her twins. Oh, Steve, she thinks, and grief almost overturns her. Oh Steve.

"Their grandfather was this rich boozer named Hal Oliphant. This priest tried to stop the wedding. I went to see him—he's crazy now, but he did say Hal had a twin. No," he says, hung up on the significance. "*Was* a twin. His brother died, if it wasn't murder, it was something else. Something weird. The family wouldn't have anything to do with Hal. He landed in California, and married this rich woman with a big house in the hills? My dad worked for the Archers and he knows."

"Billy Graver," Carroll says.

"Billy." Kurt nods. "Did you know this Hal Oliphant hit on my mother and took her away from him?"

"I'm sorry." Hearing a *click*, Carroll thinks: Please don't take it out on my girls.

"He did worse things." Kurt Graver seems to be sorting his material, figuring out what parts to lay out for her. "He used to beat Meredith up, my dad says, that poor nice lady. Finally she divorced him, but by that time she had his children. Twins."

"What does that have to do with my girls?"

He looks at her sharply. "Your girls?"

"Jane. Em. My family."

He sighs. "Please don't be in such a hurry to make them family. Just give it a little while, OK? Until I talk to their grandfather, OK? There are some things about this that we don't either of us know."

"The poor kids have lost both parents," Carroll says. "What they need now is love and a little trust."

"And you just need to be careful. *Careful.*" His next sigh sounds more like a groan.

What is most frightening about this is that in that second

of inadvertent grief, he reminded her of Steve. Shaken, she says, "Don't worry about me."

"Maybe you'll be careful if I tell you the rest of it. I'll start with the easy stuff, OK?" His face is irregular and his brows go straight across like the grease-pencil slash in a caricature but intensity makes him shine.

"About Hal's twins. We grew up together on the place. We played all over the house and the grounds and on Saturdays we took picnics across the cliff road and down the wooden steps to the observation deck on a ledge halfway down. From there you could see everything—the sky over the water, the waves, and if you wanted, you could go down the rest of the way and climb out on the rocks and swim. We did everything together. Viv was beautiful, lovely, maybe a little crazy but wonderful. But her brother. He was something else. One day—I didn't even know what I was doing, it was an accident. What happened was, I made him mad."

This is one echo too many; without wanting to Carroll recalls the warning label that accompanied her twins. She is quick, defensive. "And he took out a gun and shot you. Sure."

"No." It is at this point that he takes the left hand out of his pocket and she sees there isn't any hand at all. "He did this."

This brings tears to Carroll's eyes. "I'm so sorry." She has to squeeze the words out. "I am."

He shrugs. "It's just a cheap way to make my point. It's no big deal. It didn't even bother me much. I got over it. I even got used to it. We kept on playing together, Vivian and me and Zane. We grew up, I was in love with Vivian and I thought she loved me.

"But there was Zane. Something between them. Something so strong no outsider could understand."

He says, with some pain, "Do you know they used to have fights without even talking to each other?"

Carroll flinches. This is too close.

"I came back from college and I was seeing Vivian, I wanted to make love with her. No. I wanted to marry her. Forever. She loved me. And all the time there was Zane in the background and his shadow just kept getting bigger and bigger; it's hard to explain.

"When I wasn't around they spent all their time fighting, I couldn't hear words but I knew they were sawing back and forth. Then I started having these little accidents, cleaning fluid in my water bottle, something the matter with my car, one of the steps down the cliff was sawed halfway through and I don't know what would have happened to me—dead, I guess—if Vivian hadn't . . .

"If she hadn't . . ." He can't go on.

Then suddenly, he can. "I don't know how she knew. And then."

Carroll strains to hear words he can't bring himself to say.

"I understood what happened when I was little. Zane did what he did because I was in love with her." Finally he reaches some point he has been approaching all his life since then. "No. Because he was in love with her."

He stares into this hard truth for a long moment.

Carroll is trembling. "God."

The silence expands.

"The cliff. We were out there drinking one night, the three of us just hanging out there on the ledge. It was foggy and Zane and Viv went back to the house for more champagne. When they came back down the cliff steps they were arguing, out loud, that same old fight, you know. I think it was over me. I heard Vivian say, "No!" Then something happened in the dark and the next thing I knew I heard Zane scream. Vivian was screaming too, crying as if he was killing her, but it was Zane whose voice was going away. Down. I could hear it going down in stages, a scream coming out of him all the way down to the bottom of the cliff. Somehow he had slipped or else she'd pushed him off the steps. I heard him howl every time he hit a rock until he hit the big one and he wasn't howling any more. God, you should have seen Vivian. You'd think she'd lost everything she'd ever cared about. That's when I knew . . . Listen.

"This is the worst part." He drags his fingernails down his face. "I was nothing, compared to Zane."

Gently, Carroll touches his sleeve.

"I knew we could never be together." He rattles like a cheap machine held together with safety pins. "The widow. No. She loved Zane like part of herself."

Now he looks up at her. "Maybe he was."

Once again Carroll is struck by the shadows in Kurt's face—too much like Steve's at their first meeting; she recognizes the traces of deep grief.

"Whatever he was, his death was destroying her. With him gone, she might as well be dead. She ran away."

So they are at the intersecting point. Carroll gasps.

He ducks so she won't see him cry. "I never knew if she killed him. I never wanted to know."

"Let me get you some coffee." She feels like a fool because it's all she can find to say.

"So that's why I had to come. Even though I don't have anything certain, I knew I had to come. When I leave here I'm going to Tennessee to see Hal Oliphant. He may know what to do to keep this *thing* from happening and if he doesn't . . ." He keeps trying to find the right piece of the problem to lay out for her. "At least he can tell me what it is."

"I'm sorry," she says. "I am. But so far you've told me a lot of stuff about the family and nothing about the kids."

"It's the blood. I talked to the priest. It's something terrible in the blood."

"Not Vivian. You were in love with Vivian."

"And I was afraid of her." Drained, he sits with his elbows on his knees and his head bowed. His voice comes from a deep, murky place. "And I'm afraid of her girls."

"But they're only children." She hears her own voice break and hates herself for this weakness. "Steve's children."

He won't stop. "And somewhere deep they're Oliphants."

She hates her tears. She wants to hit him for bringing her this close to the edge. "Well that isn't enough."

"Did you know that their dolls used to fight and kill each other?"

This brings her to her feet. "I think you'd better go."

He studies her. "I guess I'd better." Rising, he looks at his watch. "I'm supposed to be on my way to the airport now. When I come back maybe I'll have something . . . Try to look at it this way—something that will keep this—" Baffled, he shakes his shaggy head. "This—*whatever it is*—from happening again."

"If you're late, you'd better hurry," she says when what she means is, *please leave*.

He lingers on the porch. "Look, I'm sorry. I'm sorry about everything but what I'm hoping is. I just want . . ." Why can't he explain? He can't. He shakes his head again.

"So thanks for coming. I'm sorry I can't." She doesn't finish. *Can't believe you*. She can't afford to believe him. This is already hard enough. Inside she hears the phone ringing—Charley, probably—she hasn't phoned in—and she hopes 'Laine will pick up. She wants to slam the screen and turn her back on him but there is something so shaky and vulnerable behind the scowl that she can't.

He seems to be being tugged in different directions—toward the car, back into the house. He waves the left arm distractedly, a gesture so earnest and unselfconscious that it completely disarms her. By this time they are both crying. Backing away he says, "Oh look, take care of yourself, OK? Please take care."

And she is sorry about everything—that they met this way, that they are at cross-purposes, that they are both so torn by circumstance that they can't just meet and be friends and maybe even something more. She is aware of 'Laine bustling and pulling her sleeve; yes it's Charley on the phone, he says it's urgent, and so even though some part of her wants to go running down the walk with Kurt Graver and get into his car, Carroll turns to her aunt. "What, 'Laine. What is it?"

When she turns back she's lost him. She hears him gunning the motor as he throws the car into gear and takes off.

27

"THE STAKES just went up," Charley says. "By tonight every major daily in the state is going to have somebody over here. Ten more minutes and we're standing in line to talk to our own sources."

Behind her in the hall Elaine is jiggling up and down in agitation. Now that Kurt is gone she wants Carroll to apologize; she wants to apologize; she wants to know what Charley Penn has to say that's so important. Carroll turns her back on her aunt, hunching over the receiver. "What's going on?"

"There's been another murder. They found him late last night. Same deal."

Carroll's voice is sharper than she intended: "What do you mean, same deal?"

"You know. No apparent marks. Local kid named Randy Hummer, fry cook at Frisch's Big Boy."

"At the mall, right?" Carroll's jaw unclenches.

"Yeah, that one," Charley says, so intent on the next thing that he mistakes her question.

OK, she thinks, misapprehending his answer. Better at the mall than. Than what? She's too pressed to name the thing she's afraid of. "Anything in common with the others?"

"Too soon to tell. He was single. Last kid in a big family. Twenty-something, went to junior college nights. I've sent Russell out to the house to try and get a picture."

She notes this and files it; Russell off in the suburbs, out of the thick of it. "Where's the body?"

"County medical examiner's working on it. They got him in on his day off because they didn't want to leave it to the weekend staff. They know this is big."

"Terrific." Carroll has the phone caught between her

shoulder and her chin so she can make notes in the reporter's notebook she packs like a revolver. It's more than a tool of the trade. Carrying it makes her feel stronger. "Cause of death?"

"They aren't saying."

"You said no marks."

"No apparent marks."

"Then how do they know it's murder?"

"They know. They just won't say. The press conference is set for noon. A canned statement, probably. We need to find out more than the chief wants to tell us."

"I'll get on it." As she makes notes Carroll is aware of a general uneasiness whose source she can't locate. She can't ask the question until she figures out what it is but there is a question nagging her. What she asks instead is, "What's going on?"

"I don't know. Nobody's used the words yet but everybody's thinking: serial killer. A first in this county. It's your job to get somebody to come right out and say it."

And it's my story. "You've got it." Question, she thinks, because this other thing is still bothering her. I need to ask Charley one more question.

"You need to work fast. We were here first, it's our town and it's your story."

"You want me to cover the press conference?"

"I'll do that. The TV guys will catch most of it anyway. You can go deeper. Get with the coroner."

"What about Russell?"

"Russell. Oh, Russell." Charley's impatience gives her a lift. "Russell can't get shit out of a baby. I need you on this."

Question, Carroll thinks, without knowing why she's so uneasy. What is it I need to ask? *Oh.* The body. "Where did you say they found the body?"

"Just about the same place as the other one."

She discovers she's leaning forward, rushing the answer she wants to hear. "In the mall parking lot, right? Somebody must have gotten him coming out of work."

"No. The beach. I thought I told you. It's the same deal as Lanny Raynor."

"The beach." There it is. It leaves her chilled and queasy. To think the girls were there yesterday; to think she was going to let them go today. "Are they going to close the beaches?"

"No. The park police came at me with the usual reasons, request from the cops and the county sheriff's office. Don't alarm anybody, don't tip off the perp, you know. Until they know what they have, it's business as usual. I . . ." He senses a disturbance at her end. "What did you say?"

"Something's come up." She can't wait to get off the phone. "That I have to do." Close, she thinks, with no way of explaining even to herself what's implied here. Too close to home. Anybody could get hurt out there. "I have to speak to my kids before I leave."

"Your kids?"

Flustered, she rushes him off the phone. "OK, OK, Steve's kids." She hurries upstairs to wake the twins.

The beach. She doesn't want her girls going anywhere near the place. She'll make 'Laine take them to Orlando if she has to, anything to keep them off the beach until this thing is over. Even if it means waking them up to tell them, she has to settle this.

It's only when she stops cold inside the door to the twins' empty bedroom that Elaine catches up with her. The beds are still neatly made with the ancient Bates spreads pulled tight, just the way 'Laine left them yesterday. The precision with which the pillows are centered and the spreads tucked on all sides makes it clear they haven't been slept in. What is unusual in the context of the twins' ritualistic neatness is the fact that the rest of the room is a mess. The top dresser drawer is open, trailing beach shirts and bathing suits, and discarded tank tops and flowered boxer trunks are strewn in a path to the mirror as if before they left for the beach the girls had tried on and discarded a dozen costumes.

"Those children," 'Laine says weakly.

"They went to bed so late I thought they'd sleep late today."

"It looks like they didn't sleep at all. At least, not here." Elaine is so pink with anxiety that it's clear she's afraid

Carroll is going to blame her. "Oh my God. What if they were out all night?"

"They were still here first thing this morning." The next thing comes out of Carroll so quickly that she almost doesn't hear what she's saying. "I heard them in the attic."

'Laine murmurs at cross-purposes, "I told them not to go to the beach alone any more, all those bikers and tough trash and nobody to protect them."

"At least I think I heard them. I was so *sleepy*."

"I told them not to go at all."

"I took something last night because I couldn't sleep and I was so grogged out that I wasn't really awake, either." Carroll shakes her head to clear it of fuzz; she can still feel the aftereffects.

"I told them not to go alone, but they went anyway." 'Laine is completely wrapped up in her own sad little recital.

"I just hope the cops aren't . . ." Carroll gets pictures in flashes: police turning up some grim evidence as her girls cross the sand and happen into one of those shocking moments people never get over. What if they accidentally stumble on a body? Or meet the murderer? "I'm going to get them."

"Why didn't they wait? Peyton promised to take them."

Carroll is worried now, rushed, but this does not go by unmarked: *Peyton*. She kept one step ahead of her uncle all through her adolescence but she was different. Being orphaned made her tough and resourceful and these girls are . . . Beautiful, she thinks. Satiny and privileged and completely unused to the rough world outside their grandmother's grounds. They're only children. *Got to keep an eye on Peyton*. "I don't want them going anywhere with Peyton."

Even though this isn't her fault Elaine is so busy trying to make amends that she doesn't hear. "Peyton can do it. I'll get him up. No, I'll go myself. I'll take an umbrella so I can sit out on the sand and keep an eye on them. It's OK, Carroll, it is. I'll keep a close eye on them."

"Thanks, but no. They have to come home."

"Then I'll go right out there and get them for you."

"Elaine, I need to do this."

"But you have all this *work!*"

"Don't tell me what to do, OK?"

She stops just long enough to call the coroner while he's still reachable. At first she thinks she's already too late because she gets the machine. But the doctor hears her leave her name and picks up. "Sorry to hear about your husband. Why did they send that kid to talk to us yesterday, instead of you?"

"Oh Sam," she says, falling into the old routine, "where were you yesterday when I needed you?"

"The fools said the *Dispatch* called."

"I am the *Dispatch*."

"Not these days. I thought it was that dumb kid they sent. Nobody said it was you."

"What's the cause of death?"

Because she and the medical examiner are friends, she gets more from him than Russell ever could. She's mulling the information as she drives to the beach. Like Lanny Raynor's, this body bears no immediately visible signs of trauma, but close investigation . . . "I don't have to tell you to let the chief think he's breaking the news," he said before he laid it out for her. "One's a coincidence, two is strange and three's a pattern. We had to check the first one pretty thoroughly before we found the puncture wound. Yesterday it was the same story, but today we knew what we were looking for."

Going on yesterday's news, Carroll asked, "The base of the skull again?"

"No. That was the first place we checked on Number Two yesterday, but no soap. It took us a while, but we found it. When we started on Number Three, we knew where to look. The puncture was right where we thought it would be."

"So they're all punctures."

"Yes."

If she can just get him to respond to this next thing, she'll have what Charley wants today. Using an old reporter's

trick she frames it as a statement. All he has to do is say yes.
"So all three deaths are related."

Instead of answering, he continues his thought. "Remember, both bodies had been in the water. The wounds were small, but they went deep, right straight into the brain. The punctures were in the eye socket."

"Ice pick?"

"I don't think so. There wasn't enough damage at the point of entry. Whatever it was, it barely grazed the eyeball."

"Who'd know that was how to do it?"

"Your guess is as good as mine," he said and that was all he'd say. "Anything else you get, you're going to have to get from the county sheriff or the chief in Jenkins. It's their territory, and they're in charge."

She pulls into the beach parking lot with a sense of familiarity that leapfrogs yesterday and puts her back in high school, Carroll Lawton, aged fifteen. She spent her summers hanging around the Dairy Queen waiting for Bobie or Skeet or somebody else from school to come along in their jacked-up beach buggies with the balloon tires, on the way to the ocean. She'd stand out there in the white summer mornings watching the shadows of the palm trees recede across the parking lot as the sun got high. Each oncoming car caught her standing on her toes, straining to see who was at the wheel because sooner or later she'd see somebody she knew. She was a younger, dumber creature in those days, parked with her elbow on the counter of the takeout window and her hip cocked, waiting for one of the boys to spot her and lean out the window, going, Hey babe, come on, life's a beach.

Memory softens her. "Poor kids. No wonder they sneaked out."

By the time she locates the twins just east of the refreshment stand she is gentle, almost apologetic. Even in the welter of Saturday beach traffic, they aren't hard to spot. The sun catches the bright hair on their identical shining heads, surrounding them with haloes, and their neat bodies lie side by side like moving parts of the same machine. By the time she reaches them, they're sitting up. They're putting suntan lotion and their little portable radio—where did they get a—into the beach bag and getting ready to go. It's as if they have consulted and decided, what: that it's too hot today? Too crowded?

Too something, it's clear. They are more than ready to go.

Without letting her know what they're thinking they pick up their blankets with sweet smiles and slip into their flip-flops so they can cross the hot parking lot without burning their feet.

Strange. Carroll doesn't have to promise to buy them clothes or jewelry to soften the blow; she doesn't even have to promise to take them for ice cream to win their acceptance. It's fait accompli. There's even an attractive little scramble over who's going to sit in front: my turn, no, *my* turn. The attention is flattering.

It's Em's turn really; they aren't wearing the slap wraps so she sneaks a surreptitious look at the rings and turns to the wearer of the sapphire. "You, Emily," she says. "It can be your turn."

They both start giggling.

"OK, guys, what is it."

"We swapped the rings."

They're so giggly that it makes her smile. It's a delight to find them so relaxed with her. She turns to the wearer of the ruby. "OK, Emily Archer, you and you alone can sit up front with me."

They cover their mouths, still laughing.

"What?"

They're so pleased with themselves that they can hardly speak. "We swapped back again."

"OK." She matches their grins. "Will the *real* Emily Archer come sit in front with me?" Then, although at times they prefer to sit together in the back, the one with the sapphire—she thinks it's Em—slides in front, settling into her seat with a little thump. The car fills with the fragrance of shampoo and scented sunscreen released by the combination of sun and the girl's body temperature. It is like an extra presence in the car.

Absorbed, Carroll is deciding which sources to see in which order after the girls are safe at home, but the silence in the car distracts her. The girls aren't talking. They're just going along fixed on something she can't see. Because this makes her uneasy she asks: "How was the beach?"

"OK," Em says.

In back, Jane says, "OK."

When she tries to explain without really explaining that they can't go to the beach for a couple of days, they sit passively and don't complain. She says, "Do you feel all right? Did you get too much sun?"

They both say, "No, we're fine."

"Look, I'm sorry you have to stay in today, but when I get home tonight, I'll explain. If you're bored, 'Laine can take you to a movie this afternoon."

"It's OK, we'll watch tapes," Jane says.

"Or MTV," Em says.

"You won't get bored?"

"We have plenty to do."

"OK, if you're sure. And when I get home tonight, we'll have some fun." She doesn't have to promise to take them to the pool at the Holiday Inn after work but she does, and they seem pleased enough. "And the three of us can have supper there. OK?" She shoots an apprehensive glance at Emily, who catches her looking and smiles. She knows without having to check in the rearview mirror that Jane is smiling too.

It is a surprise, therefore, when back at the house the twins split up, one heading for the bathroom and the other for the second floor back porch. It's Em, at least she thinks it's Em, who seems momentarily surprised that Jane is nowhere around. With her mouth making an uncertain little curlicue the child says, "You want to sit on the porch with me?"

Carroll's surprised by the rush this gives her. *I'd love to but I have to go.* She has twelve things to do before the press conference and for the moment, forgets all of them. "You bet."

So there they are sitting in the two rockers, she and Em,

creaking back and forth, back and forth more or less in silence, when she ought to be heading over to the newsroom to start on her calls. This is nice, she thinks, but if Em isn't going to talk to me, I might as well go. As if she's spoken, Emily says abruptly, "So, ah, if somebody, ah. If . . ." The sentence squeaks to a stop.

She wants to win the girl's confidence so instead of running at her with questions, the reporter's habit, or is it curse, Carroll doesn't say anything. Instead she rocks and waits.

"If," Steve's daughter says again.

So Carroll murmurs encouragingly, "So, like . . . If?"

Squirming in discomfort, Emily says, "Oh nothing. Just if."

Schooled in getting information out of people, Carroll tries another old trick: Don't ask. Tell. "Look, I know this is hard for you and all, being stuck down here with people you don't even know, but it's hard for us too. I know how hard it is. And I know how much you miss your father, it must have been terrible."

This leaves her gasping but she keeps going for the girl's sake. "It was *so fast*. I miss him too, and any time you want to talk about it . . ." She's rambling on, babbling just to maintain the illusion that they're both talking when Emily cuts her off with a swift, executive chop of the hand.

Astounded by the silence she creates so authoritatively, Carroll leans back and waits.

Em clears her throat in a little series of explosions and begins one more time. "If somebody ah, *did* something and something happened . . ." She seems to be gathering momentum. "Something that . . ." Then for no reason that Carroll can identify, she stops.

Alarmed, the girl jerks her head around so fast that Carroll sees white rings around her irises. She stands.

"If what, Em," Carroll says gently.

Nothing comes. She's watching the door.

Carroll prompts. "If what?"

But the girl remains fixed on the door. She is fixed on it for a full minute before Jane comes out.

"Oh, there you are." Jane's scrubbed face glows. Her smile is lovely, melting. "Em, come on. It's time to get ready. 'Laine is taking us to the mall."

Something makes Carroll cry, "Wait!"

Emily is already at her sister's side.

"Tomorrow. It's my day off. Let's *do* something." She has to think fast; their faces are already glazing over with impatience. "Tell you what. We'll drive to the lake."

"Lake?"

"Inland, by a couple of hours. Picnic. We'll rent a boat. What do you think?"

One says, "We don't know."

The other says, "We'd like it."

As they turn to go she calls after them because strange as they are, they're Steve's—no, hers. They're hers now and she wants more than anything to please them. "Don't forget, as soon as I get off work, we're going swimming."

—Emonamus, queen. You watch your mouth or I will watch it for you.

—*Emenaja, Janemanja, I'm so scared. Too much! I'm sick of this.*

—Not! It's only starting.

—*So many police on the beach. What if they catch us?*

—With what? We tied him to the buoy.

—*What if he floats up?*

—We tied him way *down*, OK? At the tippy bottom of the cable.

—*He was so* cute. *I liked him.*

—He disobeyed the queen.

—*But they all keep disobeying us. Nobody behaves! I don't want to do this. I want to stop. We have to stop before they catch us, and if you won't stop then I'll have to stop us. Ow!*

—Nobody stops the queen. Now shut up or I the queen will shut you.

—*Ow. Don't! Ow ow!* What are you doing?

—Changing rings, OK? Now shut up or I'll do worse to you.

—Don't, please! Stop hurting!

—Then change rings with me. That's good. Again. Again. We change so many times that we forget whose rings they are. *And which we are, OK?* OK, better.

Now you are I and I am you and if you say *one word* to *one single person* about this you know what I am going to do to you. More changing. Good now. I don't care if you don't want to. We keep changing until you forget which one you are, because if you don't, I'm going to have to kill you.

—Ow, please, ow! What if they catch us?

—Kill them too. We are the queen, and we kill who we have to. Yes.

By the time the day is out Carroll has all the victims' family records for the story. She and Charley have a statement from the chief tentatively labeling these serial killings. They have his answers to some of their questions. They have something quotable about the nature of the murder weapon, which has not been located. The chief has one other thing for her, but strictly off the record. The two bodies that washed ashore weren't wearing rings or watches in spite of tan marks that suggested they always wore them, but that wasn't the strange part. The strangeness was that they were both naked.

The mayor is on the six o'clock news live, reassuring citizens that the police are on top of the problem. He asks them to exercise caution for the next few days until Jenkins police apprehend the killer. The county sheriff turns up on the opposite channel, telling everybody that because it happened not in Jenkins but at one of the county beaches, it is the sheriff who will bring in the killer.

But Lacy has told Carroll off the record that the police don't have a clue as to where to start, much less any idea what kind of madman is doing the killings. She also says, not for publication, that details that overlap with the killing at the mall suggest that the killer comes from Jenkins.

Putting her story together, she keeps whipping her head around to look at the phone, half-expecting to have somebody call to report that they've found another body. Nothing comes in and she goes back and rewrites her lead with a sense of relief because when she's done she's done, for the day at least. Feeling generous, she lets Russell do a sidebar with quotes from the new victim's neighbors and his fellow workers at Frisch's Big Boy.

By the time she gets home the house is in deep twilight. She stands for a moment in the dim front hall. The aunts and the uncle are gone—out for their ritual Saturday night supper at the Mayflower, she supposes. For a second she's afraid she's alone here. All her losses converge and catch her in the midsection so that she staggers in place, Carroll now and at the same time that lost child here for the first time without Violet.

Then she hears the girls. The sound of their voices draws her through the front parlor to the music room. The voices go on and on, twining in a concatenation of chords and trills that transcends the ordinary. Whatever they're about, they're deeply engaged in it.

She finds them on the floor in front of Great-Great-Grandmother's gilded chair under the ancestral tapestry. The chair was shipped down to Jacksonville from New York by train after the War Between the States and it came the rest of the way overland by oxcart. Pretentious Suzy makes a big point of this. "You should be proud of your Southern heritage."

She is and she isn't. Even though growing up in this house has left Carroll with a hatred of antiques, this one is a beauty. Wooden cherubs on clouds cavort around the velvet cushion in the back, carved in fruitwood and gold-leafed by some French craftsman. Golden snakes emerge from a rosette at the crown of the design and slither down to ornament the arms, and the legs are carved to represent vine-covered trunks of trees whose leaves spread around the base that supports the velvet seat cushion.

The fight, if that's what it is the girls are engaged in, seems to be about the chair. At least she thinks so.

She has no way of knowing.

Too engrossed in the business at hand to notice her, the twins are talking. They go on and on in such recognizable cadences that it takes her a second to realize they're speaking in that weird language of theirs, not in isolated words, now, but completely. It's like nothing that she's ever heard before.

These aren't the girls she knows.

They aren't like anybody she's ever seen or heard of. They are beautiful, absorbed, completely submerged in whatever is going on between them. They might as well be two Martians, touching antennae on some alien chip of rock orbiting endlessly in the peculiar sky of an alternate universe.

They've just come in from a late dinner when the phone rings.

"Are you all right?"

"I'm fine. Who is this?" She already knows but the girls are milling in the hallway and she doesn't want to have this conversation in front of them.

"It's me."

"Oh. Hi. Can you hold a minute?"

"I just wanted to be sure you're all right." Forlorn, he seems to be trying to hold her.

Exasperation makes her brisk. "I told you, I'm fine. Now would you please hang on a minute?" Carroll props the phone and sees the girls into the TV room. She shuts the door before she picks it up again. She can't say why she keeps her voice low. "Where are you?"

"Still in Knoxville," Kurt Graver says. He sounds exasperated. "They've been giving me the runaround all day. They won't let me see him until tomorrow."

She thinks irrationally that she doesn't care if Kurt never sees him. She can't cope with the twins' grandfather right now. She doesn't want any more information than she already has. Right now it's all she can do to deal with the girls themselves. He's waiting so she says, "That's too bad. Is there anything else?"

"Not really." He can't seem to get off the phone. "I just wanted to be sure you were OK, OK?"

"Well I am, really. But thanks anyway."

"Well, great."

"But thanks for calling."

He sounds so sad when he says, "I guess that's it," that she's sorry when he hangs up, breaking the connection.

28

IN THE HILLS outside Knoxville, it's just getting light.

Sitting in the rented car in front of the posh, secluded country place where Hal Oliphant is a patient—correction: prisoner, Kurt Graver is alone with a lot of bad material he doesn't want to think about. He fled into the computer network so he wouldn't have to think about it. Living through his past was tough enough. Discovering he can't shake it is worse.

Writing elegant and sophisticated programs, he may even solve some of the world's problems. He just can't deal with his own.

He needs to get this over with. Then he can go back to Jenkins and take care of the twins for good and all. He'll get them institutionalized if that's what it takes. He'll have them put where they can't hurt anybody ever again.

Wait a minute, Kurt. As far as you know, they haven't hurt anybody. In his extreme state, facts have blurred and fused. The generations: Hal Oliphant and his unknown dead brother, Vivian and Zane, Jane and Emily Archer have become one.

Is this the puzzle or the key to its solution?

He doesn't know. So many bad times crowd him that he can't think, unbidden memories piling up in the car like layers of ghosts. On top is the night his mother ran away, riding to her death in Hal's car. His and Billy's lives were never the same.

An agonized growl makes Kurt jump. *Is that coming out of me? Idiot. Be cool. There's nothing the matter with you.*

He's itching all over. Even the inside of his mouth itches. Things he's suppressed for years are crowding him but bad as they are, they aren't as bad as the prospect of leaving the car. He seems to be OK about being outside today; he's just a little weird about getting out of the car. He can't do it until he has a certain destination. He'll be OK when the porch light switches off and the watchman opens the front door. Then he can go up and ring the bell.

Until then he's at the mercy of his past. He's like a pilgrim walking by a series of roadside shrines, forced to consider the scenes. Here's his pretty mother; he lost her and his faith in love the night of the wreck. Everything about her was negated with the discovery that she'd lied. He sees five-year-old Kurt playing outside with the twins. Zane's grin still makes him shudder. He sees Vivian crying; in spite of his bleeding arm they hug in a silent, binding pact to make it not make any difference. Daddy heard him scream. Sobbing, he fumbled with a tourniquet. Zane's mother ran out with her hair down, weeping. Vivian sent drawings to the hospital and Zane apologized. So they put themselves back together and smiled and began again. Three children, lifelong friends.

But, God! He used to come in unexpectedly to find the twins in silent communion. It was unearthly. He'd surprise them sitting with their bowed heads almost touching. Zane and Vivian, Vivian and Zane, and in the deep, ugly part of him that forever reads the bottom line, Kurt has to wonder exactly how deep and how far their strange love took them.

So the worst thing, that he can't bear to talk about, is what happened at the end. If he didn't tell Carroll Lawton this part it was for a reason. It's just too painful. It beggars the moment in which he looked down into the blossoming smoke and saw blood spurting from his wrist.

That healed. This hurts all the time.

In the end it was his fault, for making Vivian fall in love with him. For pretending she was an ordinary person. For loving her ever since they were five years old. After the accident they went on playing in the gazebo at the bottom of the grassy hill behind the Archer place, Kurt and Vivian and Zane with their heads together, laughing and colluding as if nothing bad had ever happened and nothing ever would.

He got blown up and they grew up together anyway, and

by the time he was at Stanford Kurt knew he wanted to marry Vivian. She and Zane were in Florence, studying. When the twins came back to California they had stopped being pretty kids. All three of them were grown—two grown men and a beautiful woman who loved Kurt, she did! He told her everything he hoped for and everything that had happened while she was gone and everything he knew. He was so stupid he wondered how Zane knew his secrets too.

When he charged Vivian with it she didn't explain. She only said, "He knows everything about me. He always has." Flushing, she touched his cheek. "Oh Kurt, he's my brother."

Swallowing his memories, Kurt said, "He's my brother too."

He should have paid more attention to it: how uncannily Zane *knew* without being told.

Which is what brought Zane into the gazebo one night when he was supposed to be at a party in San Francisco. He was silent and intrusive as smoke. Kurt and Vivian were together in the darkness; she burned brightly, so silky that Kurt lost himself in her, making love fiercely, as if he'd never made love before. And Vivian? For the first time they were alone together and Zane wasn't expected until sometime near dawn. Vivian murmured, "So beautiful! I want us to be this way always." But Zane? He had turned the motor off and left the car outside the gates so he could move silently through the deep grass. In the darkness he slipped down the hill and came into the gazebo so quietly that Kurt didn't know he was there until he spoke.

He knows now what at the time he refused to recognize. That the two were linked and no matter what happened or who tried to come between them, they were twins first and the bond would always prevail. Minutes before, sweet Vivian stopped moving under him. She was trembling even before her brother spoke. Before any ordinary person could have seen or heard Zane approaching, his twin sister knew.

Rigid and pale, Zane spoke out of a white fury. "OK, Viv."

She and Kurt sprang up, still clinging. Kurt couldn't

know, but it was over. "I love you," Vivian whispered anyway.

Kurt locked his forearms against her back as if he could blind her with steel. She pressed close. Foolish in love he whispered, "I'm going to take you away." She didn't speak. She had lost the power. She just raised her hands and pushed him away. As she turned to Zane and began moving him out of the gazebo, Kurt saw the sheen of tears blurring her face.

The string of coincidences began. Falling objects. Malfunctioning cars. Somebody was trying to hurt him. Vivian's color changed. When she touched his mouth her hands trembled. Kurt thinks now she killed Zane to save his life. This then, is how far the twins' strange love pushed them. Far enough to make Zane try to kill Kurt to keep Vivian from loving him. Far enough to make Vivian do what she did to save his life.

But she raged and keened like a fresh widow when he went over the cliff.

When the medics brought Zane's body up from the rocks at the bottom, Kurt looked into Vivian's eyes and saw there was no room left there for him. So he died too. It killed them all. As they carried the body across the highway and through the main gate onto the Archer place, Kurt reached for Vivian, trying to pull her to his side so they could walk up the drive together. "Don't," she cried. "Don't touch me, I'm a murderer."

"No," he said passionately, "you're fine. It was an accident."

Then, God how she pulled back and wheeled on him, Vivian, who bared her teeth in a flash of savagery; she might as well have raked them across his throat. "Get away!"

"Please," he said, "it's OK, really. Now we can be happy."

"No!" She dragged her nails across his cheek, scoring it so he would feel the sting and remember. Weeping, she hissed at him. So it's this that he can't tell Carroll. This, then, is how she demolished him:

"It could have just as easily been you."

He doesn't want to be alone with this another minute.

He wants to go past the front desk and into the modern wing where, he is told, the father of all this is in the psychiatric equivalent of Intensive Care. The first year was prepaid, they said. Committed himself. Then things happened with him, they won't say what. "Heavily sedated," they said yesterday. "Can't talk to you." He said he was from the Jenkins, Florida police. They didn't look closely when he flashed his Stanford Computer Center ID. "He has to." "You can try," they said. "We'll hold off his meds tomorrow until you get a chance to question him, but don't expect much."

He expects a lot. He expects to look into the corrupt father's eyes and see Zane Archer's face. He would like to push it in.

Stand up, you old bastard. I don't care how sick you think you are. He'll straight-arm this Hal Oliphant and put some hard questions. If the old man really stands for everything that's happened, Kurt will look into his face and know. Crazy or not, it will show.

If Kurt raises even a flicker of the power or is it truth that he can't describe but knows he'll recognize, he will press until he gets the rest. If he has to, he'll batter it out of the old man. Then maybe he'll know what to do about the twins.

At nine, they let him in.

They're courteous enough. At the rates Hal's lawyers are paying to keep him in treatment and out of jail, they'll do anything for a person. They usher Kurt through the Victorian parlors to the new part of the building, delivering him at the nurses' station. "There he is," the head nurse says, indicating an isolated figure in a wheelchair at the far end of the gleaming corridor, framed in a window through which the morning sun shines. Looking down at Hal's chart she says, "I think he's aware. Since you're from the police you already know his condition makes him immune."

"I'm not here to prosecute," Kurt says. Questions boil and he can hardly hear. "I'm here to find out."

"Don't count on much," she cautions and then adds unexpectedly, "And whatever he says, don't let him get you upset."

But he is fixed on the figure at the far end of the hall.

Passing half-open doors that offer glimpses of patients pacing, staring, turning faces to him like wearerless masks, he goes along the apparently endless hallway, skating over the shiny linoleum on silent feet. By the time he reaches Hal Oliphant he's almost figured out what he's going to say. A part of him wants to grab him by the throat and shout, *You bastard, you killed my mother,* but he won't. He'll come in from the direction of reason, hoping to get reasonable answers back.

Light frames the old man with the patrician face and the remnants of silver hair flying in wisps around the gaunt head. Hal's face is raised, half-turned to the window and he does not respond immediately, when Kurt speaks and then waits. "Mr. Oliphant?"

In the little interval when he still imagines Hal Oliphant is going to respond to his greeting, Kurt studies him: the sloping shoulders in the starched blue pajama top, the garish afghan pulled over the useless legs. *How could my mother ever have been in love with this? How could she give up her life over something like you.*

"Mr. Oliphant, I've come a long way to talk to you." When it becomes apparent Hal Oliphant isn't going to speak, Kurt begins. "You won't remember me but I am Kurt Graver. My mother was Esther Graver. You wrecked our life but you may not remember her."

The steely eyes are filmed, whether with hatred or indifference he can't know.

Kurt says, "I don't know if twins like you even remember what they do. Good. Evil. Are they all the same to you?"

He hears nothing but the faint gurgle of fluids moving through some hidden drain.

"I'm here because Father Franklin Davage told me about that girl that you probably tortured and killed. No he didn't tell me what you said in that confession but you know and I know you wrecked that person. If you want to know the truth, you wrecked Father Davage too. Priests know the devil on sight and I could tell he'd looked the devil in the face. Right, Hal?"

He imagines he sees a fly walking across the surface of one of those unblinking eyes.

"And poor Veda, that you were married to?" He leans close, trying to read some hint of an expression in his face. "She says you murdered your twin brother. So you killed your own brother and you knew what happens with twins like you but you got married and had twins anyway. And never told. And went on doing like you do."

He can't be sure exactly what kind of map of corruption this old man followed once he left the Archer place but he can see its trace in the shriveled face. But age and disease have reduced Hal Oliphant; his body has withered and his face cleaves to the skull. Has all the evil been leached away along with the flesh? Kurt hopes so. He doesn't know.

"What you don't know is that one of your own twin children was a killer—Zane. No. Vivian did it, but. No. It . . . I was there and I can tell you that one of your twins was a killer but . . ." He chokes. My God! Even today he can't say which one. "Then. Ah. Your daughter, Vivian. Ah. She got married. She had twin daughters too. Their names are Jane and Emily," he says.

The old man doesn't stir. He just breathes quietly with his thin chest going in and out under the starched pajama top. Unnerved, Kurt sees that under the afghan, his scrawny legs are bare.

"Emily and Jane." Kurt's voice is shaking. "Do you know how awful this is?"

Backlit by morning sun, the old man won't look at Kurt.

"Now Vivian is dead and the twins' father is dead and I can't prove the girls did it but somebody else is in danger and I *need to know*. I think there's something here that I don't know about and you're the only person who does. Listen," Kurt says desperately, "you have to help.

"You have to tell me before somebody else gets hurt." *Carroll,* he thinks, realizing this isn't only about stopping the twins. It's also about her. Pressed, he says, louder, "If you don't help me, somebody else is going to die."

Still the old man does not speak. Or won't speak. He just sits there with his hands folded on the afghan and his eyes fixed on some point just outside the window—the top of a tree, perhaps, or a bird circling in the blue air above the hills of Tennessee.

"Turn around and talk to me, you old bastard." Angry now, Kurt puts his hand on the arm of the wheelchair and whirls it around to confront the old man. Thus Kurt goes head to head with Hal Oliphant, shouting into his face.

When he looks into blue eyes milky with full-blown cataracts their still, shallow surfaces are stupendously blank. The old man moves his mouth all right, but there is only noise. The shapes it makes suggest cadences, like sentences, but there is no meaning here. The stroke, if that's what it is—the grim march of ischemic attacks across his brain has left Hal's consciousness intact, but trapped. Malevolent but captive, Hal Oliphant is paralyzed, unable to tell Kurt anything he needs to know.

At least he can't hurt anybody now.

Bubbling, the old man goes on in a drone that will not separate itself into syllables and in time, fades into nothing.

Still Kurt stands staring into his face for too long. Finally he turns without speaking and starts to walk away.

And is riveted in his tracks by a phlegmy, guttural shout.

"You think I don't remember her?"

Trembling, he wheels.

"The stupid little bitch."

Something inside Kurt cracks in two.

Then out it comes, words all mixed with mucus and saliva, so fast and terrible that Kurt is riveted. "You think I don't remember her, you with your agonized face cracked wide and turning grey with guilt over something you didn't even do. Don't think I don't remember. Kurt Graver, yes! Don't think I don't despise you too. I would kill you if I could. I would poison you with memories. You think I've lost all my power, well wait."

If Kurt raises his hand now to ward off what's coming, it's too late.

Contorted by missing teeth and the twisted tongue, the words keep coming out. "*Listen*. I'll tell you everything she and I ever did to each other, your mother and I, what we did

with your father's knowledge and without; oh *yes* Billy
Graver was afraid of me. I could have had you killed. His
baby boy. Which he knew. This was the nature of our
unwritten contract, see?

"His only son's safety, in exchange for which . . . I
took certain pleasures." Air rolls around somewhere inside
the old man and let itself out in what may or may not have
been a laugh. And he resumes. "Pleasures, yes."

The words are so distorted by the disability of the speaker
that they're hard to make out. Repelled as he is, Kurt finds
himself leaning forward so he can make the twisted sounds
make sense.

The old man's tongue lolls but still he speaks. "Billy
turned his back and let it happen. He did it for you. I wanted
more. I had to throw it in his face. You bet I remember
raunchy little underbred Esther Graver with that hot mouth
and her foolish hopes. I remember my wife Meredith's face
when I came into her bed without even washing Esther's
body off of me. I remember your fool of a father, the agony
of betrayal twisting his stupid, noble face, and as for you,
you were too little to factor. A baby. You were nothing to
me. Another newt wriggling across the face of the universe."

Filmed as they are by cataracts the eyes glimmer evilly.

"A speck on the world I am ordained to swarm over and
sully with my mouth and my hands until it is destroyed. I do
it in the name of US, whose destiny I alone am left to carry
out."

Hoarsely he begins the obscene litany.

"Us."

"Me and my dearest brother Evan. Paired in the womb:
dark and light. Death and life. Evil, good. Evil wears a smile
on its face, while good frets.

"All human beings are all both evil and good, but some of
us are more one thing than another. And when we come in
pairs . . .

"Well.

"When we come in pairs, we come in pairs.

"'Oh look,' Mama said, after she got over the shock,

'Twice as much of everything!' She was frightened by some of the things I did. She took my face between her hands and looked at me with those wet, weak eyes and when she said it, her voice shook. 'My darling Hal. That means you can be twice as good. Mmm hmm?'

"She couldn't know what fierce needs itched inside me, prurient, raging like scabies. Like lust.

"Evan knew.

"My brother Evan, who wanted to do *good*. D'you know he wanted to be a priest?

"That priest Davage came around, worrying it. Worrying over us. ('Oh son, *son*.') Well I showed him. Sullied and destroyed him and threw him away. Try *holiness* on my brother, will you. Your hope and God. God indeed. Never mind what lies I told to get rid of him. Got him hounded out of our church. So much for you, Father. Bye bye. I would have seduced him if I could."

Kurt flinches.

The old man sees it and his voice crackles. "Or you."

Excited by his audience, the old man has wriggled until he slides sideways in the chair so that his neck bends at a tortured angle and one foot droops off the wheelchair footrest; it's clear he doesn't know. Muscle and flesh are wasted now, everything gone except the evil spirit that drives the recital.

"And Evan, who should have known where the ugly stories about that priest came from, my poor brother was too upset to see it. Good. He prayed. 'We are two, so we contain twice as much good,' he said. He's half right.

"When we come in pairs, we contain twice as much of everything. And if one of us is lost, nothing is lost.

"Whatever the other has, the survivor takes on.

"Evil.

"Good. But good is weakness. I saw it in Evan." Something starts deep in the old man's chest and surfaces as a desperate noise—is he choking? Kurt is trying to break free of his own paralysis to pound the old man on the back when he realizes that, my God, he is laughing.

"So good is weakness," Hal Oliphant says again. "And if we discard the good?

"Then the best survives and triumphs. Evil.

"Evil. Yes. And proliferates. And makes us strong."

There is that ugly sound again. Vile laughter that makes Kurt shrink. Hal says,

"We can do anything.

"Us. Me and Evan. For I contain everything he was. First it was US, brothers in the flesh and in the bone. Brothers in the soul, and the current that flowed back and forth between us was stronger than any force outside the pair: Mother. The church. The thing that bound us came out of the major force that drives the world and in it we were bonded. Evil. Good.

"If I got drunk, my brother staggered. When I soiled a woman, he groaned in shame. He caught me with a girl we knew. I had my knife; I was laying her open like a Delaware River shad.

"*Look.* I grinned with glittering teeth. *You want?*

"Yes it was a test. He failed. My twin, who did not have to scream for me to hear him screaming. *Noooo.*

"Of course he had to die. Never mind how. And if it was like cutting out my own heart it was like something more—that itch or lust that made me squirm elevated me. I was writhing in evil joy.

"It made me howl in pleasure. 'MORE.'

"So if Evan hated the evil in us, then that evil was all mine. And if when I cultivated it, poor Evan tried to stop me . . . Well.

"So in the end it is I. I became the repository of all the good along with all the goods that we had shared and I alone harbored all the evil resident in any two people. Me. With power comes responsibility. When I finished with Evan the fucking frightened bastard wept like a baby, not because he was dying but for what I, his twin brother, his murderer, was becoming. Had become.

"Look on my works ye mighty, and despair.

"I do what I must. I will do it for as long as I can."

The old man is breathing heavily now, exhausted by his recital, and in the silence Kurt gathers himself because he's scorched by what's just happened here, raw in every nerve and fiber, dry-mouthed and beyond tears. Drained and shaking as he is, he has to pull himself together. He's just about to do it too; he's touched the wall to ground himself and has begun backing along the endless stretch of corridor between him and the nurses' station when the old man's voice catches him like a bullwhip. Paralyzed as he is, slanting sideways in the chair and unable to right himself, Hal Oliphant maims Kurt as surely and as permanently as Zane did when he took his hand. Every morning for the rest of his life Kurt will wake up trembling.

"Fuck yes I remember her, your mother, that stringy lascivious, vain little hungry bitch with the wet eyes and the dirty mouth and her heels around my neck; I remember every woman I ever did and every evil thing I do. All the evil I am meant to do.

"So I rejoice, looking at you with the blunted arm and the agonized face, because without being told I can see the marks of my only son on you. Evil lives. It makes me proud. Too bad his weak sister made Zane die, but even that . . . The evil persists. It traveled through her. He took your hand, my Zane, but that's not a patch on what I took; I took your mother and destroyed your father, yes. I am the king. I took your life. WAIT A MINUTE THERE," he gurgles as Kurt finally pulls loose and starts moving.

"Slippery, hot Esther Graver, who wanted to sing the songs I was humming. She believed everything I said. It was dropping a stone in a pond and watching the rings of pain go out like ripples, while I sat laughing on the bank. WHERE ARE YOU GOING?"

But Kurt won't answer and he won't turn back.

Still the old man's voice follows him. "For every evil act demands an audience."

Until Kurt disappears around the corner and the speaker trails off. "There is no performance without applause." The old man tries his voice again and finds that the only thing he can make come out is unbroken, unpunctuated noise.

But shit, fuck, slithering excrement and dust and my own voice struggling to get out and all I can make are these noises that make the nurses laugh. Damn you forever, you with your hurt look and all your petty urgency, you don't even hear.

Don't think I don't want to tell you about your mother. I want to watch you wince and see her sins marching across your face.

And don't think I wouldn't rub your face in the details if I could. I'd tell you everything we did to each other and all the filthy things she said to me in the middle of our secret bouts of sex. If you can imagine it, that dull-normal byproduct of some guttersnipe's coupling had hopes and dreams, she wanted me, *the foolish little pile of guts. She thought we were in love! And I? If I could I would level the halls of this hospital with my huge voice.*

Then you would know what I thought of her.

Of all of you.

But my tongue swells up in my mouth and I can't speak. My body won't obey and the selfish nurse bitches leave me in this chrome-and-plastic torture instrument, and if I slip sideways, too bad. All the evil I am *piles up inside like vomit until I gargle to let it out but my limbs fail and my throat clogs so I'm lodged sideways like a broken doll with a plastic smile on my plastic face. I HATE!*

Alone, with nobody left to notice and nobody to be hurt by what I do or say. The lust is on me; it's burning me up! The itch is killing and I can't scratch. My life is a trap! Born to destroy, and now . . .

The miserable God of that craven cleric Davage has struck me down. I'm mute as a mole snuffing along the corridors of the underworld with no way to strike and no more ways to hurt; all the hate in the world boils up in me like pus with no way to erupt, and I am powerless. I can't shoot you or stab you or lie about you or push you under a truck.

I can't tell you that I wanted to kill your mother, all right, but she was the one who wrenched the wheel.

Trapped as I am, I can't even hurt you with lies. You may think death is the ultimate punishment, but this stinking earthly prison is worse.

*If I strain at the tray I can push my food off on the floor
while they aren't looking. A pathetic means of revenge, the
only power left to me; when they remove the plastic bib I
can puke in their hands, and when they change these
miserable plastic diapers they have to throw the rag over
me fast or else—just watch, ha ha I can pee in their face.
That's all!*

And yet. And yet.

*I live again. My child has children, so it lives again. You
meant to hurt and instead you brought me hope. There is
someone to come next. My blood will follow me.*

*Two girls, nor far from here. Their parents dead, and
somebody else at risk, this fool has said. He wanted to take
help, but instead he gave such satisfaction! Yes!*

Yet they come next. Next they come.

My daughter dies but I live again.

In the next generation.

The next set of twins.

But Kurt is rushing out of the place with his eyes wild and
his mouth stretched wide, gasping for breath in a desperate
race for his life. He'll spend every day of his life from here
on trying but he can never erase the contents of the past few
minutes. Scarified as he is, tortured and miserable, he has
come away with what he flew to Knoxville to get. Trying to
murder him with words, Hal Oliphant has verified something that Kurt has suppressed ever since he first fell in love
with Vivian. In giving him the words to frame it, Hal has
brought it home.

"Oh, God!"

Nurses swivel and stare. He leaves the place at a dead
run.

Kurt is so crazed and the nurses are so distracted that
none of them will see the old man straining in his chair so
frantically that he slips sideways in his rolling daytime
prison with his face twisted and his jaw cracked so that his
mouth opens on a crazy diagonal; they won't hear the
cryptic, polysyllabic rambling that goes on and on and on.

At the airport, Kurt hurls himself out of the rental car and heads for the nearest phone. Frantic, he spends the better part of an hour dialing and redialing the house on Arbor Street in Jenkins, frustrated by a busy signal. He has to reach Carroll; he has to let her know. As his plane is called he redials for the last time. Miraculously, the phone rings and he is wild because he thinks nobody is going to answer; then at the last minute she picks up just as the final call for boarding comes over the loudspeaker, announcement and he thinks it is her voice overlapping; he has to take it on faith. He has only a minute to explain. Rushed, he shouts, "It's me." Then the urgency overtakes him and before she can say anything beyond hello, he blurts the rest in desperate haste.

"Evil," he says as the plane boards, and for a second tears strangle him. As soon as he can speak he finishes. "One of the twins is evil and from generation to generation the problem is, which one. They're so close they protect each other." He is about to die of this. "They take on each other's traits. Eventually one of them dies."

Too stricken to wait for a response or indeed understand who is listening, he finishes. He is weeping openly now. "And until one does, you have no way of knowing which is which."

29

EASY ENOUGH for Peyton Larrabie to get rid of his sisters today; they are like sheep. He needs them, but he despises them.

He's sent them off for a boat ride in the waters around Apalachicola with his boss at the insurance agency. Rudy Benson is happy to do the favor and he'll keep them occupied for hours. "I'd love to go with you," he told the girls this morning, "but I'm having a lot of pain in this back of mine."

"Oh, Peyton," Suzy said with honest regret.

"Poor Peyton." Patsy's soft jowls shook with sympathy.

"I'd hate to disappoint Rudy altogether. That's why I'm counting on you. After all, he is my boss."

Only Elaine hesitated. "A boat ride on a Sunday? What about church?"

"Oh," he said hastily, "he isn't picking you up until nine. I told him you were going to the eight o'clock." He already knew his sisters would use the hour in preparation—Elaine to pack food for armies and Suzy and Patsy to try on and discard half a dozen beach costumes. And the ammunition he used on Rudy, to set this up for his own convenience? "I think my sister Elaine has a thing for you." OK, he knew enough about his employer to know his area of vulnerability. Easy enough for Peyton to lie. Then he iced the cake. "But she won't go unless you invite the others too."

"Go ahead," he said to each of his sisters separately. "Don't tell the others, but I think Rudy has a thing for you."

So he despises his sisters, for being gullible. For making him the man of the family when all he wants is to be his own man. But he needs them too.

He needs them to look after his creature comforts—clean

shirts in the dresser, hot meals waiting every night, a ready excuse for any of the women who have tried to marry him. *I can't make any long-term commitment, I have to take care of my sisters.*

This is both true and not true. It's a two-way street. His sisters like having a man around to escort them so they don't look like hungry women, which is what they are; they feel safe sleeping with their windows open and taking the garbage out at night. It's cheap living in the family home; Peyton can spend his time off in clubs and singles bars, taking women where he can, snorting and drinking until he's completely wasted and then retreating until he's ready to fight again. It's like living in a well-run hospital.

Which has never been the real thrill.

Never mind what is the real thrill. Something Peyton does every once in a while and thinks about perpetually between times. He loves the secret slide of his hands in silky, forbidden places. He doesn't know what it is about it. He only knows it makes him feel wonderful. He never lets himself notice exactly what he's doing. Mmmmm.

When Violet's pretty daughter Carroll used to live here all the time he pursued her down hallways and stalked her at the supper table with his palms wet and his mouth watering, and if he writhes in frustration now it's because the girl was quick and wary and never trusted him. She would have hit or yelled or both. She and the guardian aunts stood between him and what he wanted.

That and the pressure: what would happen if he made a misstep and exposed his guilty secret to them. It would have been the end.

But now he's looking forward to a day alone with the twins.

Those pretty, tawny things with their sultry, veiled looks: He thinks they may even be looking forward to a day alone with him.

Ever since Carroll brought the girls into the old house, something has changed. The place is so filled with new possibilities that everybody's on edge. Peyton himself has been squirming in anticipation. His mind rings a change on the chewing gum jingle: *double the trouble, double the fun . . .*

He's been busy planning. Buying presents and taking them out to dinner with one of his sisters at the table, not a chaperone exactly. More like a beard. *Do not think my intentions are really my intentions.* Collecting their polite kisses at supper, passing them in the hallways, *this close.* Succulent girls, beautiful, and with an off-the-wall glint in the china-blue eyes that makes him think he's on to something special. He can hardly wait to be alone in the empty house with the twins, who like him by this time because of all the presents, who will sit on his lap and let him read them stories, which is the best beginning.

This, then, is the secret thrill he lives for—trying the youngest and sweetest, taking from them. This has always seemed best to him: aging Peyton, who spends his best moments not in the act with some compliant mature female, but in just this kind of crazed anticipation of the one thing he's not supposed to have.

There will be an event today. He'll see to it. It will be subtle, slight—he never goes too far with the little dears. Just far enough to get that *thrill* when, cringing, they permit his touch because they don't know enough to refuse. Never so far that they go to the police station and press charges; he never gives them anything to *tell* the officers. There will be no way for an outsider to look at them and see what's happened. All he wants is a little private, secret time in which he can get too close and do some things.

So he's sent his sisters off to Apalachicola for a day trip on his boss's Chris-Craft. The stupid, frustrated old girls can bomb around the bayous all day and come back tonight limp with exhaustion, with the skin on their Larrabie noses crisp from too much sun. And Peyton will greet them at the front door with a big smile and his face gleaming with innocence. Unless the boat drops into the Bermuda Triangle or they're blown to perdition. Then he will have the house to himself. He and these foxy girls can settle in for a *long* spell alone. There's food for the month in the larder and he has a week's worth of clean shirts and socks and underwear in his dresser.

He can do just fine without his sisters. He wishes they'd never come back.

And Violet's standoffish daughter Carroll is taken care of for now. She's off at work; she left at dawn, following a hot tip. He wouldn't mind if she never came back either, that stubborn little girl has turned into a militant woman who sees right into him. She thought her aunts would be here when she canceled her trip with the kids for today, he thinks. Too bad for you. Peyton knew what to do. He called Rudy at seven-thirty this morning, when his boss was just putting on his hat with the fish-flies and sticking a six-pack in a cooler to take on his boat.

And Peyton? "Don't you worry about the girls," he told Elaine, who was fretting as she put deviled eggs into the picnic hamper.

"But I promised Carroll I'd keep them today. All that trouble at the beach . . ."

"I won't let them get near the beach," he promised. He was already listening for their footsteps: his prey. Where were they anyway? Sprawled on their beds in their shortie nighties with the matching ruffled pants? On the screen porch with their pink feet propped on the rail, painting their toenails? Absently, he picked up a jar of celery sticks and jammed it into Elaine's hamper.

"You know they can be a handful." Elaine looked tired, torn.

He played on her weakness. "Ruby Benson would be disappointed if you didn't come." He lowered his voice, sinking the hook. "To tell the truth, he planned this whole thing especially to see you."

Poor Elaine. This is how she relinquished responsibility: in a voice shaky with uncertainty. "Carroll doesn't want them anywhere near the beach."

"No problem."

She wouldn't let go. "I promised her to keep them home today."

"Home. I promise. We'll have a *good* time."

Elaine was so intent on Rudy Benson that she didn't catch the overtones. "We need to keep them safe today. All

that . . ." Her voice broke as she repeated, ". . . trouble at
the beach."

"Don't worry, 'Laine. We're a million miles from the
beach." Peyton picked up the plastic bag of peaches and
stuffed it in the hamper without regard of bruising. "Or we
might as well be. I promise, 'Laine. I'll take good care of
them."

Now they are gone and the house is his. Standing in the
kitchen, he can hear his niece Carroll's charges stirring in
the back bedroom above him. He calls. "Oh, girls."

When they don't answer, he goes to the bottom of the
back stairs and calls again. "Oh, girls."

He hears them giggle. He hears bare feet scurrying. He
tries again. "Oh girls, I've got something for you." And
when nobody answers he starts up the stairs. "All right for
you, then," he calls. "Here I come."

As Kurt speaks the Archer twins face each other with
strange smiles. They recognize the voice. The bold twin
puts her fingers over her mouth. Her sister puts her fingers
over her mouth. They don't identify themselves. When he
hangs up, they repeat. "Eventually one of them dies." They
grin; one says, "In hell." The other parrots him. "Until one
of them does, you have no way of knowing which is which."
This is too much to consider. They shed the words like
puppies shaking to dry themselves after a shower that wets
but does not drench. They exchange looks. If one of them is
unsettled by the events of the past few days—the suddenness, the violence, now this, there is no way to tell by
looking at them which one it is. As the message finishes, the
girls grimace.

"Prince Kurt," the bold one says. She surprises them both
with a smile. "Did you hear that? He's on his way."

"Kurt! He'll be here soon," the other says apprehensively.
Jade, or is it Emerald? They have exchanged the rings again
so no outsider can be sure. "What are we going to do?"

"Take him into the kingdom, of course. It's almost ready."
The bold one says to the mute machine. "Prepare to meet
your queen . . ."

The other shrinks. "Oh cut it out. I'm afraid."

"Too late for afraid, OK?"

"But our prince. That we have always loved." They are agreed on this. Or are they? "What if he . . ." She can't finish.

"Mine," the bold one says. "He's mine."

And her sister? "No, he's mine." Unsettled, she goes on. "Maybe not either of ours. Janemanjenem. He hates us. You heard."

"I did! That's love. He's coming all this way to get us, right?"

But her twin remains apprehensive. "Get us how?"

"I don't know." The bold sister goes on with a terrible grin. "Get us in love, I think. We are the queen."

"If only he did love us. He sounds so stern, so mad!"

"He's afraid we don't love him, that's all."

"But what he said: *One of them dies.* Aren't you scared?"

"What's scared? He loves us, right? The queen. Or else . . ." She makes a gesture they both recognize.

"Oh no, not again."

"What's one more?"

"No!" Thinking fast, she builds a ladder to escape by. "He does love us. He just doesn't know it yet. We just have to make him know it, right?"

This brings a sly smile. "Mm-hmmm." The bold sister's arms describe a sensual, intricate tangle of bodies. "You and me, Emerald and Jade and him, him and Jade and Emerald."

This is moving too fast! Her twin shakes her head. "Too many too soon. He's so square? One of us, I think, just one to start with, and when he loves us enough . . ."

"We'll switch. Me first."

"No, me. It was my idea." Cleverly, she waits to see how her bold sister will take this.

She is considering. She has dark plans of her own. "But if it doesn't work . . ." Her hands slashes the air. "Got him. *Krazgo.*"

"*Krazgo nemus.* Please don't get him! We love him."

Relentless, her sister shrugs. "Or not. It all depends. Let's go fix the room."

The careful twin is biting her knuckles. "What are we going to do about the Peyton?"

"Oh, that. Our prince won't see. The Peyton was an asshole anyway."

"Too much! Too many!"

"We had to do it."

"Well I don't want to do it anymore."

"Then get Prince Kurt for us."

Therefore when the worried Kurt Graver arrives in the Larrabie house on Arbor Street near three on that sunny Sunday, the Archer twins are waiting for him. Or one of them is. Her hair is freshly washed and brushed dry in the sunshine so that it has a lemony glow. She has on a rhinestone ankle bracelet and rhinestone earrings that look like full-fledged chandeliers. Her mouth is colored and she's even put mascara on those thick black eyelashes. It has taken her a long time to prepare. She's sitting in the glider at one end of the front porch in laced sandals that twine up her long, perfect legs and a white dress that makes her look even younger and lovelier than she is. The corner is overgrown with honeysuckle and the leaves make such complicated patterns on her face that he has no way of interpreting her expression.

He says, "You remember me."

She smiles but does not speak.

"I'm looking for Carroll Lawton."

When the girl doesn't answer he tries, "Jane?"

She still doesn't answer.

Kurt says warily, "Emily?"

Her face is in shadow. When she answers, her voice is soft. "Whatever." Then she astounds him. "I'm so glad you've come."

This makes him fall back a step. "You two have always hated me."

"Oh no! We just didn't know how to let you know." Emotion makes her voice shaggy, like deep velvet. "I'm just so *glad*."

Careful, he thinks, but he also thinks he may have walked

into exactly the circumstances he needs to resolve this. He's caught one of the girls alone and if it's what, the *good* twin . . . "Where's your . . ." He doesn't know the right word for the relationship. "Where's Ms. Lawton?"

"Something came up."

"Is she at the paper?"

A series of expressions races across her face. "Yes. No. Maybe. I don't know." Then she looks at him brightly. "She'll be back soon, if you want to wait."

"How soon?"

"I don't know. You can sit with me."

He tries again. "Where is she?"

Her face is locked tight as a china box. "Something came up, I said."

Beautifully groomed and made up as she is, even with the rhinestone chandeliers glittering at her earlobes, the girl looks about twelve years old. Together, the twins have always been inscrutable, powerful because they move in tandem, the invincible matched pair. Their defenses are impregnable. Taken one at a time, Kurt thinks, they may be different. He looks at the twin, who shifts as if to make a place for him on the glider. Her sweet expression is disarming. Separated like this, they're not anything terrible. After everything, they're only little girls. He makes his voice gentle. "Can I talk to you alone?"

She greets him with a little shrug. "I am alone."

"Where's your sister?"

She does not answer. "Sit down."

Is this what I have to do to deal with them? Divide and conquer? He sits. A long time passes. He thinks he knows how to begin. "I saw your grandfather." What does he expect her to do, break down and confess everything? What's she got to confess?

She doesn't even stir. "Our grandfather is dead. Did you really come to see us, Kurt?"

"Sort of." She looks so pretty and unsullied, so pleased to have him be here that he's almost ashamed of his real reason for being here. "Yes."

She smiles and considers. The silence is profound. It is

like waiting for a clock to strike. Then in a fluid movement so swift and natural in its passion that he is astounded, she softens and relaxes against him, body pressed to body, heart close to pumping heart, "I knew you had. I knew you belonged to us."

"What!" He tries to pull back. The girl's arms tighten around his neck as he says, "I—what?"

She does not so much slide as flow closer with her mouth touching his ear. "Prince Kurt. We've been waiting for you. You don't know how long we've been waiting for you and listen, yes we do love you, yes, and if you love us . . ." Her soft lips slide down his jaw, moving toward his mouth as she keeps on murmuring hypnotically, the words flowing like warm breath mingling with his. "Please just say you love us, OK, OK?"

"Don't!"

Her hands are at his throat, sliding up, around the back of his neck and then slithering down as she murmurs, "You will be our best knight, our best, most beautiful prince."

To his horror Kurt feels his body responding and in a desperate thrust he pushed her head away with his right hand. "What are you doing?"

"Don't," she cries, and trying to pull him close she whispers harshly, "Please stay, it's important."

"I can't!" Then as she gurgles and cries out Kurt straight-arms her with his stump. And as he jumps to his feet and makes for the porch rail without regard for the drop he sees her twin sister roar out with her hair flying and her teeth bared, hurtling out the front door and thudding along the porch like a witch with skewers for fingernails, but who is she angry at anyway, lunging in his direction with her eyes wide and her mouth ajar like a beartrap ready to snap shut?

Oh God, he thinks, vaulting the rail as the girl on the swing hurls herself between them. *God,* he thinks, landing below with a thud that squeezes out all the breath he has. *What's going on?*

But on the porch above him, sister has fallen on sister now, he can hear them hissing and raging. *The good one and the bad one,* he thinks, because he thinks the one is grappling for freedom so she can pursue him and the other's struggling to hold her back so he can escape.

They're entwined now, snarling, so tightly knotted that there's no telling which is the good twin, if there is a good one, and which is the twin to fear, so that instead of staying to see how this resolves itself or to step between them and help resolve it, Kurt Graver, who has been through a lot, picks himself up almost before his breathing has jump-started and crosses the lawn and gets in the car. He locks himself in and for a second sits at the wheel and trembles, shocked by the violence and even more shocked by his own susceptibility.

Shaken and humiliated, he thinks: *Maybe it isn't them. Maybe it was me.* There he was in her arms, caught short and practically sucked in like some half-assed Lancelot, too homely and pure and stupid for his own good. And even now he doesn't know which one is good and which is bad or whether they both need to be destroyed. But how can you destroy a child, when you don't even know whether she's guilty or innocent? Can you destroy a child at all? He thinks he can hear old Hal Oliphant laughing: *I tried to tell you.* What? The whole thing makes him feel filthy, violated, soiled. Unaccountably guilty, he's so preoccupied by his own weakness here that he hardly notices when the Chinese puzzle of arms and legs and fingernails and gnashing teeth rolls across the porch and separates in a single graceful movement. For a second the girls stand, facing. Then the one twin follows the other who runs, screaming, into the Larrabie house.

Blind to this, Kurt guns the motor, and too pressed and rattled to make a K-turn, he backs down Arbor Street to the cross street, where he straightens the car and roars toward the newspaper offices, whose signs he passed on the way in. It's all he can manage right now. He needs to talk to somebody who understands, and if she doesn't understand, he has to shake her and yell into her face until she does. He should have stopped and called ahead, but there was no going into the house. Maybe he should call the police, but he's not sure what he has to report. Besides, there isn't time. Right now Carroll Lawton is the most important thing. He has to catch her before she heads home. He can see the *Dispatch* sign some blocks ahead. It seems so close!

He has no evidence to convince her, but at least he can keep her from going into that house.

Their cars will almost converge three blocks from here in a near-miss caused by Kurt's anxiety and Carroll's own informed urgency—she's headed home because she's just found out something she doesn't want to know. Each driver is so intent on the problems at hand that the acquaintances, or allies, pass without recognition and without reference, like Einsteinian streetcars hurtling into infinity on tracks that will never meet.

30

DISTURBED AND GOADED by a sickening sense of betrayal, Carroll roars toward the old house on Arbor Street. She needs an explanation from Steve's twins.

What's making her sick is the fact that she can't figure out how to begin.

If she can only do this right the girls will blink in puzzlement and prove she has nothing to worry about. They'll give chapter and verse as to their whereabouts and which of her aunts was with them at the times in question. Wasn't there a thing about Patsy taking them out for the local equivalent of Fribbles or Suzy getting them gold chains? She needs to place them at the mall with 'Laine or Patsy, or with Suzy at the jeweler's. Anywhere except where she's afraid they were.

All she needs is something definitive to tell the police. *You see? It couldn't have been them.* The trouble is, she doesn't know.

If she does this wrong, the girls will be offended by her even asking. She can see the hurt looks: Em, Jane. "You don't trust us." They'll withdraw into their innocence and shut her out for good. She'll lose everything she's gained in the past few days with them.

But in another hour or two, depending on how quickly the police move, people are going to be pressing her for an explanation. She and the twins have to be prepared. On what she thinks is slender evidence, somebody will link Steve's twins with the bad business at the beach.

It's only a matter of time before the statement of the apparent witness to the beach killings reaches Charley Penn's desk at the *Dispatch*. He's always been quick to jump to conclusions. He's going to look at the report and call her. "Twins. Didn't you say you were taking care of twins?" Then he'll call the chief.

Her fault, she supposes, for being so glad to be back that she confided in him. She should have waited to tell him about Steve's twins until . . . Until what? She isn't sure. Until she was feeling stronger? Until she got over Steve? Until she took hold of these kids and learned how to handle them? She doesn't know.

She does know. *Until I got used to them.*

She never should have come back here. She never should have gotten involved with this story. No. That isn't true. She needs this proof that she didn't die with Steve. Her copy is moving on the AP wire, which means readers all over the country are reading this story as she wrote it, under her byline. If she wants to, she can do a "special to" for one of the national news magazines or take a run at the *New York Times* or the *Washington Post.*

But before she can file today, before she can even start making calls, there is this detail she has to cope with. She doesn't know whether she's angry at the twins for running off to the beach against her orders or at the alleged witness who called the station early this morning and messed up her life.

Lacy Cotwell alerted her without even knowing what she was doing. Ignorant of Carroll's private life, she thought she was offering a hot tip. "I thought you'd like to know. This was on the night man's book when I came in this morning—call from some lady who lives at the beach. I shouldn't be telling you this and you won't let anybody know how you know, but you've done me a lot of favors and I owe you a tip. She thinks she can place this *person*—no. People. She thinks she can place them with the victims right before it happened. It's crazy, but she says the murderer is twins."

All Carroll's alarms went off at once. "Where!"

The would-be witness was a weatherbeaten old sand rat who swims a mile every day. She starts out at the north end of the public beach every day and swims to the south end and then walks back. Approaching the ramshackle box she lived in, seeing the screens punched out and door sagging on their hinges, Carroll was relieved. Just another beach crazy.

Then the caller came out on the dilapidated steps and her eyes were so clear in the delicately boned face that Carroll had to think again. The sun-browned old lady wore a faced white coverall and her white hair straggled like a heron's nest, but when she spoke the accent could have been formed at an old-fashioned girls' boarding school like Madeira or Ashley Hall. The cultivated voice commanded belief.

"You know how it is when you see something that doesn't quite make sense to you and your mind turns it around and around until you make it make sense?"

Carroll nodded.

The old lady said, "You'll go into exquisite contortions just to get comfortable with it. Well that's how it was with this. Three people go in the water and only two come out. It didn't make sense."

This was so troublesome that Carroll kept her head bent over her notebook. If she could just keep writing, maybe she could keep her distance from this.

"It was so strange that I had to keep telling myself stories to make the pieces fit. Even yesterday I told myself there was a perfectly simple explanation. The three of them were testing some kind of underwater breathing apparatus, so the third was still out there beyond the sand bar, but submerged. Or else the boy, or man, had sneaked away from the girls underwater and come out of the water farther down the beach? I thought he must have waded ashore while I wasn't looking. Still it was troublesome. I told myself all right, Babs, pass it off, you didn't see anything unusual. Until I picked up the paper today. And then!"

There was a silence. Carroll had so many questions to ask that she couldn't frame any of them. She looked up to find the old lady regarding her with those beautiful, clear eyes.

"Then it did make sense. What I saw. Each time it was the same. Three people would be coming in the water as I swam south, two beautiful girls and some third person. Boy. Or man. Then when I was on my way back up the beach on foot, I'd see them coming out. Where three went in the water, there were only two of them. The girls. Twins."

"What makes you so sure it was twins?"

"I saw them." Her certainty made Carroll feel foolish for asking. "I don't know who they are or who they belong to, but they're beautiful in their bikinis. Sweet children. Lovely tans."

"All right. Twins." Carroll was scrambling, looking for an exit. "What makes you think they were with the victims?"

"Everybody on the beach knows Lanny Raynor," the old lady said. "And I recognized the other one's picture in the paper, but yesterday's young man . . ."

"Yesterday's!" *A body I don't know about?*

"I'd never seen the boy before. He looked so young. You can never tell how many things you make up in retrospect, but looking back, I wish I'd found some way to warn him off!"

So there's this, that Carroll has to deal with, the suspicions of an old lady who doesn't seem at all senile or crazy, and who claims to have seen her girls. But look, she tells her unseen adversaries, there is the business of the puncture wounds. Too bizarre for kids. The murder at the mall was too much like something in the movies, a puncture wound in just the right spot at the base of the skull. The other two were so skillfully placed in the eye socket that they didn't even rupture the eye.

My kids would never . . . Forget it, Charley. I'll just have this out with them and then I can explain.

She pulls up in front of the house. Suzy's car is gone. Where are her aunts anyway? Even though he's her least favorite relative, she's relieved to see Peyton's car is here. She can't say why exactly, but she just doesn't want the girls to have to be alone.

She notes absently that Elaine hasn't swept the front porch. It's gritty with sand from the twin's beach shoes and still littered with stripped filters from Peyton's cigarettes and crumpled paper napkins from last night's cocktail hour.

One of the rockers is overturned but she's too distracted to give it much thought.

Opening the screen door she calls, "Girls?" The front hall is empty of everything except the Larrabie ancestral furniture: Eastlake pier table and carved mahogany side chairs clinging to the wall like huge, submissive beasts. "Janey? Em!" The girls don't answer. If she hears a faint ripple of sound, like a suppressed giggle, she can't be sure where it's coming from. *They're here,* she thinks, relieved. *At least they're safe.* The hall seems unnaturally dark today, so still that the pattern in the flocked wallpaper seems to move and the figure in the Persian runner writhes underneath her feet. Unaccountably, Carroll finds herself wrenching the oddly shaped door open so she can look into the closet under the stairs. There's nothing there that wasn't already there: rain gear, dressy coats her aunts bought and stored for special events that never took place. She calls her aunts. "Elaine?" When there's no answer she tries Suzy, Patsy.

Reluctantly, she calls her uncle. "Peyton?" She's glad when he doesn't answer. Better alone than alone in the house with him.

Still she is aware of a stir in the air as if of somebody moving somewhere just out of sight and so she calls the twins. "Emily? Jane?" Everything is so still that the house might have been deserted by the last Larrabie some time in the 'Twenties but kept preserved, a diorama of the way America used to live. She checks the downstairs rooms: formal living room with its velvet portieres, music room, something different but what; dining room with the surface of the long table completely bare, family TV room looking too neat for an ordinary Sunday, with the crisply folded Sunday papers unread. She flashes on the lost colony in Virginia. History books say they just disappeared. Did searchers come in and find warm pillows bearing indentations from the heads of late sleepers, and pots still bubbling on the stove? It must have been something like this.

She ends in the kitchen, where she finds Aunt 'Laine's excited little note.

Apalachicola excursion!!!

Back soon. I left lunch for the girls.

Don't worry, the note concludes, oh Elaine, you fool! *Peyton's taking care of them.*

Peyton, she thinks with her teeth on edge. She's left them alone with Peyton. Oh Elaine, how could you?

If that yellow-haired old bastard has taken them off somewhere, Carroll's going to kill him. If he lays even one finger on them . . . If he's tried anything with her girls either here or out in some restaurant, she's going to cut out his heart and hand it to the police. Anger propels her back into the main hall and up the wide staircase to the front of the house, where she skids into Peyton's room. There's nothing. She sees a few of those yellowing white hairs on the satin bolster, that's all. She doesn't have the heart to check his sister's rooms. They are too filled with sad memories and dated dresses the Larrabie sisters have cherished like discarded shells. Instead she stands on the worn green carpet that runs from the front of the house back into the new rooms her grandfather built above the kitchen, and she calls again.

"All right, Peyton, where are you?"

When he doesn't answer she goes through the back hall, calling for the girls. Every few steps she stops and listens but there's no repetition of the murmurous noise she thought she heard when she first came into the house. For the moment, there's nothing: no muttering, no ghostly giggles, no thumping as if of somebody trying so hard to hold still that she twitches accidentally and thumps the wall with her elbow. It's as if the house is holding its breath.

Even though she's certain the twins' room is empty, she knocks. She waits for a few seconds too long to open the door. What is she afraid of? Nothing. Something. Not knowing. Finding out.

The shades are down, making a yellow light in the room. She stands in the doorway for a moment longer and then she goes inside.

The twins' room is in disorder, the beds tumbled as if they've just gotten up. Their ruffled nighties are strewn across the rag rug, joining the trail of discarded clothes they'd left the day before. Upset without knowing why, Carroll tries the dresser. She can't know whether she's looking for some clue to the girls' character or whether she simply wants to count the bathing suits, to assure herself that they haven't disobeyed and taken off for the beach.

In spite of the litter on the floor, the dresser drawers are as neat as though the girls were preparing for inspection at summer camp. In the top drawer they've piled underpants here, bras there, night things here. Most are folded the way they were when they came home from the stores at the mall, with price tags still attached. Of course she slips her hand underneath the pile of shortie nighties and of course she finds a notebook. She thinks it may be a diary. All girls keep diaries and they all keep them in the underwear drawer. The only difference here is that the girls have put their secret thoughts into one of those old-fashioned granite-finished composition books with lined pages. She remembers now that they had notebooks with them when she picked them up in the hospital. Poor things, she thinks. When they lost Steve they lost everything. But. They pick up and begin again. Girls are the same everywhere, she thinks, debating whether to open it.

It doesn't take her long to win that battle against her honor.

"Jane?" she calls, just to be sure they won't walk in on her. "Em?" Then she stands there riffling the pages until the thing just falls open in her hands. She is at the last entry.

For all the good it does. The book is dense with ink. The writer or writers were so intent on getting everything in that when they finished the page they turned the book sideways to get everything in, discarding the lines. The writing is so small that it takes her a minute to realize that it's incomprehensible. The girls' secrets are written here, all right, but they're laid out in no language Carroll has ever heard of, inscribed in ideograms and letters so complex that most of what's on the page bears no recognizable resemblance to the Roman alphabet. It's as if somebody has chased a flock of gulls across an ink pad and turned them loose on the neatly ruled and formerly pristine page.

She sighs and puts it down.

Then she moves on to the second drawer. The new T-shirts are here, along with some gaudy, silky shifts completely inappropriate for fourteen-year-olds. Only Suzy could have imagined these would look right on her girls. Her aunt seems determined to trick Steve's daughters out like a pair of little hookers. A look into the new velvet jewelry case bears this out. Suzy has burdened the girls with costume jewelry that is surprising in its vulgarity. *Well,* Carroll thinks just like a convicted mother, making a note to herself, *have to do something about that.* The third drawer yields nothing but shorts and slacks and she's about to turn to the closet when she realizes that she's stopped short of the bottom drawer, with its yellowed varnish stained with rust where the handles sit.

She has to ask herself why.

Creepy, she thinks, and she doesn't know whether it's her suspicions or her fear of finding something that makes her back hairs prickle and her teeth clench as she bends to open the bottom drawer.

There's nothing at first: a pair of T-shirts, the ones the twins had on yesterday. The only thing strange about it is that as far as Carroll can make out, everything else the twins have worn in the past few days is knotted on the rug or thrown on a chair. She puts her hand in the drawer to feel underneath the shirts and yips.

She's stuck herself on something sharp.

Sucking her finger, she stoops to see what it is. She's trying to disengage the shirts from the other contents when she becomes aware of a shadow behind her, something caught out of the corner of the eye that makes her breath sharp as a little knife.

"What are you doing in our room?"

The mess in the drawer rattles as she drops it guiltily. She stands so fast that she cracks her head on the open top drawer.

"What are you doing here?"

"I'm sorry, I . . ."

After everything, after all her anxious calling, the girls are standing right here. "Carroll?"

They look fierce, judgmental. This is getting off to a bad start. She tries again. "Thank heaven you're all right."

"All right?"

Carroll's eyes flick back and forth between them looking for the rings but they've turned them so only the gold shows, which means she has no way of knowing which twin says, "We're fine."

"Why wouldn't we be fine?"

"And what are you doing here?"

They are lovely, flawless, cold as a pair of china shepherdesses in their Laura Ashley dresses—the flowery, girlish clothes she thought they hated, that she was so eager to replace. They have put them on today and fluffed up the sleeves and carefully tied the sashes, completing their costumes with the sweet little sandals Patsy bought for them and the gold chains they must have gotten from Suzy yesterday before Carroll came in from work. They are beautifully dressed as if put together for some ceremony whose meaning they must know, that she can't even guess at. Their smooth blonde hair is brushed and the ends have been combed into little curls. Their bearing is so regal that for a moment, she falls back.

Then Carroll thinks: *Wait a minute. Who are they to question me?*

They see her falter. "What are you doing in our room?"

They are so cold-looking, almost arrogant in the way they stand and judge that even though it's not the way she planned this, Carroll feels anger flare. "What do you mean what am I doing here? This is my house. And what the hell have you girls been doing?"

Murmuring, they fall back a step.

She snaps, "What have you been doing anyway?"

All their greedy demands, these girls, all the anxiety they've cost her so far and now their coldness when all she's

trying to do is help them. She has to prepare them to refute
the surprise witness, and here they are giving her a hard
time—it's just too much. "Come *on!*"

Their heads swivel so their eyes lock.

She hears herself barking, "And don't you go talking in
your goddamn sinister secret language. Something's come
up here, and we have to get together and work this out."

There is a little buzz in the air between the girls. Carroll
thinks it is a push-pull situation but she can't know what the
girls want, or don't want, only that the twins move a little
closer like figurines bonded by contact cement. (Is one
holding the other in place? Is one of them good and one of
them bad?) They move in close, standing shoulder to
shoulder, flank to flank, and they turn to her as one, blinking
those perfect eyes.

"Why Carroll, what is it?"

"What's the matter, Carroll?"

"Something. Well I don't know exactly. Oh God," Carroll
groans, pushed beyond the limit. "It may be something
awful." She blurts, "There's this lady at the beach who says
you were out there when those people got hurt."

"But you don't think . . ." The eyes are blue.

"I have to ask." God, she thinks. They can't both be bad.

"You couldn't possibly think . . ." The eyes are blue and
innocent. But is one pair slightly rimmed in red, bearing
faint traces of a recent fight? If only she knew whether she
had an ally here!

What was the child, she thinks it was Jane, trying to tell
her yesterday? "Jane?" If one of them is her ally here, she
needs to find out which. "Or is it Em?"

They say in unison. "It's us."

"Cut it out!"

They are so cool! "Us, OK? So tell. Just tell us what you
think."

She isn't exactly crying; it's more of a howl. "I don't
know any more. I don't know what I think. I . . ." Through
this exchange she's been nagged by something—oh, it's
her finger, still bleeding from something in the drawer.

It's . . . Their next word slashes through her thoughts. It's so sharp and ugly that she lifts her head as if at the sound of a shot.

"Krazgo!"

Carroll cries, "What?"

One of the girls is barking at the other, "Nemo krazgo!"

"I told you girls not to . . ."

But they are deep in a frenzy of language. "Fronamus glebo. Krazgo. Hemus. Mot!"

She shouts, "You can damn well quit it with the language."

They don't even hear her. "Nemo naja."

Or else they hear and it doesn't matter. "Krazgo. Mot! Mot! Mot!"

"I said stop!"

It doesn't matter in the least. Lost in their fury, the twins have turned away from her and in on each other. Hissing and snarling, they are gripped in a moment so complete and intense, so powerful and exclusive that they exist only for each other. Locked in twinship, they are the only thing in each other's world. They have clamped hands on each other's forearms now, so deeply engaged in a fierce, emotional tug-of-war that Carroll has to wonder if they know she's in the room.

The girls are tweeting and clicking, talking fast, muttering through clenched teeth in that weird and hateful language that leaves Carroll helpless and mesmerized. They fade through the doorway in a vise-like tangle of anger, kicking the door shut so they can continue their pitched battle elsewhere in the apparently deserted house. But in the second before the door slams they respond to her at last, hurling a single spiteful word at her: "You!" It's like a gauntlet thrown down.

"Come back!" Carroll goes to the door to open it and finds it locked. She shouts, "I haven't finished with you, so come back." Where there had been a flurry of sound, squabbling and angry thumping, there is a silence so profound that it strikes her cold. What replays in her head then is not their angry squalling but a speech remembered. Meredith Archer's warning. Enough!

"Cut it out!" she says loud enough to be heard through the locked door. "You're only kids."

Whatever you do . . .

She pulls herself together. "And this door is not the only way out of this room."

This is what finds Carroll Lawton lifting the drawn window shade and raising the back window so she can climb out. This puts her on the screened back porch that runs across the back of the house. She'll go along the porch. Passing the hall door, which the girls have probably locked, she'll duck through the window into her room. If she has to break glass to do it, fine. She's in a mood to break a little glass.

She is so intent on this that it takes her a minute to notice that she's not alone on the porch. Then she sees him sitting moodily in a rocker at the far end, like a retired captain looking out to sea. He looks downcast with his head bowed and his arms in the white coat hanging so his knuckles brush the floor, but the sight of him makes her teeth grind; an ugly taste forces itself up her throat.

"Peyton!" It figures, she thinks. Still he doesn't move and he doesn't turn. She's tolerated her uncle all these years but she's always hated him and somehow his presence here makes sense. "I should have known this was your fault. All right you old bastard, what did you do to set them off?"

When he still doesn't respond she goes the rest of the distance. She'll push him out of the chair if she has to. She wants her uncle standing when she has it out with him so he won't try one of his old tricks and try to pull her onto his lap. "Are you afraid to face me? Is that it?" She's hung up on a sentence from her morning's interview. *When you find something that doesn't make sense, your mind will do anything to make sense of it.* Over the years she's found Peyton asleep in his chair so many times that OK, maybe he really doesn't hear. Maybe he really is asleep. She's always hated touching him, so instead of shaking him awake she says, loud, "OK, Pay, I know you've done something you're ashamed of, would you rather admit it to me or do you want to tell the police?"

And finally comes around in front of him and sees what she has probably known all along, that her uncle is dead. She doesn't have to grab his head by that yellow-white hair and pull it back to know that she'll find a puncture wound right where the pathologist located the ones on the floaters, at the outside corner of the left eye. Nor does she have to go back to the girls' room to know what's underneath the shirts in the bottom dresser drawer. Not ice picks. Hatpins, the clutch of pins she remembers from her childhood forays into the attic, larger than life, long, rusty but still sharp.

"Who was it, Pay," she shouts, outraged. "Who did it? Why in hell don't you tell me which one?" Without even knowing how she arrives at the next thing she finds herself vibrating with urgency. *My God, I've got to save the other one.*

She's too smart to think she can do this alone. She's in the upstairs hall, just discovering that somebody's pulled the phone out of its jack and removed it; she's just about to throw herself downstairs to dial 911 when an uncanny whistle that she does not immediately recognize arrests her where she stands.

"Caaaaa . . ."

It's so thin and shrill that it will take her a minute to identify it as a scream. In the next second, it's cut off. Whirling, she sees the attic door stands open. Whatever is going on is happening up there. The scream unfurls like a black ribbon.

". . . rooollll . . ." The voice is relentless, piercing, terrible. At first she can't make it out. Then she can. Faint as it is, almost drowned out by the sounds of thudding feet, overturning furniture and the sound of a struggle, it sounds like a plea. Her name.

She is riveted, frightened, torn. She needs to call for help but whatever is going on overhead is going on so swiftly and so violently that she has to hurry. A girl is shrilling in agony, tortured, caught between life and death. "Jane!" she cries. "Emily!" Which is villain and which is victim? She doesn't know.

All she knows is that there's a life at risk. If she wastes time running for the phone, somebody's going to die. She has no choice.

"I'm coming," she cries. Foolhardy as it is, terrifying and dangerous, she has to go up there and stop whatever is going on.

31

THE MINUTE she starts up the narrow attic stairs the wailing stops. Nothing moves. Instead of rushing to the rescue with a clear-cut sense of what to do and how to help the crying girl, Carroll is climbing into the unknown.

At the wedge-shaped landing where the stairs make a sharp turn, she hesitates. Until she completes the corner, she can't see the rest of the way. What if something terrible has happened to the girl so she can't cry any more? What can she do against the enemy? She is reluctant to go forward. She calls.

"Jane? Em?"

There is no answer.

She hates the attic. Even when she fled here in adolescence, dodging chores or hiding from Uncle Peyton, the place made her uneasy. The old clothes and pictures abandoned here, the discarded furniture reflect several generations of frustrated ambitions and wasted lives. Building this house, the early Larrabies intended to make their fortune and conquer society. They bought grand furniture to ornament rooms where the powerful would come to beg favors. The entire attic would be finished off and furnished for an expanding staff. Instead their best things ended up here, shelved, along with the family's hopes.

Now the amalgam of half-finished rooms and unfinished spaces is filled with pitfalls, scorpions' nests and uncharted areas where the flooring gives way to naked beams and only a thin skin of lath and plastic separates the unwary from the downstairs bedrooms. Carroll doesn't know which is more frightening, the shadowy crawlspaces between rooms and eaves or the dingy, raw-looking maids' rooms, identical as slots in an egg carton. With their ruined mattresses and stained window shades and cracked plaster they speak of sorrow, like abandoned movie sets or staging areas for unspeakable crimes waiting to be committed. The open spaces in the attic are even worse. They're hung with racks of old gowns and stacked with paintings and chests and trunks and cartons all crowded by grotesquely ornamented furniture covered in tattered velvet and encrusted with rosettes and angels, all these bits and pieces of the Larrabie family past shoved under the eaves and covered with canvas like so many guilty secrets.

The twins could be anywhere.

It could be too late.

She isn't breathing. Even so, she can't hear anything.

Fueled by the climbing Florida sun, the heat in the attic is staggering. When she does breathe again, it takes a minute to get used to. *God,* she thinks, *what am I doing?*

But even though there's an uncanny absence of sound she's certain that somewhere up here, one of Steve's girls is trapped with her beautiful eyes flooding and her mouth stretched wide in a silent cry for help. She can't let anything stop her. She needs to find the twins and see them up close. She needs to look them in the face and bore in, staring, until she knows once for all which twin she has to save.

And which one is the enemy.

She doesn't know what she has to do then, only that she has to do it. *Steve,* she thinks, and feels her heart being pulled inside out. *I'm trying, Steve.*

The top of the mean little staircase is partially blocked by a big, troublingly familiar shape. She has to suck in her breath to slide past it and up into the attic. Clearing the staircase Carroll stands, trembling, in the storehouse of her family's secrets.

She just has time to recognize the object before somebody tilts it and sends it toppling. Oh, it's the . . . With a shattering crash the thing crunches into the stairwell, effectively sealing the exit.

Arrested by the crash and the dust rising from the wreckage that closes off the staircase, Carroll is only half-aware of the sound of footsteps, the girl or girls retreating. The object that blocks the way down is the oversized, incongruously carved chair from the music room. *Why didn't I see what was wrong down there?* High and wide as a throne, with its double seat and paired lions' heads, the thing is so big she wonders how the girls managed to get it this far. What did they do, make Peyton help them haul it up the stairs and then turn on him? What did they have to promise him to get him to bring the chair this far? Shuddering, she can imagine, and is sickened by dislike for the old lecher, who came on to the girls and then let them lure him into some—what. Something that caused his own death.

But they couldn't both be . . . One of them is acting against her will, she thinks. No. Knows. Her breach catches.

Has to be.

"Jane? I've come to help."

Jane doesn't answer. She tries again. "It's me, Emily. If you can't talk, at least thump so I can find you."

She listens.

"If you would just try and make some kind of noise!"

This time she's almost certain she hears laughter.

"Please. God, no tricks!"

Laughter again. Chilled, she understands. They've lured her here as surely as they lured Peyton. Or one of them has.

For all she knows, the cry for help was a fake. Oh God, was it their way of getting her attention? She goes on in a low, level voice that she knows will carry even to the recesses under the eaves. "OK, girls. That's enough. This has to end."

Something above her shifts—birds in the rafters? She feels sand sifting into her hair and into her eyes.

She lifts her voice. "You might as well come out. You know I won't leave until I find you."

The space between her and the finished rooms where the Larrabies kept their maids is filled with furniture. She advances steadily but cautiously, skirting the neatly piled forties modern chairs and tables at a slight distance, speaking as she goes. She is in the main part of the attic now. She calls.

"OK. It's time. I'm coming after you."

For the moment there is a complete absence of sound.

Cautious but determined, she advances. "I want to help."

There is a little stir, a disturbance in the stifling air. The sound she hears could be somebody sobbing. Or somebody snickering. It could be coming from the row of abandoned maids' rooms or the area beyond, which is dark and heaped with discarded treasures. Or it could come from the treacherous space near the front of the house where the skin of the place is thin and easily broken.

"You might as well come out."

A light goes on in the last bedroom. She sees it coming from under the closed door.

"If you don't, I'm coming to get you."

Then the hears the girls, or one of them. The voice is neither hysterical nor threatening. It is clear and chilling.

"Very well, Lady Carroll. This way."

Approaching, she passes the open door to the adjacent room. Unlike the one where the twins are hiding, where a lamp glows, it is only partially lighted. Sunshine filters through the grimy window shade. From here she sees objects have been tugged into the room from the attic and turned to the twins' purposes: portraits, a mounted horsehead she's never seen before; a dressmaker's dummy with its bared muslin breast studded with Great-Grandmother's pearl-handled fruit knives. And in the center of the room a little marble table with vigil lamps in place but not yet lighted.

She does not go in. When she sees what's enshrined there she doesn't want to. Something silver lies half-covered by a piece of cloth. It's probably just as well she doesn't get close enough to recognize it as her dead husband's bracelet; she already has too much to deal with. Rags that might be the victims' bathing suits lie in a little heap, and wiped clean and lying next to them in a sun-burst pattern are four of her great-aunt's longest, fiercest-looking hatpins.

The reporter in her clicks: This is how they did it. She wishes to God this were just another story she could phone in and have done with, but it isn't.

She knocks on the last door. Her voice is low, grave. "I'm here."

As she tries the knob and finds it locked, one or both of the twins will say in an elevated tone of authority that is both incongruous and chilling, "Very well. You may come into the presence."

Damn, damn, goddamn; kicking the rented car along the dusty, nearly deserted streets to the Larrabie house, Kurt Graver leans forward in anger, hatred and anxiety. The rest of the world seems to be at home with the shades down or out to lunch, so what is this town, the last place in the world to honor blue laws? Everything is closed. He found the offices of the *Dispatch* shuttered and he had to hammer on the back door for ten minutes before Charley Penn came down and told him Carroll hadn't reported in yet. Damn all those people out there at the beach or rereading the Sunday funnies without a clue as to what's about to come down here. Damn all stupid inefficiency, damn ignorant Carroll Lawton for ignoring his warnings and most of all damn his own susceptibility, damn craven Kurt Graver for being so thunderstruck by his own unbidden lust that he fled the Larrabie house and those *eerie girls* instead of planting himself on the front steps like a troll with an axe to keep anything worse from happening.

Damn his eyes for not throttling Hal Oliphant until he came back to his senses and disgorged the truth, and damn every minute it's taking him to get back to the house where he's certain something ugly is happening.

And double-damn stupid Kurt for going looking for Carroll Lawton at her office when any fool would have known that forewarned or not, it was the house she would come back to.

He is trembling with insufficiency. Did he live through everything and hunt down Hal Oliphant just to let the twins get away with this? Confronting the incomprehensible, he's spent his life to now trying to make sense of it. Everything depends on what comes next. It is this that makes him hurtle down the main drag toward Arbor Street in the sleepy large town or small city of Jenkins, Florida, with an undeniable sense of urgency.

The feeling that he is fated. No, ordained. To do what? Something. More. It bubbles up in his throat; all his memories converge and he can taste it.

Die, if I have to. Or kill someone.

Inside the biggest of the maids' rooms, the girls wait side by side on the draped cartons they have assembled to substitute for the gold chair with the lions' heads, which they couldn't manage to wrestle the rest of the distance into their makeshift throne room. One thinks, or both of them think: *audience platform.*

"You may come into the presence." They know she can't. The door is locked. But as long as Carroll stands outside, they have her located. They need to keep her in place until they can decide what to do about her. What one wants, the other fears. But to survive as an entity, they both need it. Closer than Chang and Eng, who were joined at the belly, these two are bonded by hate and blood and a terrible sense of urgency, so tightly linked in this moment of crisis that their thoughts flow back and forth in a rush of sound that needs no words to complete the intentions.

—*Not.*

—*Will.*

Desperately they push back and forth—*Not yet.*

—*Have to, yes.* This one is pushing harder. *Want to.*

His sister resists.—*Not if we don't have to.* Which is the stronger?

Which is the queen, really? The bold one presses forward.—*Our life is at issue. We are the queen. We need the execution.*

The other temporizes.—*No execution without trial. Besides, we need her.*

Which twin is smarter?

—*For what?*

—*She gave us the rings.*

And which more dangerous?

—*No trial without its execution.* The bold one is breathless, almost lascivious, in her drive toward completion.

There is a pause before the other continues. *Trial first, yes?* Cleverly, then, but is she effective?—*We like trials.*

Her twin agrees grudgingly.—*If you say so.*

—*The queen is fair.*

His sister stands.—*And we are the queen.*

She goes to the door and turns the key in the lock. Then with a thunderous look at her twin, she resumes her place on the throne.

They repeat then, "OK, Lady Carroll. It's open."

At Greycrest in the wooded foothills just outside Knoxville the staff is riveted by a huge inarticulate howl, an apparently unending river of pain and rage that winds through corridors and penetrates even the private offices. It is coming from the private room where that lewd-eyed, blathering, pinchy old bastard has just been put down for his nap today. He hasn't said a comprehensible word since he got here; instead, he screams. He mutters angrily sometimes, just noise, but it's nothing like this. The ugly open-throated wail is accompanied by thudding sounds and the crash of a metal bedpan being hurled against the wall which is a puzzle to the nurses pounding toward the scene of the crime as so far as they know, his strokes have left Hal Oliphant half-paralyzed, speechless and disabled. "Don't worry," they tell each other, rushing for the room. "He can't hurt anybody."

But he can offend. The room is foul. In spite of the security bars on the bed he has managed to get out. Lashing around like an angry lizard, he writhes on the floor. In the absence of words to express his violent rage and loathing, Hal Oliphant has spread himself around—human waste in every possible form, and when they rush to keep him from hurting himself, the old man collects all his anger—what set it off?—in one final explosion of hatred before his eyes glaze over and his body jerks once and then goes rigid in the ultimate coma.

"It lives!" he gargles, and they have no way of knowing

that he means: evil. It is a hideous outcry that will leave the staff puzzled and shaken. "I live!" *In the next generation.*

When she tries the door again it is unlocked.

"Hello Carroll."

"Hello Carroll."

Their voices are as sweet as their aspect, two pretty girls with shining hair looking at her out of Steve Harriman's blue eyes, with her lost love Steve's expression shimmering just below the surface, Steve's smile writing itself across their lovely, regular features. How can they hurt her? They look beautifully put together, out of place here in this garishly papered maid's room with its pattern of stained poppies and even younger than they are in their little gold chains and their full-skirted flowered dresses.

Standing in the doorway, Carroll feels crowded. There are heavy mahogany pedestals flanking her like the pillars in the palace of Samson's enemies. The girls have used them to hold vases filled with dying flowers. An old bridge lamp stands behind the makeshift throne, striking highlights in their hair. They have put on velvet capes and artificial wreaths left over from some Christmas pageant. They wear them like queens. They are secure here in this place they've made for themselves, serene. How could she have thought they were anything other than lovely?

Yet one has done the murders. The evidence is in the next room, neatly arranged on the little marble tables. When she gets out of here she has to call the police and turn them in. Or one of them in. The knowledge gives her the dry swallows.

They smile at her as if they know none of this. As if they don't even guess there is anything behind her pursuit but simple curiosity. She looks at the velvet-draped boxes where they perch, at the clutter of bronze maquettes and camphorwood boxes and onyx eggs on the Queen Anne side tables and the family portraits dragged in from under the rafters and propped against the violently patterned wallpaper. The room looks bizarre enough but strangely elegant, as if in assembling all these objects the girls had been acting on instinct, in the same kind of prescience that makes the infant Dalai Lama select the objects belonging to his predecessor. If they are not descended from royalty, they might as well be. Graciously, they greet her.

"Welcome," Jane says, if it is Jane.

"Welcome into the kingdom."

"Welcome to Amadamaland."

"No. To the colony. Later we'll take you into the kingdom."

Jane says, "After we explain." She seems honestly pleased to have Carroll here. "It's hard to tell now because we don't have the throne in place yet, but this is the throne room."

"Audience hall."

"Where the trials begin. Whatever."

"Yes." This one's eyes glitter. "The trials."

She swallows hard. "It's very nice." How strange they are, Carroll thinks and, trying to bore deeper and divine what's going on here, she thinks: how cold the eyes are, looking from one to the other. But she does not know. Is this the case or is she projecting the evil of one on the innocence of the other?

"And later," one says, blindsiding her with the information, "an altar to our King, Saint Stephen."

She cries out in pain.

They say as if it's the most natural thing in the world, "Our dear father."

How bizarrely savage, closed as they are inside a circle of their own making.

How sinister.

She is so fuddled by pain and confusion that she falls back on a cliche. "We have to talk."

"See," the one says knowingly, "I told you she'd be glad to see us."

"We'll see," the other says, glaring not at her sister but at Carroll.

"Emily." Carroll does not quite know how to begin. "Jane."

But the bold twin cuts her off. "No. The queen. And we'll

see how well you do with this. After we explain to you.
Even our courtiers must survive the trials."

Her sister echoes, "Yes, the trials."

"But first." She slips down from the makeshift throne
while her sister holds back. She's holding a pair of scarves.
"You have to prove you trust us."

What's she going to do, offer to bind and gag me? "No
way." Shaking her head, Carroll steps back. "You have to
prove you trust me. Otherwise I can't help you. I said we
have to talk."

The girl retreats. "No we don't. Not that way. We talk."

"She and I talk," Jane, if it is Jane, says to her.

So it may be Emily who says firmly, "And you listen."

Thus it is that Carroll hears the tale of Amadamaland and
of Queen Jade—Jane, she supposes, and Emily must be
Queen Emerald. Strange how it spins itself out, frightening
and hypnotic, an uncommon duet in which the girls' voices
intertwine until they are inextricable, quiet from violent,
sweet from malevolent, the Queen of Amadamaland who
has lost their beloved king, Saint Stephen, and to com-
memorate his death has tried to collect knights to fight the
wicked stepmother in his honor.

"Not his fault it went wrong," Em says.

"And not our fault either."

Oh my God, Carroll thinks. *Did they kill Steve?* Tears
have begun sliding down her face. She may understand that
she is approaching the intolerable. Before she can think
about that—Steve—she has to hear this. She has to get
them out of this room. She has to get them to the ground
floor, where she can call the police. "Can we talk about this
downstairs?"

"No," Emily says. That's all. When she goes on it is
reflectively, shaking her head as if surprised by the news she
has to deliver. "They brought it on themselves. Bad knights.
But you never know a knight is bad . . ."

Regretfully, Jane completes it, ". . . until he's bad."

"You have to know your men before you knight them.
You know, the knightly ordeals. Not our fault that some
were found wanting and others . . ." Emily's voice slashes

through everything. "Others tried to defile the queen." Rage makes her chin tremble.

In an angry flash, Carroll sees it clearly. *Peyton.*

"Nobody defiles the queen," she says. "Nobody crosses us."

The twins make their own world, and in it everybody marches to their imperatives. *Whatever you do, don't make them angry.*

Jane, if it is Jane, says, "So we didn't *mean* bad things. But what happened—happened."

"And now it is over with, OK?" The girl fixes her with those irreproachably blue eyes and says, "So no problem, right? As long as you let it rest right here."

Her twin is entreating. "So please let's let it rest right here. Right, Carroll?"

Carroll keeps her tone level but she *will not say* what they want to hear. "I think we'd better go downstairs."

The other is firm. "Not now. Not yet. Not until you promise."

Jane, if it is Jane, says hurriedly, "So no harm meant and no harm done and this is our secret, OK?"

"Look at it this way, yes OK?" Her twin's voice is coming and going in little hiccoughs that devolve into a giggle. "The queen can't help it."

Jane prods gently, "And you love us, right, Carroll? So you promise. You said you came to help us."

Carroll is rattling like a jar full of marbles. She doesn't know why the girls don't hear all of the parts of her clinking against each other. "I don't know what I came to do." She draws herself up. "But I do know what we have to do. As soon as we get the chair out of the stairwell."

"Our throne!"

"We have to talk to the police. I think you'd better take the wreaths off first."

"But the queen promised if we explained to you . . ."

"Yes if we *explained*, that you would, you know. Understand?"

"Understand," the sister says. "So it's OK, right?"

Carroll says, "No it's not OK. Something awful's going

on and I can't help either of you unless you'll say who did it."

The one is pleading. "No."

The other is emphatic. "No." Her face darkens; it's like a solar eclipse. Then something unexpected happens. It's like catching the werewolf in the middle of the change. The sound is savage, abrupt. "Krazgo." It is ugly, wolfish. Commanding. She is reaching in her pocket. "Krazgo!"

Her sister is crying. "Neemo!"

"Krazgo!" The word, if it is a word, dissolves into a fierce, wet snarl of sheer hatred. The two rise as one.

Anything can happen now.

Then before Carroll can turn and hurl herself through the door the girls are upon her, the dominant one first. In the next second the other hurtles after her sister, clawing at her back. Attacking Carroll, they turn on each other at the same time, locked in a pitched battle over what to do here. With nails raking and foam flying, they disappear into their frenzy so completely that Carroll manages to extricate herself. Trembling, she sees as they tangle that the one has her hand raised with something so sharp—a kitchen knife!—that fear makes her teeth clash even as the other shouts "Noooo."

And Carroll throws herself against them, knocking them off balance. It's like trying to break up a dogfight. Her voice whistles in pain as the knife rakes her forearm. All fingernails and gnashing teeth, the girl turns on her sister. "You!"

"No!" Desperate, the victim hurls herself against the attacker with her hand raised—is that a rock she brings down on her sister's temple? The other shrieks and drops the knife. Then they all go down together in a knot of arms and legs, rolling and thrashing until the pedestals wobble and fall into each other: wild twins and desperate woman, tumbling vases, dead flowers, all, in a crash that leaves Carroll dazed and frightened as the twins clear the room and flee into the attic. She discovers that she can't get up.

"Watch out," she cries, not quite sure what she means. She calls out in warning. "It isn't safe!"

Then she hears them rolling down the hall and away from

her; she hears the continuing struggle, pleas for help and guttural outcries and then the terrified, childlike shrilling that drew her up here in the first place, so that once again she is plunged into doubt and confusion.

She doesn't know who they are. Or where they are.

They could be rushing into the unfinished space above the front of the house where there are hazards, bent spikes and broken glass panels, paper-thin flooring. She struggles to raise herself on one elbow. "Watch out," she cries again. "Watch out!"

She hears a voice trailing back. "Carroll . . . Help!"

What's expected of her here? Who can she trust? She is so drained by the events of the past few days, so leveled and shaken that she finds herself stuck to the floor, dizzy and trembling.

Then she hears another sound: thumping and cursing. The noise is coming from the bottom of the attic stairs.

Stunned, she tries to stand. "What is it? What?"

She can't make out the words but she recognizes Kurt Graver's voice. He is hurling himself against the unwieldy, ruined chair that bars the stairway, pounding and desperate.

Carroll is on her feet now, with a pageant of fireworks breaking behind her eyes. She touches her hair and feels blood and understands that in the seconds when the twins made their escape, a toppling vase has bashed her into unconsciousness. She becomes aware as she staggers into the attic that the twins could be anywhere—in the crawl-spaces, behind the heaped furniture, hidden in the shadows, waiting to lurch out at her or sneak up from behind with an ancestral sword or a poker and club her senseless.

But the clatter of footsteps is receding. If the girls were heading for the stairs when they broke away from her, the sound of Kurt's voice stampeded them.

She hears Kurt hacking at the chair with something heavy and then she hears:

"Carroll, please help!"

It comes from the unfinished space near the front of the house. Carroll follows, and with a gasp, stops short. She's at the point where the attic floor gives way to naked lath and a shell of plaster. From here exposed beams make a narrow path over the master suite and MorMama's bedroom.

In the shadows, one of the girls calls, "Out here, Carroll."

The other cries, "No, don't come out here, it's scary!"

She can't see clearly, but she knows what's happened. In their fury the girls ran out on the beams before they realized they were in danger. They are teetering, still locked in unholy opposition. Any distraction, any blow, any hurled object will destroy their concentration. A breath could throw them off balance and send them crashing through the amalgam of lath and brittle, weakened plaster that is all that separates them from the high-ceilinged bedroom that has been sealed ever since MorMama died there.

Jane's voice quivers. "I can't come back!"

"Wait," Carroll says foolishly, "Wait there. I'll help you."

The other girl's voice is like a whip. "Krazgo, bitch!"

"Oh please help me, Carroll!"

So here she is, Carroll Lawton, close to the end and brought up against it: What to do, who needs her help here. She can arm herself and try to bring down the enemy with a curtain rod or throw a brick and hit her, or she can stand here at the brink of the open space and try to reason the girls back to safety.

But they are clinging, whether for safety or in combat, she can't know. They sway precariously.

"Don't," she pleads. "Wait. Don't move. Now if you'll just let go of each other."

"We can't! Come help us!"

"Don't come!"

"Please help us!"

"Wait!" She casts around for a curtain rod, anything to steady them. "I'll find something for you to hang onto."

"There isn't time. Come get us."

Then she hears the most seductive sound. One of them starts to whimper. Whatever they've done, they're still children.

Steve's children. Her toes curl over the edge of the floor. In another second she's going to launch herself. "Oh please don't cry. I'm coming to get you."

His voice is so big it staggers her. "In hell!" Kurt Graver has cleared the stairs. The floor shakes as he thuds toward them.

Hearing, the girls hiss like cornered cats.

Carroll teeters.

"DO YOU BELIEVE ME NOW?" Kurt pushes her out of the way. Carroll falls to one side, safely short of the spot where the flooring gives way to open rafters.

She cries "Kurt, don't!"

Before she can stop him Kurt Graver shakes her off. He's running so fast that he flies off the finished floor and his foot comes down so hard on the beam that the house shudders. He's angry enough to do anything to end this, even kill the girls. Instead his violent footfall hits the beam with such force that the sisters panic and their arms fly. As Kurt realizes where he is and pulls himself up short, shuddering, the twins let go, terrified and furious. Off balance, Kurt extends his arms and pulls himself upright like a rope walker as the girls note his presence and scream as if at the first sight of a conquering army. Embattled, they back away chattering and before Carroll can do anything to stop them the girls hurl themselves on each other in a frenzy of recriminations, and in the strange dark-light entanglement that has driven them all their lives each fights to save herself and finish the other.

Cursing to the skies in their strange language the twins tangle, grappling and rolling without regard for the beams or what lies between them.

For Carroll, every backward step Kurt takes seems eternal. To wait is torture. She won't understand until later that all this unfolds in seconds. Finally Kurt is standing beside her.

And in their transport of fury the girls have hurled themselves off the beam, toppling, deaf to her cries and blind to what lies below them. In that second, they seem to be suspended over nothing. Locked in hatred, they fall on the thin skin of lath and plaster in a frenzy of flailing fists and sharp knees and elbows that shakes the flimsy surface until it shatters and they plunge in a cloud of plaster dust, screaming as they disappear beneath the shattered surface.

Trembling, Carroll hears a single knife-like scream as they fall into the high-ceilinged master bedroom below. She turns to Kurt in horror. He nods as if for him at least, something has clicked into place.

In seconds they clear the attic stairs and run the length of the house, sprinting along the worn green carpeting. The door to the oversized bedroom where MorMama died is closed. There is no sound coming from the room. Nobody cries for help and nobody comes running out to greet her. Unsteady now, she takes Kurt's arm and does not know why he puts her aside when they reach the door, settling her with a firm hand so he can go in first.

When he comes out his face is white with plaster dust and he is coughing. "It's OK," he says. "They aren't going to hurt anybody."

And it is OK, she supposes. Instead of landing on the bed, which might have saved their lives, the girls have landed in the middle of the floor, or one has. The other is sprawled over the splintered towel rack with her spine cracked so she lies at a terrible angle and her blank blue eyes stare at the ruined ceiling. The floor is a morass of broken lath and chunks of plaster and, horrifyingly enough, the tiny skeletons of rats or squirrels that must have died in the attic over the last century. The air in the violet room is thick with dust and as Carroll approaches the form huddled on the floor in the middle of the littered carpet, more plaster sifts down from the splintered hole in the ceiling. One of the children is moaning. The girl may not know that her sister has died or—and it is this that chills Carroll and sets her teeth on edge forever—or she may have had something to do with it. The surviving twin hears Carroll's little sob of grief. Sighing like a waking princess, she rolls over and sits up, rubbing her eyes and blinking.

She does not speak.

Oh God, let it be the right one. "Jane?" she says cautiously.

The girl sits up.

"Careful," Kurt says in a low voice. "OK?"

"Shh." She's hardly aware she has spoken.

The girl tries to smile. "Carroll?"

Approaching, she has no way of knowing which of the girls has risen out of the carnage to greet her.

The child rubs her face and then looks at her right hand.

Carroll says uncertainly, "Emily?"

The girl rubs the ring finger and then looks up, blinking. "It's me, Carroll," she says. "Jane."

Is it? The tone is right. At least she thinks it is. "Jane?"

"See, it's me. I have the ring!" She holds out her hand and Carroll sees the ruby.

She puts out her arms. "Oh God, sweetie!"

But as they hug Carroll is aware of Kurt Graver stirring behind her. "Right or wrong," he says urgently, and as the girl in her arms stiffens at the sound of his voice she knows exactly what he means. "Carroll, right or wrong?"

"Why, right. I think." Standing back, she helps the girl step through the wreckage. "It's Jane," she says with her eyes filling, and as she does so she understands as she never before has the near-impossibility of making, in this world at least, absolute and final distinctions between good and evil. Taking her hand, the girl smiles up at her as Carroll gathers the strength to go forward, saying, "It has to be."